I0660112

RAYMOND F. JONES
RESURRECTED

Selected Science Fiction Stories of Raymond F. Jones

By Raymond F. Jones
Edited by Greg Fowlkes

Includes the Special Preview of
THE BLOOD RED SANDS OF MARS
A Science Fiction Novel by Greg Fowlkes

RAYMOND F. JONES RESURRECTED

Selected Science Fiction Stories of Raymond F. Jones

© 2012 Resurrected Press
www.ResurrectedPress.com

Published by Resurrected Press

This classic book was handcrafted by Resurrected Press. Resurrected Press is dedicated to bringing high quality classic books back to the readers who enjoy them. These are not scanned versions of the originals, but, rather, quality checked and edited books meant to be enjoyed!

Please visit ResurrectedPress.com to view our entire catalogue!

ISBN 13: 978-1-937022-41-9

Printed in the United States of America

FOREWORD

Raymond F. Jones (1915-1994) had an active career that spanned nearly three decades. His most famous work is the novel *This Island Earth* (1952) which in 1955 was made into a movie of the same name. This movie provides one of the classic images from science fiction cinema, the alien with the outside head. Unlike many of the science fiction movies of the day that film actually had a message. The aliens recruit a group of earth scientists in the hopes of forestalling the destruction of their own planet. In the end, their efforts fail, with their failure serving as a cautionary tale for mankind to avoid destroying Earth in a nuclear Armageddon.

The story typifies much of Jones's fiction. Most of his work was not of the "Space Opera" genre, but rather an investigation of the impact of alien worlds and alien situations on humanity. His stories were meant to invite reflection rather than just serve as pure entertainment. Much of his work was written before the advent of the Space Age when writers were much more concerned with "What are we going to do when we get there?" rather than "How are we going to get there?"

When I was twelve, my mother gave me two books of science fiction as a birthday present. One was a collection of seven of H. G. Wells's novels including *The War of the Worlds, The Time Machine, and The Invisible Man*. The other was *Adventures in Time and Space*, edited by Raymond J. Healy and J. Francis McComas. The latter was a collection of 35 stories by some of the best names in science fiction. It included stories such as Campbell's "Who Goes There" and Heinlein's "By His Bootstraps." It was the best birthday present I've ever gotten. Over the years I've read every story in that volume many times, some so many times I have them practically memorized.

One of the stories from that book is the oft anthologized "Correspondence Course," which was written in the immediate post World War II period. A soldier recovering from his wounds is begins a correspondence course and eventually realizes that it is instructing him in a technology that must come from an alien source. Predating the saucer scare of the early 50's the story's message is one of hope rather than fear. It exemplifies that "sense of wonder" the best science fiction of the era produced.

At about the same time as I received *Adventures in Time and Space*, I was reading just about any science fiction I could find in the public library. One story that made a lasting impression was "Tools of the Trade" the tale of a man with a problem, how to fix an alien spaceship when you can understand neither the technology or the culture that produced it. I first read that story some fifty years ago and its memory has stuck with me though I didn't reread it until a few years ago when I was able to track down on the internet a copy of the too neglected anthology "Space, Space, Space."

During his career, Jones published over seventy-five stories and a number of novels. In this collection we have brought together nine of his longer works that were first published in magazines. Each of these stories examines a particular question, questions such as "What sort of man will it take to travel to the stars and colonize other worlds?" or "How does man learn create new ideas?" A number of his works posed the question "Are we ready to join the galactic civilization?" and the corollary "Are they ready for us?"These were definitely questions from a particular time and place, and I don't agree with all the answers that Jones comes up with, but the important thing was that he was asking the questions and making his readers think about them.

While Jones's stories ask you to think, they can entertain as well, the hallmark of a good science fiction writer. Each of them is capable of producing that sense of wonder that unfortunately is missing from much of modern science fiction. In an autobiographical piece, Jones gave the opinion that man in the future would be pretty much like man of today with all his quirks, foibles and virtues. The characters in these stories are very much human (with a few exceptions) with human reactions. This is what makes his stories worth reading. Resurrected Press is proud to bring you this collection of his works.

About the Author

Raymond Fisher Jones (November 15, 1915-January 24, 1994) was an American science fiction author. He was born in Salt Lake City and studied radio engineering. He worked as a telephone switch installer before taking a job with the weather bureau. His first science fiction story was published in 1941but the bulk of his writing was done in the 1950's. He is best known for the novel *This Island Earth* which was later made into a movie of the same name. His story "The Children's Room" was later made into an episode of the television series *Tales of Tomorrow*.

Greg Fowlkes
Editor-In-Chief
Resurrected Press
www.ResurrectedPress.com

TABLE OF CONTENTS

Correspondence Course

Originally Published in *Astounding Science Fiction*
April 1945

CORRESPONDENCE COURSE

The old lane from the farmhouse to the letter box down the road was the same dusty trail that he remembered from eons before. The deep summer dust stirred as feet moved slowly and haltingly. The marks of his left foot were deep and firm as when he had last walked the lane, but where his right foot had moved there was a ragged, continuous line with irregular depressions and there was the sharp imprint of a cane besides the dragging footprints.

He looked up to the sky a moment as an echelon of planes from the advanced trainer base fifty miles away wheeled overhead. A nostalgia seized him, an overwhelming longing for the men he had known—and for Ruth.

He was home; he had come back alive, but with so many gone who would never come back, what good was it?

With Ruth gone it was no good at all. For an instant his mind burned with pain and his eyes ached as if a bomb-burst had blinded him as he remembered that day in the little field hospital where he had watched her die and heard the enemy planes overhead.

Afterwards, he had gone up alone, against orders, determined to die with her, but take along as many Nazis as he could.

But he hadn't died. He had come out of it with bullet-shattered leg and sent home to rust and die slowly over many years.

He shook his head and tried to fling the thoughts out of his mind. It was wrong. The doctors had warned him—

He resumed his slow march, half dragging the all but useless leg behind him. This was the same lane down which he had run so fast those summer days long ago. There was a swimming hole and a fishing pond a quarter of a mile away. He tried to dim his vision with half-shut eyes and remember those pleasant days and wipe out all fear and bitterness from his mind.

It was ten o'clock in the morning and Mr. McAfee, the rural postman, was late, but Jim Ward could see his struggling, antique Ford raising a low cloud of dust a mile down the road.

Jim leaned heavily upon the stout cedar post that supported the mailbox and when Mr. McAfee rattled up he managed to wave and smile cheerfully.

Mr. McAfee adjusted his spectacles on the bridge of his nose with a rapid trombone manipulation.

"Bless me, Jim, it's good to see you up and around!"

"Pretty good to be up," Jim managed to force enthusiasm into his voice. But he knew he couldn't stand talking very long to old Charles McAfee as if everything had not changed since the last time.

"Any mail for the Wards, today?"

The postman shuffled his fistful of mail. "Only one."

Jim glanced at the return address block and shrugged. "I'm on the sucker lists already. They don't lose time when they find out there are still bones left to pick on. You keep it."

He turned painfully and faced towards the house. "I've got to be getting back. Glad to have seen you, Mr. McAfee."

"Yeah, sure, Jim. Glad to have seen you. But I...er ...got to deliver the mail—" He held out the letter hopefully.

"O.K." Jim laughed sharply and grabbed the circular.

He went only as far as the giant oak whose branches extended far enough to overshadow the mailbox. He sat down in the shade with his back against the great bole and tried to watch the echelon still soaring above the valley through the rifts in the leaves coverage above him. After a time he glanced down at the circular letter from which his fingers were peeling little fragments of paper. Idly, he ripped open the envelope and glanced at the contents. In cheap, garish typograph with splattering of red and purple ink the words seemed to be trying to jump out at him.

SERVICEMAN-WHAT OF THE FUTURE?

You have come back from the wars. You have found life different than you knew it before, and much that was familiar is gone. But new things have come, new things that are here to stay and are a part of the world you are going to live in.

Have you thought of the place you will occupy? Are you prepared to resume life in the ways of peace?

WE CAN HELP YOU

Have you heard of the POWER CO-ORDINATOR? No, of course you haven't because it has been a hush-hush secret source of power that has been turning the wheels of war industries for many months. But now the secret of this vast source of new power can be told, and the need for hundreds, no, thousands of trained technicians—such as you, yourself, may become—will be tremendous in the next decade.

LET US PROVE TO YOU

Let us prove to you that we know what we are talking about. We are so certain that you, as soldier trained in the operation of the intricate machines of war, will be interested in this most miraculous new source of power and the technique of handling it that we are willing to send you absolutely FREE the first three lessons of our twenty-five lesson course that will train you to be a POWER CO-ORDINATOR technician.

Let us prove it to you. Fill out the enclosed coupon and mail it today!

Don't just shrug and throw this circular away as just another advertisement. MAIL THE COUPON NOW!

Jim Ward smiled reminiscently at the style of the circular. It reminded him of Billy Hensley and the time when they were thirteen. They sent in all the clipped and filled-out coupons they could find in magazines. They had samples of soap and magic tricks and catalogues and even a live bird came as a result of one. They kept all the stuff in Hensley's attic until Billy's dad finally threw it all out.

Impulsively, in whimsical tribute to the gone-forever happiness of those days, Jim Ward scratched his name and address in pencil and told the power co-ordinators to send him there three free lessons.

Mr. McAfee had only another mile to go up the road before he came to the end and returned past the Ward farm to Kramer's Forks. Jim Ward waited and hailed him.

"Want to take another letter?"

The postman halted the clattering Ford and jumped down. "What's that?"

Jim repeated his request and held up the stamped reply card. "Take this with you?"

Mr. McAfee turned it over and read every word on the back of the card. "Good thing," he grunted. "So you're going to take a correspondence course in this new power what-is-it? I think that's mighty fine, Jim. Give you new interests—sort of take your mind off things."

"Yeah, sure." Jim struggled up with the aid of his cane and the bole of the oak tree. "Better see if I can make it back to the house now."

All the whimsy and humor were suddenly gone out of the situation.

It was a fantastically short time—three days later—that Mr. McAfee stopped at the Ward farm again. He glanced at the thick envelope in his pack and the return address block it bore. He could see Jim Ward on the farmhouse porch and turned the Ford up the lane. Its rattle made Jim turn his head and open his eyes from the thoughtless blankness into which he had been trying to sink. He removed the pipe from his mouth and watched the car approach.

"Here's your course," shouted Mr. McAfee. "Here's your first lesson!"

"What lesson?"

"The correspondence course you sent for. The power what-is-it? Don't you remember?"

"No," said Jim. "I'd forgotten all about it. Take the thing away. I don't want it. It was just a silly joke."

"You hadn't ought to feel that way, Jim. After all, your leg is going to be all right. I heard the Doc say so down in the drugstore last night. And everything is going to be all right. There's no use letting it get you down. Besides—I got to deliver the mail."

He tossed the brown envelope on the porch besides Jim. "Brought it up special because I thought you'd be in a hurry to get it."

Jim smiled an apology. "I'm sorry, Mac. Didn't mean to take it out on you. Thanks for bringing it up. I'll study it good and hard this morning right here on the porch."

Mr. McAfee beamed and nodded and rattled away. Jim closed his eyes again, but he couldn't find the pleasing blankness he'd found before. Now the screen of his mind showed only the sky with thundering, plummeting engines—and the face of a girl lying still and white with closed eyes.

Jim opened his eyes and his hands slipped to his sides and touched the envelope. He ripped it open and scanned the pages. It was the sort of stuff he had collected as a boy, all right. He glanced at the paragraph headings and tossed the first lesson aside. A lot of obvious stuff about comparisons between steam power and waterfalls and electricity. It seemed all jumbled up like a high school student's essay on the development of power from the time of Archimedes.

The mimeographed pages were poorly done. They looked as if the stencils had been cut with a typewriter that had been hit on the type faces with a hammer.

He tossed the second lesson aside and glanced at the top sheet of the third. His hand arrested itself midway in the act of tossing the lesson beside the other two. He caught a glimpse of the calculations on an inside page and opened up the booklet.

There was no high school stuff there. His brain struggled to remember the long unused methods of integral calculus and the manipulation of partial differential equations.

There were pages of the stuff. It was like a sort of beacon light, dim and far off, but pointing a sure pathway to his mind and getting brighter as he progressed. One by one, he followed the intricate steps of the math and the short paragraphs of description between. When at last he reached the final page and turned the book over and scowled heavily the sun was halfway down the afternoon sky.

He looked away over the fields and pondered. This was no elementary stuff. Such math as this didn't belong in a home study correspondence course. He picked up the envelope and concentrated on the return block.

All it said was: M. H. Quilcon Schools, Henderson, Iowa. The lessons were signed at the bottom with the mimeographed reproductions of M. H. Quilcon's ponderous signature.

Jim picked up lesson one again and began reading slowly and carefully, as if hidden between the lines he might find some mystic message.

By the end of July his leg was strong enough for him to walk without the cane. He walked slowly and with a limp and once in a while the leg gave way as if he had a trick knee. But he learned quickly to catch himself before he fell and he reveled in the thrill of walking again.

By the end of July the tenth lesson of the correspondence course had arrived and Jim knew that he had gone as far as he could alone. He was lost in amazement as he moved in the new scientific wonderland that had opened up before him. He had known that great strides had been made in techniques and production, but it seemed incredible that such a basic discovery as power co-ordination had been producing war machines these many months. He wondered why the principle had not been applied more directly as a weapon itself—but he didn't understand enough about it to know whether it could or not. He didn't even understand yet from where the basic energy of the system was derived.

The tenth lesson was as poorly produced as the rest of them had been, but it was practically a book in its thickness. When he had finished it Jim knew that he had to know more of the background of the new science. He had to talk to someone who knew something about it. But he knew of no one who had ever heard of it. He had seen no advertisements of the M. H. Quilcon Schools. Only the first circular and these lessons.

As soon as he had finished the homework on lesson ten and had given it into Mr. McAfee's care, Jim Ward made up his mind to go down to Henderson, Iowa, and visit the Quilcon School.

He wished he had retained the lesson material because he could have taken it there faster than it would arrive via the local mail channels.

The streamliner barely stopped at Henderson, Iowa, long enough to allow him to disembark. Then it was gone and Jim Ward stared about him.

The sleepy looking ticket seller, dispatcher, and janitor eyed him wonderingly and spat a huge amber stream across his desk and out the window.

"Looking for somebody, mister?"

"I'm looking for Henderson, Iowa. Is this it?" Jim asked dubiously.

"You're here, mister. But don't walk too fast or you'll be out of it. The city limits only go a block past Smith's Drugstore."

Jim noticed the sign over the door and glanced at the inscription that he had not seen before: Henderson, Iowa, Pop. 806.

"I'm looking for Mr. M. H. Quilcon. He runs a correspondence school here somewhere. Do you know of him?"

The depot staff shifted its cud again and spat thoughtfully. "Been here twenty-nine years next October. Never heard a name like that around here, and I know 'em all."

"Are there any correspondence schools here?"

"Miss Marybell Anne Simmons gives beauty operator lessons once in a while, but that's all the school of that kind that I know of."

Disconcerted, Jim Ward murmured his thanks and moved slowly out of the station. The sight before him was dismaying. He wondered if the population hadn't declined since the estimate on the sign in the station was made.

A small mercantile store that sagged in the middle faced him across the street. Farther along was a tiny framed building labeled Sheriff's Office. On his side Jim saw Smith's drugstore a couple of hundred feet down from the station with a riding saddle and a patented fertilizer displayed in the window. In the other direction was the combined post office, bank and what was advertised as a newspaper and printing office.

Jim strode toward this last building while curious watchers on the porch of the mercantile store stared at him trudging through the dust.

The postmistress glanced up from the armful of mail that she was sorting into boxes as Jim entered. She offered a cheery hello that seemed to tinkle from the buxom figure.

"I'm looking for a man named Quilcon. I thought you might be able to give me some information concerning him."

"Kweelcon?" She furrowed her brow. "There's no one here by that name. How do you spell it?"

Before he could answer, the woman dropped a handful of letters on the floor. Jim was certain that he saw the one he had mailed to the school before he left.

As the woman stooped to recover the letters a dark brown shadow streaked across the floor. Jim got the momentary impression of an enormous brown slug moving with lightning speed.

The postmistress gave a scream of anger and scuffed her feet to the door. She returned in a moment.

"Armadillo," she explained. "Darn thing's been hanging around here for months and nobody seems to be able to kill it." She resumed putting the mail in the boxes.

"I think you missed one," said Jim. She did not have the one that he recognized as the one he'd mailed.

The woman looked about her on the floor. "I got them all, thank you. Now what did you say this man's name was?"

Jim leaned over the counter and looked at the floor. He was sure—But there was obviously no other letter in sight and there was no place it could have gone.

"Quilcon," Jim said slowly. "I'm not sure of the pronunciation myself, but that's the way it seemed it should be."

"There's no one in Henderson by that name. Wait a minute now. That's a funny thing—you know it was about a month ago that I saw an envelope going out of here with a name something like that in the upper left corner. I thought at the time it was a funny name and wondered who put it in, but I never did find out and I thought I'd been dreaming. How'd you know to come here looking for him?"

"I guess I must have received the mail you saw."

"Well, you might ask Mr. Herald. He's in the newspaper office next door. But I'm sure there's no one in this town by that name."

"You publish a newspaper here?"

The woman laughed. "We call it that. Mr. Herald owns the bank and a big farm and puts this out free as a hobby. It's not much, but everybody in town reads it. On Saturday he puts out a regular printed edition. This is the daily."

She held up a small mimeographed sheet that was moderately legible. Jim glanced at it and moved towards the door. "Thanks, anyway."

As he went out into the summer sun there was something growing in his brain, an intense you-forgot-something-in-there sort of feeling. He couldn't place it and tried to ignore it.

Then as he stepped across the threshold of the printing office he got it. That mimeographed newssheet he had seen—it bore a startling resemblance to the lessons he had received from M. H. Quilcon. The same purple ink. Slightly crooked sheets. But that was foolish to try to make a connection there. All mimeographed jobs looked about alike.

Mr. Herald was a portly little man with a fringe around his baldness. Jim repeated his inquiry.

"Quilcon?" Mr. Herald pinched his lips thoughtfully. "No, can't say as I ever heard the name. Odd name—I'm sure I'd know it if I'd ever heard it."

Jim Ward knew that further investigation here would be a waste of time. There was something wrong somewhere. The information in his correspondence course could not be coming out of this half dead little town.

He glanced at a copy of the newssheet lying on the man's littered desk beside an ancient Woodstock. "Nice little sheet you put out there," said Jim.

Mr. Herald laughed. "Well, it's not much, but I get a kick out of it, and the people enjoy reading about Mrs. Kelly's lost hogs and the Dorius kid's whooping cough. It livens things up."

"Ever do any work for anybody else—printing or mimeographing?"

"If anybody wants it, but I haven't had an outside job in three years."

Jim glanced about searchingly. The old Woodstock seemed to be the only typewriter in the room.

"I might as well go on," he said. "But I wonder if you'd mind letting me use your typewriter to write a note and leave it at the post office for Quilcon if he ever shows up."

"Sure, go ahead. Help yourself."

Jim sat down before the clanking machine and hammered out a brief paragraph while Mr. Herald wandered to the back of the shop. The Jim rose and shoved the paper in his pocket. He wished he had brought a sheet from one of the lessons with him.

"Thanks," he called to Mr. Herald. He picked up a copy of the latest edition of the newspaper and shoved it in his pocket with the typed sheet.

On the trip homeward he studied the mimeographed sheet until he had memorized every line, but he withheld conclusions until he reached home.

From the station he called the farm and Hank, the hired man, came to pick him up. The ten miles out to the farm seemed like a hundred. But at last in his own room Jim spread out the two sheets of paper he'd brought with him and opened up lesson one of the correspondence course.

There was no mistake. The stencils of the course manuals had been cut on Mr. Herald's ancient machine. There was the same nick out of the side of the o, and the b was flattened on the bulge. The r was minus half its base.

Mr. Herald had prepared the course.

Mr. Herald must then be M. H. Quilcon. But why had he denied any knowledge of the name? What had he refused to see Jim and admit his authorship of the course?

At ten o'clock that night Mr. McAfee arrived with a special delivery letter for Jim.

"I don't ordinarily deliver these way out here this time of night," he said. "But I thought you might like to have it. Might be something important. A job or something, maybe. It's from Mr. Quilcon."

"Thanks. Thanks for bringing it, Mac."

Jim hurried into his room and ripped open the letter. It read:

Dear Mr. Ward:

Your progress in understanding the principles of power co-ordination are exceptional and I am very pleased to note your progress in connection with the tenth lesson which I have just received from you.

An unusual opportunity has arisen which I am moved to offer you. There is a large installation of a power co-ordination engine in need of vital repairs some distance from here. I believe that you are fully qualified to work on this machine under supervision which will be provided and you would gain some valuable experience. The installation is located some distance from the city of Henderson. It is about two miles out on the Balmer road. You will find there the Hortan Machine Works at which the installation is located. Repairs are urgently needed and you are the closest qualified student able to take advantage of this opportunity which might lead to a valuable permanent connection. Therefore, I request that you come at once. I will meet you there.

Sincerely,
M. H. Quilcon

For a long time Jim Ward sat on the bed with the letter and the sheets of paper spread out before him. What had begun as a simple quest for information was rapidly becoming an intricate puzzle.

Who was M. H. Quilcon?

It seemed obvious that Mr. Herald, the banker and part-time newspaper publisher, must be Quilcon. The correspondence course manuals had certainly been produced on his typewriter. The chance of any two typewriters having exactly the same four or five disfigurements in type approached the infinitesimal.

And Herald—if he were Quilcon—must have written this letter just before or shortly after Jim's visit. The letter was certainly a product of the ancient Woodstock.

There was a fascination in the puzzle and a sense of something sinister, Jim thought. Then he laughed aloud at his own melodrama and began repacking the suitcase. There was a midnight train he could get back to Henderson.

It was hot afternoon when he arrived in the town for the second time. The station staff looked up in surprise as he got off the train.

"Back again? I thought you'd given up."

"I've found out where Mr. Quilcon is. He's at the Hortan Machine Works. Can you tell me exactly where that is?"

"Never heard of it."

"It's supposed to be about two miles out of town on Balmer Road."

"That's the main street of town going on down through the Willow Creek district. There's no machine works out there. You must be in the wrong state, mister. Or somebody's kidding you."

"Do you think Mr. Herald could tell me anything about such a machine shop. I mean, does he know anything about machinery or things related to it?"

"Man, no! Old Man Herald don't care about nothing but money and that little fool paper of his. Machinery! He can't hook up anything more complicated than his suspenders."

Jim started down the main street toward the Willow Creek district. Balmer Road rapidly narrowed and turned, leaving the town out of sight behind a low rise. Willow Creek was a glistening thread in the midst of meadow land.

There was no more unlikely spot in the world for a machine works of any kind, Jim thought. Someone must be playing an utterly fantastic joke on him. But how or why they had picked on him were mystifying.

At the same time he knew within him that it was no joke. There was a deadly seriousness about it all. The principles of power co-ordination were right. He had slaved and dug through them enough to be sure of that. He felt that he could almost build a power co-ordination engine now with the proper means— except that he didn't understand from where the power was derived!

In the timelessness of the bright air about him, with the only sound coming from the brook and the leaves on the willow trees beside it, Jim found it impossible to judge time or distance.

He paced his steps and counted until he was certain that at least two miles had been covered. He halted and looked about almost determined to go back and re-examine the way he had come.

He glanced ahead, his eyes scanning every minute detail of the meadowland. And then he saw it.

The sunlight glistened as if on a metal surface. And above the bright spot in the distance was the faintly readable legend:

HORTAN MACHINE WORKS

Thrusting aside all judgment concerning the incredibility of a machine shop in such a locale, he crossed the stream and made his way over the meadow toward the small rise.

As he approached, the machine works appeared to be merely a dome-shaped structure about thirty feet in diameter and with an open door in one side. He came up to it with a mind ready for anything. The crudely painted sign above the door looked as if it had been drawn by an inexpert barn painter in a state of intoxication.

Jim entered the dimly lit interior of the shop and set his case upon the floor beside a narrow bench that extended about the room.

Tools and instruments of unfamiliar design were upon the bench and upon the walls. But no one appeared.

Then he noticed an open door and a steep, spiral ramp that led down to a basement room. He stepped through and half slid, half walked down to the next level.

There was artificial lighting be fluorescent tubes of unusual construction, Jim noticed. But still no sign of anyone. And there was not an object in the room that appeared familiar to him. Articles that vaguely resembled furniture were against the walls.

He felt uneasy amid the strangeness of the room and he was about to go back up the steep ramp when a voice came to him.

"This is Mr. Quilcon. Is that you, Mr. Ward?"

"Yes. Where are you?"

"I'm in the next room, unable to come out until I finish a bit of work I have started. Will you please go on down to the room below? You will find the damaged machinery there. Please go right to work on it. I'm sure that you have a complete understanding of what is necessary. I will join you in a moment?"

Hesitantly, Jim turned to the other side of the room where he saw a second ramp leading down to a brilliantly lighted room. He glanced about once more, then moved down the ramp.

The room was high-ceilinged and somewhat larger in diameter than the others that he had seen and it was almost completely occupied by the machine.

A series of close fitting towers with regular bulbous swellings on their columns formed the main structure of the engine. These were grouped in a solid circle with narrow walkways at right angles to each other passing through them.

Jim Ward stood for a long time examining their surfaces that rose twenty feet from the floor. All that he had learned from the curious correspondence course seemed to fall into place. Diagrams and drawings of such machines had seemed incomprehensible. Now he knew exactly what each part was for and how the machine operated.

He squeezed his body into the narrow walkway between the towers and wormed his way to the center of the engine. His bad leg made it difficult, but he at last came to the damaged structure.

One of the tubes had cracked open under some strain and through the slit he could see the marvelous intricate wiring with which it was filled. Wiring that was burned now and fused to a mass. It was in a control circuit that rendered the whole machine functionless, but its repair would not be difficult, Jim knew.

He went back to the periphery of the engine and found the controls of a cranelike device which he lowered and seized the cracked sleeve and drew off the damaged part.

From the drawers and bins in the walls he selected parts and tools and returned to the damaged spot.

In the cramped space he began tearing away the fused parts and wiring. He was lost and utterly unconscious of anything but the fascination of the mighty engine. Here within this room was machine capacity to power a great city.

The basic function rested upon the principle of magnetic currents in contrast to electric currents. The discovery of magnetic currents has been announced only a few months before he came home from the war. The application of the discovery had been swift.

And he began to glimpse the fundamental source of the energy supplying the machine. It was in the great currents of gravitational and magnetic force flowing between the planets and the suns of the universe. As great as atomic energy and as boundless in its resources, this required no fantastically dangerous machinery to harness. The principle of the power co-ordinator was simple.

The pain of his cramped position forced Jim to move out to rest his leg. As he stood beside the engine he resumed his pondering on the purpose it had in this strange location. Why was it built here and what use was made of its power?

He moved about to restore the circulation in his legs and sought to trace the flow of energy through the engine, determine where and what kind of a load was placed on it.

His search led him below into a third sub-basement of the building and there he found the thing he was searching for, the load into which the tremendous drive of the engine was coupled.

But here he was unable to comprehend fully, for the load was itself a machine of strange design, and none of its features had been covered in the correspondence course.

The machine upstairs seized upon the magnetic currents of space and selected and concentrated those flowing in a given direction.

The force of these currents was then fed into the machine in this room, but there was no point of reaction against which the energy could be applied.

Unless—

The logical, inevitable conclusion forced itself upon his mind. There was only one conceivable point of reaction.

He stood very still and a tremor went through him. He looked up at the smooth walls about him. Metal, all of them. And this room—it was narrower that the one above—as if the entire building was tapered from the dome protruding out of the earth to the basement floor.

The only possible point of reaction was the building itself.

But it wasn't a building. It was a vessel.

Jim clawed and stumbled his way up the incline into the engine room, then beyond into the chamber above. He was halfway up the top ramp when he heard the voice again.

"Is that you, Mr. Ward? I have almost finished and will be with you in a moment. Have you completed the repairs? Was it very difficult?"

He hesitated, but didn't answer. Something about the quality of that voice gave him a chill. He hadn't noticed it before because of his curiosity and his interest in the place. Now he detected its unearthly, inhuman quality.

He detected the fact that it wasn't a voice at all, but that the words had been formed in his brain as if he himself had spoken them.

He was nearly at the top of the ramp and drew himself up on hands and knees to the floor level when he saw the shadow of the closing door sweep across the room and heard the metallic clang of the door. It was sealed tight. Only the small windows— or ports—admitted light.

He rose and straightened and calmed himself with the thought that the vessel could not fly. It could not rise with the remainder of the repair task unfinished—and he was not going to finish it; that much was certain.

"Quilcon!" he called. "Show yourself! Who are you and what do you want of me?"

"I want you to finish the repair job and do it quickly," the voice replied instantly. "And quickly—it must be finished quickly."

There was a note of desperation and despair that seemed to cut into Jim. Then he caught sight of the slight motion against the wall beside him.

In a small, transparent hemisphere that was fastened to the side of the wall lay the slug that Jim had seen at the post office, the thing the woman had called an "armadillo." He had not even noticed it when he first entered the room. The thing was moving now with slow pulsations that swelled its surface and great welts like dark veins stood out upon it.

From the golden-hued hemisphere a maze of cable ran to instruments and junction boxes around the room and a hundred tiny pseudo-pods grasped terminals inside the hemisphere.

It was a vessel—and this slug within the hemisphere was its alien, incredible pilot. Jim knew it with startling cold reality that came to him in waves of thought that emanated from the slug called Quilcon and broke over Jim's mind. It was a ship and a pilot from beyond Earth—from out of the reaches of space.

"What do you want of me? Who are you?" said Jim Ward.

"I am Quilcon. You are a good student. You learn well."

"What do you want?"

There was something wrong with the creature. Intangibly, Jim sensed it. An aura of sickness, a desperate urgency came to his mind.

But something else was in the foreground of Jim's mind. The horror of the alien creature diminished and Jim contemplated the miracle that had come to mankind.

"I'll bargain with you," he said quietly. "Tell me how to build a ship like this for my people and I will fix the engines for you."

"No! No—there is no time for that. I must hurry—"

"The I shall leave without any repairs."

He moved toward the door and instantly a paralyzing wave took hold of him as if he had seized a pair of charged electrodes. It relaxed only as he stumbled back from the door.

"My power is weak," said Quilcon, "but it is strong enough for many days yet—many of your days. Too many for you to live without food and water. Repair the engine and then I shall let you go."

"Is what I ask too much to pay for my help?"

"You have had pay enough. You can teach your people to build power co-ordination machines. Is that not enough?"

"My people want to build ships like this one and move through space."

"I cannot teach you that. I do not know. I did not build this ship."

There were surging waves of troubled though that washed over his mind, but Jim Ward's tenseness eased. The first fear of totally alien life drifted from his mind and he felt a strange affinity for the creature. It was injured and sick, he knew, but he could not believe that it did not know how the ship was built.

"Those who built this ship come often to trade upon my world," said Quilcon. "But we have no such ships of our own. Most of us have no desire to see anything but the damp caves and sunny shores of our own world. But I longed to see the worlds from which these ships came.

"When this one landed near my cave I crept in and hid myself. The ship took off then and we traveled an endless time. Then an accident to the engine killed all three of those who manned the ship and I was left alone.

"I was injured, too, but I was not killed. Only the other of me died."

Jim did not understand the queer phrase, but he did not break into Quilcon's story.

"I was able to arrange means to control the flight of the ship, to prevent its destruction as it landed upon this planet, but I could not repair it because of the nature of my body."

Jim saw then that the creature's story must be true. It was obvious that the ship had been built to be manned by beings utterly unlike Quilcon.

"I investigated the city of yours near by and learned of your ways and customs. I needed help of one of you to repair the ship.

By force I could persuade one of you to do simple tasks, but none so complex as this requires.

"Then I discovered the peculiar customs of learning among you. I forced the man Herald to prepare the materials and send them to you. I received them before the person at the post office could see them. I got your name from the newspapers along with several others who were unsatisfactory.

"I had to teach you to understand the power co-ordinator because only by voluntary operation of your highest faculties will you be able to understand and repair the machine. I can assist but not force you to do that."

The creature began pleading again. "And now will you repair the engine quickly. I am dying—but shall live longer than you— it is a long journey to my home planet, but I must get there and I need every instant of the time that is left to me."

Jim caught a glimpse of the dream vision that was the creature's home world. It was a place of security and peace—in Quilcon's terms. But even its alienness did not block out the sense of quiet beauty that Quilcon's mind transmitted to Jim's. They were a species of high intelligence. Exceptionally developed in the laws of mathematics and theory of logic, they were handicapped in bodily development from inquiring into other fields of science whose existence was demonstrated by their logic and their mathematics. The more intellectual among them were frustrated creatures whose lives were made tolerable only by an infinite capacity for stoicism and adaptation.

But of them all, Quilcon was among the most restless and rebellious and ambitious. No one of them had ever dared such a journey as he had taken. A swelling pity and understanding came over Jim Ward.

"I'll bargain with you," he said desperately. "I'll repair the engine if you'll let me have its principle. If you don't have them, you can get them to me with little trouble. My people must have such a ship as this."

He tried to visualize what it would mean to Earth to have space flight in a century or perhaps five centuries before the slow plodding of science and research might have revealed it.

But the creature was silent.

"Quilcon—" Jim repeated. He hoped it hadn't died.

"I'll bargain with you," said Quilcon at last. "Let me be the other of you and I'll give you what you want."

"The other of me?" What are you talking about?"

"It is hard for you to understand. It is a union—such as we make upon our world. When two or more of us want to be together we go together in the same brain, the same body. I am alone now, and it is an unendurable existence because I have known what it is to have another of me.

"Let me come into your brain, into your mind and live there with you. We will teach you people and mine. We will take this ship to all the universes of which living creatures can dream. It is either this or we both die together, for too much time has gone for me to return. This body dies,."

Stunned by Quilcon's ultimatum, Jim Ward stared at the ugly slug on the wall. Its brown body was heaving with violent pulsations of pain and a sense of delirium and terror came from it to Jim.

"Hurry! Let me come!" it pleaded.

He could feel sensations as if fingers were probing his cranium looking, pleading for entrance. It turned him cold.

He looked into the years and thought of an existence with this alien mind in his. Would they battle for eventual possession of his body and he perhaps be subject to slavery in his own living corpse?

He tried to probe Quilcon's thoughts, but he could find no sense or intent of conquest. There was almost human amenities intermingled with a world of new science and thought.

He knew Quilcon would keep his promise to give the secrets of the ship to the men of Earth. That alone would be worth the price of his sacrifice—if it should be a sacrifice.

"Come!" he said quietly.

It was as if a torrent of liquid light were flowing into his brain. It was blinding and excruciating in its flaming intensity. He thought he sensed rather than saw the brown husk of Quilcon quiver in the hemisphere and shrivel like a brown nut.

But in his mind there was union and he paused and trembled with the sudden great reality of what he knew. He knew what Quilcon was and gladness flowed into him like light. A thought soared through his brain: Is sex only in the difference of bodily function and the texture of skin and the tone of voice?

He thought of another day when there was death in the sky and on the Earth below, and in a little field hospital. A figure on a white cot had murmured, "You'll be all right, Jim. I'm going on, I guess, but you'll be all right. I know it. Don't miss me too much."

He had known there would be no peace for him ever, but now there was peace and the voice of Quilcon was like that voice from long ago, for as the creature probed into his thoughts its inherent adaptability matched in feelings and thought to his and said, "Everything is all right, isn't it, Jim Ward?"

"Yes . . . yes it is." The intensity of his feelings almost blinded him. "And I want to call you Ruth, after another Ruth-"

"I like that name." There was shyness and appreciation in the tones, and it was not strange to Jim that he could not see the speaker, for there was a vision in his mind far lovelier than any Earthly vision could ever have been.

"We'll have everything," he said. "Everything that your world and mine can offer. We'll see them all."

But like the other Ruth who had been so practical, this one was, too. "First we have to repair the engine. Shall we do it, now?"

The solitary figure of Jim Ward moved toward the ramp and disappeared into the depths of the ship.

Tools of the Trade

Originally Published in *Astounding Science Fiction*,
November 1950

Tools of the Trade

There are a lot of tools in any good garage. But what if the garage was for spaceships, and if the ships came in for repair from every corner of the universe? And suppose that they had been built by hundreds of different races, each with its own set of living requirements, its own special kind of intelligence, and its own sciences never developed on Earth. Running that kind of garage will be an art.

Politics, too, is an art. We Terrans have not developed it very highly as yet. Our sciences are far ahead of our political institutions, and it's a favorite game to assign responsibility for what goes wrong with the machinery of our government to politicians. When men have made their contacts with the races of other planets they may discover that for all Earth's skills and knowledge the inhabitants of other worlds are wiser in certain respects than Man.

Anyway, here is a story with something to think about in it. It starts with a super garage, but it is up to the reader to decide just where it ends. That depends, in part, on what he thinks of those dopes in City Hall and the muddleheads in Washington. Or are they?

The desert sun was slowly lighting the sleek, lazy backs of the ships on the field of "Joe's Service and Repair." It lit the distant hills, too, promising a day of greater splendor than it could possibly deliver in this barren land. But Joe didn't mind. He liked big plans.

From the window of his second-story office he watched. His normal working day began at dawn and in the outer office he heard the entrance of his secretary, Mary Barnes. She was devoted him, but her quick heel taps registered the irritation of having to rise so early.

Joe stoked the big cigar in his mouth with long, pleasurable draughts. The field was getting too small. Time for another expansion, almost, but he wondered if this time he should set up a separate location somewhere else. Concentration meant efficiency but the bureaucrats who had to keep tabs on him worried about "Joe's Service and Repair" becoming too big. Steadily, however, they were becoming smaller and smaller fry. Soon they wouldn't matter at all—he hoped.

He marveled at the colors of the hulls. At midday most would be dingy, space-pocked gray, but now they seemed to glow with bright yellow and pink hues of shining metal.

There was the big Nadian. She was having a new drive, atomic, Class Six, he recalled. Besides her was the much smaller Iban with new atmosphere pumps to be installed—half the crew had died getting her into the repair depot. Most of them represented tragedy, but that tragedy was less because of him.

He looked beyond the Nadian to the fine, golden hull that loomed even bigger a little way beyond. He squinted for recognition, bending forward until his cigar almost touched the windowpane. The he recognized it.

"Mary! How did that royal barge get on our field? Mary—!"

She came from the outer office at her own pace, but with her morning coiffure adjustments only half completed. "I have the entry slip on the Martremant, if that's what you're worrying about," she said. "It was in the hopper this morning—came in during the night. It is a very big job. She was rammed by a freighter that got out of control at Capitol Field just as the First Administrator was about to take off."

"I can refuse service to anyone, and I refuse to have anything to do with those junketing politicians. Goodwill tour—bah!"

The Montremant was the personal ship of the Galactic Union's First Administrator. With two hundred of his commissioners, he was making a good-will tour through member galaxies. Since it was, of course, impossible to visit all, the party had honored Earth greatly, her galaxy being one of the most remote from Administration Central.

Joe looked up sharply as he became aware of Mary's silence. "Well, I can, can't I—?

"I'm afraid not, Joe." Her brown eyes watched him seriously. "Your charter forbids discrimination, except by government ban or permission. I'm sure there will be neither in this instance.

The job carries a special government contract straight from the Capitol."

"Not only do I have to fix this barge, but, as a tax-payer, I have to foot my own bill?"

"Stripped to its bare essentials, that's about it. The government is half panicky about the accident. Up to now the junket went off as rehearsed, It looked as if the support of the First Administrator had been assured for Earth's candidate when the Administrator's term expires in six months."

"Now the political plums have all turned sour because some chowderhead rams the royal barge, is that it?"

"That's it. You can bet nobody slept on Capitol Hill last night."

Joe chuckled suddenly. "Tough, isn't it? The vips will have to wait for repairs or a new ship. Wouldn't it be tough if we couldn't find or make one essential part? Of course, it would take a long time to find that out. I think I'll take this job after all."

"Why don't you just get it fixed as quickly as you can," said Mary crossly, "and get it off your mind? You breed ulcers this way."

Joe's face sobered. "All right, Mary. We'll do it your way. I think the efficiency of this office has picked up thirty percent since you came—but I wonder if we have as much fun—"

"It's not fun to hate anything as much as you do politicians."

"A person can't be sweet all the time. I don't know of much more suitable use to be made of the pompous windbags."

"If I remember elementary history correctly there was a time of technological government."

"A bunch of plumber's apprentices," growled Joe. "The gang that got in was worse than the politicians."

"That's what everybody else thought, too."

"Look, you're changing the subject." He took her arm with fatherly gentleness and led her closer to the window. "That hulk out there cost a billion, at least. Its operating expenses on this hundred-day junket are a quarter-million every day. Who pays it? Little guys like me and you. A tax on this, a tax on that— half our life and substance are dribbled away supporting those . . . those junketeers!"

"Little guys like me an you—! That calls for an increase next Thursday. Here comes Mr. Litchfield. He looks as if he has troubles on his mind. Ten to one it's Martremant trouble."

She retreated to her own office as the chief repair engineer parked his scooter outside the building and started up the stairs.

Howard Litchfield looked more like a professional wrestler than a crack engineer. He carried his elbows slightly away from his body as if perpetually waiting for someone to photograph his strong-man pose

"You've seen it, I suppose," he said.

"The Martremant?"

We're going to have trouble on this job.

"Why—what is it?"

"This is one of the eight third-order ships in existence. We've never had a third-order job in here before."

"So what? There are twenty other jobs out there that are the first we've seen of their exact kind. The crew of the Martremant can give enough of their cerebral analogues to pin it down."

"They could—if they were alive."

Joe slowly removed his cigar. "What happened to them?"

"The freighter that knocked the ship out drove through the side of the officer's quarters, and ended up by almost splitting the drive chambers in two.   Only twenty percent of the machinery is good. All crew-men with technical knowledge are dead. The only ones left are the cooks and stewards, and they're not Radalians, who built the vessel."

"And politicians—" added Joe.

"Who won't move out."

"What?"

"That's right. The First and his commissioners are still aboard."

"What about the atmosphere machinery?"

"That's the twenty percent that's left. Each state suite is self-contained and independent. None of them got damaged."

"Well, why doesn't the government just give them a new ship and junk the old one? It would be cheaper. Don't forget who pays this bill."

Litchfield chook his head and sat down on the polished desk. "There was some mention of it, I gather, but the First wants his personal barge back in Grade A shape with not a scratch showing, so that's what he was promised. We have to deliver."

"It's not his ship, anyway. It belongs to the Galactic Commission."

"Sure—but who's going to remind him? He's the F. A."

"I'd like to remind him! I'd—" Joe sensed the uselessness of another tirade. He recalled Mary's advice—get the ship fixed.

"I'll help you," he announced decisively. "Let's get that thing off the field by the end of the week."

"This is already Monday!"

"A man could breed a pretty good-sized ulcer in six days."

On the small scooters used for transportation about the vast field, they sped towards the hulk of the Martremant. It was a squat tube of a hull about twenty stories high and three times as long. Joe gasped at the great gash in the rear third of it.

"It would have been easier to take the tools to the job than bring that piece of junk here. The freighter must have rammed clear inside and then turned and come out sidewise."

"It exploded. That's why nobody will know for sure what happened."

Lights had been placed and Litchfield's analysis crew were already deep in the process of photographing and carefully dismantling the wreckage.

As Joe looked about, he became aware that there were others present who had no business to be—but he knew who they were.

You could tell them by the crease of their clothes, the glistening shine upon their shoes, the dainty way they reached down every so often to dust imaginary specks from their knees.

There were four of them this time. The leader approached with outstretched hand, and recognition slowly flamed in Joe's eyes.

"I'm Mr. Johnson of the President's office. Perhaps you recall I used to be in Field Inspection," he said. "These men are—"

"I remember," said Joe slowly, glancing at Johnson's graying temples. "You're the Capitol's current wonder boy. You write speeches now."

The man flushed, but he went on. "These men are Mr. Burns, Mr. Cornwall, and Mr. Hansen, who are of the Presidential Advisory Office."

Joe took the hand of each in sullen challenge.

"We tried to locate you last night to discuss the repair of the Martremant. We finally authorized its entry, since it had already arrived, anyway."

"I was home asleep until five and down here by five-thirty. You didn't look very hard for me."

"Perhaps you have been acquainted with the tremendous significance of this job," said Johnson.

"I have. You want it done promptly so you can all get your fingers in the big pie to be cut next election day."

The advisers' faces grew masklike. "The ship must be repaired with dispatch and accuracy, in order to minimize the inconvenience to the Commissioners and the First Administrator. We are authorized to place every government facility required at your disposal and issue a blank check for the work."

"On my account!" cried Joe. "You offer me a blank check on my own bank account just like you were Santa Claus.

"I'm afraid, Mr. Williams, that you don't understand the matter of appropriations."

"I'm afraid I do. But if you want this hulk fixed, my advice is to get out and stay out. Every hour you clutter up the field delays the work another day."

"It is necessary that we remain. The President had delegated us to be on the site and issue him hourly reports on the progress of the work."

Groaning, Joe turned away. About their heads, he could see successive floors blasted upward and torn with jagged holes. Swaying lights and miniature shadows of crewmen showed the analysis work going on in those far levels.

"Did you check the files for Radalian analogues?"

"Yes. We've never had any in here before of that race. The First and his Radalian Commissioners have already been asked. They refused, of course."

"Naturally," Joe growled. "Who could expect a politician to let his brains be poked into? We'd find out what was behind the double-talk we get. Get a transcript of the plans from Radal then."

"We already tried. They report the plans are confidential, top-secret and super secret. Therefore, they cannot be given out."

Joe stood for perhaps five seconds while his blood pressure mounted. Then he walked quietly to where the four advisors were watching. He spoke to them for approximately thirty seconds. They held a consultation and then moved towards the front end of the ship where the officials held forth in their luxurious suites.

Fifteen minutes later they emerged and went to the communications office. Within an hour the transcript of the plans was on Litchfield's desk.

It made Joe feel good. He smiled expansively at the stack of sheets.

"That is the first time I ever saw a politician who was any good in a pinch. Now, we ought to be able to go on without any trouble. We won't even need an analogue. Maybe I ought to go back to the office and see what Mary's got for me. If you need me—"

Litchfield listened absently. The responsibility for repair was his. The stack of sheets describing the drive was three feet high. It would be necessary to resort to cerebral absorption methods to comprehend all that mass of data, but that didn't worry him. He had opened the broad structural schematic and the stereoscopic representation of the engines as they were in place.

The tan of his face became suddenly a shade lighter. "Wait a minute, Joe. Our troubles aren't over yet. This may be the time that we don't make it—"

"What's the matter now? We've got the plans of the ship. All we need to do is follow them. Anything a critter can build, we can fix."

"Providing we have the tools."

"Tools? We've got a tool department. Art Rawlins can build any tool you need."

"Think Art ever heard of the molecular spray technique?"

Joe slowly dropped his cigar into a spittoon and retreated from the doorway. "Molecular spray—it's only a rumor. You hear it at least once a week."

"Not any more is it just a rumor. These plans specify it."

Joe bent over the charts. They had been given English titling automatically during transmission. Litchfield was right. The engines were designed to be constructed by spray technique.

He knew what that meant. It was the only way they could be built. Any other construction method would require a new design for the whole power plant.

Joe knew virtually nothing of the technique. He had never found anyone who had even seen it. According to rumor, however, it was remotely akin to the printing of electrical circuits which had been common for hundreds of years.

It was a means of building up three-dimensional objects of unlimited complexity by spraying on molecules in precise streams of variable constituency. The spray was keyed by an intricate matrix system that steered automatically the tool mechanism and changed the quality of the molecules from uranium to soft putty if that was called for. It was possible to leave channels, build in wiring, and assemble parts in any degree of intimacy required by design, a degree far surpassing that possible by clumsy nut and bold or welding techniques.

"There ought to be spray equipment aboard the ship," said Joe. "If repairs were required, I understand they would have to tear the thing down and build it up again."

"Could be, but any sigh of a machine shop was volatilized. As it stands, we'd have to build a factory to build the tool before we could even start on the ship—provided we could get plans for the tools."

"That shouldn't be hard. We could get them the same way we got the drive data."

"Let's try once more to get them to settle for conventional drive. We can set them up with a good second-order outfit. Maybe the Presidential Advisors can put some pressure in that direction.

Joe called them in and explained the situation. They tried to look as if they comprehended what spray technique was all about, but Johnson shook his head.

"I guess we should have mentioned it first," he said, "that the Administrator asked if you understood the spray methods. We said you did, because we felt sure you would have no trouble with construction methods. He said that was fine, because his people only rented the equipment from the makers—some other race who won't let it out of their hands. The tool design is not available."

"Then we'll have to substitute," said Litchfield. "There's no possible way to obtain spray tools in any reasonable time. We can install a good second-order drive. You'll have to make it right with the First."

"You want to substitute a simpler, less efficient drive?"

"If the junketeers want to get under way in the next six years."

"We can't allow it," said Johnson. "This represents the thing the President sent us to guard against. The ship has to be repaired as it was."

"That represents the political mind at work under a full head of steam!" exclaimed Joe. "We can't be given the tools, but we have to do the job anyway! Now, listen—"

"Suppose you listen, Mr. Williams. How would it look for the First Administrator to go limping around the galaxy explaining that he was behind schedule because his ship got wrecked on Sol III and the Terrestrians were incapable of matching his drives?

"How would it look, not only from our own political viewpoint, but from the standpoint of your technical abilities, your business? Consider the effect if it got spread around that 'Joe's Service and Repair' had muffed the First Administrator's job? In spite of my own personal distress in the matter, it is with a great pleasure I view you position over a very rickety barrel.

"Good day, Mr. Williams—Mr. Litchfield."

"All right—here's the last word," said Joe. "We'll fix the Martremant so well that the original builders won't know it's been repaired—and by the end of the week. You may include that in the next hourly report to the President."

Litchfield didn't look up when they had gone. He continued to stare down at the drawing, but he spoke to Joe. "You know what you just said?"

"You bet I do! Call in all three crew shifts who'll be on the repair job. We'll give them cerebral on the drive plans. Get Art Rawlins and his whole tool crew down here. Start them making matrices from these plans.

"Then tell them to make some spray tools and get to work."

"Just like that?"

Joe's face was suddenly more bitter than Litchfield remembered it for a long time. He leaned over the table of drawings to look out the window. The quartet of advisors seemed in a jovial mood as they went towards the ship.

"They may not represent the President's views," said Joe, "but for themselves they've already written off this crop of plums. They have given up, but they think they're going to watch us lose our shirts in this deal.

"Remember the times we beat Johnson when he was Field Inspection? He hates our guts. They all do, because we produce, and they can't do anything but sit on the sidelines. They make believe they run the show while inside they eat their hearts out because they are so incompetent in the ordinary business of living.

"If we fail on this job, they'll see that we're black-balled in every port in the Union. The fact that we represent Terra in the field of service and repair doesn't matter any more. They figure we can be replaced."

From long custom Litchfield gave only half an ear to Joe's political tirades, but he saw that Joe was completely right this time. The politicians whose strangling regulations had been loosed by Joe's persistence were not going to let this golden opportunity go by.

Suddenly he was mad, too. "The end of the week," he muttered.

Art Rawlins considered himself the biggest man on the place. Physically, he was. Joe wouldn't have tolerated the huge, slow-moving bulk in any lesser man, but Rawlins was probably the best tool engineer on the planet.

"You can't make things without tools," was his motto, "and I'm the man who makes the tools that make the machines," he finished modestly. "Without me, nobody works."

He was given the problem without the political angles. There was no dismay in his reaction. Rather, he scented in it the challenge of his career. He exhaled a happy snort of enthusiasm as Joe finished outlining the details.

"Molecular spray!" he exclaimed. "I've heard of it half a dozen times in the last three months. But no crew that has come in has ever seen it. Now we've got a ship that uses it!"

"But without analogues of the designing race, and with no plans of the spray, can you build it?"

"I don't see why not. There's not an artifact made that doesn't leave tool marks indicating the mental processes of the mind that made it—and the tools with which he built. There should be enough information in the plans of the ship to identify and build the tools."

"All right. I hope so. We're setting up a cerebral for the repair crews this morning. You'll want to get in on that with your crew. Get them into the cerebral room in fifteen minutes."

Cerebral indoctrination was a method of short-circuiting the acquiring of data. It implanted items of information directly into the cortex without sending it through the long, circuitous, interference-filled channels of the senses.

From the original data, scanning machines produced impulses exactly like the waves of a perfectly healthy brain as it thought through the problem. These impulses acted directly upon the molecules of the recipient's brains, imposing the data within.

Joe and Litchfield sat in on the session, absorbing the vast flood of information regarding the design of the Martremant. When it was over, they felt sure they could have designed the tools by which the engine would have to be built. But they knew it was an illusion. There was still a tremendous job of analysis to be done, and they lacked Art Rawlins' special skill in evaluating the data they had.

The repair crew filed out of the room at the end of the two-hour session. Rawlins and his men continued to sit there in their chairs, their headpieces in their laps. It was when he saw them that Joe felt the intense sinking inside him.

"What's the matter?" he said thinly. "Wasn't it any good?"

Art Rawlins' wide jowls circled downward to rest against his upper chest. "Let's run through it again, Joe. This time change the differential to get fabrication analysis instead of design and function."

The smaller group of men sat there for another two hours while the machine went through the thousands of drawings and stereoscopes once more. When the lights were on again, Rawlins was slumped still lower.

"I was right the first time," he muttered. "It's no wonder the spray technique is so scarce if the inventors want to keep it hidden. Nobody could figure it out from scratch."

"Why?"

"The tools . . . the tools to make the spray—we can't make them."

For about three-quarters of a minute Joe thought he hadn't heard right. Then he saw that Rawlins wasn't joking, but was perfectly serious in his absurd-sounding statement.

"What do you mean?" Joe asked. "I don't understand."

"We'd have to go down through four or five separate derivations to try to get to the basic technologies involved. By then the trail would be so faint and the variables so large that it would be meaningless.

"I never heard of taking four or five derivatives of a cerebral," said Litchfield.

"Neither has anyone else. It's never come up in such a series as this before. Look: We now have an understanding of what the third-order-drive engines are like. We know what the molecular spray tools to build them are like—but we don't know how to build the tools to build the tools with which to build the spray—and maybe one order of tools below that. See what I mean?"

Joe's voice sounded awed by this complexity that he had never imagined. "It still sounds crazy."

"That's the way it is. Take our tools. Suppose an aborigine could utilize cerebral processes to analyze a sawed block of wood, for example."

"He would first discover the need of a steel saw and would get a pretty good idea of what it was like. His next derivative would be the machine tools to make the saw. That would be pretty faint. He'd go on down to steel-making processes and discover the necessity for iron ore—but he'd never reach any geological knowledge that would show him how to locate it. He'd never get as far as the technology of smelting it or tempering it. Those items just wouldn't be there in the sawing process.

"So it is with the spray. There are at least five separate and unknown technologies that step down to any level with which we are now familiar. The chances of our discovering how to build a molecular spray are absolutely, mathematically zero. The information has got to come from outside, or not at all."

"Nevertheless, the ship has to be repaired and off the field by the end of the week," said Joe.

The others in the room stared at him with a sort of pity as if his mind had slipped into a rut from which it would never escape.

"Go over it again," he said. "Try it down on the hundredth differential if necessary. Drain it of everything it's got, and then have a try at it again. I'll see you later."

Litchfield followed him out of the analysis building into the hot sunlight of the field. Dingy, dust-colored haze hung over all the desert now and the distant hills were shaded a dirty color. He remembered the splendor of the morning and looked accusingly skyward. If any day was ever a bust, this one was.

They walked half of the mile to the site of the wrecked Martremant before either spoke. Then Joe stopped, looking toward the ship with grim defiance shaping his face.

"Howard," he said slowly, "in all the rumors you've heard about the molecular spray, whose name has been connected with it? Did you ever hear before of this mysterious, secret race that's supposed to have concocted it?"

"Why, no. It's always mentioned in connection with the Radalians, but I suppose that was because the Radalians appear to be the only ones using it in their third-order ships—after what Johnson reported about the First."

"I don't believe it. It's too thin. I think the Radalians themselves built it."

"That's crazy! Why would they be withholding it when we can't fix their ship without it?"

"Only the special gods of the politicians could answer that one. The whole thing reeks of the thinking of the political mind. Wherever a political deal is going on there are always lies and counterlies. In this deal, one of them is a story of the mysterious builders of the molecular spray. And there is one way we can find out with absolute certainty."

"How?"

"We'll get us a Radalian analogue."

There was a white plume of dust growing slowly in their direction from the damaged Martremant. At its head were twin scooters bearing two of Litchfield's analysis crew. The illusion of slowness disappeared as the little carriers crackled up and stopped with a burst of gray dust.

"Have you got trouble?" Litchfield asked.

"Trouble!" one exclaimed. "Those crazy politicians—you've got to get them out of there."

"Where?"

"Everywhere. They're loose all over the place. They got tired of sitting in their plush staterooms so they put on pressure suits and now they're kibitzing all over the place—telling us how to do our jobs! The windbags—!"

"At least our friend's from the President's office ought to be able to keep the vips out of our hair while we work," said Litchfield.

"Not only that," continued his crewman, "but their suit exhausts smell up the place until we can't breathe."

"You say they're trying to tell you how to do the job—?" said Joe.

"Yeah—I finished a picture of an assembly and was starting to tear it apart when one of these walking nightmares suddenly sticks out ten of his arms or legs and garrmps in his own language and then says, not on my world, young man, we perform such an operation this way!"

"Were any of them Radalians?"

"I don't know, but you've got to get them out of the way."

Joe turned to Litchfield. "They're trying to show the man how to do his job. What more could we want?"

"A bunch of junketing, kibitzing commissioners won't do us much good. They couldn't run the ship, let alone build it."

"No, but I'll bet if we had an analogue—a Radalian one—we'd know how to build the tools to build the tools to build it. We could differentiate all the way down to the most basic technology required."

"I suppose you'll just step up to the First Administrator and ask him for it."

"Something like that. I've sparred with them long enough to know something about how political minds tick. One thing they can't resist is a Tour."

The atmosphere inside the ship was foul. There were at least a score of clumsy, alien pressure suits within range of their vision as they climbed in through the rent in the hull.

Some suits were squat, some tall, some with eight appendages, some with three or four. Some were filled with liquid, others with gas of chemistry and pressure that would be instant death to a Terrestrian.

It was the exhaust from some of these that Joe and Litchfield smelled immediately. Methane, chlorine, and fluorine were the least deadly that they recognized.

And every one of the politicians was equipped with a cerebropath by which he could make himself heard and understood in order to inflict his opinions on the helpless workman nearest him.

Close by, a six-appendaged creature was earnestly instructing a workman in his job—and exuding a foul aroma that Joe didn't recognize at once. While they watched, the workman quietly rolled over with his staring face upward.

The alien commissioner straightened in perplexity. "That fellow is incompetent. We can't allow such work on our vessel. See that he is replaced."

And the creature marched austerely away.

Funny, Joe thought. You travel a million light-years and find creatures that look like something that should be crawling on the bottom of the sea. Even among them a politician is a politician—arrogant, demanding, and wholly ignorant of ninety-nine percent of the subjects upon which he essays to pontificate.

Joe and Litchfield hunted up the advisors and explained the problem.

"Sorry," said Johnson. "It is their ship, you know. If you can't stand their breathing methane down your necks, you'll just have to work in pressure suits yourselves."

In the eyes of Johnson and the three others Joe could see the grinning faces of all the host of inspectors and bureaucrats he had bested in his long career. They hated him because they belonged to a dying race of bureaucrats and he was their successor. But they had never had him bound so tightly in their red tape as now.

Direct appeal to the foreign commissioners was, of course, useless. They might retreat from their kibitzing, but they would put Earth down as an unfriendly planet of sub-sentient life on which it was not safe to have a space vessel repaired.

"Al right, will you do this, then?" said Joe. "Will you convey my respects to the First Administrator and ask him if he would care for a personally conducted tour of my place? Since the repair work is well in hand, I find myself free and would be glad to be at his service."

The advisors gave him uniform, startled glances. Johnson blinked. "I don't see why not," he said, slowly turning over the idea to find the catch. "You're sure the work is in hand? We should like to report that to the President."

"You may assure him that he has nothing to worry about, but a good deal depends upon my friendly relations with the First Administrator. Will you be so kind as to introduce me?"

Suspicious still, he left and returned in a moment with a grotesque, armored hulk.

"Lockneil, the Radalian, First Administrator of the Galactic Union," said Johnson.

The creature extended one of two stubby appendages. Two others he kept wrapped around his waist—as if he were afraid he'd get his shirt stolen, Joe thought.

"And this is Joe Williams, owner and operator of 'Joe's Service and Repair'—"

Be nice to him, Joe told himself fiercely. This is the guy that can make the field look like another archeological site if he's rubbed the wrong way.

"Glad to know you," said Joe.

"And I," said the Radalian. "Your name is known widely in many galaxies."

The old oil, Joe muttered to himself and smiled appreciatively. "Yes, we get customers from a variety of ports."

"It's comforting to know that our vessel is in such good hands. You are experiencing no unusual difficulties, I trust?"

"Oh, no. Everything's going along fine. We are old hands at working with strange machinery. We have quite a complete system for analyzing cultural artifacts foreign to our own system."

"That's what I've been told," said Lochneil with interest. "In fact, I had hoped during this good-will tour to investigate your place. Time would not have permitted, but this unfortunate accident has forced the delay upon us. Your offer of which Mr. Johnson spoke is extremely welcome. That is, if you're not too busy, of course."

Was there ever a politician who didn't ask that fool question while he consumed the time and energies of his betters, Joe wondered. The tools to make the tools to make the tools—

It kept ringing through his head like a stupid jingle that had no end or meaning. He had to get a Radalian analogue. He was sure he was right—but if his hunch were a bust—

"We have a carrier that will make it easier than trying to walk in the pressure suit," he offered.

"Not at all. Your gravity is light. I shall enjoy a stroll."

You and who else, Joe thought, glancing towards the dust-covered pavement that seemed to be faintly smoking in the heat of the mid-afternoon. But already the Radalian was striding away.

Joe caught up with him. "That building directly across the field is the hospital. We attempt to give medical attention to all who are sick or injured when they arrive."

"Your depot is extremely advanced to have such."

He introduced the First Administrator to Dr. Yates, in charge of the hospital. Immediately it was like old home week, and Joe was startled at the ease with which Lochneil conducted himself in Yates' presence. The old doctor was crotchety and hated people asking silly questions.

But he showed Lochneil the pressure suites where natural accommodations of temperature, pressure, and atmosphere could be supplied in an infinite variety of combinations.

For an hour the Administrator pressed him with questions about the mechanical and biological functions of the complex hospital—how they operated on creatures that couldn't be depressurized, that had to be continually in atmospheres deadly to Earthmen—

Yates answered them all with obvious pleasure.

A political trick, Joe thought irritably, the ability to appear interested in something about which you didn't give a single, minute damn. But that wasn't the answer, either, he recognized with a start. The First Administrator was actually interested in these things. He acted like a creature with a mind that could absorb such technical information.

He found himself almost pleased with the company of the First Administrator, and chafed irritably against this breach of principle.

They went from there to the great machine shops where Lochneil grilled the official in charge in a way that made old Mortenson enjoy it. The Administrator insisted on operating some of the complex fabricating tools—a twenty-ton shear, an eighty-foot planer, the giant lathes.

Next came the library and museums where vast accumulations of encyclopedic data on a hundred thousand races was stored.

"This is most complete," said the First Administrator in frank awe. "It almost is superior to our Union facilities."

The afternoon was nearly over and the sun was setting with an unembarrassed attempt to re-enact some of the morning's glory. Evening crews had come on, but Lochneil showed no signs of giving up. Joe was hungry and tired. He was afraid the First Administrator would want to read the whole library—or worse, yet, that he would suddenly decide to quit.

They had to make one more stop—just one more.

"Engineering analysis is last," said Joe wearily. "Outside of administration, that about completes what we have here—except the hotel, of course, and you wouldn't care to see that now, I'm sure."

"I must see you analysis section," said Lochneil. "That is almost legendary among starmen."

Joe led him into the building and showed him the files of tapes. "We have better than a hundred thousand analogues of members of foreign races. These have all been gathered since I started the depot when I was young.

"You are aware, of course, of the basis of analogue work. It depends upon the fact that in the brain of each race are typical neural structures. The artifacts of the race are always analogues to portions of these structures. If we have so much as one percent of the data relative to a certain artifact, we can usually determine the rest by interpolation from neural analogues."

"Without the analogue your whole establishment would be virtually helpless, would it not?"

"Right. That's the key that allows the whole place to operate."

"May I see the Radalian analogues that you have on hand?"

"We have none at all of your race."

"That is most unfortunate—and even more so that we are unable to allow specimens from those who are present. Your request was relayed to us, but of course it was not necessary in order to repair the ship."

"Oh, no. We just wanted to increase our files. The repair work was well under way when we made the request."

"Fortunately—otherwise it might have been delayed."

Joe felt the tension of fatigue growing strong within him. "Over here," he said, "are the chambers used for interviewing and analogue taking. Would you care to see what we can do in the way of duplicating your environment?"

"Of course."

Lochneil recited the atmospheric constituents and required pressures and temperatures.

"When the green light glows you may remove you pressure suit. I will be on the other side of this transparent wall."

Would the fool actually do it? Joe was so tired he was almost trembling. He feared his anxiety showed, but Lochneil seemed oblivious to all but the mechanical intricacies of the chamber.

Joe sealed the door and took his place in the interviewer's chair. As the green light flashed Lochneil cautiously opened the panel at the side of his face.

"Very agreeable. Like a spring day on my home world."

He stripped off the pressure suit while Joe sat as if paralyzed. The Radalian was a sleek creature who seemed covered with bright green velvet. Great wild eyes shifting at random in the bulging sockets. Scanning vision, Joe thought. He had seen it twice before, but didn't know it was in the Radalians.

The First Administrator strode about, flexing his short and long arms with pleasurable freedom from the suit.

Like a politician strutting around on a platform, Joe thought. But that wasn't right, he knew somehow. Lochneil was of a different cast from the local politicians. He spoke and talked like a man who could perform—

He sat down opposite Joe. "Extremely well done," he said. "I have not seen anything to compare with it in all my travels. I only regret our visit was at the expense of the lives of our crew."

He began fingering the panel at his side. He picked up the helmet used for analogue taking. "This is what, now?" he said.

"That picks up the neural pulses and sends them on to the recorder."

Lochneil gave a pompous grmmf and eyed the gadget closely.

Joe fingered the row of controls on the arm of his chair. His hands were sweaty.

If he puts it on, I'll let him have it—

He did—

And Joe did.

He blasted the brain of Lochneil with one quick flash that went deep to extract millions of neural patterns. It was a bitter technique seldom used, but possible. It differed from the ordinary recording in the same way a photograph by intense flash differs from a time picture. And it always knocked the patient out—sometimes seriously.

For a long time Joe just sat there. The great eyes of Lochneil were staring wildly and still scanning slowly—but utterly vacant.

He would be all right—Joe hoped and prayed. But he prayed also for the impossible—that Lochneil might be as completely stupid as the run of the mill politicians in regard to technical matters.

It was already much too late for that, for the First Administrator had displayed many times the comprehension of his Terrestrian kind. And, much as he hated to admit it to himself, Joe liked the man.

He called Yates, who swore at him and left his dinner table. Then he called Litchfield and explained what he had done. The engineer swore, too, and called him a fool for pulling such a stunt.

Then Joe sat down and waited for them to come, almost convinced that their opinions of him were correct.

Yates came first and took the stiff Lochneil away with scarcely a word to Joe. When Litchfield came, Joe was examining the tapes.

"You really put the fat in the fire."

"I don't know. I couldn't think of anything else."

"You shouldn't think at all after a day like this. Let's get a drink and go home to bed."

"No—we've got to examine these analogues. If I'm right, we can start making tools to make the tools to make . . . oh, hell! We can start tonight."

"And I suppose the First won't even know what hit him?"

"Let's not speak of it now."

They took the tape into the scanning room and placed it in one of the machines. Beside it, they placed the data take from the Radalian plans. Then Joe pressed the button and watched the screen. After a moment he sat back with a sigh. This was it. The Radalian analogue nailed down the molecular spray to the lowest technical level.

They didn't sleep that night, and by morning it was raining. That was appropriate, Joe thought, for the events that would certainly transpire this day.

Art Rawlins had slaved beside them all night and by morning his eyes were as baggy as his grin was wide. "We can make a spray, now," he said. "You watch!"

By dawn Lochneil had still not awakened. Joe went over to the hospital suite while Litchfield and Rawlins got things under way. Joe wanted to be alone with the First Administrator. He didn't want anyone else to have to share the brunt of Lochneil's wrath.

But the First Administrator awoke without wrath of indignation. He sat up so suddenly it almost shocked Joe. Then he grinned ruefully. At least Joe took it for a Radalian grin.

"That was a foolish thing for me to do," said Lochneil. "I didn't even give you time to warn me, did I?"

Joe exhaled—long and deep—and a slow, grim tension began building up anew within him. The Radalian intended to pose as innocent of understanding what had taken place. But Joe knew that was a lie. The question he had heard yesterday could not have come from one too ignorant to know his analogue had been taken.

Lochneil was still playing a lying political game, and to what purpose Joe could not guess.

"Are you hurt?" he said solicitously. "We're deeply sorry a thing like this should happen. The current—"

"A slight headache is all. I'd like to return to the ship now. I feel hungry."

"Stay right where you are. Breakfast is coming up!"

On Wednesday they had the tools to make the tools to make the tools to make the spray.

On Thursday they had the tools to make the tools to make the spray.

Friday, they had the spray.

In the process, Art Rawlins had filled a hangar fifteen hundred feet long with machinery. He had taken advantage of the offer of Johnson to use available government facilities. For two solid days fleets of ships had poured machines and technicians into the place.

On the third day the single piece of equipment required to rebuild the Martremant emerged.

The evening shift on Friday began the rebuilding. The ship was moved a considerable distance and shielded heavily—but the junketeers refused to move. Of them all, only Lochneil was on hand to watch the process.

It was wholly automatic, but Joe had the honor of pressing the button to start the process. Inside the ship, a great backing plate had been prepared. In front of it, an intricate scaffolding held the nozzle that sprayed out a great machine, molecule by molecule.

Simultaneously, on each floor, the process went on, building the units that would drive the ship at third-order velocities.

And Joe had not yet solved the lie of Lochneil. But he was about to, he thought. It was now or never.

He fed the heavy piles of matrix plates into the scanning chambers of the molecular spray. While Lochneil—and only Lochneil—was looking, he switched a pair of matrices.

He stepped back then, absently watching the functioning of the machine. On tube faces, they could watch the building as it proceeded inside the ship. Joe was aware of Lochneil's eyes upon him. The great scanning eyes of the First Administrator were spinning back and forth like mad radar beams.

At last, with a cry of dismay, the Radalian leaped for the controls of the machine just as the scanning of the erroneous matrix began.

He cut the power and gestured helplessly towards the matrix.

"I thought . . . it seemed . . . are you sure it's working all right?"

"Now how about the full story?" said Joe. "You've been pulling our legs ever since you came here. Why?"

"You knew perfectly well how the molecular spray was to be built. You could have told us, but you played dumb. Then you deliberately sat down in the analogue chair and gave me the analogue I had tried so hard to get. There must be a reason, and even if you are the First Administrator, it ought to be a good one."

Lochneil smiled slowly and turned to the controls. He changed the matrix and started the machine again. Then he faced Joe.

"I was quite sure you never would get the Martremant repaired in any reasonable time without the analogue. That's why I gave it to you. You see, I happen to be the inventor of the spray process."

Joe swallowed hard. "You . . . the spray—?"

"We came here for the prime purpose of getting information first-hand from your people about your people. The conference and dinners and polite exchanges we were subjected to in you Capitol seemed like a deliberate barrier to prevent that. So we had planned a secret mission to accomplish what a straight-forward visit seemed unable to do.

"Then, suddenly, the accident made it possible. Our kibitzing, as you called it, was quite deliberate. We wanted to observe you in natural circumstances. We wanted to observe your attempts to solve the problem without knowing you were being given the molecular spray. Your results were admirable."

"But why all this?" said Joe. "It still makes no sense. You— the spray designer, and First Administrator. We haven't a single being on our whole planet who could occupy correspondingly similar positions."

"I know," said Lochneil. "That is the tragedy of your people. We have studied and marveled over you organization since you entered the Union. You will not be flattered, I'm sure, to know that among the sociologists of more advanced civilizations you are classified as 'political primitives.' Hundreds of theses have been written to describe and explain how a culture can advance in such a lopsided manner as yours.

"Good government is simply good living, and we are taught how to live with one another. Therefore, it is hardly startling among us that I, the inventor of the spray, should also serve a term as First Administrator. The implications of your term 'political' do not exist among us."

"Then there is no intention of choosing an Earthman for First Administrator?" said Joe.

"On the contrary, we are seriously considering the appointment. It would give you considerable political confidence as a people.

"We have watched with pleasure your progress since entering the Union. Your bureaucracy is dying at an increasing rate, and we should like to offer assistance in its replacement. There is in you language a term, I believe, that expresses somewhat the situation—wheels within wheels."

Joe got it then. The faint implications that had been present in the Lochneil analogue.

Wheels within wheels—

Concentric coteries of increasingly tight and advanced organizations with the vast Galactic Union. Primitive worlds, such as Earth, were allowed to believe there was only a loose federation. But they were thinking now of inviting Earth to join one of the inner circles—

"I hope if you choose an Earthman you will get a man who can beat a politician at his own game," said Joe.

"I shall. I surely shall. He will be handpicked and trained for the position, and I have a positive recommendation already to make as soon as we return to Administration Central.

"It has been a pleasure to know you and watch you at work. Exhausting all lesser alternatives, you resorted to extremities only when necessary. You operate according to correct political principles, Mr. Williams. In fact, I would say you are an excellent politician."

Noise Level

Originally Published in *Astounding Science Fiction*
December 1952

NOISE LEVEL

I

Dr. Martin Nagle studied the paint on the ceiling of the outer anteroom of the Office of National Research. After ten minutes he was fairly certain which corner had been painted first, the direction of advance across the ceiling, and approximately how long it had taken.

It was a new building and a new paint job, but these facts were evident in the brush marks and brush hairs left in the paint. On the whole, the job was something of an indication of how things were in general, he thought somewhat sadly.

He studied the rug. Specifications should have been higher. The manufacturer undoubtedly operated on the principle of "Don't throw away seconds; you can always sell them to the Government."

His watch showed twenty-five minutes spent in the study of the anteroom. It was all he was going to give it. He picked up his briefcase and top coat and moved towards the door.

He almost collided with a grey-suited figure, then backed away in pleasant recognition.

"Berk!"

The face of Dr. Kenneth Berkeley lighted as he gripped Martin Nagle's free hand and clapped him on the shoulder.

"What are you doing out here in the waiting room, Mart?"

"I got invited to some conference with all the top dogs and high brass, but the boys in blue wouldn't let me in. I was just on my way back to California. But you're one of the last I expected to meet here. What are you doing, Berk?"

"I work on ONR. I'm on this conference myself. They sent me out to look for you. Everybody else has arrived."

"I saw the parade from here, Dykstra from MIT, Collins from Harvard, and Mellon from Cal Tech. A high-powered bunch."

"It is. And they're all waiting on you! Come on. We'll talk later."

Mart jerked a thumb towards the office opening off of the anteroom. "The boys in there seem to have doubts as to whether I can be trusted not to pass things on to the Comrades. I can't wait around. It'll probably take six weeks to clear me. I thought all that would have been taken care of. Evidently it wasn't. Give my regards to everybody, and tell Keyes I'm sorry I hadn't been cleared for classified projects. I guess he didn't know it."

"No, wait—this is absolutely silly," said Berk. "We've got to have you in there. Sit down and we'll have this thing cleared in five minutes!"

Mart sat down again. He had never worked on any classified projects. The fingerprinting and sleuthing into the past of his colleagues had always seemed distasteful to him. He knew Berk didn't have a chance now. He'd seen more than one good man twiddle his thumbs for six months or a year while his dark past was unearthed.

Rising voices from the inner office of the FBI agent became audible. Mart caught snatches of Berk's baritone roar. "Utterly ridiculous . . . top-drawer physicist . . . electro fields . . . got to have this man—"

After the FBI office there were still the offices of Military Intelligence and Naval Intelligence to hurdle. It was a fantastic triple barrier they had woven about the conference. On coming in he had chuckled at this further evidence of frantic bureaucrats trying to button up the secrets of nature which lay visible to the whole world.

In a moment Berk came striding out, red-faced and indignant. "You stay right there, Mart," he said furiously. "I'm going to get Keyes on this thing, and we'll find out who's got a right to get into this place besides the janitor!"

"Look, Berk—I don't mind. I don't think you ought to bother Keyes with this—"

"I'll be right back. This thing has gone too far."

Mart felt rather foolish. It was not his fault he couldn't get by the security officers, but that failure induced a faint sense of guilt.

Berk returned within minutes. With him were two men in uniform, a brigadier general, and a naval captain. With them was Dr. Keyes, Director of ONR. Martin knew him only by reputation—which was very top-drawer indeed. Keyes approached with a direct friendly smile and offered his hand.

"I'm very sorry, Dr. Nagle, regarding this delay. I had no idea that you would be stopped at the security desk. I issued instructions in plenty of time for the conference that everyone invited be properly cleared. Somehow this formality was overlooked in your case. But I am sure that we shall be able to make satisfactory emergency arrangements within a few moments. If you will wait here while I confer with these gentlemen—"

They closed the door of the inner office, but Mart could not help straining his ears at the rumble of sounds that filtered through. He caught a phrase in a voice that belonged to one of the security officers: " . . . Demanded these triple security screens yourself—"

And another from Keyes: " . . .The one man who may be able to crack this thing for us—"

Mart had come reluctantly. His wife had protested, and the two children had set up a tremendous wail that it meant no summer vacation at all.

He rather wished he had heeded their protests. The moment a man became involved in something so classified it required triple passes from the Army, Navy, and FBI he could say goodbye to freedom. He wondered how Keyes had become involved in such a circuitous business. Keyes had done monumental work on electromagnetic radiation.

And he wondered, too, what Kenneth Berkeley was doing here. It was way out of his field. Berk was a top psychologist in the mechanics of learning, and experimental training procedures.

It looked to Mart as if both of them were wasting their time in security clearance wrangles.

He was not particularly intrigued by the possible magnitude of the problem under consideration. A man sitting by a mountain stream under an open summer sky had the most ponderous problems of nature before him if he chose to consider them. None couched in the hush-hush terms behind closed doors could have any greater import.

At last the door opened. Mart arose. Dr. Keyes led the procession out of the room. All of the men were a little more strained in their expressions than when they went in, but Keyes took mart's arm.

"It's all right. You have full clearance now. Your papers will be issued and ready when you come out. But let's get to the conference at once. We've kept the others waiting."

As Mart stepped inside the conference room he caught his breath involuntarily. Besides the brilliant array of his colleagues in fields closely allied to his own, there was a display of gold-splashed uniforms of all military services. He had quick recognition of several lieutenant generals, vice admirals, and at least one member of the JCS.

Berk ushered him to a seat in the front row. He felt doubly guilty that these men had been kept waiting, although it was no fault of his.

At the front of the room a projection screen was unrolled on the wall. A sixteen mm. projector was set up near the rear. On a table on the far side a tarpaulin covered some kind of irregular object.

Keyes stepped to the front of the room and cleared his throat briefly.

"We will dispense with the formality of introducing each of you gentlemen. Many of you are acquainted, professionally or personally, and I trust that all will be before this project is many hours old.

"The top classification nature of the material we are about to discuss has been emphasized to you by the triple filter of security officers who have passed upon your admission to this room. That which is discussed here you will properly regard as worthy of protection with you own life, if such an extreme consideration should be forced upon you at some future time."

The military members of the audience remained immobile, but Martin Nagle observed an uneasy shifting among his fellow scientists. All of them were to some degree uncomfortable in the presence of the military assumption that you could lock up secrets of nature when they lay all about like shells upon the seashore.

But Keyes wasn't a military man. Mart felt his muscles become a little more rigid as the significance of this penetrated.

"Ten days ago," said Keyes very slowly, "we were approached by a young man, an inventor of sorts, who claimed to have produced a remarkable and revolutionary invention.

"His name was Leon Dunning. He had an unusual regard for his own abilities, and expected, apparently, that everyone else would have the same regard on sight. This trait led him to a rather unpleasant presentation of himself. He would talk with no one but the Director of the Office, and made such a nuisance that it became a question of seeing him or calling the police.

"His case was drawn to my attention, and I finally chose to see him. He had some rather startling claims. He claimed to have solved the problem of producing an anti-gravity machine."

Martin Nagle felt a sudden sinking sensation within him—and an impulse to laugh. For this he had cancelled the kids' summer vacation! Maybe it wasn't too late to get back—

He glanced at his colleagues. Dykstra was bending over and rubbing his forehead to hide the smile that appeared on his lips. Lee and Norcross gave each other smiles of pitying indulgence. Berkeley, Mart noted, was almost the only scientist who did not move or smile. But, of course, Berk was a psychologist.

"I see that some of you gentlemen are amused," continued Keyes. "So was I. I wondered what was the best means of getting rid of this obnoxious crackpot who had forced his way into my office. Again, it was a question of listening until the ridiculousness of his claims became self-evident, or having him thrown out. I listened.

"I tried to draw him out regarding the theories upon which the device operated, but he refused to discuss this in detail. He insisted such discussions could be held only after a demonstration of his device.

"With a free Saturday afternoon that week, I agreed to watch. Dunning insisted that certain military personnel also be invited and that film and tape recording equipment be available. Having gone as far as I had, I agreed to this and rounded up some of the gentlemen who were with us this afternoon.

"He wanted no other kind of publicity, and so we arranged to meet at the small private airfield at the Dover club. That was just one week ago today. He demonstrated.

"A small pack was attached to his shoulders by straps. I assisted him in putting it on. It weighed perhaps thirty-five or forty pounds. It had no visible means of propulsion such as propeller or jets, and no connection to an external power source. Seeing it, I felt ridiculous for having invited my military guests to such a futile performance.

"We stood in a circle about ten feet in diameter around him. When the pack was fastened, he gave us a kind of pitying smile, it seemed, and pressed a switch at his belt.

"Instantly, he rose straight up into the air in a smoothly accelerated climb. We spread apart to watch him. At about five hundred feet, he came to a stop and hung motionless for a moment. Then he dropped back down to the centre of the circle."

Keyes paused. "I see a variety of expressions on you faces. I presume some of you consider us who observed it as victims of hallucinations or out and out liars. We agreed afterward that it was very fortunate that Dunning insisted on motion pictures of the demonstration. These we have for your inspection. If you will, please—"

He signaled to his assistants. The shades were drawn and the projector at the rear started to whirr. Mart found himself leaning forward, his hand clutching the desk arm of the chair. This was something he didn't even want to believe, he thought.

On the screen there appeared a scene of encircling men. In the centre. Dunning appeared to be in his late twenties. Mart could detect at once the type that Keyes had described—a snotty young jerk who knew he was good and figured others better catch on to that real fast. Mart knew the type. You run into them in senior engineering classes in every school in the country.

He watched the circle back from Dunning. There was a clear shot of the alleged inventor standing with the weird pack on his back. He fumbled a moment with the key switch at his belt, then rose abruptly from the ground.

Mart stared. The picture panned up jerkily as the operator evidently retreated for a longer range view. He watch closely for any sign of emanation from the pack. He had to remind himself of the foolishness of looking for such. There was certainly no type of jet that could operate this way.

But anti-gravity—Mart caught a feeling that was a cross between a prickle and a chill moving slowly along the upper length of his spine.

The motion on the screen came to a halt. Then slowly Dunning lowered himself to the middle of the circle once more.

The screen went dark, and lights flashed on in the room. Mart jerked as if waking from a hypnotic spell.

"We paused at this point," said Keyes. "Dunning became more talkative and discussed somewhat the basic theories of his machine. For this we used the tape recorder he had insisted on us bringing along.

"Unfortunately, the record is so poor due to high noise level and distortion that it is next to unintelligible, but we will play it for you in a moment.

"Following the discussion, he agreed to make another demonstration showing an additional factor, horizontal flight control. We'll have the movie of this, now."

He touched the light button. The scene appeared once more. This time the circle opened at one side and Dunning rose in a rather steep arc and leveled off. Against the background, he seemed about as high as the roof of the hangar beyond. For about a hundred feet he drifted slowly, then accelerated his pace. Mart felt a wholly irrational impulse to laugh. It was Buck Rogers in full attack.

Abruptly the screen flared. A puff of light exploded from the pack on Dunning's back. For a terrible moment he seemed suspended in an attitude of violent agony. Then he plunged like a dropped stone.

The camera lost him for an instant, but it caught the full impact of his body on the field. During the fall, he turned over. The pack was beneath him as he crashed. His body bounced and rolled a short way and lay still.

Keyes moved to the light switch, and signaled for the raising of the shades. Someone rose to do this. No one else moved. The room seemed caught in a suspension of time.

"There you have it, gentlemen," said Keyes in a quiet voice. "You will begin to understand why you were called here today. Dunning had it—anti-gravity. Of that we are absolutely sure, And Dunning is dead."

He drew a corner of the canvas from the table by the far wall. "The remains of the device are here for your examination. So far, we see only burned and bloody wreckage in it. Under your supervision it will be carefully photographed and dismantled."

He dropped the cover and returned to the centre of the platform. "We went immediately to Dunning's home with a crew of investigators from ONR assisted by security officers of the services.

"Dunning quite evident paranoia was carried out in an utter lack of notes. He must have lived in constant fear that his work would be stolen. His laboratory was excellent for a private worker. What his income was we don't know as yet.

"He also had an astonishing library—astonishing in that it covered almost every occult field as well. This, too, remains somewhat of a mystery.

"We investigated his college background. He appears to have had a difficulty in getting along at any one college, and attended at least four. His curriculum was as varied as his library. He studied courses in electrical engineering, comparative religion, advanced astronomy, Latin, the theory of groups, general semantics and advanced comparative anatomy.

"We managed to contact about twenty of his instructors and fellow students. Their uniform opinions described him as paranoid. He was utterly without intimates of any kind. If he communicated his theories to anyone, we do not know about it.

"So the only record we have of the expressions of the man who first devised an anti-gravity machine is this poor-quality tape."

He nodded again to the operator at the rear of the room. The latter turned on the recorder whose output was fed to a speaker on the table in front.

At once the room was filled with a hissing, roaring garble. The sound of planes taking off—the everyday noise of the airport. Beneath the racket was the dead man's voice, a thin, rather high-pitched sound carrying through the background noise a tone of condescension and impatient tolerance.

Mart listened with ears strained to make sense of the garble. His eyes caught Berk's and reflected his despair of ever getting anything out of the mess. Keyes signaled the operator.

"I see that you are impatient with this recording, gentlemen. Perhaps there is no purpose in playing it in this conference. But each of you will be given a copy. In the privacy of your own laboratories you will have opportunity to make what you can of it. It is worth your study simply because, as far as we know, it contains the only clues we possess."

Mart raised a hand impatiently. "Dr. Keyes, you and the others at the demonstration heard the original discussion. Can't you give us more than is on the tape?"

Keyes smiled bitterly. "I wish that we could, Dr. Nagle. Unfortunately, at the time it seemed that the semantic noise in Dunning's explanation was as high as the engineering noise on the tape. We have, however, filled in to the best of our recollection on the written transcript, which we will give you.

"This transcript gives what has been pieced together by phonetic experts who have analyzed the tape. Observers' additions are in parentheses. These were added only if all observers agreed independently, and may or may not be accurate. Is there any other question?"

There were, they all knew, but for the moment the impact seemed to have stifled the response of the whole audience.

Keyes took a step forward. "I wonder if there is any of you who underestimates the seriousness of this problem now. Is there anyone who does not understand that this secret must be regained at all cost?

"We know that within the field of present knowledge there lies the knowledge necessary to conquer gravity—to take us beyond the Earth, to the stars, if we wish to go.

"We know that if one young American could do it, some young Russian could also. We have to duplicate that work of Dunning's

"The full facilities of ONR are at your disposal. Access to Dunning's laboratory and library and the remains of his machine will be granted, of course. Each of you has been selected, out of all whom we might have called, because we believed you possess some special qualification for the task. You cannot fail.

"We will meet again this evening, gentlemen. I trust you understand now the necessity for absolute security on this project."

II

A long time afterwards, Martin Nagle recalled that he must have been in a partial stupor when he left that conference room. He felt a vague and unpleasant sensation about his head as if it had been beaten repeatedly with a pillow.

He and Kenneth Berkeley went out together. They paused only long enough to make polite greetings to his fellow physicists whom he had not seen for a long time. But he was in a hurry to leave. To get rid of that feeling in his head.

In front of the ONR building he stopped with his hands in his pockets and looked over the unpleasant grey of the city's buildings. He could close his eyes and still see a man rising up into the air—soaring at an angle—dropping like a plummet.

All at once he realized he hadn't even stopped to examine the remains of the instrument under the tarpaulin. He turned suddenly on Berkeley.

"The psychology of this thing—is that where you're in on it, Berk?"

His companion nodded. "Keyes called me in when he wanted an investigation into Dunning's past. I'm staying, I guess."

"You know it's impossible, don't you?" said Mart. "Utterly and completely impossible! There's nothing in our basic science to explain this thing, let alone duplicate it."

"Impossible? Meaning what?"

"Meaning that I've got to . . . that every one of us has got to shift gears, back up, retrace who knows how far—twenty years of learning—five hundred years of science? Where did we go off the track? Why was it left to a screwball like Dunning to hit it right?"

"He was an odd character," mused Berk. "Astrology, mysticism, levitation. There's quite a bit in the tape about levitation. That's not so far removed from the concept of anti-gravity at that, is it?"

Mart made a rough noise in his throat. "I expect to hear any moment that his first successful flight was aboard a broomstick."

"Well, there's quite a bit of lore about broomsticks—also magic carpets and such. Makes you wonder how it all got started."

The shock was slowly wearing down. Martin returned to the hotel after the evening conference, which was spent mostly in examining the wreckage.

It was as Keyes had said, hopeless. But there was an indefinable something about gazing upon the remains of what had been the realization of an impossible dream. Mart felt a kind of frantic yearning to reach out and touch that mass and convert it back to the instrument it had once been by sheer force of will. As if believing it possible would make it so.

And wasn't there some essence of truth in this, he thought? Dunning had believed it could be done and had done it. Reputable men in science didn't believe such things possible—

Now, in his hotel room, Mart sat on the edge of the bed looking out of the window and across the night lights of the city. There were certain things you had to accept as impossible. The foundation of science was built upon the concept of the impossible as well as the possible.

Perpetual motion.

The alchemist's dream—as the alchemist dreamed it, anyway.

Anti-gravity—

All man's experience in attempting to master nature showed these things could not be done. You had to set yourself some limitations. You had to let your work be bounded by certain Great Impossibles or you could spend a lifetime trying to solve the secret of invisibility or of walking though a brick wall.

Or trying to build a magic carpet.

He stood up and walked to the window. There had been growing all afternoon a sense of faint panic. And now he identified it. Where could you draw the line? It had to be drawn. He was sure of that.

It had been drawn once before, quite definitely. In the 1890s they had closed the books. Great minds believed then that science had encompassed the universe. All that was not known belonged to the Great Impossibles.

Then had come radium, the Roentgen tube, relativity, cosmic rays.

The line vanished. Where was it now? A few hours ago he would have said he could define it with fair accuracy. Tonight he did not know.

He went to bed. After an hour he got up and called Kenneth Berkeley. The clock said almost midnight. It didn't matter.

"Berk," he said into the phone. "Mart, I've just been thinking. The whole crowd will be going through Dunning's lab and his library. What's the chance of your getting me out there first thing in the morning? Just the two of us. I'd like to beat the crowd."

"I think I can arrange it," said Berk. "Keyes wants each of you to work as you wish. I'll tell you more about that tomorrow. I'll call you as early as I can."

It rained during the night, and when Berk called for Mart in his car, the city was dismal with fog, lessening even further the reality surrounding them.

"Keyes wasn't much in favour of this," said Berk as they drove away from the hotel. "It's liable to make some of the others mad, but frankly, I'm sure he's convinced that you're the member of the class most likely to succeed."

Mart grunted. "Least likely, I'd say. I'm not sure that I'm convinced yet that Dunning didn't have some terrific joker in here somewhere."

"I know what you mean, but you will. It comes gradually. And easier for you. You're the youngest of the group. Keyes thinks some of the older men may spend all their time proving Dunning couldn't do it. How do you feel about that? Is that the way you're heading, or are you going to try to find out what Dunning did?"

"Anything a jerk like Dunning can do, Nagle can do double— once Nagle is convinced that Dunning did it."

Berk threw back his head and laughed. "Keyes will love you, boy. He's been afraid he wouldn't find a single top John in the country who would really try."

Dunning's place was in the shabby, once fashionable sector of town where the owners of the gingerbread monsters were no longer able to meet the upkeep or sell them to anyone who was.

It had been learned that the house actually belonged to an uncle of Dunning, but so far he had not been located.

A guard was on duty at the front entrance. He nodded as Berk and Mart showed their passes.

"Dunning's laboratories and shops are on the first floor," said Berk. "Upstairs, is his library. He slept in one of the third floor bedrooms, but the rest are vacant. A lot of cooking seems to have been done in the back kitchen. He left a well stocked larder. Where do you want to start?"

"A quick look through the labs to begin. I want to get the feel of the layout."

On the right of the entrance hallway, they came into a small but extremely well equipped chemistry laboratory. The place seemed well used, but immaculate. A complex fractionating setup was on the worktable.

"Almost the only piece of writing in the whole place was found on a small pad here," said Berk. "A bit of scratch work computation without any formulas or reactions."

Mart grunted and moved on to the adjacent room. Here was the more familiar hodgepodge of the electronic experimenter, but even in this there was instantly apparent the mark of a careful workman. Breadboard layouts were assembled with optimum care. Test leads were carefully made of rubber-covered or shielded wire and equipped with clips instead of being the usual random lengths of coloured connecting wire hastily stripped and tied to a terminal.

A sizeable bank of rack and panel mounted equipment was not recognizable at once as to function. It appeared to be a set-up that might belong to any careful experimenter who had no regard for his bank account.

This would need further study, but Mart continued moving through to the next room, a machine shop, as well equipped for its functions as the previous rooms. A six-inch lathe, a large drill press, and a milling machine were the chief items.

Mart whistled softly as he stood in the middle of the room and looked back the way they had come.

"When I was a kid in high school," he said, "this is exactly the kind of place I thought Heaven would be."

"And it had to belong to a person like Dunning, eh?" said Berk with a slow smile.

Mart turned sharply. His voice became low and serious. "Berk—whatever Dunning may have been, he was no jug-head. A paranoid, maybe, but not a jug-head. He could do things. Look at this."

He picked up a weird looking assembly from a nearby table and held it up to the light. It gleamed with a creamy sheen. A silver-plated bit of high-frequency plumbing.

"That's beautiful," said Mart. "There're not more than three or four university shops in the whole country that can turn out a piece like that. I've had to fight for weeks to get our machinists to come up with anything that complex and then it would be way out of tolerance."

He hefted the piece of plumbing lightly. He knew it was just right. It had the feel of being made right.

Berk led the way across the hall. He opened the door for Mart. There, against the walls of the room, were panels of a compact digital computer, and on the other side an analogue computer.

"But you haven't seen anything yet," said Berk. "The surprise of your life is upstairs."

"Gravity was a force, Mart thought as he climbed the stairs. You only lick force with force—in the world of physics, at least. In politics and human relations, force might yield to something more subtle, but if Dunning had licked gravity it was with some other—and presently known—force. Physics was at least aware of every force that existed. There were no gaps except perhaps the one temporarily occupied by the elusive neutrino.

Dunning's machine was ingenious. But it could be nothing but a clever application of well-known laws and forces. There was no miracle, no magic in it. Having decided this on a slow, verbal basis, Mart felt somewhat more at ease. He followed Berk into the library.

There was not simply one room of it, but an entire suite had been converted and shelved. There were certainly several thousand volumes in the place.

"This is the one that may interest you most." Berk stepped into the nearest room on his left. "A is for astrology," he said. He gestured towards a full section of shelving.

Mart scanned the titles: Astrology for the Novice, Astrology and the Infinite Destiny, The Babylonian Way, The Course of the Stars.

He hopefully pulled the latter volume from the shelf against the possibility it might be an astronomy text. It wasn't. He quickly put it back with its fellows.

"Well read, too," said Berk. "We examined quite a number and they have copious notations in Dunning's handwriting. This may be the one place we can find real clues to his thinking—in such marginal notes."

Mart waved a hand in violent rejection of the somber volumes and shoved his hands deep in his pockets. "Junk!" he muttered. "This has no bearing on Keyes' problem at all, of course. But it certainly ought to be a problem of interest to you.

"A guy would need two separate heads to hold an interest in the things downstairs and in this nonsense at the same time."

"But Dunning had only a single head," said Berk quietly. "Maybe it's all part of a whole that we don't see—and that Dunning did."

Mart pursed his lips and looked at the psychologist.

"I'm serious," said Berk. "My field is primarily the human mind, and only secondarily the subjects with which the mind deals. But we see in Dunning a single mind that can whip the matter of anti-gravity, that can hold an interest in the fields represented by the laboratories below, and can digest the material of this library.

"Now, actually, there is no true schizophrenia. In the skull of each of us is only a single individual, and anyone examined closely enough can be found to have a remarkably consistent goal, no matter how apparently erratic his activities.

"Perhaps much of the material Dunning found in both the library and in the laboratory proved redundant, but I would say that Dunning's genius apparently lay in his ability to extract relevant material from the redundant without categorically rejecting entire areas of human thought."

Mart smiled tolerantly and turned away. He found himself facing a section of shelves covered with works on East Indian philosophy. Six of eight feet space was devoted to the subject of Levitation. Mart jabbed a finger at the titles.

"Anything those boys can do by hocus-pocus Nagle can do twice as fast by x's and y's and by making electrons jump through hoops."

"That's all Keyes wants. How soon can you deliver?"

III

After lunch, they returned to ONR. Mart was assigned an office and given a copy of the Dunning tape. He put aside the prepared transcript, as Keyes had suggested, and prepared to listen, unbiased.

He turned on the recorder and winced at the garble of sound that blared forth again. With one hand on the volume control he rested his chin on his arm in front of the speaker and strained to hear through the noise the scarcely audible voice of Dunning.

Near the beginning, he caught the word "levitation" mentioned many times. There was a full phrase, "levitation which was first successfully demonstrated to the Western world by the English medium—" The buzz of a plane cut off the rest of it.

Mart rewound the tape and listened to that much of it again. At each mention of levitation an image flared up in Mart's mind. An image of a dirty, scrawny Indian fakir equipped with a filthy turban. A coil of rope over one arm, and a basket with a snake in the other hand.

But Dunning had produced anti-gravity.

What semantic significance had he found in the word?

Mart growled to himself in irritation and let the tape run on. There was nothing more in those first few feet of it. He perked up his ears at a phrase "earth effect" separated by a garble from "distribution of sunspots unexplained to date by astronomers, and politely ignored by all experts—"

It struck a faint bell of recollection in Mart's mind. He scratched a note on a pad to check on it.

The sound dissolved again to hissing and roaring, through which the dead man seemed to taunt him. He gathered that much talk was on the subject of "planetary configurations—," Astrology. He groaned aloud and closed his eyes through a comparatively long stretch of audibility: "Magnetic storms on Earth predictable through movements of the planets in terms of quadrature—fields of data observed through thousands of years and do not fit explanations now accepted for other phenomena."

It shifted apparently, after many minutes, to comparative religion. "Galileo and Newton," Dunning said, "affected man's thinking more than they knew. The clipped from religion its miracles and from physics its imagination . . . of India there's more conquest of the physical universe than in a score of American research laboratories."

And that was the last of it. The tape fizzled out in a long garble of buzzing planes and faulty recording. Mart turned off the machine.

That was it. The mind and work of the first man to directly conquer gravity!

With an almost physical weariness he turned to the transcript and scanned through it. There was more, but it was astonishing how little additional information was actually added from the memories of the original observers. Mart supposed Dunning's words were such a shock to those military and scientific minds that they were stunned into semi-permanent amnesia in respect to the things he said.

He leaned back in the chair, summing up what he had heard. Dunning's thesis seemed to be that much sound data had been excluded by conventional scientists from standard theories. The dead man had believed much of this data could be found and explained in the various realms of astrology, East Indian mysticism, movements of sunspots, the levitation of mediums, and a host of other unorthodox areas.

Where was the thread of rational thought that could find its way through this? He closed his eyes again, trying to fell for a starting point.

There came a knock on the door, and a voice, "May I come in, Dr. Nagle?"

It was Keyes. Mart rose and offered a chair. "I have just finished the tapes and transcription. There is very little to go on."

"Very little indeed," said Keyes. "When you were a youngster entering a contest for the first time you had a feeling for it. You know what I mean. It's in your throat and chest, and in your stomach. It goes all the way through your legs to your toes.

"It's the feeling of your entire organism—a feeling that you haven't got a chance to win—or that you are going to acquit yourself to the maximum ability within you, regardless of the strength of others. Do you understand me?"

Mart nodded.

"What kind of a feeling do you have about this. Dr. Nagle?"

Mart relaxed and leaned back with his eyes half closed. He understood Keyes. He had gone through a range of all possible feelings since yesterday afternoon. Which one of them had remained with him?

"I can do it," he said quietly to Keyes. "I could wish for more data, and I'm not wholly in sympathy with Dunning's approach. But I can examine the data he had, and reexamine the data I have. And I can do it."

"Good!" Keyes stood up. "That's what I came in to find out. And your answer is what I hoped to hear. You may expect that your reaction is not quite universal among your colleagues, although I feel all will co-operate. But some of them will be licked before they start, because they will feel, and persist in feeling that the thing ought not to be."

Dr. Kenneth Berkeley had never ceased to wonder at the constitution of man. When he was very young he had wondered why some of his fellows believed in fairies, and others did not. He wondered why some could believe the moon was made of green cheese and others were equally sure it could not be so.

He grew to wonder intensely just how man knew anything for sure, and that long road of wonder led to the present moment of his status as fellow in psychology at ONR.

He was grateful for the privilege of being on this project under the leadership of Dr. Keyes. Keyes appreciated more than any other physicist that he had known the importance of the fact that an individual is a man first and a scientist second—that there is no true objectivity in science. There is no divorcing the observer from the observed, and every scientific theory and law, no matter how conscientiously propounded and objectively proved, is nevertheless coloured by the observer.

Berkeley was intrigued by the study of the physicists' reactions to the situation in which Dunning's discovery and death had placed them.

Martin Nagle had reacted approximately as Berkeley expected. They had known each other well during undergraduate days in college, drifting apart later as their professions diverged.

Through the day Berkele6y conducted the rest of the scientists through the house. A number of them had made requests to go privately as Mart had done. Others went in groups of three or four. But by the end of the day all had visited the place except Professor Wilson Dykstra.

During the first day, Dykstra confined himself to a study of the tape and transcription. He did not present himself for a visit to the Dunning house until the following morning.

Berk called at his hotel. He kept the psychologist waiting fifteen minutes before he finally appeared through the revolving doors.

Dykstra was a small, round man in his late sixties, owlish in heavy framed glasses. His jutting lower lip seemed to signify his being perpetually on the defensive, as if he couldn't believe the world were really as he saw it. But Berk knew he was a great man in his own field. He had contributed much to the elucidation of Einstein's work in relation to gravity, which was the reason for his being invited to participate in the project.

The sky was threatening, and Dykstra clutched a black umbrella to his chest as he emerged from the hotel. Berk waited with the car door open.

"Good morning, Dr. Dykstra. It looks as if we'll be alone this morning. Everyone else took a visit to Dunning's yesterday."

Dykstra grunted and got in. "That's the way I wanted it. I spent a full day yesterday going over that ridiculous tape recording."

Berk moved the car out into the line of traffic. He had rather felt from the very first that the project could get along just as well without Dykstra.

"Were you able to derive anything at all from it?"

"I have reached no conclusion as yet, Dr. Berkeley. But when I do, I do not believe it is going to be that young Dunning was the unadulterated genius some of you people consider him. Surely you, a psychologist, can understand the type of mind that would produce such a mixture of unrelated and irrelevant, not to say mythological material!"

"There are many strange things about the human mind which we do not know," said Berk. "One of the least understood is the point at which genius ends and nonsense begins."

"In physics the march is steadily upwards! We have no doubt as to which way lies progress."

Berk let that one ride. A man who saw in the world such terrible simplicity might ultimately find Dunning's mystery completely transparent. He couldn't risk that possibility by arguing.

They drew up to the old mansion Dunning had occupied. Dykstra surveyed it from the car. "The kind of a place one would expect," he grunted.

It was difficult to estimate what was going on in the physicist's mind as he came into the laboratories.

In the first room he scanned the shelves of reagents. He took down a dozen bottles and examined their labels closely. Of some he removed the stoppers and sniffed cautiously, then replaced them all on the shelf in mild disdain.

He spent a long time examining the fractionating set-up in the centre of the room. He spotted the pad of computations left there and drew an old envelope from his pocket and did some comparison scribbling.

In the electronics room he turned to look through the doorway. "Why would any man want two such laboratories as these?"

His inspection was much more thorough than that of any of the others, including Martin Nagle. Berk supposed that Mart and many of the others would be back, but Dykstra was going through with a fine-toothed comb the first time.

He poked through the machine shop. "Well equipped," he muttered, "for a man who likes to tinker."

But he was highly impressed by the computer room. He examined the settings of the instruments and the chart paper. He opened up every desk drawer and shuffled through the scattering of papers inside.

Red-faced, he turned to Berk. "This is absurd! Certainly there would be charts, papers, or something showing the man's calculations. These instruments are not here for show; they've obviously been used. Someone has removed the computational material from this room!"

"It's just as we found it," said Berk. "We don't understand it any better than you."

"I don't believe it," said Dykstra flatly.

The reaction of the physicist to the library was the thing Berk was most interested in. He let Dykstra look at will over the strange and exotic collection of volumes.

At first Dykstra reacted like a suddenly eager animal. He ran from the shelves of mythology, got a glance at the section on astrology, hurried from there to the books on faith-healing, and made a spiral turn that brought him up against the region of material on East Indian philosophy.

"What is this," he bellowed hoarsely, "a joke?"

The pudgy figure seemed to swell visibly with indignation.

"The next room would interest you most, perhaps," said Berk.

Dykstra almost ran through the adjoining door as if escaping some devil with whom he had come face to face. Then, catching sight of the titles here, he began to breathe easily and with an audible sigh of relief. He was among friends."

With an air of reverence, he took down a worn copy of Weyl's Space Time Matter, and a reissue of the relativity papers.

"It isn't possible," he murmured, "that Dunning owned and understood both of these libraries."

"He understood and conquered gravity," said Berk. "And this is the last of the clues we have to show you."

Dykstra put the books carefully back on the shelves. "I don't like it." He glanced back to the other room as if it were a place of terror.

"There's something wrong," he murmured. "Anti-gravity! Whoever heard of such a thing? And how could it come out of a place like this?"

IV

That afternoon, they met again in conference. There was agreement that they would tackle the problem. Only Professor Dykstra exhibited a continuing belligerence towards the affair, yet he made no move to withdraw.

Full co-operation of military facilities was pledged by the representatives of the services. The centre of investigation was to be at ONR, however, with branching research wherever needed.

No one had conceived even a tentative starting point which he cared to discuss with his colleagues. Most of them had spent the morning re-reading the relativity papers and staring at the ceiling of their respective offices. They agreed to work as loosely or as closely as the problem demanded. Until some working programme could be initiated by some of them, it was decided to hold daily seminars to try to spark each other into creative thought.

A minor honour came to Mart in his election as chairman of the seminar. It gave him uneasiness because he was junior in age and profession to all of them. But his eminence in electro-fields made him a likely co-ordinator of the project.

Mart selected a representative sample from the occult section of Dunning's library and took it to his own office. He settled down amid an aura of astrology, spiritualism, mysticism, religion, sunspot data, and levitation. He had no specific purpose, only to expose his own mind to the atmosphere in which Dunning had operated. Dunning had found the goal. The tracks he walked in had to be located, no matter where they were picked up.

Some of the stuff was boring, much could be nothing but sheer delusion. Yet his dogged pursuit left him intrigued by some of the material.

The reports on poltergeism at Leander Castle near London, for example. They were well reported. Independent cross references verified each other very well. The works on levitation were far more difficult to credit. There was a hodgepodge about purification of the body and the soul, of reaching assorted states of exaltation above the ordinary degree of mortal.

Yet levitation had occurred, according to reports of witnesses who might not be considered too unreliable.

And what did this have to do with religion—in which Dunning had had tremendous interest, to judge by the notations he made?

There were miracles in religion, Mart reflected.

Anti-gravity was a miracle.

Miracle: that which is considered impossible and which cannot be duplicated by the observers, even after it has been seen.

In scientific law there is a difference. It can be applied by anyone with sufficient IQ. But the worker of miracles does not come out of the laboratory of halls of learning.

He rises spontaneously out of the mountains or out of the wilderness, and gathers novices who seek with all their hearts to equal the Master. But they never do. Always there is a difference. The magic of miracles seems unteachable. It has its own spontaneous majesty, or is nothing but old-fashioned hoodwinking. There seemed, to Mart, no in-between.

Anti-gravity.

Was it natural law, or miracle? Had Dunning found the bridge that made only a single category of the two? Or was he a performer of miracles, whose art could not be taught, but would arise spontaneously, full blown?

Mart slammed the books shut and pushed them to the rear of the desk. He pulled a scratch pad out of the drawer and began penciling furiously the basic Einstein equations.

By the end of the first week there was little to report. The daily seminars had been held, but outside of reeducating each other in the exotic concepts of the relativity world they had achieved nothing.

Or so it seemed to Mart. Keyes seemed quite pleased, however, and Berk mentioned that they should be congratulated on their progress. As if they had taken a major step forward in merely meeting and agreeing to undertake the project.

And maybe they had, Mart thought.

He found himself in difficulty as chairman of the seminar. Invariably, in such a group there is a member who undertakes to educate his colleagues anew in all the basic sciences. In this case, it was made doubly difficult because the self-appointed instructor was Professor Dykstra.

That he was capable of teaching them a good deal, there was no question. But on Saturday at the end of this first week he arose with a particularly triumphant expression and strode to the blackboard where he began scrawling his barely legible chicken marks.

"I have achieved the thing for which I have been looking, gentlemen," he said. "I am able to show that no instrument as we have had described to us is possible without a violation of Dr. Einstein's postulate of equivalence. If we admit the correctness of this postulate—as we all do, of course—then you will see from Equation One that—"

Mart stared at—and through—the equations that Dykstra had scrawled. He listened with half an ear. It looked and sounded all right. But something had to be done about Dykstra.

Dykstra was wrong—even with his equations being right. Where was it, thought Mart. It was something you couldn't name or scarcely define. Maybe it was in the feeling that Keyes talked about, the feeling that goes all through you down to your toes. He knew what Dykstra's feeling was, all right. It touched him like the proximity of a thousand-ton refrigeration unit going full blast. Dykstra thought they were fools to be monkeying with this project, and remained with it only because he considered it his solemn duty to show them this irrefutable fact.

He was dragging the feet of the whole group. But in spite of him, all the rest were pulling in the other direction, Mart knew. In this week, they had all achieved an acceptance of the validity of Dunning's accomplishment. And that, after all, was something of an achievement, he decided.

In Mart's vision, the equations on the board became surrounded by fuzzy signs of the Zodiac. Dykstra had completed his argument and Mart stood up.

"Since you have presented us with such elegant proof of your thesis, doctor," he said, "and since we have all become aware of the reality of Dunning's accomplishment, the only conclusion we can make is that the basic premise is at fault. I could say you have submitted very excellent reasons for doubting the validity of the postulate of equivalence!"

Dykstra stood a moment as if he could not believe his ears. He turned to his seat indecisively as if trying to make up his mind to ignore or answer the statement. Finally, he grew red and his body seemed to swell as he faced mart.

"My dear Dr. Nagle, if there is anyone in this room who does not understand that the postulate of equivalence has been established beyond any possibility of refutation I would suggest that he resign from this project immediately!"

Mart restrained a grin, but warmed to his subject. He had no purpose but to needle Dykstra, and yet—

"Seriously, doctor—and I throw this out to all of you: what would happen if the postulate of equivalence were not true?

"You've been as shocked as I by the items from Dunning's library, but I would like to ask: what is the significance of the postulate of equivalence in the accomplishment of the medium who is able to rise unsupported from a couch, in what is certainly a well authenticated instance of levitation?

"Why is the literature of the East so full of material on levitation? I think Dunning asked that question and got some sensible answers. If the postulate of equivalence doesn't fit those answers, perhaps we had better re-examine the postulate. As a matter of fact, if we ever expect to duplicate Dunning's work, we will have to examine every postulate we've got that pertains in any way to gravity."

Professor Dykstra abandoned what he considered had been a disorderly argument. He resumed his seat with a grandiose appeal to the equations on the board.

Unexpectedly, Jennings, a thin dry man from Cal Tech, took the floor.

"I agree wholeheartedly with Dr. Nagle," he said. "Something has been happening to me this past week. I see it in most of you, also, whether you are aware of it or not.

"By the age of forty the average research physicist seems to acquire an intuitive ability to fend off anything that doesn't jibe with the laws as he knows them.

"Then we become heads of departments while the younger fellows come along and assimilate the data that doesn't fit in our generation, and get credited with the discoveries we have passed over.

"We seem to establish a sort of gateway in our minds, floodgates if you will, through which the mass of physical universe data flows. As we become older and more learned we adjust the setting of this gate to the point where nothing new can be trapped behind it. We cling to that which we had in our youth and abruptly we are creatures of history.

"I feel the experiences of the past week have jarred my mental floodgates on their very hinges. Once more, I feel able to accept and retain data which I have not encountered before. I think Dr. Nagle is right. We have to reexamine all we have learned to this point concerning gravity. If any factors of East Indian lore or spiritualism prove relevant, I do not think physics will be shattered to its foundations if we assibilate such data.

"We cannot escape the fact that one man solved anti-gravity. Eight days ago not one of us would have admitted the possibility. Today we are charged with the responsibility of moving forward in time and catching up with it."

Mart was tired after that seminar. It became a stormy affair. There seemed a kind of anger submerged not far below the surface of each of them. An anger at themselves for having been on the wrong track for so long, a kind of diffused rage at the whole physical universe for playing such tricks when asked a straightforward question.

More than one had balked at Mart's drastic suggestion. Sanders had said, ". . . and there can be no revision of the postulate of equivalence. Any data which indicates it automatically leaves the observer of that data suspect."

Mart called Kenneth Berkeley's office as soon as the seminar was ended.

"Hi, Berk," he said.

"Yeah—how's it coming? I've been wanting to get over your way the last couple of days. I haven't noticed any of you boys moving out into the machine shops yet. I suppose you are still in the paper-work stage."

"We haven't got there, yet," muttered Mart. "I have more important things than anti-gravity to discuss with you. How are you set up for a couple of days' fishing?"

"Fishing? I could probably make it. All work and no play and that sort of thing—I don't need to remind you, of course, of the need for top speed on this Project Levitation—"

"I'm going fishing," said Mart. "You coming along or not?"

"I'm coming. I can get the loan of a cabin on the best trout stream the other side of Fulton Fish Market. When will you be ready?"

"I'll have to rent some gear. If you know of a good place, I can be ready in an hour and we can pick it up on the way."

"I'll have to check my own gear, provided Judith hasn't thrown it out in the last three years since I used it. It's about a two hundred mile drive. We can make it by midnight."

Mart and Berk had done a good deal of fishing together one summer following their Junior year. They had spent much of that year and all of the summer settling the abstruse problems of the Universe and with quite divergent results.

At the end of the summer Mart had been of the total conviction that life was wholly soluble in terms of the external world. If a man had something good and useful to do in shaping the world to his own dream, he would be a sane and happy man.

Berk had arrived at the opposite pole in the conviction that man's life lay within the thin shelter of his own skin. Now each of them had moved a good way towards the other's camp.

Mart thought of this as they drove through the night. He reminded Berk of it.

"If the world were as college Juniors see it, all out troubles would be over," said Berk. "There is probably no time in a man's life when he is so completely of a single-minded point of view."

"I don't know. There's Dykstra. He hasn't changed an opinion since he was a Junior. He's going to prove Dunning didn't have anti-gravity or bust. He knows it can't be done."

"How about the others?"

"This week has been a period of metamorphosis. They've changed. We're where we can do some work, now."

There was a caretaker on the property Berk had borrowed. He had things ready when the two men arrived. Mart determined to put everything connected with ONR out of his mind while he was there. He sat down and wrote a letter home, which helped in that direction.

In the morning he arose in the clear mountain air, and to the enormous song of birds in the pines beyond the house, and he felt that he had truly forgotten all else but this. The smell of bacon and eggs floated in from the kitchen as he met Berk outside the door.

"It's nice to know a psychologist who knows a millionaire. Could we have had breakfast in bed if we had ordered it?"

Berk laughed. "Not on your life. Wait till Joe gets you out in the woods. Then you'll see how much coddling you'll get."

"Let's not take him along," said Mart. "I'd like to be alone as much as possible."

"Sure. Joe won't mind. He's the one who knows all the good fishing holes, though—"

"The fish don't matter." Said Mart.

The forest was moist with dew, and the pre-dawn chill remained in the ravines through which they descended towards the river. It was still shadowed by the mountains here, and quiet except for the few birds who had not abandoned its grey light for the pink-tipped hills above.

Mart knew at once that this was what he needed. He donned the hip boots and tested the spring of the new glass rod he had rented.

"I guess I'm old-fashioned," he said. "I like the feel of the old ones better."

"I'm still using mine," said Berk. "Matter of fact, I believe it's the same one I had the last summer we were together."

They sloshed out into the water a little way above a quiet pool. It wasn't wide enough for both of them there, so Mart moved along upstream, "Some guy published an article the other day," he said, "in which he claimed the average time of catching a fish in a stream like this is two hours and nineteen minutes. Didn't we do better than that?"

"Seems like we did a lot better. If we don't we'll have to get Joe to make a lunch today."

They did considerably better. By noon, Mart had six and Berk had seven good trout.

"I'll write the fish researcher a letter," said Mart, "and your family will eat trout for a week."

After lunch they sat with their backs against a tree on the bank and watched the water flowing past.

"Have you got any attack on the project at all?" said Berk.

Mart told him about the last seminar. "Dykstra may be entirely right. His math makes a pretty picture. But I was serious when I suggested the re-examination of the postulate of equivalence—at least as it now stands."

"You're ahead of me," said Berk. "What is the postulate of equivalence?"

"It was proposed by Einstein in one of his first papers, the 1907 one, I think. He postulated the effects of inertia are equivalent to those of gravity.

"That is, in an object propelled at a constant rate of acceleration, a man would feel effects that could not be distinguished from those of gravity. He could walk, function, and would have weight just as if he were on a large mass having gravitational attraction.

"Conversely, an observer inside a freely falling elevator in Earth's gravitational field would observe no effects of gravity inside that elevator. He could stand on a scale, and would register no weight. Liquid would not pour from a glass. It has been stated that no mechanical experiment could ever reveal the presence of Earth's gravitational field in the interior of any such frame of reference moving freely in this field of gravitation. We have accepted this assumption for a long time.

"There are good reasons for accepting it, good, sound mathematical reasons. Yet we have not empirically exhausted all possible means of detecting a gravitational field under such conditions, and it is foolish to exclude the possibility.

"So—Dykstra has made a good point in his fairly rigorous demonstration that a mechanism such as Dunning would demand the abandonment of the postulate of equivalence. It may well be that the postulate is an unwarranted assumption, based upon inadequate data. If so, that's a good starting point. What the next step might be, I don't know."

"Is gravity a kind of something that can be identified otherwise than as a mathematical symbol—or through the observation of a falling apple?"

"No. That's all it is, actually. A symbol in our formulas that stands for an unidentified something which manifests itself in the attraction between masses."

"How about a flowing something, like this stream?"

"Could be. Nobody knows."

The water eddied about a projecting rock near the bank. Berk threw in a handful of sticks he had been idly breaking, in his hand. Swiftly, they flowed together and converged in the centre of the whirlpool by the rock.

"Might be a point of view," he said, "in which it could be postulated that those sticks gravitated towards each other under a mutual attraction."

"It wasn't attraction in them," said mart thoughtfully. "It was forces pushing and pulling on them. Gravity—a pushing and pulling, maybe. But a pull or a push of what? That Dunning! He knew!"

Sitting on the porch in the dark, after dinner, Mart had a feeling of satisfaction, a vague sense of having accomplished something during the day. He didn't know what, but it didn't matter. It was something—

"You know," he said suddenly, "the thing we need to know, and that you psychologists ought to be able to tell us is where ideas come from.

"Take the first cave man with two brain cells big enough to click together. Where did he get the idea to put a fire in his cave? I think that's the problem you and I tried to solve a long time ago. Where do they come from—inside or outside?" He paused and gave the mosquitoes his attention.

"Keep going," said Berk.

"I haven't any further to go. I'm thinking about gravity again."

"What are you thinking?"

"How to get a new idea concerning it. What does man actually do when he cooks up a new theory, a new mechanism? I feel like I'm being sucked into that problem constantly, instead of the one I'm supposed to be attacking."

"Well, what are you doing? You're trying to cook up a new idea—"

"I'm thinking right now about this afternoon. Something flowing—but it would be something you couldn't get a picture of—like space-time. Now that it's been brought into the open, I think I really have never liked the postulate of equivalence. Just a feeling knocking around through a few molecules in my cranium. The postulate is wrong.

"Then I try to picture something flowing through the dark of space. It couldn't be a three-dimensional flow like a river."

He sat up straighter and slowly withdrew the cigar from his mouth. "It couldn't be—But it could be a flow—" He stood up suddenly and turned towards the house. "Look, Berk, you've got to excuse me, if you don't mind. I've got some math to do."

"Berk's cigar tip brightened in a long, glowing moment. Don't mind me," said the psychologist.

V

Berk had no idea what time Mart went to bed that night. In the morning he found him in the same position working furiously, and had the impression Mart had not retired at all. He observed he'd changed clothes, at least.

"The fish are calling," said Berk.

Mart glanced up. "Give me another half hour. Look, the fish can wait. I've got to get back the office as soon as possible. There's something here I want to keep on with."

Berk grinned agreeably. "Go to it, boy. I'll get the car packed. You say when."

In town he went directly to his own office without seeing anyone. There, he continued the work begun the night before. As he proceeded, some of his initial enthusiasm waned. It would be two or three days before he would be ready to invite inspection. One of his manipulations several pages back turned out to be in error. He retraced slowly through the maze.

A little after three there came a knock. He looked up in irritation as Dykstra walked in.

"Dr. Nagle! I'm glad you're in. I tried and couldn't find you yesterday."

"I took a day off for fishing. Can I help you?"

Dykstra slid into the chair on the other side of the desk with an almost furtive motion. Mart frowned.

"I have something of extreme importance to discuss regarding the project," said Dykstra. He leaned forward confidentially, his eyes squinting a little behind the owlish glasses.

"Do you realize," he said, "that this entire project is a fraud?"

"Fraud! What are you talking about?"

"I have been over the Dunning house, so called, with a fine-toothed comb. I proved to you in our last seminar that the postulate of equivalence denied the possibility of any such device as this Dunning is supposed to have invented. Now, I can assure you that Dunning never existed! We are the victims of a base fraud."

He clapped the palms of his hands upon the top of the desk in triumphal finality and leaned back.

"I don't understand," murmured Mart.

"You shall. Go over that laboratory. There is no consistency. Examine the shelves of reagents. Ask what possible chemical endeavor could be carried out with such a random selection of materials. The electronics section is as hodgepodge as the corner television shop. The computers have never been used in the room they are in. And that library—it is obvious what an intellectual packrat's nest that is!

"No, Dr. Nagle, for some inconceivable reason we are the victims of a base fraud. Anti-gravity! Do you suppose that anyone here actually thought they could make us believe it?

"Now, what I want to know is why we have been sent on this fool's errand when the nation needs the talents of each one of us so badly?"

Mart felt a faint sickness in the pit of his stomach. "I'll admit there are strange things about this presentation. If what you say should be true, how can the eyewitness accounts be explained?"

"Perjury!" snapped Dykstra.

"I can hardly imagine a member of the JCS involved in such. I am sorry, but I do not share your opinion. As a matter of fact, I have done a good deal of work toward our goal.

"As of this moment, I am prepared to say definitely that the postulate of equivalence is not going to hold."

Red-faced, Dykstra stood up. "I'm extremely sorry you hold such views, Dr. Nagle. I had always believed you a young man of great promise. Perhaps you shall yet be when proper light is thrown upon this abominable fraud perpetuated upon us. Good day!"

Mart didn't bother to rise as Dykstra stomped out of the door. The visit bothered him. Absurd as the accusations were, they threatened the foundation upon which he worked. If he could not be sure that Denning's device had performed as described he was subject to the buffeting of all his prior assurance that anti-gravity was nonsense.

But the JCS involved in a reasonless and silly fraud as Dykstra proposed—!

He turned back to his sheets of computations with almost frantic energy. When it was almost time that most of them would be leaving he reached for the phone and called Jennings. The man was an able mathematician and could work this through if anyone could. It was not as far along as Mart would have liked, but he had to know if he were at the entrance of a blind alley.

"Can you come over for a moment?" he said. "I've got something I'd like to show you."

In a few moments Jennings appeared. As he came in he gave Mart the momentary impression of an old-time country preacher ruffled with righteous indignation at the sins of this congregation.

He blurted out before Mart had a chance to speak. "Did you see Dykstra this afternoon running around with some cock and bull story about the project being a fraud?"

Mart nodded.

"Why Keyes ever let an old fool like him in here—Dykstra has been a fine man. But he's shot his wad. I called Keyes at once."

"I guess all of us have had natural suspicions like Dykstra's," said Mart, "but not enough to go completely overboard as he has."

"I've talked to several of the others. They are upset, some of them. I tried to lift them out of it. But what is it you've got? Anything that looks like an answer?"

Mart slid the sheets across the desk. "The postulate of equivalence is out, I'm pretty sure of that. I've been computing the possible field of motion circulating through curved space. It turns out to be an eight-dimensional thing, but it makes sense. I'd like you to look it over."

Jennings' eyebrows raised. "Very good. Of course, it's not easy for me to accept the renunciation of the postulate of equivalence, you understand. That has been around for forty-five years now."

"We may find something to fit in its place."

"You have no other copy of this?"

Mart shrugged, "I can do it again."

"I'll take good care of them." Jennings put the papers in an inside pocket. "But suppose you do demonstrate the possibility of such a flow? Where do we go from there? Have you any idea?"

"Some," said Mart. "I've watched a whirlpool yesterday. Ever watch what happens to sticks when they are thrown into one. They go towards each other. That's gravity."

Jennings frowned. "Now wait a minute, Mart—"

Mart laughed. "Don't get me wrong. Consider this flow. I don't know what properties it might have. It would have to take place through four of the dimensions involved. But when we get through, we'll develop the expression for the curl of such a flow through material substance.

"Suppose such a curl exists. Whirlpools appear. It's a crude analogy. Your mind can't get hold of it. We need the math. But perhaps we can show that the curl is in such a direction as to cause a reduction of spatial displacement between masses causing the curl. Could that make sense?"

Jennings had been sitting very still. Now he smiled and spread his hands on the desk top. "It could. The curl of an eight-dimensional flow would be fairly complex. But if it develops all right, what then?"

"Then we build a device to streamline matter through this flow, so that curl will not develop."

Jennings sat back in his chair as if suddenly limp. "Holy smoke, you've got it all figured out! But wait a minute, that would simply nullify gravity. How about anti-gravity?"

Mart shrugged. "We find a way to introduce a reverse curl vector."

"That does it, boy, that does it."

Mart laughed and walked to the door with him. "Yeah, I know how the thing sounds, but, look—I'm really not kidding. If this gravitational flow expression works out, the test of it could follow. It could, Jennings."

Jennings faced him with all amusement gone out of his face. "I'm not laughing, Mart," he said, "not at you anyway. If we get the answer to this whole thing it's going to be something like that. It's just that everything we've postulated up to now has so completely blocked any thinking of this kind that a man has to be prepared to consider himself slightly rocky to even talk about it."

It was a day later when Berk called him. "Hey, Mart, why didn't you let us know right away about Dykstra? If Jennings hadn't called, we might have got to him too late."

"What do you mean?"

"This story he's been giving about the project being a fraud. I hope you weren't bothered by it."

"Not much. Are you going to kick him off the project?"

"That follows, naturally. He's in a rest home now. His mind was so congealed that he couldn't accept the reality of Dunning's work. He flipped his lid in a mild sort of way. He'll be all right in a few weeks and can go back to teaching."

"I'm sorry about it. We almost have the answer he was afraid to face, I believe."

Impatiently, Mart threw his thesis open to the whole seminar that day. It was a bit hard to take for some who had been inclined somewhat in Dykstra's direction, but the math was clean enough to appeal to all of them. They pitched in almost as a solid unit to try to obtain a formulation convertible to metal and electrons and fields.

Jennings was the one who carried it all the way. He rushed into Mart's office three days later without knocking and slapped some sheets on the desk.

"You were right, Mart," he exclaimed. "Your field does show curl in the presence of material substances. We're on our way to Dunning's flying belt!"

But when it came, Mart was dismayed. The entire group worked in a thirty-six hour seminar to whip the work into final shape. The result was that an anti-gravity machine could be built. But it would be the size of a hundred-ton cyclotron!

Mart told Keyes what they had. "It's a far cry from Dunning's flying belt," he said. "We'll continue trying to boil it down if you want us to, or we can submit a practical design that will work now in the shape we've got it in."

Keyes glanced at the sketches mart had prepared. "It isn't exactly what we'd expected, but I think we'd better build it. The important thing how is to get a practical anti-gravity machine functioning. Refinements can come later. The shops are yours. How long will it take?"

"It depends on what you wish to put into it in the way of men and machines. With a round-the-clock crew I believe the model could be ready in about three weeks."

"It's yours," said Keyes. "Build it."

It was actually over four weeks before the first demonstration was scheduled in the big machinery shop protected by the triple security seal that had shrouded the whole project.

Those in attendance were the ones present at the first conference plus a few of the workmen who had helped build the massive device.

The demonstration was simple, almost anti-climactic after the hectic seminars they had sweated out the past weeks. Mart stepped to the switchboard that seemed diminutive under the high, steel-arched ceiling of the shop. He threw the main power switches and then adjusted slowly a number of dials.

Almost imperceptibly, and without wavering, the enormous disk-like mass rose in the centre of the shop. It hovered without visible support three feet above the floor.

The disk was thirty feet in diameter and three feet thick. Its tonnage was evident in the long crack in the concrete floor beneath the I-beams laid temporarily to support it.

Dr. Keyes reached out a hand to touch the mass. He pushed with all his might.

Mart smiled and shook his head. "It'll move if you push it long enough and hard enough. But it has almost the inertia of a small battleship. A far cry, as I said, from Dunning's flying belt. But we'll keep trying."

"It's a monumental achievement," said Keyes, "and I congratulate you all."

While they watched, Mart touched the controls again and slowly lowered the mass to the I-beam supports. He cut the power.

"I would like all of you to return to the conference room at this time," Keyes said. "There, we have some additional data to give you."

Mart fell in step besides Berk on the way out. "What's up now?" he said. "Are you going to pin tin medals on us?"

"Better than that," said Berk. "You'll see."

Once more they found themselves seated almost as they had been that eventful day weeks ago. Keyes took his usual position at the head.

"There is no need of telling any of you gentlemen what this achievement means to our country and for all mankind. Anti-gravity will revolutionize the military and peacetime transport of the world—and in time will take man to the stars.

"Now—I have someone I would like to introduce to you."

He stepped aside and beckoned through the doorway to the next room behind him. Someone came through in response. Then Keyes stood aside.

A startled gasp went through the audience. Before them stood Leon Dunning.

He smiled at the group a little wryly. "I see you know me, gentlemen. I hope none of you will bear me any bad feelings or consider me the repulsive character I have been painted. The script called for it. An unpleasant young jerk, is the way it was described I believe."

Jennings was on his feet. "What is the meaning of this, Dr. Keyes? I think we are entitled to an explanation!"

"Indeed you are, Dr. Jennings. And you shall have one." Keyes replaced Dunning who took a seat. "To a considerable extent, our friend, Professor Dykstra, was correct. The original data given you at the beginning of this project was a hoax."

A wave of startled cries and protests arose from the assembly. Keyes raised a hand. "Just a moment, please. Hear me out. I said that the initial data was a hoax. There was no Leon Dunning, inventor of anti-gravity devices. We put on a show, and faked a film. There was no anti-gravity.

"Today, there is an anti-gravity machine in existence. I want you to consider very carefully, gentlemen, just where the hoax in this matter truly lies." He paused for a moment, looking into the eyes of each of them, then stepped aside. "Our chief psychologist, Dr. Kenneth Berkeley, will give you the remainder of the story."

Berk got to his feet and moved to the front as if reluctant to do what had to be done.

"If any of you are angry," he said. "I am the person to whom it should be directed. Project Levitation was the direct result of my proposal.

"Do not think, however, that I am apologizing. I object to the term hoax, or fraud, which Professor Dykstra called it. How can we call it a hoax when out of it has come a thing with potentialities that cannot be grasped by any of us at this time?"

"But why, man, why?" Jennings exploded impatiently. "Why this hocus-pocus, this nonsense, this irrelevance about astrology, levitation, and mysticism! Why wasn't it set up as a straightforward project. We aren't a bunch of high school kids to be tricked into something we don't want to do!"

"Suppose you give me the answer to that?" said Berk. "How would you have responded to a letter from Dr. Keyes inviting you to take part in a project to build an anti-gravity machine? How many of you would have remained in your safe and sane universities where crackpots are not allowed to spend the people's money as they are in Government institutions?

"We are thankful we had no more than one Professor Dykstra on the project. He refused to accept the data we provided and his goal became to prove anti-gravity Impossible. How many of you would have come with the same goal if our little make-believe had not spurred you on?

"Dykstra could not face the data in a rational manner. As a result he suffered a nervous breakdown, which was, of course, the result of a long chain of previous incidents.

"On the other hand, those of you who could accept the data we handed you were able to knock out the preconceptions about anti-gravity and achieve that which you had considered impossible.

"Essentially, this was a project in psychology, not physics. We could have chosen something besides anti-gravity. The results, I predict, would have been the same. I have observed many scientists at work in the laboratory and library. I have studied the educational preconceptions they bring to their work. Before a problem is tackled, a decision is already made as to whether it is possible or impossible. In many cases, as exemplified by Professor Dykstra, the interest in the problem is only to the extent of proving the decision correct.

"If you will forgive me for using you for guinea pigs in my project, I submit to you that I have given a far more powerful technique for scientific investigation than you have ever possessed before. The technique of the conviction that any desired answer can be found. You have not been hoaxed at all. You have been shown a new and powerful scientific method.

"If you could and did lick a problem previously impossible to you, in a matter of weeks, how many more of your own research problems are just waiting for this new approach?"

There was a good deal more said at the meeting. Some of it was highly confused. Berk's explanation was not understood by several of them.

It would take a long time for it to sink in thoroughly, even for him, Mart thought. There was just a trace of anger within him that he found hard to put down. But he chuckled at the smooth way in which Berk had engineered the project. He'd bet the psychologist had had some uneasy moments because of Dykstra!

There was a sort of stunned feeling in his mind as he began to recognize the absolute truth of what Berk had demonstrated.

He saw it reflected in the faces of some of the others, a sort of blank, why-didn't-somebody-tell-me-this-before look.

It was finally agreed they would meet again the next day to thresh out their reactions to what had been done.

As soon as they were able to break away, Berk took Mart's arm. "I almost forgot to tell you, you are invited to dinner tonight."

"That had better not be a hoax," said Mart.

After dinner, the two of them went out into the patio with which Berk struggled to give his city lot the dignity of an estate. They sat down on a garden seat and watched the moon come up through the neighbour's television antenna.

"I want the rest of it," said Mart.

"The rest of what?"

"Don't be coy. The rest of the guys are going to get it out of you in the morning, but I want it first."

Berk was silent for a while then started speaking. He lit a pipe and got it going well. "Jennings almost had it in that speech about the floodgates of the mind which you mentioned. You and I almost had it back there when we were trying to solve the problems of the Universe in school.

"It boils down to the thing you asked me up in the mountains: what is the process of thinking? Where does original thought come from?

"Consider the abstruse equations you cooked up in a matter of days on the gravitational flow around the curvature of space. Why didn't you do it ten years ago? Why didn't somebody else do it a long time ago? Why you, and nobody else?

"I wanted you on the project especially, Mart, because I want you to give me a hand with this thing, if you will. It's a little more than I can handle. I don't know whether it's physics or psychology or some weird cross between the two.

"Anyway, here's where I started: you know communications theory. You know that any kind of data can be put in code form consisting of pulses. For example, a complex photograph codified in terms of half-tone dots. There are many possible methods of coding information into pulses. The code can be dot-dash, it can use time-separation between pulses, it can use pulse amplitude, a thousand different factors and combinations of factors. But any information can be expressed as a special sequence of pulses.

"One such sequence is: 'Every body in the universe attracts every other body in the universe'; another, 'The secret of immortality is—', and still another, 'Gravity is itself the result of the action of—and it can be nullified by—'

"Any answer to any question can be expressed in terms of a special sequence of pulses, wherein some relationship between the pulses is a codified expression of the information.

"But, by definition, pure noise is a completely random sequence of pulses, containing pulses in all possible relationships.

"Therefore any information-bearing message is a special subclass of the class 'noise.' Pure noise, therefore, includes all possible messages, all possible information. Hence, pure noise, which is actually another term for pure probability, is omniscient!

"Now, that isn't just an exercise in scholastic logic. It is a recognition that all things can be learned, all things can be achieved."

Mart stirred and blew a violent cloud of cigar smoke at the moon. "Hold it!" he exclaimed. "There's got to be some limit to the territory you take in."

"Why? Is my logic wrong in regard to noise and information?"

"God, I don't know. It sounds good. It's right, of course, but exactly what does that have to do with the operation of the human mind and Project Levitation?"

"From a structural standpoint, I can't answer that question—yet. Functionally, it appears that there must be in the human mind a mechanism which is nothing but a pure noise generator, a producer of random impulses, pure omniscient noise.

"Somewhere else there must be another mechanism which is set to either filter the production of random noise or control its production so that only semantically meaningful forms are allowed to come through. Evidently, the filter is capable of being set at any level to filter out anything we choose to define as noise.

"So we go through the rough process of growing up, we go to school, and get educated, we get a red line setting on the noise filter which rejects all buy a bare minimum of data presented by the external universe, and our internal creativeness as well.

"Facts in the world around us are rejected from then on when they don't fit. Creative imagination is whittled down. The filter takes care of it automatically once we give it a setting."

"And your project here," said Mart, "the stuff on Babylonian mysticism, astrology, and the rest of that crud—"

"The whole pattern was set to be as noisy as possible," said Berk. "We didn't know how to produce anti-gravity, so we gave you a picture of a man who did, and made it as noisy as possible to loosen up you own noise filters on the subject. I offered you a dose of omniscient

noise on the subject of anti-gravity, and the one inescapable conclusion that it had been done.

"Everyone of you had previously set your filters to reject the idea of anti-gravity. Nonsense! No use looking for that. Work on something useful.

"So I suggested to Keyes we assemble a bunch of you doubledomes and slap you solidly with the fact that it ain't nonsense, it can be done, Bud. Give you some omniscient noise to listen to, loosen up you filters, and let the answer come through out of your own mental productiveness.

"It worked. It always will work. All you've got to do is get the lead out of your pants and the rocks out of your head, and the arbitrary noise filter settings corrected on a few of the other things you've always wanted to do—and you can find a proper answer to any problem you care to investigate!"

Mart glanced up at the moon spreading silver across the sky. "Yeah—there's the stars," he said. "I've always wanted the stars. Now we've got anti-gravity—"

"And so you can go to the stars—if you want to."

Mart shook his head. "You and Dunning—first we've got it, then we haven't.

"You get us to produce anti-gravity. And it becomes a mere gimmick! Sure we could see the planets, maybe even go beyond the solar system before we die. But I guess I'm going to stay here and work with you. A paltry planet or two isn't so much, after all. If we could learn to utilize the maximum noise level of the human mind we could master the whole Universe!"

THE COLONISTS

ILLUSTRATED BY PAUL ORBAN
ORIGINALLY PUBLISHED IN *IF WORLDS OF SCIENCE
FICTION*, JUNE 1954

If historical precedent be wrong—what qualities, then, must man possess to successfully colonize new worlds? Doctor Ashby said: "There is no piece of data you cannot find, provided you can devise the proper experimental procedure for turning it up." Now—about the man and the procedure....

THE COLONISTS

This was the rainy year. Last year had been the dry one, and it would come again. But they wouldn't be here to see it, Captain Louis Carnahan thought. They had seen four dry ones, and now had come the fourth wet one, and soon they would be going home. For them, this was the end of the cycle.

At first they had kept track of the days, checking each one off on their calendars, but the calendars had long since been mingled indistinguishably with the stuff of the planet itself—along with most of the rest of their equipment. By that time, however, they had learned that the cycle of wet and dry seasons was almost precisely equivalent to a pair of their own Terran years, so they had no more need for the calendars.

But at the beginning of this wet season Carnahan had begun marking off the days once again with scratches on the post of the hut in which he lived. The chronometers were gone, too, but one and three-quarters Earth days equalled one Serrengian day, and by that he could compute when the ships from Earth were due.

He had dug moats about the hut to keep rain water from coming in over his dirt floor. Only two of the walls were erected, and he didn't know or much care whether he would get the other two up or not. Most of the materials had blown away during the last dry period and he doubted very much that he would replace them. The two available walls were cornered against the prevailing winds. The roof was still in good shape, allowing him a sufficient space free of leaks to accommodate his cooking and the mat which he called a bed.

He picked up a gourd container from the rough bench in the center of the room and took a swallow of the burning liquid. From the front of the hut he looked out over the rain swept terrain at the circle of huts. Diametrically across from him he could see Bolinger, the little biologist, moving energetically about. Bolinger was the only one who had retained any semblance of scientific interest. He puttered continually over his collection, which had grown enormously over the eight year period.

When they got back, Bolinger at least would have some accomplishment to view with pride. The rest of them—?

Carnahan laughed sharply and took another big swallow from the gourd, feeling the fresh surge of hot liquor already crossing the portals of his brain, bringing its false sense of wisdom and clarity. He knew it was false, but it was the only source of wisdom he had left, he told himself.

He staggered back to the bed with the gourd. He caught a glimpse of his image in the small steel mirror on the little table at the end of the bed. Pausing to stare, he stroked the thick mat of beard and ran his fingers through the mane of hair that had been very black when he came, and was now a dirty silver grey.

He hadn't looked at himself for a long time, but now he had to. He had to know what they would see when the ships of Earth came to pick up the personnel of the Base and leave another crew. The image made him sick.

At the beginning of this final season of the rains, all his life before coming to Serrengia seemed like a dream that had never been real. Now it was coming back, as if he were measuring the final distance of a circle and approaching once again his starting point. He kept remembering more and more. Watching his image in the mirror, he remembered what General Winthrop had said on the day of their departure. "The pick of Earth's finest," the General said. "We have combed the Earth and you are the men we have chosen to represent Mankind in the far reaches of the Universe. Remember that wherever you go, there goes the honor of Mankind. Do not, above all, betray that honor."

Carnahan clenched his teeth in bitterness. He wished old fatty Winthrop had come with them. Savagely he upended the gourd and flung it across the room. It meant a trip to Bailey's hut to get it replenished. Bailey had been the Chief Physicist.

Now he was the official distiller, and the rotgut he produced was the only thing that made existence bearable.

The Captain stared again at his own image. "Captain Louis Carnahan," he murmured aloud. "The pick of Earth's finest—!" He smashed a fist at the little metal mirror and sent it flying across the room. The table crashed over, one feeble leg twisting brokenly. Then Carnahan hunched over with his face buried against the bed. His fists beat against it while his shoulders jerked in familiar, drunken sobs.

After it was over he raised up, sitting on the edge of the bed. His mind burned with devastating clarity. It seemed for once he could remember everything that had ever happened to him. He remembered it all. He remembered his childhood under the bright, pleasant sky of Earth. He remembered his ambition to be a soldier, which meant spaceman, even then. He remembered his first flight, a simple training tour of the Moon installations. It convinced him that never again could he consider himself an Earthman in the sense of one who dwells upon the Earth. His realm was the sky and the stars. Not even the short period when he had allowed himself to be in love had changed his convictions. He had sacrificed everything his career demanded.

Where had it gone wrong? How could he have allowed himself to forget? For years he had forgotten, he realized in horror. He had forgotten that Earth existed. He had forgotten how he came to be here, and why. And all that he was meant to accomplish had gone undone. For years the scientific work of the great base expedition had been ignored. Only the little biologist across the way, pecking at his tasks season after season, had accomplished anything.

And now the ships were coming to demand an accounting.

He groaned aloud as the vision became more terrible. He thought of that day when they had arrived at the inhospitable and uninhabited world of Serrengia. He could close his eyes and see it again—the four tall ships standing on the plateau that was scarred by their landing. The men had been so proud of what they had done and would yet do. They could see nothing to defeat them as they unloaded the mountains of equipment and supplies.

Now that same equipment lay oozing in the muck of leafy decomposition, corroded and useless like the men themselves.

And in the dry seasons it had been alternately buried and blasted by the sands and the winds.

He remembered exactly the day and the hour when they had cracked beyond all recovery. With an iron hand he had held them for three years. Weekly he demanded an appearance in full dress uniform, and hard discipline in all their relationships was the rule. Then one day he let the dress review go. They had come in from a long trek through a jungle that was renewing itself after a dry season. Too exhausted in body and spirit, and filled with an increasing sense of futility, he abandoned for the moment the formalities he had held to.

After that it was easy. They fell apart all around him. He tried to hold them, settling quarrels that verged on mutiny. Then in the sixth month of the fourth year he had to kill with his own hands the first of his crazed and rebellious crew. The scientific work disintegrated and was abandoned. He remembered he had locked up all their notes and observations and charts, but where he had hidden the metal chest was one of the few things he seemed unable to recall.

The more violent of the expedition killed each other off, or wandered into the jungle or desert and never came back. On the even dozen who were left there had settled a kind of monastic hermitage. Each man kept to himself, aware that a hairbreadth trespass against his neighbor would mean quick challenge to the death. Yet they clung to membership in this degenerate community as if it represented their last claim to humanness.

This is what they would see though. They would see his personal failure. It *was* his, there was no question of that. If he had been strong he could have held the expedition together. He could have maintained the base in all the strength and honor of military tradition that had been entrusted to him. He hadn't been strong enough.

The ships would come. The four of them. They might come tomorrow or even today. A panic crept through him. The ships could land at any time now, and their men would come marching out to greet him in his failure and cowardice and his dishonor. It must not happen. Old fatty Winthrop had said one thing that made sense: "—there goes the honor of Mankind. Do not, above all, betray that honor."

Fatty was right. The only thing he had left was honor, and in only one way could he retain it.

With the fiery clarity burning in his brain he struggled from where he lay and picked up the metallic mirror and hung it from the post near the bed. He turned up the broken table against the wall. Then, with the air of one who has not been on the premises for a long time he began searching through the long unused chests stacked in the corner. The contents were for the most part in a state of decay, but he found his straight edged razor in the oiled pouch where he had last placed it.

There should have been shaving detergent, but he couldn't find it. He contented himself with preparing hot water, then slowly and painfully hacked the thick beard away and scraped his face clean. He found a comb and raked it through his tangled mat of hair, arranging it in some vague resemblance to the cut he used to wear.

From the chests he drew forth the dress uniform he had put away so long ago. Fortunately, it had been in the center, surrounded by other articles so that it was among the best preserved of his possessions. He donned it in place of the rags he wore. The shoes were almost completely hard from lack of care, but he put them on anyway and brushed the toes with a scrap of cloth.

From underneath his bed he took his one possession which he had kept in meticulous repair, his service pistol. Then he stood up, buttoning and smoothing his coat, and smiled at himself in the little mirror. But his gaze shifted at once to something an infinity away.

"'Do not, above all, betray that honor.' At least you gave us one good piece of advice, fatty," he said.

Carefully, he raised the pistol to his head.

*   *   *   *   *

Hull number four was erect and self-supporting. Its shell enclosure was complete except for necessary installation openings. And in Number One the installations were complete and the ship's first test flight was scheduled for tomorrow morning.

John Ashby looked from the third story window of his office toward the distant assembly yards on the other side of the field. The four hulls stood like golden flames in the afternoon sunlight. Ashby felt defeated by the speed with which the ships were being completed. It was almost as if the engineers had a special animosity toward him, which they expressed in their unreasonable speed of construction. This was nonsense, of course. They had a job to do and were proud if they could cut time from their schedule.

But there was no cutting time from *his* schedule, and without the completion of his work the ships would not fly. He had to find men capable of taking them on their fantastic journeys. To date, he had failed.

He glanced down at the black car with government markings, which had driven in front of the building a few moments before, and then he heard Miss Haslam, his secretary, on the interphone. "The Colonization Commission, Dr. Ashby."

He turned from the window. "Have them come in at once," he said.

He strode to the door and shook hands with each of the men. Only four of them had come: Mr. Merton, Chairman; General Winthrop; Dr. Cowper; and Dr. Boxman.

"Please have seats over here by the window," Ashby suggested.

They accepted and General Winthrop stood a moment looking out. "A beautiful sight, aren't they, Ashby?" he said. "They get more beautiful every day. You ought to get over more often. Collins says you haven't been around the place for weeks, and Number One is going up tomorrow."

"We've had too much to occupy us here."

"*My* men are ready," said the General pointedly. "We could supply a dozen crews to take those ships to Serrengia and back, and man the base there."

Ashby turned away, ignoring the General's comment. He took a chair at the small conference table where the three Commissioners had seated themselves. Winthrop followed, settling in his chair with a smile, as if he had scored a major point.

"Number One is ready," said Merton, "and still you have failed to offer us a single man, Dr. Ashby. The Commission feels that the time is very near when definite action will have to be taken. We have your reports, but we wanted a personal word with you to see if we couldn't come to some understanding as to what we can expect."

"I will send you the men when I find out what kind of man we need," said Ashby. "Until then there had better be no thought of releasing the colonization fleet. I will not be responsible for any but the right answers to this problem."

"We are getting to the point," said Boxman, "where we feel forced to consider the recommendations of General Winthrop. Frankly, we have never been able to fully understand your objections."

"There'll never be a time when I cannot supply all the men needed to establish this base," said Winthrop. "We spend unlimited funds and years of time training personnel for posts of this kind, yet you insist on looking for unprepared amateurs. It makes no sense whatever, and only because you have been given complete charge of the personnel program have you been able to force your views on the Commission. But no one understands you. In view of your continued failure, the Commission is going to be forced to make its own choice."

"My resignation may be had at any time," said Ashby.

"No, no, Dr. Ashby." Merton held up his hand. "The General is perhaps too impulsive in his disappointment that you have failed us so far, but we do not ask for your resignation. We do ask if there is not some way in which you might see fit to use the General's men in manning the base."

"The whole answer lies in the erroneous term you persist in applying to this project," said Ashby. "It is not a base, and never will be. We propose to set up a colony. It makes an enormous difference with respect to the kind of men required. We've been over this before—"

"But not enough," snapped Winthrop. "We'll continue to go over it until you understand you can't waste those ships on a bunch of half-baked idealists inspired by some noble nonsense about carrying on the torch of human civilization beyond the stars. We're putting up a base, to gather scientific data and establish rights of occupancy."

"I don't think I agree with your description of my proposed party of colonists," said Ashby mildly.

"That's what they'll be! Were colonists ever anything but psalm singing rebels or cutthroats trying to escape hanging? You're not going to establish a cultural and scientific base with such people."

"No, you're quite right. That's not the kind."

"What is it you're looking for?" said Merton irritably. "What kind of men do you want, if you can't find them among the best and the worst humanity offers."

"Your terms are hardly accurate," said Ashby. "You fail to recognize the fact that we have never known what kind of man it takes to colonize. You ignore the fact that we have never yet successfully colonized the planets of our own Solar System. Bases, yes—but all our colonies have failed to date."

"What better evidence could you ask for in support of my argument?" demanded Winthrop. "We've *proved* bases are practical, and that colonies are not."

"No matter how far away or how long the periods of rotation, a man assigned to a base expects to return home. Night or day, in the performance of any duty, there is in his mind as a working background the recognition that at some future time he can go home. His base is never his home."

"Precisely. That is what makes the base successful."

Ashby shook his head. "No base is ever successful from the standpoint of permanent extension of a civilization. By its very nature it is transitory, impermanent. That is not what we want now."

"We have the concept of permanent bases in military thinking," said Winthrop. "You can't generalize in that fashion."

"Name for me a single military or expeditionary base that continued its permanency over any extended period of history."

"Well—now—"

"The concept is invalid," said Ashby. "Extensions of humanity from one area to another on a permanent basis are made by colonists. Men who do not expect to rotate, but come to live and establish homes. This is what we want on Serrengia. Humanity is preparing to make an extension of itself in the Universe.

"But more than this, there are limitations of time and distance in the establishment of bases, which cannot be overcome by any amount of training of personnel. Cycles of rotation and distances from home can be lengthened beyond the capacity of men to endure. It is only when they go out with *no* expectation of return that time and distance cease to control them."

"We do not know of any such limitations," said Winthrop. "They have not been met here in the Solar System."

"We know them," said Ashby. "The thing we have not found and which we must discover before those ships depart is the quality that makes it possible for a man to ignore time and distance and his homeland. We know a good deal about the successful colonists of Earth's history. We know that invariably they were of some minority group which felt itself persecuted or limited by conditions surrounding it, or else they were fleeing the results of some crime."

"If that is what you are looking for, it is no wonder you have failed," said Dr. Cowper. "We have no such minority groups in our society."

"Very true," Ashby replied. "But it is not the condition of fleeing or being persecuted that generates the qualities of a perfect colonist by any means! We have examples enough of adequately persecuted groups who failed as colonists. But there is some quality, which seems to appear, if at all, only in some of those who have courage enough to flee their oppression or limiting conditions. This quality makes them successful in their colonization.

"We are looking first, therefore, for individuals who would have the courage to resist severe limitations to the extent of flight, if such limitations existed. And among these we hope to find the essence of that which makes it possible for a man to cut all ties with his homeland."

"So you are making your search," said Merton, "among the potentially rebellious and criminal?"

Ashby nodded. "We have confined our study to these individuals as a result of strict historical precedent so that we might narrow the search as much as possible. You must understand, however, that to choose merely the rebellious and staff our ships with these would be foolhardy. It would be a ridiculous shotgun technique. *Some* of them would succeed, but we would never know which it would be. We might send twenty or a thousand ships out and establish one successful colony.

"We have to do much better than that. Our consumption of facilities on this project is so great that we have to *know*, within a negligible margin of error, that when these groups are visited in eight or fifty years from now we will find a community of cooperative, progressive human beings. We cannot be satisfied with less!"

"I'm afraid the majority of sentiment in the Commission is not in agreement with you," said Mr. Merton. "To oppose General Winthrop's trained crews with selected cutthroats and traitors may have historical precedent, but it scarcely seems the optimum procedure in this case!

"We are willing to be shown proof of your thesis, Dr. Ashby, but we have certain realities of which we are sure. If we can do no better, we shall take the best available to us at the time the ships are ready. If you cannot supply us with proven crews and colonists by then we shall be forced to accept General Winthrop's recommendations and choose personnel whose reactions are at least known and predictable to a high degree. I'm sorry, but surely you can understand our position in this matter."

For a long time Ashby was silent, looking from one to the other of the faces about the table. Then he spoke in a low voice, as if having reached the extremity of his resources. "Yes—the reactions of Winthrop's men are indeed known. I suggest that you come with me and I will show you what those reactions are."

He stood up and the others followed with inquiring expressions on their faces. Winthrop made a short, jerky motion of his head, as if he detected a hidden sting in Ashby's words. "What do you mean by that?" he demanded.

"You don't suppose that our examinations would neglect the men on whom you have spent so much time and effort in training?"

The General flushed with rage. "If you've tampered with any of my men—! You had no right—!"

The other Commission members were smiling in faint amusement at the General's discomfiture.

"I should think it would be to your advantage to check the results of your training," said Mr. Merton.

"There is only one possible check!" exclaimed General Winthrop. "Put these men on a base for a period of eight years and at a distance of forty seven light years from home and see what they will do. That is the only way you can check on them."

"And if you know anything about our methods of testing, you will understand that this, in effect, is what we have done. Your best man is about to be released from the test pit. He can't have more than an hour to go."

"Who have you got in your guinea pig pen?" the General demanded. "If you've ruined him—"

"Captain Louis Carnahan," said Ashby. "Shall we go down, gentlemen?"

*   *   *   *   *

It had been a grisly business, watching the final minutes of Carnahan's disintegration. General Winthrop's face was almost purple when he saw the test pit in which Carnahan was being examined. He tried to tear out the observation lens with his bare hands as he saw the Captain lift the loaded pistol to his head in the moment before the safety beam cut in.

And now Ashby kept hearing Winthrop's furious, scathing voice: "You have destroyed one of the best men the Service has ever produced! I'll have your hide for this, Ashby, if it's the last act of my life."

Merton and the others had been shocked also by the violence and degradation of what they saw, but whether he had made his point or not, Ashby didn't know. Carnahan, of course, would be returned to the Service within twenty four hours, all adverse effects of the test completely removed. He would be aware that he had taken it and had not passed, but there would be no trace of the bitter emotions generated during those days of examination.

Ashby looked out again at the four hulls now turning from gold to red as the sun dropped lower in the sky. He had not asked Merton if the ultimatum was going to stick. He wondered how they could insist on it after what they had seen, but he didn't *know*.

Impatiently, he turned from the window as Miss Haslam's voice came on the intercom once more. "Dr. Ashby, Mr. Jorden is still waiting to see you."

Jorden. He had forgotten. The man had been waiting during his conference with the Commissioners. Jorden was the one who had been rejected for examination two weeks ago and insisted he had a *right* to be examined for colonization factors. He had been trying to get in ever since. He might as well get rid of the man once and for all, Ashby decided reluctantly.

"Show him in," he said.

Mark Jorden was a tall, blond man in his late twenties. Shaking hands with him, Ashby felt thick, strong fingers and glimpsed a massive wrist at the edge of the coat sleeve. Jorden's face was a pleasant Scandinavian pink, matched by blue eyes that looked intently into Ashby's face.

They sat at the desk. "You want to be a colonist," said Ashby. "You say you want to settle forty seven light years from Earth for the rest of your life. And our preliminary psycho tests indicate you have scarcely a vestige of the basic qualities required. Why do you insist on the full examination?"

Jorden smiled and shook his head honestly. "I don't know exactly. It seems like something I'd enjoy doing. Maybe it's in my people—they liked to move around and see new places. They were seamen in the days when there weren't any charts to sail by."

"It's certain that this is a situation without charts to sail by," said Ashby, "but I hardly think the word 'enjoy' is applicable. Have you thought at all of what existence means at that distance from Earth, with no communication whatever except a ship every eight years or so? Qualifications just a trifle short of insanity are required for a venture of that kind."

"I'm sure you don't mean that, Dr. Ashby," said Jorden reprovingly.

"Perhaps not," said Ashby. His visitor's calm assurance irritated him, as if *he* were the one who knew what a colonist ought to be. "I see by your application you're an electrical engineer."

Jorden nodded. "Yes. My company has just offered me the head of the department, but I had to explain I was putting in an application for colonist. They think I'm crazy, of course."

"Does taking the examination mean giving up your promotion?"

"I'm not sure. But I rather think they will pass me up and give it to one of the other men."

"You want to go badly enough to risk giving up that chance in order to take an examination which will unquestionably show you have no qualifications whatever to be a colonist?"

"I think I'm qualified," said Jorden. "I insist on being given the chance. I believe I have the right to it."

Ashby tried to restrain his irritation. What Jorden said was perhaps true. No one had ever raised the point before. Those previously rejected by the preliminary tests had withdrawn in good grace. It seemed senseless to waste the time of a test pit and its large crew on an obviously hopeless applicant. On the other hand, he couldn't afford to have Jorden stirring up trouble with the Colonization Commission at this critical time—and he could guess that was exactly what Jorden's next move would be if he were turned down again.

"Our machines will find out everything about you later," said Ashby, "but I'd like you to tell me about yourself so that I may feel personally acquainted with you."

Jorden shrugged. "There's not much to tell. I had the usual schooling, which wasn't anything impressive. I had my three year hitch in the Service, and I suppose that's where I began to feel there was something available in life which I had never anticipated. I suppose it sounds very silly to you, but when I first put a foot on the Moon I felt like crying. I picked up a handful of pumice and let it sift through my fingers. I looked out toward Mars and felt as if I could go anywhere, that I ought to go everywhere.

"The medicos told me later that it was a crazy sort of feeling that everyone gets his first time out, but I didn't believe them. I didn't believe it was quite the same with anyone else. When I got out to Mars finally, and during my one tour on Pluto, it seemed to get worse instead of decreasing as they told me it would. When I got out I took a job in my profession, and I've been satisfied, but I've never been able to get rid of the feeling there's something I'm missing, something I ought to be doing. It's connected with everything out there." He lifted a broad hand and gestured to the horizon beyond the windows.

"Perhaps your career should have been in the Service," suggested Ashby.

"No. That was good enough while it lasted, but they didn't have anything I wanted permanently. When I heard about the proposed colonization on Serrengia that seemed to be it."

"Your application indicates you are not married."

"That's right," said Jorden. "I have no ties to hold me back."

"You understand, of course, that as a colonist you will be expected to marry, either before leaving or soon after arrival. Colonial life is family life."

"I hadn't thought much about that, but it can't be too bad, I suppose. I presume my choice would be quite severely limited to a fellow colonist?"

"Correct."

"There is a story about my third or fourth grandfather who was given a girl to marry the night before he sailed from his homeland to settle in a new country. They had seventeen children and were said to be extraordinarily happy. My family still owns the homestead they cleared. I was born there."

"It can be done, but it doesn't conform closely with our currently accepted social mores," said Ashby hopefully.

"I'm sure that won't stand in my way. If there's a woman who's willing to take a chance, I certainly will be."

"There's one more thing we have to know," said Ashby. "What are you running away from? Who or what are your enemies?"

Jorden laughed uncertainly. "I'm sorry, but I'm not running away from anything. As far as I know I have no enemies."

"*All* colonists are running from something," said Ashby. "Otherwise they would stay where they are."

Jorden regarded him a moment in silence, then smiled slowly. "I think you are going to have occasion to revise that thesis," he said.

"A great deal of history would also have to be revised if we did," said Ashby. "At any rate, let's go down to the test pits. I'll show you what's in store for you there, and you can further decide if you insist on going through with it."

*   *   *   *   *

The laboratories of the Institute of Social Science were spread over a forty acre area, consisting mostly of the test pits where experimental examination of proposed colonists was being conducted. Ashby led his visitor to the ground floor where they took a pair of the electric cycles used for transportation along the vast corridors of the laboratory.

A quarter of a mile away they stopped and entered a glassed-in control room fitted with a number of desks and extensive banks of electronic equipment.

"This almost looks like a good sized computer setup," said Jorden admiringly.

"We use computers extensively, but this equipment is merely the recording and control apparatus for the synthetic environment established in the test pit. Please step this way."

The control room was empty now, but during a test it was occupied by a dozen technicians. It was a highly unorthodox procedure to show a prospective colonist the test pit setup before examination, but Ashby still had hopes of shunting Jorden aside without wasting the facilities on a useless test.

They moved to an observation post and Ashby directed Jorden's attention to the observation lenses. "We cleaned out here this afternoon," he said. "A Captain of the Service last occupied the pit."

Jorden looked up inquiringly. "Did he—?"

"No. He didn't make it. Tomorrow morning you will be given a preconditioning which will set up the basic situation that you have traveled to Serrengia and are now established there in the colony. We will begin the test at a period of some length after establishment there, when difficulties begin to pile up. Other members of the party will be laboratory staff people who will provide specific, guiding stimuli to determine your reaction to them."

"Are they there constantly, night and day?"

"No. When you are asleep their day's work is over and they go home."

"What if I wake up and find the whole setup is a phony?"

"You won't. We have control beams constantly focussed upon the persons being tested. These are used to keep him asleep when desirable, and to control him to the extent of preventing him doing physical harm to himself or others."

"Is that necessary?" said Jorden dubiously. "Why should anyone wish to do harm?"

"The Captain, whom we released today, was pushed to the point of suicide," said Ashby. "We find it *quite* necessary to assure ourselves of adequate control at all times."

"How can you set up the illusion of distance and a whole new world in such a comparatively small area?"

"It *is* illusion, a great deal of it. Some is induced along with the initial preconditioning, other features are done mechanically, but when you are there you will have no doubt whatever that you are a colonist on the planet Serrengia. You will act accordingly, and respond to the stimuli exactly as if you had been transported to the actual planet. In this way, we are sure of finding colonists who will not blow up when they face the real situation."

"How many have you found so far?"

"None."

Jorden was shaken for a moment, but he smiled then and said, "You have found one. Put my name down on the books."

"We'll see," said Ashby grimly. "Your colony will be in the limited belt of the planet's northern hemisphere where considerable agriculture is possible. You'll be in the midst of a group trying to beat a living from a world which is neither excessively hostile nor conducive to indolence. Some of the people will be bitter and wish they had never come. They will break up in groups and fight each other. They will challenge every reason you have for your own coming. You will face your own personal impoverishment, the death of your child—"

"Child?" said Jorden.

"Yes. You will be provided with a wife and three children. One of these will die, and you will react as if it were your own flesh. Your wife will oppose your staying, and demand a return to Earth. We will throw at you every force available to tear down your determination to build a colony. We shall test in every possible way the validity of your decision to go. Do you still wish to go through with it?"

Jorden's grin was somewhat fainter. He took a deep breath as he nodded slowly. "Yes, I'll go through with it. I think it's what I want."

*   *   *   *   *

When Ashby finally returned alone to the office, Miss Haslam had gone home. He put in a call anyway for Dr. Bonnie Nathan. She usually remained somewhere in the laboratory until quite late, even when not assigned to a test.

In a few minutes her voice came over the phone. "John? What can I do for you?"

"I thought I could let you off for a few days," said Ashby, "but we've got another one that's come up rather suddenly." He told her briefly about Mark Jorden. "It's useless, but I don't want him running to the Commission right now, so we'll put him through. You'll be the wife. We'll use Program Sixty Eight, except that we'll accelerate it."

"Accelerate—!"

"Yes. It won't hurt him any. Whatever happens we can wipe up afterwards. This is simply a nuisance and I want it out of the way as quickly as possible. After that—perhaps I can give you those few days I promised you. O.K.?"

"It's all right with me," said Bonnie. "But an accelerated Sixty Eight—"

*　　*　　*　　*　　*

They stood on a low hillock overlooking the ninety acres of bottom land salvaged from the creek grass. Mark Jorden shaded his eyes and squinted critically over the even stand of green shoots emerging from the bronzed soil. Germination had been good in spite of the poor planting time. The chance of getting a crop out was fair. If they didn't they'd be eating shoe plastic in another few months.

The ten year old boy beside him clutched his hand and edged closer as if there were something threatening him from the broad fields. "Isn't there any way at all for Earth to send us food," he said, "if we don't get a crop?"

"We have to make believe Earth doesn't exist, Roddy," said Jorden. "We couldn't even let them know we need help, we're so far away." He gripped the boy's shoulders solidly in his big hands and drew him close. "We aren't going to need any help from Earth. We're going to make it on our own. After all, what would they do on Earth if they couldn't make it? Where would they go for outside help?"

"I know," said the boy, "but there are so many of them they can't fail. Here, there's only the few of us."

Jorden patted his shoulder gently again as they started moving toward the rough houses a half mile away. "That makes it all the easier for us," he said. "We don't have to worry about the ones who won't cooperate. We can't lose with the setup we've got."

It was harder for Roddy. He remembered Earth, although he had been only four when they left. He still remembered the cities and the oceans and the forests he had known so briefly, and was cursed with the human nostalgia for a past that seemed more desirable than an unknown, fearful future.

Of the other children, Alice had been a baby when they left, and Jerry had been born during the trip. They knew only Serrengia and loved its wild, uncompromising rigor. They spent their abandoned wildness of childhood in the nearby hills and forests. But with Roddy it was different. Childhood seemed to have slipped by him. He was moody, and moved carefully in constant fear of this world he would never willingly call home. Jorden's heart ached with longing to instill some kind of joy into him.

"That looks like Mr. Tibbets," said Roddy suddenly, his eyes on the new log house.

"I believe you're right," said Jorden. "It looks like Roberts and Adamson with him. Quite a delegation. I wonder what they want."

The colony consisted of about a hundred families, each averaging five members. Originally they had settled on a broad plateau at some distance from the river. It was a good location overlooking hundreds of miles of desert and forest land. Its soil was fertile and the river water was lifted easily through the abundant power of the community atomic energy plant which had been brought from Earth.

Three months ago, however, the power plant had been destroyed in a disastrous explosion that killed almost a score of the colonists. Crops for their next season's food supply were half matured and could not be saved by any means available.

The community was broken into a number of smaller groups. Three of these, composed of fifteen families each, moved to the low lands along the river bank and cleared acreage for new crops in a desperate hope of getting a harvest before the season ended. They had not yet learned enough of the cycle of weather in this area to predict it with much accuracy.

Mark Jorden was in charge of one of the farms and the elected leader of the village in which he lived.

Tibbets was an elderly man from the same village. In his middle sixties, he presented a puzzle to Jorden as to why he had been permitted to come. Roberts and Adamson were from the settlements farther down the river.

Jorden felt certain of the reason for their visit. He didn't want to hear what they had to say, but he knew he might as well get it over with.

They hailed him from the narrow wooden porch. Jorden came up the steps and shook hands with each. "Won't you come in? I'm sure Bonnie can find something cool to drink."

Tibbets wiped his thin, wrinkled brow. "She already has. That girl of yours doesn't waste any time being told what to do. It's too bad some of the others can't pitch in the way Bonnie does."

Jorden accepted the praise without comment, wondering if no one else at all were aware of the hot, violent protests she sometimes poured out against him because of the colony.

"Come in anyway," Jorden said. "I have to go back to the watering in a little while, but you can take it easy till then." He led the way into the log house.

Their homes on the plateau had been decent ones. With adequate power they had made lumber and cement, and within a year of their landing had built a town of fine homes. Among those who had been forced to abandon them, no one was more bitter than Bonnie. "You're no farmer," she said. "Why can't those who are be the ones to move?"

Now, when he came into the kitchen, she was tired, but she tried to smile as always at her pleasure in seeing him again. He couldn't imagine what it would be like not having her to welcome him from the fields.

"I'll get something cool for you and Roddy," she said. "Would you gentlemen like another drink?"

When they were settled in the front room Tibbets spoke. "You know why we've come, Mark. The election is only a couple of months away. We can't have Boggs in for another term of governor. You've got to say you'll run against him."

"As I told you last time, Boggs may be a poor excuse for the job, but I'd be worse. He's at least an administrator. I'm only an engineer—and more recently a farmer."

"We've got something new, now," said Tibbets, his eyes suddenly cold and meaningful.

"The talk about his deliberately blowing up the power plant? Talk of that kind could blow up the whole colony as well. Boggs may have his faults but he's not insane."

"We've got proof now," said Tibbets. "It's true. Adamson's got the evidence. He got one of the engineers who escaped the blast to talk. It's one of them who were supposed to have been killed. He's so scared of Boggs he's still hiding out. But he's got the proof and those who are helping him know it's true."

"Tibbets is right," said Adamson earnestly. "We know it's true. And something like that can't stay hidden. It's got to be brought out if we're going to make the colony survive. You can't just shut your eyes to it and say, 'Good old Boggs would never do a thing like that.'"

Jorden's eyes were darker as he spoke in low tones now, hoping Roddy would not be listening in the kitchen. "Suppose it is true. Why would Boggs do such an insane thing?"

"Because he's an insane man," said Tibbets. "That's the obvious answer. He wants to destroy the colony and limit its growth. He was satisfied to come here and be elected governor and run the show. He saw it as means of becoming a two-bit dictator over a group of subservient colonists. It hasn't turned out that way. He found a large percentage of engineers and scientists who would have none of his nonsense.

"He saw the group becoming something bigger than himself. He had to cut it down to his own size. He's willing to destroy what he can't possess, but he believes that by reducing us to primitive status he can keep us in line. In either case the colony loses."

"If what you say is true—if it's actually true," Jorden said, his eyes suddenly far away, "we've got to fight him—"

"Then we can count on you?"

"Yes—you can count on me."

*   *   *   *   *

He stood in the doorway watching the departure of the three men, but he was aware of Bonnie behind him. She rushed to him as he turned, and put her face against his chest.

"Mark—you can't do it! Boggs will kill you. This is no concern of ours. We don't belong to Maintown any more. It's their business up there. I'd go crazy if anything happened to you. You've got to think of the rest of us!"

"I am thinking," said Mark. He raised her chin so he could look into her eyes. "I'm thinking that we are going to live here the rest of our lives, and so are the children. If the story about Boggs is true, we're all concerned. We wouldn't be down here if the power plant hadn't been destroyed. We'd be living in our good home in Maintown. Would you expect me to let Boggs get away with this without raising a hand to stop him?"

"Yes—I would," said Bonnie, "because there is nothing anyone can do. You know he has Maintown in the palm of his hand. He's screened out every ruffian and soured colonist in the whole group and they'll do anything he says. You can't fight them all, Mark. I won't let you."

"It won't be me alone," said Jorden. "If it develops into a fight the majority of the colony will be with us. Earth will be with us. Boggs will be facing the results of the whole two billion year struggle it took to make man what he now is."

*   *   *   *   *

In the lounge off the lab cafeteria, Ashby indulged in a late coffee knowing he wouldn't sleep anyway. Across the table Bonnie ate sparingly of a belated supper.

"The threat of having to fight Boggs didn't give him much of a scare," said Ashby thoughtfully.

"It'll take a lot more than a bogey man like Boggs to scare Mark," said Bonnie. "You've got yourself a bigger quantity of man than you bargained for."

"This might turn out to be more interesting than we thought. I wish there were more time to spend on him. But Merton called up again today to verify the ultimatum I told you about. We produce colonists by the time Hull Four is complete or they turn the personnel problem over to Winthrop—even after they saw Carnahan go to pieces before their eyes."

"Has it ever occurred to you," said Bonnie slowly, "that we might just possibly be off on the wrong foot? How do you know that any of the colonists of Earth's history could have stood up to the demands of Serrengia? I'm beginning to suspect that the Mayflower's passenger list would have folded quite completely under these conditions. They had it comparatively easy. So did most other successful colonists."

"Yes—?" said Ashby.

"Maybe they succeeded in *spite* of being rebels. If they could have come to the new lands without the pressure of flight, but in complete freedom of action, they might have made an even greater success."

"But why would they have come at all, then?"

"I don't know. There must be another motive capable of impelling them. In great feats of exploration, creation—other human actions similar to colonization—"

"There are *no* other human actions similar to colonization," said Ashby. "Surely you realize we're dealing with something unique here, Bonnie!"

"I know—all I'm trying to say is there could be another valid motive. I think Mark Jorden's got it. There's something different about this test, and I think you ought to look in on it yourself."

"What's so different about him?"

"He doesn't act like the rest. He hasn't any apparent reason for being here."

Ashby looked at the girl closely. She was one of his top staff members and had been with him from the beginning. The incredible strain of working day after day in the test pits was showing its effects, he thought.

"I shouldn't have let you get started on this one," he said. "You're fagged out. Maybe it would be better to erase what we've done and start over, so that you can drop out."

She shook her head with a quickness that surprised him. "I want to finish it, and see how Mark turns out. I'm so used to working with the bitter, anti-social ones that it's a relief to have someone who is halfway normal and gregarious. I want to be around when we find out why he's here."

"Especially if he should go all the way to the end. But he won't—"

*   *   *   *   *

Ashby was genuinely concerned about Bonnie's condition when he looked in on her the next morning. The strain on her face was real beyond any matter of make-up or acting. He wondered just why she should be giving in to it now. Bonnie was well trained, as were all the staff members who worked in the test pits. The emotional conflicts mocked up there were not allowed to penetrate very deeply into their personal experience, yet it looked now as if Bonnie had somehow lost control of the armor to protect against such invasion. She seemed to be living the circumstances of the test program almost as intensely as Mark Jorden was doing.

Such a condition couldn't be permitted to continue, but he was baffled by it. Her physical and emotional check prior to the test had not shown her threshold to be this low. Evidently there was emotional dynamite buried somewhere in the situation they had manufactured.

Through the observation lens of the test pit Ashby watched Jorden begin a tour of the villages, making a quiet investigation of the situation, which he had all but ignored until it was forced to his attention. Jorden spent an hour with Adamson, listening carefully to the atomic engineer's story, and then was led to the hiding place of the engineer who claimed direct evidence that Boggs had instigated the explosion at the power plant.

As Adamson left them, Ashby signaled him through the tiny button buried in the skin behind his right ear. "This is Ashby," he said. "How does it look? Do you think he's going to tackle Boggs?"

"No question of that." Adamson's words came back, although he made no movement of his mouth or throat. "Jorden is one of these people with a lot of inertia. It takes a big push to get him moving, but when he really gets rolling there isn't much that can stop him, either. You're really going to have to put the pressure on to find his cracking point."

"I'm afraid we're likely to find Bonnie's first. There's something about this that's hitting her too hard. Do you know what it is?"

"No," said Adamson. "I thought I noticed it a little yesterday, too. Maybe we ought to check her out."

"She insists on completing the program. And I'd like to go all the way with Jorden. I'm becoming rather curious about him. Keep an eye on Bonnie and let me know what you think at the end of the shift."

"I'll do that," said Adamson.

$$*\quad*\quad*\quad*\quad*$$

Jorden followed his guide for more than a mile beyond the last village on the bank of the river. There, in a willow hidden cave in the clay bank, he found James, the atomic engineer who was reported to know of Boggs' attack on the power plant.

"I told him you were coming," said Adamson, "but I'm going to leave. You can make out better if you're alone with him. He's bitter, but he isn't armed, and he'll go along with you if you don't push him too hard."

Jorden watched Adamson disappear along the bank in the direction from which they had come. He had a feeling of utter ridiculousness. This wasn't what they had come for! They had come to build an outpost of human beings, to establish man's claim in this sector of the Universe. And they were ending in a petty conflict worthy of the politics of centuries before, back on Earth.

His face took on a harder set as he approached the mouth of the cave and whistled the signal notes that Adamson had taught him. If the establishment of the colony demanded this kind of fight then he was willing to enter the battle. He had not dedicated the remainder of his life to a goal only to abandon it to a petty tyrant like Boggs.

A bearded face peered cautiously through parted willows and James' voice spoke. "You're Jorden? I suppose by now everybody in the villages knows where I'm hiding out. I'm the world's prize fool for letting this parade come past my place. Come in and I'll tell you what I know. If you help get Boggs it will be worth anything it costs me."

Jorden followed the man through the screening willows to the mouth of the cave. There the two of them squatted on rocks opposite each other.

"I remember you now," said James. "You set up the electric plant when we were assembling the pile, didn't you? I thought we'd worked together."

Jorden nodded, hoping James would go on, remembering Adamson's caution not to push him too hard, but the engineer seemed to have nothing more to say. He rubbed a hand forcibly against his other arm and looked beyond the mouth of the cave to the slow moving river.

"This business concerning Boggs' destruction of the plant— how did it start?" said Jorden finally.

"How does anything of that kind start?" said James. "Boggs came to some of us and remarked in casual conversation what a shame it would be if the colony were to duplicate all over again the mistakes that Earth have made during the past thousands of years. A few of us were sympathetic with that thought—it would indeed be a shame. Some of the engineers thought that this was the perfect chance to set up a truly scientific society. They didn't agree that Boggs was the ideal leader, but he *was* the leader and the obvious one to work through. They all became convinced that a rapid industrialization and a highly technological society built upon the old rusty foundations would be most difficult to overcome in building a society on truly adequate sociological principles. You can take it from there."

Yes, he could, Jorden thought. Anybody could take it from there. It was the oldest lie that men of power and position had ever concocted. Why had those particular colonists fallen for it?

"What about you?" he asked James. "Were you sucked in by Boggs' arguments?"

The engineer nodded. "He took all of us. And all along he never intended that more than a couple would get out alive—by double crossing the others."

"Why?" said Jorden.

"Why? I've thought a lot about that, living here in this mudhole. You get to thinking about things like that when you realize there's no going back, that Boggs would kill me on sight for what I could tell—and that the other colonists would also, because of what I've done. Adamson says I can trust him. He says I can trust you. But I don't trust anybody. I know that someday soon I'm going to get a bullet in the head from one of you. All I'm hoping is that some of you hate Boggs enough to get him first."

"Why did you come to Serrengia in the first place?"

"To get away. Why did anyone come? You don't give up everything you've got in order to go to some strange world and spend the rest of your life unless you've got a reason. Unless you hate what you've got so much you're willing to try anything else. Unless you're so terribly afraid of what could happen to you back there that you're willing to face any kind of dangers out here. We all had our reasons. I'm not asking yours. It makes no difference to you what mine were. But they're all alike. We came because we were so afraid or full of hate we couldn't stay."

"How did you expect to build a new world out of hate and fear of the old one?"

"Who worried about what we'd build here? All we wanted to do was get away. You can't tell me *you* came for any other reason!"

*   *   *   *   *

Jorden made no answer. He continued to stare in wonder at the atomic engineer. To what extent were James' words actually true? How completely was the colony riddled with unpredictable, purposeless characters like him?

If they had fled Earth with a purpose to create something better than they left, there was a chance. But if James was right that most of them had come in blind flight with no goal at all then the Earth colony of Serrengia would be dead long before the ships came again.

But Jorden did not believe this. He did not believe that any but a small fraction of the colonists had any feeling toward Earth except that of love. Most had come because they wanted to do this particular thing with their lives. Nothing had driven or forced them to it.

"Tell me what Boggs did, and what he persuaded you to do," said Jorden.

In detail, James told him how Boggs had gained influence with the technicians necessary to prepare the plant for destruction, how he had persuaded them that a new, idealistic social order demanded their obedience to this fantastic plan. Then, under the Governor's direction, two of the men betrayed the rest. Only James, who was at a slight distance from his normal operating post that night, had escaped with non-fatal injuries.

"I know how you feel," said James. "You'd like to stick a knife into me now. But until you succeed in disposing of Boggs, you need to be sure I'm alive. When that's over you'll send someone around to take care of the traitor, James. But you may be sure I won't be here. I'll get through your guards!"

The man was half crazed, Jorden thought, from infection and fever in half treated wounds, and probably from the effects of radiation itself. "We aren't going to set up any guards," he said. "We're going to send you medical care. Don't try to get away down the river. I'll have some men who'll take you where you'll be safe and have care."

Jorden left, on the hope that James would not attempt further flight until he was assured of Boggs' defeat. But the colony could not quickly administer the kind of defeat James wanted. They had to be orderly, even if it was a frontier community. There had to be a trial. There had to be evidence, and James had to be called to give it.

He returned to the village and made arrangements with Adamson to get medical care for James. Dr. Babbit, one of the four physicians with the colony, was sufficiently out of sympathy with Boggs to be trusted.

Then, with his family, he accompanied Tibbets to Maintown. On the bulletin board outside the Council Hall he hung an announcement of his candidacy for the governorship, which Tibbets had prepared for him. Tibbets made a little speech to the handful of people who gathered to read what was on the bulletin, but Jorden declined to make any personal statement just now. He had enough to say when it came time to accuse Boggs of the crimes involved in destruction of the power plant.

But among those who squinted closely at Tibbets' fine, black printing there came a look of mild awe. It had been generally assumed that Boggs would go unopposed for re-election.

On the way back Tibbets' car passed the length of Maintown and took them by the deserted house which Jorden had built in their first year on Serrengia. Bonnie gave it a covetous look, contrasting its spaciousness with the primitive cabin in which she now lived.

Tibbets caught her glance. "If it were not for Boggs you would still be living there," he said.

Bonnie made no answer. Both she and Roddy stared ahead, as if unable to bring their attention to bear upon the present, because of the fear incited by everything about them. Jorden was also silent, but his eyes wandered incessantly over the surrounding hills and distant farmlands. He hadn't bargained for anything like this. He had expected to find himself in a society of cooperative and uniformly energetic human beings. He knew now, without any further persuasion, that this had been a vision strictly from an ivory tower.

He should have anticipated that in a group like this there would be a sprinkling of small time thugs and dictators and generally shiftless individuals who could not make a go of it in the society they had left. At home you could live and work with such without ever being more than vaguely aware of their eccentricities. Here, their deviation from required cooperation was enough to disrupt the whole community.

He could understand the terror in Bonnie and Roddy. They had come only because of him, with no understanding of the colony's purpose. The present turmoil underlined their conviction that it had been pure folly to come. Somehow he'd have to show them. He'd have to make them understand there was a reason for being on Serrengia. But at the moment he did not know how to do it.

*   *   *   *   *

The program called for a continuation well into the night with a long scene at the cabin, but Ashby interrupted it as soon as they returned from Maintown. He ordered a twenty four hour rest, because of Bonnie. The extended period of sleep wouldn't harm Jorden.

Bonnie, however, was furious at the interruption as she came out of the test pit.

"If you're going to let it go to the end, why don't you get on with it?" she demanded. "The whole thing is so far off the track that you might as well find out as soon as possible that you're not getting anywhere."

"I think we're beginning to find out a great deal. But I want you to have a rest. The hours of this shift are much too long for you."

"You think you know what's going on inside Mark Jorden by watching the dials and meters, but you don't, because it's not himself he's concerned about. It's a goal outside and bigger than himself. The colony *means* something to him. It never meant anything at all to any of the others."

"Then this is the kind of situation we've been looking for."

"But we haven't the techniques or insight to understand it. We can analyze a man who's running away—but we're not prepared for one who's running *toward*."

*   *   *   *   *

The night after they returned from Maintown a terrific storm broke over the plateau. It began at supper time and for an hour poured torrents of water on the land. Jorden wanted to go down to the river to see if their diversion dams were holding. If they went out it meant long days of hard hand labor restoring them.

He gave in, however, to Bonnie's plea to stay in the house with them. Roddy was frightened of the storm and looked physically ill when thunder made the walls of the cabin shake. It wouldn't change the actual facts of the damage to the dams whether Jorden examined them now or in the morning. He tried to think up stories to tell the children, but it was hard to make up some dealing only with Serrengia and ignoring Earth, as he had to do for Roddy's sake.

After the rain finally stopped and Bonnie had put the children to bed there came a knock at the door. Bonnie opened it. Governor Boggs and two Council members moved into the room. Little pools of water drained to the floor about their feet.

The Governor turned slowly and grinned at Bonnie and Mark Jorden as the light from the lamp and the fireplace fell upon him. "Nasty night out," he said. "For a time I was afraid we weren't going to make it."

Boggs was a short, stout man and carried himself very erect. He seemed to exaggerate his normal posture as he moved toward the chairs Bonnie offered the men.

Jorden remained seated in his big wooden chair by the fireplace glancing up with cold challenge in his face as his visitors settled on the opposite side of the fire.

"I'm sorry we missed you when you were in town today," said Boggs. "It was not until late this afternoon that I became aware of your visit."

He reached to an inner coat pocket and drew forth a paper which he unfolded carefully. Jorden recognized it as the announcement he had tacked on the bulletin board. Boggs passed it over.

"I felt sure you would wish to withdraw this, Jorden, after you had given it a little fuller consideration. I'm sure that by now you have had time to think over the matter a little more calmly and find a good many reasons why you should withdraw your announcement."

"I haven't thought much about it," said Jorden, "but now that you call it to my attention I am becoming aware of an increasing number of reasons why I should not withdraw. I assure you I have no intention of doing so."

Boggs smiled and folded up the paper and slipped it into the fire. "I have not been such a bad administrator during my first term of office, have I Jorden?"

"That is for the people to decide—on election day."

"But why should they want to change a perfectly capable administrator," said Boggs in an injured tone, "and put in a very capable engineer and farm manager—who has no qualifications in administrative matters?"

"That too is a question to be answered on election day."

Boggs shifted in his chair, dropping the deliberately maintained smile from his face. "There have been some stories circulating about the colony recently," he said. "It is possible that you have heard them and believe them."

"Possibly," said Jorden.

"I wouldn't. I wouldn't believe them if I were you. I wouldn't even listen to them because it might lead to dangerous and erroneous conclusions, which would cause you to convict in your mind an honest man."

"That would be my error then, wouldn't it?" said Jorden.

The Governor nodded. "A grave one as far as it concerns the welfare of yourself and your family, Jorden."

Jorden's face hardened. "Threats of that kind aren't appropriate to your position, Governor."

"Perhaps you are not aware of my exact position."

"I think I am! And I intend to do everything in my power to change it. You are a small time chiseler who saw a good chance to set yourself up for life in a cushy situation where five hundred other people would obey your slightest whim. That's an old fashioned situation, Boggs, and you can't set it up here even if you are willing to resort to sabotage and murder."

Boggs eyes narrowed and he looked at Jorden for a long time. "I am afraid, then," he said, "that there is nothing I can do except put a stop to your repeating these lying stories about me."

The Governor's eyes never moved, but Jorden shifted in sudden, wild indecision. Almost simultaneously there were two shots exploding in the narrow cabin, and then a third. Jorden and Boggs leaped out of their chairs.

From the kitchen doorway came the steel-taut voice of Bonnie. "Don't move any further, Mr. Boggs. Put your hands in the air. Get his gun, Mark—in the pocket on this side."

For a moment Jorden hesitated, his eyes held by the sight of Boggs' two gunmen on the floor, blood spreading in tiny rivulets. He took the pistol from the Governor's pocket and held it in readiness.

"I ought to kill you now, Boggs," he said. "Fortunately, or unfortunately, we have to set a precedent in such matters if the colony is to survive. We have to go through the formality of a trial for sabotaging the power plant and murdering those killed there. Actually, it would be a good idea if you just took off over the hills and went as far as you could before the jungle got you. It would save us all a great deal of trouble."

Hope surged in Boggs' eyes as he recognized that Jorden was incapable of shooting him down. Then bitterness mingled with that hope. "You won't get away with this, Jorden. We'll see what the people have to say about your wife shooting my men down while my back is turned."

"*Their* backs weren't turned," said Jorden. "Get them out of here now. If you want to save explanations as to why you came here tonight you might find a convenient spot and bury them— before you take out over the hills yourself."

Watching until they could no longer see the lights of Boggs' car, they closed the door. Bonnie collapsed with a moan, cringing in Jorden's arms.

"Now they'll kill us all," she said in a lifeless voice. "We haven't got a chance. For this we followed your great dream of colonizing an outpost of the Universe!"

*   *   *   *   *

That night Roddy was sick. Six days later he was dead. Before they decided to go through with this section of the program there were long and heated conferences between Bonnie and Ashby and the staff working at the test pit. Bonnie insisted the program should be dropped here. They already knew that Jorden was what they were searching for. They had only to analyze the factors that had brought him to the test and they would have what they needed to identify as many colonists as the project required. He didn't need to be broken down any further.

Ashby knew this was not true. Jorden's basic purpose as a colonist had not yet been brought into sight. Ashby recognized that his goal was almost certainly the perpetuation of the colony—and he was the first one who had maintained such a goal this far—but they had to know the drive that existed behind the goal. If it should develop a basis wholly in flight it would still crack before completion of the program.

But Ashby continued to be hesitant on Bonnie's account. Roddy's illness and death meant a continuous tour in the test pit for the full six days. And this was cut from the scheduled eight it normally occupied. Why it was impossible for Bonnie to reduce her own personal tension on the project, Ashby didn't know, but she had become increasingly susceptible as time went on.

Word of Jorden's persistence was spreading among the staff personnel of other sections of the lab. A subdued excitement was stirring among them. In most cases so far examined, the colonist had by now either knuckled under to Boggs or engaged in a futile personal duel with him. If they went further, they almost invariably collapsed under the pressure of Bonnie's blame and began cursing Serrengia as well as the Earth from which they fled.

Ashby ordered resumption of the program. It was an agony for him, too, watching Bonnie during the long hours of Roddy's illness. It seemed every bit as much a test of her strength and endurance as it was of Mark Jorden's. With the televiewer Ashby brought an image of her face up close, studying her from every angle during the long nights when she and Mark Jorden exchanged vigil over Roddy. He scanned her face by the firelight of the rough cabin.

After three days, Jorden was running close to exhaustion, but in spite of the strain Bonnie seemed capable of remaining there forever. Her eyes watched Jorden's face, taking in his every movement and expression.

And after three days of watching Bonnie's face in close-up, Ashby suddenly murmured aloud to himself in disbelief and astonishment.

Dr. Miller, who was Tibbets in the program, came up to his side. "What is it, Ashby? Has something gone wrong?"

Ashby shook his head slowly in wonder and pointed to the image in the viewer. "Look at her," he said. "Can't you see what has happened to Bonnie? We should have caught it long ago. No wonder this job is tearing her apart—no wonder she doesn't want it to end the way it must—or end at all, for that matter!"

"I still don't see what you are talking about," said Miller in exasperation. "I don't see that anything has happened to her. She looks like the same old Bonnie to me."

"Does she?" said Ashby. "Watch her when she looks at Jorden. Can't you see she has fallen in love with him?"

*   *   *   *   *

There was probably a whole class of people like Roddy, Jorden thought. People incapable of surviving beyond the world on which they were born. Since the day of his coming Roddy had fought an unceasing battle with this hated, alien world of Serrengia. He awoke each morning to renew the unequal contest before he was even out of bed—and knowing fully that he was beaten before he started.

Jorden had tried every way he knew to instill into his son some of his own love for this new world. It was a good world and the men who grew up on it in the years to come would love it with all their hearts. But Roddy could not give up his reaching back, his longing for Earth. He shrank before the problem of their doubtful food supply. He caught snatches of adult worries and nourished them with a dark agony that made it appear to Jorden sometimes as if the boy were walking in a nightmare.

It had been cruel and brutal to bring him. But there was no use blaming himself for that. If only Bonnie would stop blaming him! He couldn't have known ahead of time that Roddy was one of those who could not be—transplanted. Fervently, he prayed for the boy's life now and vowed that when the ships came again he would be free to go home.

And always Bonnie's eyes were upon him. Sitting in the firelight of the cabin, he could feel her staring at him, accusing him, hating him for bringing them to Serrengia.

Once he looked up and caught her glance. "Don't hate me so much, Bonnie!" he said. "You're driving Roddy down. I can feel it. Reach out to him with your love and don't let him go."

But Roddy said later that same evening, "Maybe I'll go back to Earth now, Daddy. Do you think that's where little boys go when they die?"

He wanted to return so badly that he was willing to dic to achieve it, Jorden thought. That's what Dr. Babbit said: "Roddy doesn't even want to live, Jorden. As incredible as it seems, he's literally dying of homesickness. I'm afraid there's not a thing I can do for him. I'm sorry, but it's up to you. You and Bonnie are the only ones who can give him a desire to remain, if anyone can."

Roddy's hate for Serrengia was greater than any desire they could induce in him to live. With ease, he conquered all the miracle drugs Dr. Babbit lavished from the colony's restricted store. He died on the sixth night after Boggs' visit.

*　　*　　*　　*　　*

The funeral was held in the little community church built when the colonists first laid out Maintown. Mark and Bonnie Jorden were almost oblivious to the words spoken over the body of Roddy by the Reverend Wagner, who had come as the colonists' spiritual adviser.

Bonnie's hands were folded on her lap, and she kept her eyes down throughout the service. She was aware of the agony within Mark Jorden. It was a real agony, and its strength almost frightened her, for she had never before seen such a response in any man who had gone through the test this far. They were men concerned only with themselves, incapable of the love that Jorden could feel for a son.

He reached out and took one of her hands in his own. She could feel the emotion within him, the tightening and trembling of his big, hard-muscled arm.

Ashby was watching. Over the private communication system that linked them he murmured, "Cry, Bonnie! Make it real. Make him hate himself and everything he's done since he decided to become a colonist—if you can! This is where we've got to find out whether he can crack or not—and why."

"You can't break him," said Bonnie. "He's the strongest man I've ever known. If you find his breaking point it will be when you destroy him utterly. You've got to quit before you reach that point!"

"All that we've done will be useless if we quit now, Bonnie. Just a few more hours and then it will all be over—"

As if his words had touched a hidden trigger, she did begin to cry with a deep but almost inaudible sound and a heavy movement of her shoulders. Mark Jorden put his arm about her as if to force away her grief.

"I *know*, Bonnie," said Ashby softly. "I can see in your face what's happened to you. It's going to be all right. Everything doesn't end for you when the test is over."

"Oh, shut up!" said Bonnie in a sudden rage that made her tears come faster. "If I ever work on another of your damned experiments it will be when I've lost my senses entirely! You don't know what this does to people. I didn't know either— because I didn't care. But now I know—"

"You know that no harm results after we've erased and corrected all inadequate reactions at the end of the test. You're letting your feelings cover up your full awareness of what we're doing."

"Yes, and I suppose that when it's over I had better submit to a little erasing myself. Then Bonnie can go back to work as a little iced steel probe for some more of your guinea pigs!"

"Bonnie—!"

She made no answer to Ashby, but lay her head on Jorden's shoulder while her sobbing subsided. How did it happen? she asked herself. It wasn't anything she had wanted. It had just happened. It had happened that first day when he came in from the field at the beginning of the experiment with all of the planted background that made him think he was meeting Bonnie for the thousandth time instead of the first.

She was supposed to be an actress and receive his husbandly kiss with all the skilled mimicry that made her so valuable to the lab. But it hadn't been like that. She had played sister, mother, daughter, wife—a hundred roles to as many other tested applicants. For the first time she saw one as a human being instead of a sociological specimen. That's the way it was when she met Mark Jorden.

There was no answer to it, she thought bitterly as she rested her face against his shoulder. Ashby was right—just a few more hours and it would all be over. All Jorden's feeling for her as his wife was induced by the postulates of the test, just as were his feelings for Roddy. His subjective reactions were real enough, but they would vanish when their stimulus was removed with the test postulates. He would look upon the restored Roddy as just another little boy—and upon Bonnie, the Doctor in Sociology, as just another misemployed female.

She raised her head and dried her eyes as she sensed that the service was ending. Actually, Ashby was right, of course. They had to go on, and the sooner it came to an end the better it would be for her. She *would* submit to alteration of her own personal data after the test, she thought. She would let them erase all feelings and sentiments she held for Mark Jorden, and then she would be as good as new. After all, if a sociologist couldn't handle his own reactions in a situation of this kind he wasn't of much value in his profession!

*   *   *   *   *

The sun was hot as they returned from the little burial ground near the church. There were quite a number of other graves besides Roddy's, but his was the loneliest, Jorden thought. He had never forgiven them for robbing him of his home and the only world in which he could live.

He felt the growing coldness of Bonnie as they came up to their shabby cabin that had once looked so brave to him.

Serrengia had cost him Bonnie, too. Even before Roddy. She had remained only because it was her duty.

He took her hand as she put a foot on the doorstep. "Bonnie—"

She looked at him bitterly, her eyes searching his face as if to find something of the quality that once drew her to him. "Don't try to say it, Mark—there's nothing left to say."

He let her go, and the two children followed past him into the house. He sat down on the step and looked out over the fields that edged the river bank. His mind felt numbed by Roddy's passing. Bonnie's insistent blame made him live it over and over again.

The light from the green of the fields was like a caress to his eyes. I should hate it, he thought. I should hate the whole damned planet for what it's taken from me. But that's not right—Serrengia hasn't taken anything. It's only that Bonnie and I can't live in the same world, or live the same kind of lives. Roddy was like her. But I didn't know then. I didn't know how either of them were.

We have to go on. There's no going back. Maybe if I'd known, I would have made it different for all of us. I can't now, and it would be crazy to start hating Serrengia for the faults that are in us. Who could do anything but love this fresh, wild planet of ours—?

He ought to go down and take a look at the field, he thought. He rose to go in and tell Bonnie. The crops hadn't had water since Roddy took sick.

He found Bonnie in the bedroom with the drawers of their cabinets open and their trunk in the middle of the floor, its lid thrown back. Clothes lay strewn on the bed.

He felt a slow tightening of his scalp and of the skin along the back of his neck. "Bonnie—"

She straightened and looked into his face with cold, distant eyes. "I'm packing, Mark," she said. "I'm leaving. I'm going home. The girls are going with me. You can stay until they dig your grave beside Roddy's, but I'm going home."

Jorden's face went white. He strode forward and caught her by the arms. "Bonnie—you know there's no way to go home. There won't be a ship for six years. This is home, Bonnie. There's no other place to go."

For a moment the set expression of her face seemed to melt. She frowned as if he had told her some mystery she could not fathom. Then her countenance cleared and its blank determination returned. "I'm going home," she repeated. "You can't stop me. I've done all a wife can be expected to do. I've given my son as the price of your foolishness. You can't ask for more."

He had to get out. He felt that if he remained another instant just then something inside him would explode under the pressure of his grief. He went to the front door and stood leaning against it while he looked over the landscape that almost seemed to reach out for him in hate as it had for Roddy. So you want her, too! he cried inside himself.

Alice came up and tugged at his hand as he stood there. "What's the matter, Daddy? What's the matter with Mama?"

He bent down and kissed her on the forehead. "Nothing, honey. You go and play for a moment while I help Mother."

"I want to help, too!"

"Please, Alice—"

He moved back to the bedroom. Bonnie was carefully examining each item of apparel she packed in the big trunk. She didn't look up as he came in.

"Bonnie," he said in a low voice, "are you going to leave me?"

She put down the dress she was holding and looked up at him. "Yes I'm leaving you," she said. "You've got what you wanted—all you've ever wanted." She looked out towards the fields, shimmering in the heat of the day.

"That's not true, Bonnie. You know it isn't. I've always loved you and needed you, and it's grown greater every hour we've been together."

"Then you'll have to prove it! Give up this hell-world you want us to call home, and give us back our Earth. If you love me, you can prove it."

"It's no test of love to make a man give up the goal that means his life to him. You'd despise me forever if I let you do that to me. I'd rather you went away from me now with the feeling you have at this time, because I'd know I had your love—"

Bonnie remained still and unmoving in his arms, her face averted from his. He put his hand to her chin and turned her face to him. "You do love me, Bonnie? That hasn't changed, has it?"

She put her head against his chest and rocked from side to side as if in some agony. "Oh, no—Mark! That will never change. Damn you, Ashby, damn you—"

*   *   *   *   *

In the control room Ashby and Miller groaned aloud to each other, and a technician looked at them questioningly, his hand on a switch. Ashby shook his head and stared at the scene before him.

Jorden shook Bonnie gently in his arms. "Ashby?" he said. "Who's Ashby?"

Bonnie looked up, the blank despair on her face again. "I don't remember—" she said haltingly. "Someone I used to—know—"

"It makes no difference," Jorden said. "What matters is that you love me and you're going to stay with me. Let's put these things away now, darling. I know how you've felt the past week, but we've got to put it behind us and look forward to the future. Roddy would want it that way."

"There's no future to look forward to," said Bonnie dully. "Nothing here on Serrengia. There's no meaning to any of us being here. I'm going back to Earth."

"It does have a meaning! If I could only make you see it. If you could only understand why I had to come—"

"Then tell me if you know! You've never tried to tell me. You live as if you know something so deep and secret you can live by it every hour of your life and find meaning in it. But I can only guess at what it is you've chosen for your god. If it's anything but some illusion, put it into words and make me know it, too!"

"I've never tried," said Jorden hesitantly. "I've never tried to put it into words. It's something I didn't know was in me until I heard of the chance to colonize Serrengia. And then I knew I had to come.

"It's like a growing that you feel in every cell. It's a growing out and away, and it's what you have to do. You're a sperm—an ovum—and if you don't leave the parent body you die. You don't have to hate what you leave behind as James and Boggs and so many of the others do. It gave you life, and for that you're grateful. But you've got to have a life of your own.

"It's what I was born to do, Bonnie. I didn't know it was there, but now I've found it I can't kill it."

"You have to kill it—or me."

"You don't mean that. You're part of me. You've been a part of me so long you feel what I feel. You're lying, Bonnie, when you say you're going away. You don't want to go. You want to go on with me, but something's holding you back. What is it, Bonnie? Tell me what it is that holds you back!"

Her eyes went wide. For a moment she thought he was talking out of the real situation, not the make-believe of the test. Then she recognized the impossibility of this. Her eyes cast a pleading glance in the direction of the observation tubes.

Ashby spoke fiercely: "Go on, Bonnie! Don't lose the tension. Push him. We've got to know. He's almost there!"

She moved slowly to the dresser where she had laid Jorden's hunting knife previously, as if with no particular intent. Now, out of sight of Jorden, her hand touched it. She picked it up.

Ashby's voice came again. "Bonnie—move!"

She murmured, "Lost—"

And then she whirled about, knife in hand. She cried aloud. "I can't go on any further! Can't you see this is enough? Stop it! Stop it—"

Jorden leaped for the knife.

In the observation room a technician touched a switch.

*   *   *   *   *

Ashby felt the subdued elation of success reached after a long and strenuous effort. Bonnie was seated across the desk from him, but he sat at an angle so that he could see the four hulls out of the corner of his eye. One and Two had made their test flights and the others would not be far behind. The expedition would be a success, too. There was no longer any doubt of that, because he knew now where to look for adequate personnel.

"I'm glad I didn't foul up your test completely, anyway," said Bonnie slowly. "Even if what you say about Mark shouldn't turn out to be true."

Ashby moved his chair around to face her directly. She was rested, and had gone through a mental re-orientation which had removed some of the tension from her face.

"You didn't foul it up at all," he said. "We went far enough to learn that he would have survived even your suicide, and would have continued in his determination to carry the colony forward. Nothing but his own death will stand in his way if he actually sets out on such a project. Are you completely sure you want to be tied to such a single purposed man as Mark Jorden is?"

"There's no doubt of that! But I just don't feel as if I can face him now—with his knowing.... How can I ever be sure his feeling for me was not merely induced by the test experience, and might change as time goes on? You should have wiped it all out, and let us start over from scratch. It would have been easier that way."

"There isn't time enough before the ships leave. But why should we have erased it all? We took away the postulates of the test and left Bonnie in his memory. His love for you didn't vanish when the test postulates went. As long as he has a memory of you he will love you. So why make him fall in love with you twice? No use wasting so much important time at your age. Here he comes—"

Bonnie felt she couldn't possibly turn around as the door opened behind her. She heard Mark's moment of hesitation, his slow steps on the carpet. Ashby was smiling a little and nodding. Then she felt the hard grip of Mark's hands on her shoulders. He drew her up and turned her to face him. Her eyes were wet.

"Bonnie—" he said softly.

*   *   *   *   *

Ashby turned to the window again. The gantry cranes were hoisting machinery in Hull Three. Maybe he had been wrong about there not being enough time between now and takeoff for Mark and Bonnie to discover each other all over again. They worked pretty fast. But then, as he had mentioned, why waste time at their age?

They were smiling, holding tight to each other as Ashby turned back from the window.

"They tell me I passed," said Jorden. "I'm sorry about taking your best Social Examiner away from you—but as you told me in the beginning this colonization business is a family affair."

"Yes—that happens to be one of the few things I was right about." Ashby motioned them to the chairs. "Through you we located our major error. It was our identifying rebellion with colonization ability. Colonization is not a matter of rebellion at all. The two factors merely happen to accompany each other at times. But the essence of colonization is a growth factor—of the kind you so very accurately described when Bonnie pushed you into digging up some insight on the matter. It is so often associated with rebellion because rebellion is or has been, historically, necessary to the exercise of this growth factor.

"The American Colonists, for example, were rebels only incidentally. As a group, they possessed a growth factor forcing them beyond the confines of the culture in which they lived. It gave them the strength for rebellion and successful colonization. And it is so easy to confuse colonists of that type with mere cutthroats, thugs, and misfits. The latter may or may not have a sufficiently high growth factor. In any case, their primary drive is hate and fear, which are wholly inadequate motives for successful colonization.

"The ideal colonist does not break with the parent body, nor does he merely extend it. He creates a new nucleus capable of interchange with the parent body, but not controlled by it. He wants to build beyond the current society, and the latter is not strong enough to pull him back into it. Colonization may take everything else of value in life and give nothing but itself in return, but the colonists' desire for new life and growth is great enough to make this sufficient. It is not a mere transplant of an old life. It is conception and gestation and birth.

"Our present society allows almost unlimited exercise of the growth factor in individuals, regardless of how powerful it may be. That is why we have failed to colonize the planets. They offer no motive or satisfaction sufficient to outweigh the satisfactions already available. As a result we've had virtually no applicants coming to us because of hampered growth. You are one of the very few who might come under our present approach. And even a very slight change of occupational conditions would have kept you from coming. You didn't want the department leadership offered you, because it would limit the personally creative functions you enjoyed. That one slim, hairbreadth factor brought you in."

"But how do you expect now to get any substantial number of colonists?" exclaimed Jorden.

"We'll put on a recruiting campaign. We'll go to the creative groups—the engineers, the planners, the artists—we'll show that opportunity for creative functioning and growth will be far greater in the work of building colonial outposts than in any activity they now enjoy. And we won't have to exaggerate, either. It's true.

"We'll be able to send out a colony of whom we can be certain. In the past, colonies have invariably failed when they consisted only of members fleeing from something, without possessing an adequate growth factor.

"When this becomes thoroughly understood in my field, I shall probably never live down my initial error of assuming that a colonist had to hate or fear what he left behind in order to leave it forever. The exact opposite is true. Successful colonization of the Universe by Earthmen will occur only when there is a love and respect for the Homeland—and a capacity for complete independence from it."

Ashby pressed his fingers together and looked at his visitors soberly. "There is only one thing further," he said. "We've found out also that Bonnie is not essentially a colonist—"

Bonnie's face went white. She pushed Jorden's arm away and leaned across the desk. "You knew—! Then we can't—Why didn't you tell me this in the beginning?"

"Please don't be hasty, Bonnie," said Ashby. "As I was about to say, we have found, however, that another condition exists in which you can become eligible and stable through a genuine love for a qualified colonist, to the extent you are willing to follow him completely in his ambitions and desires. This is strictly a feminine possibility—a woman can become a sort of second order colonist, you might say.

"Of course, Jorden, you still have to make the basic decision as to whether you want to go to Serrengia or not. We have found out merely that you *can*."

"I think there's no doubt about my wanting to," said Jorden.

He turned Bonnie around in his arms again, and Ashby chuckled mildly. "I have always said there is no piece of data you cannot find, provided you can devise the proper experimental procedure for turning it up," he said.

The Unlearned

Illustrated by Ed Emsh
Originally Published In *IF Worlds of Science
Fiction*, August 1954

The scientists of Rykeman III were conceded by all the galactic members to be supreme in scientific achievement. Now the Rykes were going to share their vast knowledge with the scientists of Earth. To any question they would supply an answer—for a price. And Hockley, of all Earth's scientists, was the stubborn one who wanted to weigh the answers with the costs....

THE UNLEARNED

The Chief Officer of Scientific Services, Information and Coordination was a somewhat misleading and obscure title, and Dr. Sherman Hockley who held it was not the least of those whom the title misled and sometimes obscured.

He told himself he was not a mere library administrator, although he was proud of the information files built up under his direction. They contained the essence of accumulated knowledge found to date on Earth and the extraterrestrial planets so far contacted. He didn't feel justified in claiming to be strictly a research supervisor, either, in spite of duties as top level administrator for all divisions of the National Standardization and Research Laboratories and their subsidiaries in government, industry, and education. During his term of supervision the National Laboratories had made a tremendous growth, in contrast to a previous decline.

Most of all, however, he disclaimed being a figurehead, to which all the loose strings of a vast and rambling organization could be tied. But sometimes it was quite difficult to know whether or not that was his primary assignment after all. His unrelenting efforts to keep out of the category seemed to be encountering more and more determination to push him in that direction.

Of course, this was merely the way it looked in his more bitter moments—such as the present. Normally, he had a full awareness of the paramount importance of his position, and was determined to administer it on a scale in keeping with that importance. His decision could affect the research in the world's major laboratories. Not that he was a dictator by any means, although there were times when dictation was called for. As when a dozen projects needed money and the Congress allotted enough for one or two. Somebody had to make a choice—

His major difficulty was that active researchers knew it was the Congressional Science Committee which was ultimately responsible for their bread and butter. And the Senators regarded the scientists, who did the actual work in the laboratories, as the only ones who mattered. Both groups tended to look upon Hockley's office as a sort of fulcrum in their efforts to maintain balance with each other—or as referee in their sparring for adequate control over each other.

At that, however, things research-wise were better than ever before. More funds and facilities were available. Positions in pure research were more secure.

And then, once again, rumors about Rykeman III had begun to circulate wildly a few days ago.

Since Man's achievement of extra-galactic flight, stories of Rykeman III had tantalized the world and made research scientists sick with longing when they considered the possible truth of what they heard. The planet was rumored to be a world of super-science, whose people had an answer for every research problem a man could conceive. The very few Earthmen who had been to Rykeman III confirmed the rumors. It was a paradise, according to their stories. And among other peoples of the galaxies the inhabitants of Rykeman III were acknowledged supreme in scientific achievement. None challenged them. None even approached them in abilities.

What made the situation so frustrating to Earthmen was the additional report that the Rykes were quite altruistically sharing their science with a considerable number of other worlds on a fee basis. Earth scientists became intoxicated at the mere thought of studying at the feet of the exalted Rykes.

Except Dr. Sherman Hockley. From the first he had taken a dim view of the Ryke reports. Considering the accomplishments of the National Laboratories, he could see no reason for his colleagues' half-shameful disowning of all their own work in favor of a completely unknown culture several hundred million light years away. They were bound to contact more advanced cultures in their explorations—and could be thankful they were as altruistic as the Rykes!—but it was no reason to view themselves as idiot children hoping to be taught by the Rykes.

He had kept his opinions very much to himself in the past, since they were not popular with his associates, who generally regarded his attitudes as simply old-fashioned. But now, for the first time, a Ryke ship was honoring Earth with a visit. There was almost hysterical speculation over the possibility that Earth would be offered tutelage by the mighty Ryke scientists. Hockley wouldn't have said he was unalterably opposed to the idea. He would have described himself as extremely cautious. What he did oppose wholeheartedly was the enthusiasm that painted the Rykes with pure and shining light, without a shadowy hue in the whole picture.

Since his arrival, the Ryke envoy had been closeted with members of the Congressional Science Committee. Not a word had leaked as to his message. Shortly, however, the scientists were to be let in on the secret which might affect their careers for better or for worse during the rest of their lives, and for many generations to come. The meeting was going to be—

Hockley jumped to his feet as he glanced at the clock. He hurried through the door to the office of his secretary, Miss Cardston, who looked meaningfully at him as he passed.

"I'll bet there isn't a Senator on time," he said.

In the corridor he almost collided with Dr. Lester Showalter, who was his Administrative Assistant for Basic Research. "The Ryke character showed up fifteen minutes ago," said Showalter. "Everyone's waiting."

"We've got six minutes yet," said Hockley. He walked rapidly beside Showalter. "Is there any word on what the envoy's got that's so important?"

"No. I've got the feeling it's something pretty big. Wheeler and Johnson of Budget are there. Somebody said it might have something to do with the National Lab."

"I don't see the connection between that and a meeting with the Ryke," said Hockley.

Showalter stopped at the door of the conference room. "Maybe they want to sell us something. At any rate, we're about to find out."

The conference table was surrounded by Senators of the Committee. Layered behind them were scientists representing the cream of Hockley's organization. Senator Markham, the bulky, red-faced Chairman greeted them. "Your seats are reserved at the head of the table," he said.

"Sorry about the time," Hockley mumbled. "Clock must be slow."

"Quite all right. We assembled just a trifle early. I want you to meet our visitor, Special Envoy from Rykeman III, Liacan."

Markham introduced them, and the stick-thin envoy arose with an extended hand. His frail, whistling voice that was in keeping with his bird-like character spoke in clear tones. "I am happy to know you, Dr. Hockley, Dr. Showalter."

The two men sat down in good view of the visitor's profile. Hockley had seen the Rykes before, but had always been repelled by their snobbish approach. Characteristically, the envoy bore roughly anthropomorphic features, including a short feather covering on his dorsal side. He was dressed in bright clothing that left visible the streak of feathering that descended from the bright, plumed crown and along the back of his neck. Gravity and air pressure of Earth were about normal for him. For breathing, however, he was required to wear a small device in one narrow nostril. This was connected to a compact tank on his shoulder.

Markham called for order and introduced the visitor. There was a round of applause. Liacan bowed with a short, stiff gesture and let his small black eyes dart over the audience. With an adjustment of his breathing piece he began speaking.

"It is recognized on Earth," he said, "as it is elsewhere, that my people of Rykeman III possess undisputed intellectual leadership in the galaxies of the Council. Your research is concerned with things taught only in the kindergartens of my world. Much that you hold to be true is in error, and your most profound discoveries are self-evident to the children of my people."

Hockley felt a quick, painful contraction in the region of his diaphragm. So this was it!

"We are regarded with much jealousy, envy, and even hatred by some of our unlearned neighbors in space," said the Ryke. "But it has never been our desire to be selfish with our superior achievements which make us the object of these feelings. We have undertaken a program of scientific leadership in our interstellar neighborhood. This began long before you came into space and many worlds have accepted the plan we offer.

"Obviously, it is impractical to pour out all the knowledge and basic science we have accumulated. Another world would find it impossible to sort out that which was applicable to it. What we do is act as a consultation center upon which others can call at will to obtain data pertaining to any problem at hand. Thus, they are not required to sort through wholly inapplicable information to find what they need.

"For example, if you desire to improve your surface conveyances, we will supply you with data for building an optimum vehicle suitable for conditions on Earth and which is virtually indestructible. You will of course do your own manufacturing, but even there we can supply you with technology that will make the process seem miraculous by your present standards.

"Our services are offered for a fee, payable in suitable items of goods or raw materials. When you contemplate the freedom from monotonous and unending research in fields already explored by us, I am certain you will not consider our fees exorbitant. Our desire is to raise the cultural level of all peoples to the maximum of which they are capable. We know it is not possible or even desirable to bring others to our own high levels, but we do offer assistance to all cultures in accord with their ability to receive. The basic principle is that they shall ask—and whatever is asked for, with intelligence sufficient for its utilization, that shall be granted.

"I am certain I may count on your acceptance of the generous offer of my people."

The envoy sat down with a jiggling of his bright plume, and there was absolute silence in the room. Hockley pictured to himself the dusty, cobweb laboratories of Earth vacated by scientists who ran to the phone to call the Rykes for answers to every problem.

Senator Markham stood up and glanced over the audience. "There is the essence of the program which has been submitted to us," he said. "There is a vast amount of detail which is, of course, obvious to the minds of our friends on Rykeman III, but which must be the subject of much deliberation on the part of us comparatively simple minded Earthmen." He gave a self-conscious chuckle, which got no response.

Hockley felt mentally stunned. Here at last was the thing that had been hoped for by most, anxiously awaited by a few, and opposed by almost no one.

"The major difficulty," said Markham with slow dignity, "is the price. It's high, yes. In monetary terms, approximately twelve and a half billions per year. But certainly no man in his right mind would consider any reasonable figure too high for what we can expect to receive from our friends of Rykeman III.

"We of the Science Committee do not believe, however, that we could get a commitment for this sum to be added to our normal budget. Yet there is a rather obvious solution. The sum required is very close to that which is now expended on the National Standardization and Research Laboratories."

Hockley felt a sudden chill at the back of his neck.

"With the assistance of the Rykes," said Markham, "we shall have no further need of the National Laboratories. We shall require but a small staff to analyze our problems and present them to the Rykes and relay the answers for proper assimilation. Acceptance of the Ryke program provides its own automatic financing!"

He glanced about with a triumphant smile. Hockley felt as if he were looking through a mist upon something that happened a long time ago. The National Lab! Abandon the National Lab!

Around him there were small nods of agreement from his colleagues. Some pursed their lips as if doubtful—but not very much. He waited for someone to rise to his feet in a blast of protest. No one did. For a moment Hockley's own hands tensed on the back of the chair in front of him. Then he slumped back to his seat. Now was not the time.

They had to thrash it out among themselves. He had to show them the magnitude of this bribe. He had to find an argument to beat down the Congressmen's irrational hopes of paradise. He couldn't plead for the Lab on the grounds of sentiment—or that it was sometimes a good idea to work out your own problems. The Senators didn't care for the problems or concerns of the scientists. It appeared that even the scientists themselves had forgotten to care. He had to slug both groups with something very solid.

Markham was going on. "We are convinced this is a bargain which even the most obstinate of our Congressional colleagues will be quick to recognize. It would be folly to compute with building blocks when we can gain access to giant calculators. There should be no real difficulty in getting funds transferred from the National Laboratory.

"At this time we will adjourn. Liacan leaves this evening. Our acceptance of this generous offer will be conveyed to Rykeman III directly upon official sanction by the Congress. I wish to ask this same group to meet again for discussion of the details incident to this transfer of operations. Let us say at ten o'clock in the morning, gentlemen."

*   *   *   *   *

Hockley said goodbye to the envoy. Afterwards, he moved through the circle of Senators to his own group. In the corridor they tightened about him and followed along as if he had given an order for them to follow him. He turned and attempted a grin.

"Looks like a bull session is in order, gents. Assembly in five minutes in my office."

As he and Showalter opened the door to Miss Cardston's office and strode in, the secretary looked up with a start. "I thought you were going to meet in the conference room."

"We've met," said Hockley. "This is the aftermeeting. Send out for a couple of cases of beer." He glanced at the number surging through the doorway and fished in his billfold. "Better make it three. This ought to cover it."

With disapproval, Miss Cardston picked up the bills and turned to the phone. Almost simultaneously there was a bellow of protest and an enormous, ham-like hand gripped her slender wrist. She glanced up in momentary fright.

Dr. Forman K. Silvers was holding her wrist with one hand and clapping Hockley on the back with the other. "This is not an occasion for beer, my boy!" he said in an enormous voice. "Make that a case of champagne, Miss Cardston." He released her and drew out his own billfold.

"Get somebody to bring in a couple of dozen chairs," Hockley said.

In his own office he walked to the window behind his desk and stood facing it. The afternoon haze was coming up out of the ocean. Faintly visible were the great buildings of the National Laboratories on the other side of the city. Above the mist the sun caught the tip of the eight story tower where the massive field tunnels of the newly designed gammatron were to be installed.

Or *were* to have been installed.

The gammatron was expected to make possible the creation of gravitational fields up to five thousand g's. It would probably be a mere toy to the Rykes, but Hockley felt a fierce pride in its creation. Maybe that was childish. Maybe his whole feeling about the Lab was childish. Perhaps the time had come to give up childish things and take upon themselves adulthood.

But looking across the city at the concrete spire of the gammatron, he didn't believe it.

He heard the clank of metal chairs as a couple of clerks began bringing them in. Then there was the clink of glassware. He turned to see Miss Cardston stiffly indicating a spot on the library table for the glasses and the frosty bottles.

Hockley walked slowly to the table and filled one of the glasses. He raised it slowly. "It's been a short life but a merry one, gentlemen." He swallowed the contents of the glass too quickly and returned to his desk.

"You don't sound very happy about the whole thing," said Mortenson, a chemist who wore a neat, silvery mustache.

"Are you overjoyed," said Hockley, "that we are to swap the National Lab for a bottomless encyclopedia?"

"Yes, I think so," said Mortenson. "There are some minor objections, but in the end I'm certain we'll all be satisfied with what we get."

"Satisfied! Happy!" exclaimed the mathematician, Dr. Silvers. "How can you use words so prosaic and restrained in references to these great events which we shall be privileged to witness in our lifetimes?"

He had taken his stand by the library table and was now filling the glasses with the clear, bubbling champagne, sloshing it with ecstatic abandon over the table and the rug.

Hockley glanced toward him. "You don't believe, then, Dr. Silvers, that we should maintain any reserve in regard to the Rykes?"

"None whatever! The gods themselves have stepped down and offered an invitation direct to paradise. Should we question or hold back, or say we are merely happy. The proper response of a man about to enter heaven is beyond words!"

The bombast of the mathematician never failed to enliven any backroom session in which he participated. "I have no doubt," he said, "that within a fortnight we shall be in possession of a solution to the Legrandian Equations. I have sought this for forty years."

"I think it would be a mistake to support the closing of the National Laboratories," said Hockley slowly.

As if a switch had been thrown, their expressions changed. There was a sudden carefulness in their stance and movements, as if they were feinting before a deadly opponent.

"I don't feel it's such a bad bargain," said a thin, bespectacled physicist named Judson. He was seated across the room from Hockley. "I'll vote to sacrifice the Lab in exchange for what the Rykes will give us."

"That's the point," said Hockley. "Exactly what are the Rykes going to give us? And we speak very glibly of sharing their science. But shall we actually be in any position to share it? What becomes of the class of scientists on Earth when the Lab is abandoned?"

Wilkins stood abruptly, his hands shoved part way into his pockets and his lower jaw extended tensely. "I don't believe that's part of this question," he said. "It is not just we scientists who are to share the benefits of the Rykes. It is Mankind. At this time we have no right to consider mere personal concerns. We would betray our whole calling—our very humanity—if we thought for one moment of standing in the way of this development because of our personal concern over economic and professional problems. There has never been a time when a true scientist would not put aside his personal concerns for the good of all."

Hockley waited, half expecting somebody to start clapping. No one did, but there were glances of self-righteous approval in Wilkins' direction. The biologist straightened the sleeves of his coat with a smug gesture and awaited Hockley's rebuttal.

"*We* are Mankind," Hockley said finally. "You and I are as much a part of humanity as that bus load of punch machine clerks and store managers passing on the street outside. If we betray ourselves we have betrayed humanity.

"This is not a sudden thing. It is the end point of a trend which has gone on for a long time. It began with our first contacts beyond the galaxy, when we realized there were peoples far in advance of us in science and economy. We have been feeding on them ever since. Our own developments have shrunk in direct proportion. For a long time we've been on the verge of becoming intellectual parasites in the Universe. Acceptance of the Ryke offer will be the final step in that direction."

Instantly, almost every other man in the room was talking at once. Hockley smiled faintly until the angry voices subsided. Then Silvers cleared his throat gently. He placed his glass beside the bottles on the table with a precise motion. "I am sure," he said, "that a moment's thought will convince you that you do not mean what you have just said.

"Consider the position of pupil and teacher. One of Man's greatest failings is his predilection for assuming always the position of teacher and eschewing that of pupil. There is also the question of humility, intellectual humility. We scientists have always boasted of our readiness to set aside one so-called truth and accept another with more valid supporting evidence.

"Since our first contact with other galactic civilizations we have had the utmost need to adopt an attitude of humility. We have been fortunate in coming to a community of worlds where war and oppression are not standard rules of procedure. Among our own people we have encountered no such magnanimity as has been extended repeatedly by other worlds, climaxed now by the Ryke's magnificent offer.

"To adopt sincere intellectual humility and the attitude of the pupil is not to function as a parasite, Dr. Hockley."

"Your analogy of teacher and pupil is very faulty in expressing our relation to the Rykes," said Hockley. "Or perhaps I should say it is too hellishly accurate. Would you have us remain the eternal pupils? The closing of the National Laboratories means an irreversible change in our position. Is it worth gaining a universe of knowledge to give up your own personal free inquiry?"

"I am sure none of us considers he is giving up his personal free inquiry," said Silvers almost angrily. "We see unlimited expansion beyond anything we have imagined in our wildest dreams."

On a few faces there were frowns of uncertainty, but no one spoke up to support him. Hockley knew that until this vision of paradise wore off there were none of them on whom he could count.

He smiled broadly and stood up to ease the tension in the room. "Well, it appears you have made your decision. Of course, Congress can accept the Ryke plan whether we approve or not, but it is good to go on record one way or the other. I suppose that on the way out tonight it would be proper to check in at Personnel and file a services available notification."

And then he wished he hadn't said that. Their faces grew a little more set at his unappreciated attempt at humor.

*   *   *   *   *

Showalter remained after the others left. He sat across the desk while Hockley turned back to the window. Only the tip of the gammatron tower now caught the late afternoon sunlight.

"Maybe I'm getting old," Hockley said. "Maybe they're right and the Lab isn't worth preserving if it means the difference between getting or not getting tutelage from the Rykes."

"But you don't feel that's true," said Showalter.

"No."

"You're the one who built the Lab into what it is. It has as much worth as it ever had, and you have an obligation to keep it from being destroyed by a group of politicians who could never understand its necessity."

"I didn't build it," said Hockley. "It grew because I was able to find enough people who wanted the institution to exist. But I've been away from research so long—I never was much good at it really. Did you ever know that? I've always thought of myself as a sort of impressario of scientific productions, if I might use such a term. Maybe those closer to the actual work are right. Maybe I'm just trying to hang on to the past. It could be time for a jump to a new kind of progress."

"You don't believe any of that."

Hockley looked steadily in the direction of the Lab buildings. "I don't believe any of it. That isn't just an accumulation of buildings over there, with a name attached to them. It's the advancing terminal of all Man's history of trying to find out about himself and the Universe. It started before Neanderthal climbed into his caves a half million years ago. From then until now there's a steady path of trial and error—of learning. There's exultation and despair, success and failure. Now they want to say it was all for nothing."

"But to be pupils—to let the Rykes teach us—"

"The only trouble with Silvers' argument is that our culture has never understood that teaching, in the accepted sense, is an impossibility. There can be only learning—never teaching. The teacher has to be eliminated from the actual learning process before genuine learning can ever take place. But the Rykes offer to become the Ultimate Teacher."

"And if this is true," said Showalter slowly, "you couldn't teach it to those who disagree, could you? They'd have to learn it for themselves."

Hockley turned. For a moment he continued to stare at his assistant. Then his face broke into a narrow grin. "Of course you're right! There's only one way they'll ever learn it: go through the actual experience of what Ryke tutelage will mean."

Most of the workrooms at Information Central were empty this time of evening. Hockley selected the first one he came to and called for every scrap of data pertaining to Rykeman III. There was a fair amount of information available on the physical characteristics of the world. Hockley scribbled swift, privately intelligible notes as he scanned. The Rykes lived under a gravity one third heavier than Earth's, with a day little more than half as long, and they received only forty percent as much heat from their frail sun as Earthmen were accustomed to.

Cultural characteristics included a trading system that made the entire planet a single economic unit. And the planet had no history whatever of war. The Rykes themselves had contributed almost nothing to the central libraries of the galaxies concerning their own personal makeup and mental functions, however. What little was available came from observers not of their race.

There were indications they were a highly unemotional race, not given to any artistic expression. Hockley found this surprising. The general rule was for highly intellectual attainments to be accompanied by equally high artistic expression.

But all of this provided no data that he could relate to his present problem, no basis for argument beyond what he already had. He returned the films to their silver cans and sat staring at the neat pile of them on the desk. Then he smiled at his own obtuseness. Data on Rykeman III might be lacking, but the Ryke plan had been tried on plenty of other worlds. Data on *them* should not be so scarce.

He returned the cans and punched out a new request on the call panel. Twenty seconds later he was pleasantly surprised by a score of new tapes in the hopper. That was enough for a full night's work. He wished he'd brought Showalter along to help.

Then his eye caught sight of the label on the topmost can in the pile: Janisson VIII. The name rang a familiar signal somewhere deep in his mind. Then he knew—that was the home world of Waldon Thar, one of his closest friends in the year when he'd gone to school at Galactic Center for advanced study.

Thar had been one of the most brilliant researchers Hockley had ever known. In bull session debate he was instantly beyond the depth of everyone else.

Janisson VIII. Thar could tell him about the Rykes!

Hockley pushed the tape cans aside and went to the phone in the workroom. He dialed for the interstellar operator. "Government priority call to Janisson VIII," he said. "Waldon Thar. He attended Galactic Center Research Institute twenty-three years ago. He came from the city Plar, which was his home at that time. I have no other information, except that he is probably employed as a research scientist."

There was a moment's silence while the operator noted the information. "There will be some delay," she said finally. "At present the inter-galactic beams are full."

"I can use top emergency priority on this," said Hockley. "Can you clear a trunk for me on that?"

"Yes. One moment, please."

He sat by the window for half an hour, turning down the light in the workroom so that he could see the flow of traffic at the port west of the Lab buildings. Two spaceships took off and three came in while he waited. And then the phone rang.

"I'm sorry," the operator said. "Waldon Thar is reported not on Janisson VIII. He went to Rykeman III about two Earth years ago. Do you wish to attempt to locate him there?"

"By all means," said Hockley. "Same priority."

This was better than he had hoped for. Thar could really get him the information he needed on the Rykes. Twenty minutes later the phone rang again. In the operator's first words Hockley sensed apology and knew the attempt had failed.

"Our office has learned that Waldon Thar is at present on tour as aide to the Ryke emissary, Liacan. We can perhaps trace—"

"No!" Hockley shouted. "That won't be necessary. I know now—"

He almost laughed aloud to himself. This was an incredible piece of good luck. Waldon Thar was probably out at the space port right now—unless one of those ships taking off had been the Ryke—

He wondered why Thar had not tried to contact him. Of course, it had been a long time, but they had been very close at the center. He dialed the field control tower. "I want to know if the ship from Rykeman III has departed yet," he said.

"They were scheduled for six hours ago, but mechanical difficulty has delayed them. Present estimated take-off is 1100."

Almost two hours to go, Hockley thought. That should be time enough. "Please put me in communication with one of the aides aboard named Waldon Thar. This is Sherman Hockley of Scientific Services. Priority request."

"I'll try, sir." The tower operator manifested a sudden increase of respect. "One moment, please."

Hockley heard the buzz and switch clicks of communication circuits reaching for the ship. Then, in a moment, he heard the somewhat irritated but familiar voice of his old friend.

"Waldon Thar speaking," the voice said. "Who wishes to talk?"

"Listen, you old son of a cyclotron's maiden aunt!" said Hockley. "Who would want to talk on Sol III? Why didn't you give me a buzz when you landed? I just found out you were here."

"Sherm Hockley, of course," the voice said with distant, unperturbed tones. "This is indeed a surprise and a pleasure. To be honest, I had forgotten Earth was your home planet."

"I'll try to think of something to jog your memory next time. How about getting together?"

"Well—I don't have very long," said Thar hesitantly. "If you could come over for a few minutes—"

Hockley had the jolting feeling that Waldon Thar would just as soon pass up the opportunity for their meeting. Some of the enthusiasm went out of his voice. "There's a good all-night interplanetary eatery and bar on the field there. I'll be along in fifteen minutes."

"Fine," said Thar, "but please try not to be late."

On the way to the field, Hockley wondered about the change that had apparently taken place in Thar. Of course, *he* had changed, too—perhaps for much the worse. But Thar sounded like a stuffed shirt now, and that is the last thing Hockley would have expected. In school, Thar had been the most irreverent of the whole class of irreverents, denouncing in ecstasy the established and unproven lore, riding the professors of unsubstantiated hypotheses. Now—well, he didn't sound like the Thar Hockley knew.

He took a table and sat down just as Thar entered the dining room. The latter's broad smile momentarily removed Hockley's doubts. The smile hadn't changed. And there was the same expression of devilish disregard for the established order. The same warm friendliness. It baffled Hockley to understand how Thar could have failed to remember Earth was his home.

Thar mentioned it as he came up and took Hockley's hand. "I'm terribly sorry," he said. "It was stupid to forget that Earth meant Sherman Hockley."

"I know how it is. I should have written. I guess I'm the one who owes a letter."

"No, I think not," said Thar.

They sat on opposite sides of a small table near a window and ordered drinks. On the field they could see the vast, shadowy outline of the Ryke vessel.

Thar was of a race genetically close to the Rykes. He lacked the feathery covering, but this was replaced by a layer of thin scales, which had a tendency to stand on edge when he was excited. He also wore a breathing piece, and carried the small shoulder tank with a faint air of superiority.

Hockley watched him with a growing sense of loss. The first impression had been more nearly correct. Thar hadn't wanted to meet him.

"It's been a long time," said Hockley lamely. "I guess there isn't much we did back there that means anything now."

"You shouldn't say that," said Thar as if recognizing he had been too remote. "Every hour of our acquaintance meant a great deal to me. I'll never forgive myself for forgetting—but tell me how you learned I was aboard the Ryke ship."

"The Rykes have made us an offer. I wanted to find out the effects on worlds that had accepted. I learned Janisson VIII was one, so I started looking."

"I'm so very glad you did, Sherm. You want me to confirm, of course, the advisability of accepting the offer Liacan has made."

"Confirm—or deny it," said Hockley.

Thar spread his clawlike hands. "Deny it? The most glorious opportunity a planet could possibly have?"

Something in Thar's voice gave Hockley a sudden chill. "How has it worked on your own world?"

"Janisson VIII has turned from a slum to a world of mansions. Our economic problems have been solved. Health and long life are routine. There is nothing we want that we cannot have for the asking."

"But are you *satisfied* with it? Is there nothing which you had to give up that you would like returned?"

Waldon Thar threw back his head and laughed in high pitched tones. "I might have known that would be the question you would ask! Forgive me, friend Sherman, but I had almost forgotten how unventuresome you are.

"Your question is ridiculous. Why should we wish to go back to our economic inequalities, poverty and distress, our ignorant plodding research in science? You can answer your own question."

They were silent for a moment. Hockley thought his friend would have gladly terminated their visit right there and returned to his ship. To forestall this, he leaned across the table and asked, "Your science—what has become of that?"

"Our science! We never had any. We were ignorant children playing with mud and rocks. We knew nothing. We had nothing. Until the Rykes offered to educate us."

"Surely you don't believe that," said Hockley quietly. "The problem you worked on at the Institute—gravity at micro-cosmic levels. That was not a childish thing."

Thar laughed shortly and bitterly. "What disillusionment you have coming, friend Sherman! If you only knew how truly childish it was. Wait until you learn from the Rykes the true conception of gravity, its nature and the part it plays in the structure of matter."

Hockley felt a sick tightening within him. This was not the Waldon Thar, the wild demon who thrust aside all authority and rumor in his own headlong search for knowledge. It couldn't be Thar who was sitting passively by, being *told* what the nature of the Universe is.

"Your scientists—?" Hockley persisted. "What has become of all your researchers?"

"The answer is the same," said Thar. "We had no science. We had no scientists. Those who once went by that name have become for the first time honest students knowing the pleasure of studying at the feet of masters."

"You have set up laboratories in which your researches are supervised by the Rykes?"

"Laboratories? We have no need of laboratories. We have workshops and study rooms where we try to absorb that which the Rykes discovered long ago. Maybe at some future time we will come to a point where we can reach into the frontier of knowledge with our own minds, but this does not seem likely now."

"So you have given up all original research of your own?"

"How could we do otherwise? The Rykes have all the answers to any question we have intelligence enough to ask. Follow them, Sherman. It is no disgrace to be led by such as the Ryke teachers."

"Don't you ever long," said Hockley, "to take just one short step on your own two feet?"

"Why crawl when you can go by trans-light carrier?"

Thar sipped the last of his drink and glanced toward the wall clock. "I must go. I can understand the direction of your questions and your thinking. You hesitate because you might lose the chance to play in the mud and count the pretty pebbles in the sand. Put away childish things. You will never miss them!"

They shook hands, and a moment later Hockley said goodbye to Thar at the entrance to the field. "I know Earth will accept," said Thar. "And you and I should not have lost contact—but we'll make up for it."

Watching him move toward the dark hulk of the ship, Hockley wondered if Thar actually believed that. In less than an hour they had exhausted all they had to say after twenty years. Hockley had the information he needed about the Ryke plan, but he wished he could have kept his old memories of his student friend. Thar was drunk on the heady stuff being peddled by the Rykes, and if what he said were true, it was strong enough to intoxicate a whole planet.

His blood grew cold at the thought. This was more than a fight for the National Laboratories. It was a struggle to keep all Mankind from becoming what Thar had become.

If he could have put Thar on exhibition in the meeting tomorrow, and shown what he was once like, he would have made his point. But Thar, before and after, was not available for exhibit. He had to find another way to show his colleagues and the Senators what the Rykes would make of them.

He glanced at his watch. They wouldn't like being wakened at this hour, but neither would the scientists put up much resistance to his request for support in Markham's meeting. He went back to the bar and called each of his colleagues who had been in the meeting that day.

*   *   *   *   *

Hockley was called first when the assembly convened at ten that morning. He rose slowly from his seat near Markham and glanced over the somewhat puzzled expressions of the scientists.

"I don't know that I can speak for the entire group of scientists present," he said. "We met yesterday and found some differences of opinion concerning this offer. While it is true there is overwhelming sentiment supporting it, certain questions remain, which we feel require additional data in order to be answered properly.

"While we recognize that official acceptance can be given to the Rykes with no approval whatever from the scientists, it seems only fair that we should have every opportunity to make what we consider a proper study and to express our opinions in the matter.

"To the non-scientist—and perhaps to many of my colleagues—it may seem inconceivable that there could be any questions whatever. But we wonder about the position of students of future generations, we wonder about the details of administration of the program, we wonder about the total effects of the program upon our society as a whole. We wish to ask permission to make further study of the matter in an effort to answer these questions and many others. We request permission to go as a committee to Rykeman III and make a first hand study of what the Rykes propose to do, how they will teach us, and how they will dispense the information they so generously offer.

"I ask that you consider this most seriously, and make an official request of the Rykes to grant us such opportunity for study, that you provide the necessary appropriations for the trip. I consider it most urgent that this be done at once."

There was a stir of concern and disapproval from Congressional members as Hockley sat down. Senators leaned to speak in whispers to their neighbors, but Hockley observed the scientists remained quiet and impassive. He believed he had sold them in his telephone calls during the early morning. They liked the idea of obtaining additional data. Besides, most of them wanted to see Rykeman III for themselves.

Senator Markham finally stood up, obviously disturbed by Hockley's abrupt proposal. "It has seemed to us members of the Committee that there could hardly be any need for more data than is already available to us. The remarkable effects of Ryke science on other backward worlds is common knowledge.

"On the other hand we recognize the qualifications of you gentlemen which make your request appear justified. We will have to discuss this at length, but at the moment I believe I can say I am in sympathy with your request and can encourage my Committee to give it serious consideration."

*   *   *   *   *

A great deal more was said on that and subsequent days. News of the Ryke offer was not given to the public, but the landing of the Ryke ship could not be hidden. It became known that Liacan carried his offer to other worlds and speculation was made that he offered it to Earth also. Angry questions were raised as to why the purpose of the visit was not clarified, but government silence was maintained while Hockley's request was considered.

It encountered bitter debate in the closed sessions, but permission was finally given for a junket of ninety scientists and ten senators to Rykeman III.

This could not be hidden, so the facts were modified and a story given out that the party was going to request participation in the Ryke program being offered other worlds, that Liacan's visit had not been conclusive.

In the days preceding the take-off Hockley felt a sense of destiny weighing heavily upon him. He read every word of the stream of opinion that flowed through the press. Every commentator and columnist seemed called upon to make his own specific analysis of the possibilities of the visit to Rykeman III. And the opinions were almost uniform that it would be an approach to Utopia to have the Rykes take over. Hockley was sickened by this mass conversion to the siren call of the Rykes.

It was a tremendous relief when the day finally came and the huge transport ship lifted solemnly into space.

Most of the group were in the ship's lounge watching the television port as the Earth drifted away beneath them. Senator Markham seemed nervous and almost frightened, Hockley thought, as if something intangible had escaped him.

"I hope we're not wasting our time," he said. "Not that I don't understand your position," he added hastily to cover the show of antagonism he sensed creeping into his voice.

"We appreciate your support," said Hockley, "and we'll do our best to see the time of the investigation is not wasted."

But afterwards, when the two of them were alone by the screen, Silvers spoke to Hockley soberly. The mathematician had lost some of the wild exuberance he'd had at first. It had been replaced by a deep, intense conviction that nothing must stand in the way of Earth's alliance with the Rykes.

"We all understand why you wanted us to come," he said. "We know you believe this delay will cool our enthusiasm. It's only fair to make clear that it won't. How you intend to change us by taking us to the home of the Rykes has got us all baffled. The reverse will be true, I am very sure. We intend to make it clear to the Rykes that we accept their offer. I hope you have no plan to make a declaration to the contrary."

Hockley kept his eyes on the screen, watching the green sphere of Earth. "I have no intention of making any statement of any kind. I was perfectly honest when I said our understanding of the Rykes would profit by this visit. You all agreed. I meant nothing more nor less than what I said. I hope no one in the group thinks otherwise."

"We don't know," said Silvers.

"It's just that you've got us wondering how you expect to change our views."

"I have not said that is my intention."

"Can you say it is not?"

"No, I cannot say that. But the question is incomplete. My whole intention is to discover as fully as possible what will be the result of alliance with the Rykes. If you should conclude that it will be unfavorable that will be the result of your own direct observations and computations, not of my arguments."

"You may be sure that is one thing that will not occur," said Silvers.

*　　*　　*　　*　　*

It took them a month to reach a transfer point where they could change to a commercial vessel using Ryke principles. In the following week they covered a distance several thousand times that which they had already come. And then they were on Rykeman III.

A few of them had visited the planet previously, on vacation trips or routine study expeditions, but most of them were seeing it for the first time. While well out into space the group began crowding the vision screens which brought into range the streets and buildings of the cities. They could see the people walking and riding there.

Hockley caught his breath at the sight, and doubts overwhelmed him, telling him he was an utter and complete fool. The city upon which he looked was a jewel of perfection. Buildings were not indiscriminate masses of masonry and metal and plastic heaped up without regard to the total effect. Rather, the city was a unit created with an eye to esthetic perfection.

Silvers stood beside Hockley. "We've got a chance to make Earth look that way," said the mathematician.

"There's only one thing missing," said Hockley. "The price tag. We still need to know what it's going to cost."

Upon landing, the Earthmen were greeted by a covey of their bird-like hosts who scurried about, introducing themselves in their high whistling voices. In busses, they were moved half way across the city to a building which stood beside an enormous park area.

It was obviously a building designed for the reception of just such delegations as this one, giving Hockley evidence that perhaps his idea was not so original after all. It was a relief to get inside after their brief trip across the city. Gravity, temperature, and air pressure and composition duplicated those of Earth inside, and conditions could be varied to accommodate many different species. Hockley felt confident they could become accustomed to outside conditions after a few days, but it was exhausting now to be out for long.

They were shown to individual quarters and given leisure to unpack and inspect their surroundings. Furniture had been adjusted to their size and needs. The only oversight Hockley could find was a faint odor of chlorine lingering in the closets. He wondered who the last occupant of the room had been.

After a noon meal, served with foods of astonishingly close approximation to their native fare, the group was offered a prelude to the general instruction and indoctrination which would begin the following day. This was in the form of a guided tour through the science museum which, Hockley gathered, was a modernized Ryke parallel to the venerable Smithsonian back home. The tour was entirely optional, as far as the planned program of the Rykes was concerned, but none of the Earthmen turned it down.

Hockley tried to concentrate heavily on the memory of Waldon Thar and keep the image of his friend always before him as he moved through the city and inspected the works of the Rykes. He found it helped suppress the awe and adulation which he had an impulse to share with his companions.

It was possible even, he found, to adopt a kind of truculent cynicism toward the approach the Rykes were making. The visit to the science museum *could* be an attempt to bowl them over with an eon-long vista of Ryke superiority in the sciences. At least that was most certainly the effect on them. Hockley cursed his own feeling of ignorance and inferiority as the guide led them quietly past the works of the masters, offering but little comment, letting them see for themselves the obvious relationships.

In the massive display showing developments of spaceflight, the atomic vessels, not much different from Earthmen's best efforts, were far down the line, very near to the earliest attempts of the Rykes to rocket their way into space. Beyond that level was an incredible series of developments incomprehensible to most of the Earthmen.

And to all their questions the guide offered the monotonous reply: "That will be explained to you later. We only wish to give you an overall picture of our culture at the present time."

But this was not enough for one of the astronomers, named Moore, who moved ahead of Hockley in the crowd. Hockley saw the back of Moore's neck growing redder by the minute as the guide's evasive answer was repeated. Finally, Moore forced a discussion regarding the merits of some systems of comparing the brightness of stars, which the guide briefly showed them.

The guide, in great annoyance, burst out with a stream of explanation that completely flattened any opinions Moore might have had. But at the same time the astronomer grinned amiably at the Ryke. "That ought to settle that," he said. "I'll bet it won't take a week to get our system changed back home."

Moore's success loosened the restraint of the others and they beseiged the guide mercilessly then with opinions, questions, comparisons—and even mild disapprovals. The guide's exasperation was obvious—and pleasant—to Hockley, who remained a bystander. It was frightening to Markham and some of the other senators who were unable to take part in the discussion. But most of the scientists failed to notice it in their eagerness to learn.

After dinner that night they gathered in the lounge and study of their quarters. Markham stood beside Hockley as they partook cautiously of the cocktails which the Rykes had attempted to duplicate for them. The Senator's awe had returned to overshadow any concern he felt during the events of the afternoon. "A wonderful day!" he said. "Even though this visit delays completion of our arrangements with the Rykes those of us here will be grateful forever that you proposed it. Nothing could have so impressed us all with the desirability of accepting the Ryke's tutelage. It was a stroke of genius, Dr. Hockley. And for a time I thought you were actually opposed to the Rykes!"

He sipped his drink while Hockley said nothing. Then his brow furrowed a bit. "But I wonder why our guide cut short our tour this afternoon. If I recall correctly he said at the beginning there was a great deal more to see than he actually showed us."

Hockley smiled and sipped politely at his drink before he set it down and faced the Senator. "I was wondering if anyone else noticed that," he said.

*   *   *   *   *

Hockley slept well that night except for the fact that occasional whiffs of chlorine seemed to drift from various corners of the room even though he turned the air-conditioning system on full blast.

In the morning there began a series of specialized lectures which had been prepared in accordance with the Earthmen's request to acquaint them with what they would be getting upon acceptance of the Ryke offer.

It was obviously no new experience for the Rykes. The lectures were well prepared and anticipated many questions. The only thing new about it, Hockley thought, was the delivery in the language of the Earthmen. Otherwise, he felt this was something prepared a long time ago and given a thousand times or more.

They were divided into smaller groups according to their specialties, electronic men going one way, astronomers and mathematical physicists another, chemists and general physicists in still another direction. Hockley, Showalter and the senators were considered more or less free floating members of the delegation with the privilege of visiting with one group or another according to their pleasure.

Hockley chose to spend the first day with the chemists, since that was his own first love. Dr. Showalter and Senator Markham came along with him. As much as he tried he found it virtually impossible not to sit with the same open-mouthed wonder that his colleagues exhibited. The swift, free-flowing exposition of the Ryke lecturer led them immediately beyond their own realms, but so carefully did he lead them that it seemed that they must have come this way before, and forgotten it.

Hockley felt half angry with himself. He felt he had allowed himself to be hypnotized by the skill of the Ryke, and wondered despairingly if there were any chance at all of combating their approach. He saw nothing to indicate it in the experience of that day or the ones immediately following. But he retained hope that there was much significance in the action of the guide who had cut short their visit to the museum.

In the evenings, in the study lounge of the dormitory, they held interminable bull sessions exchanging and digesting what they had been shown during the day. It was at the end of the third day that Hockley thought he could detect a subtle change in the group. He had some difficulty analyzing it at first. It seemed to be a growing aliveness, a sort of recovery. And then he recognized that the initial stunned reaction to the magnificence of the Rykes was passing off. They had been shocked by the impact of the Rykes, almost as if they had been struck a blow on the head. Temporarily, they had shelved all their own analytical and critical facilities and yielded to the Rykes without question.

Now they were beginning to recover, springing back to a condition considerably nearer normal. Hockley felt a surge of encouragement as he detected a more sharply critical evaluation in the conversations that buzzed around him. The enthusiasm was more measured.

It was the following evening, however, that witnessed the first event of pronounced shifting of anyone's attitude. They had finished dinner and were gathering in the lounge, sparring around, setting up groups for the bull sessions that would go until long after midnight. Most of them had already settled down and were talking part in conversations or were listening quietly when they were suddenly aware of a change in the atmosphere of the room.

For a moment there was a general turning of heads to locate the source of the disturbance. Hockley knew he could never describe just what made him look around, but he was abruptly conscious that Dr. Silvers was walking into the lounge and looking slowly about at those gathered there. Something in his presence was like the sudden appearance of a thundercloud, his face seemed to reflect the dark turbulence of a summer storm.

EMSH -

He said nothing, however, to anyone but strode over and sat beside Hockley, who was alone at the moment smoking the next to last of his Earthside cigars. Hockley felt the smouldering turmoil inside the mathematician. He extended his final cigar. Silvers brushed it away.

"The last one," said Hockley mildly. "In spite of all their abilities the Ryke imitations are somewhat less than natural."

Silvers turned slowly to face Hockley. "I presented them with the Legrandian Equations today," he said. "I expected to get a straightforward answer to a perfectly legitimate scientific question. That is what we were led to expect, was it not?"

Hockley nodded. "That's my impression. Did you get something less than a straightforward answer?"

The mathematician exhaled noisily. "The Legrandian Equations will lead to a geometry as revolutionary as Riemann's was in his day. But I was told by the Rykes that I 'should dismiss it from all further consideration. It does not lead to any profitable mathematical development.'"

Hockley felt that his heart most certainly skipped a beat, but he managed to keep his voice steady, and sympathetic. "That's too bad. I know what high hopes you had. I suppose you will give up work on the Equations now?"

"I will not!" Silvers exclaimed loudly. Nearby groups who had returned hesitantly to their own conversations now stared at him again. But abruptly he changed his tone and looked almost pleadingly at Hockley. "I don't understand it. Why should they say such a thing? It appears to be one of the most profitable avenues of exploration I have encountered in my whole career. And the Rykes brush it aside!"

"What did you say when they told you to give it up?"

"I said I wanted to know where the development would lead. I said it had been indicated that we could have an answer to any scientific problem within the range of their abilities, and certainly this is, from what I've seen.

"The instructor replied that I'd been given an answer to my question, that 'the first lesson you must learn if you wish to acquire our pace in science is to recognize that we have been along the path ahead of you. We know which are the possibilities that are worthwhile to develop. We have gained our speed by learning to bypass every avenue but the main one, and not get lost in tempting side roads.'

"He said that we've got to learn to trust them and take their word as to which is the correct and profitable field of research, that 'we will show you where to go, as we agreed to do. If you are not willing to accept our leadership in this respect our agreement means nothing.' Wouldn't that be a magnificent way to make scientific progress!"

The mathematician shifted in his chair as if trying to control an internal fury that would not be capped. He held out his hand abruptly. "I'll take that cigar after all, if you don't mind, Hockley."

With savage energy he chewed the end and ignited the cigar, then blew a mammoth cloud of smoke ceilingward. "I think the trouble must be in our lecturer," he said. "He's crazy. He couldn't possibly represent the conventional attitude of the Rykes. They promised to give answers to our problems—and this is the kind of nonsense I get. I'm going to see somebody higher up and find out why we can't have a lecturer who knows what he's talking about. Or maybe you or Markham would rather take it up— through official channels, as it were?"

"The Ryke was correct," said Hockley. "He *did* give you an answer."

"He could answer *all* our questions that way!"

"You're perfectly right," said Hockley soberly. "He could do exactly that."

"They won't of course," said Silvers, defensively. "Even if this particular character isn't just playing the screwball, my question is just a special case. It's just one particular thing they consider to be valueless. Perhaps in the end I'll find they're right—but I'm going to develop a solution to these Equations if it takes the rest of my life!

"After all, they admit they have no solution, that they have not bothered to go down this particular side path, as they put it. If we don't go down it how can we ever know whether it's worthwhile or not? How can the Rykes know what they may have missed by not doing so?"

"I can't answer that," said Hockley. "For us or for them, I know of no other way to predict the outcome of a specific line of research except to carry it through and find out what lies at the end of the road."

*   *   *   *   *

Hockley didn't sleep very well after he finally went to bed that night. Silvers had presented him with the break he had been expecting and hoping for. The first chink in the armor of sanctity surrounding the Rykes. Now he wondered what would follow, if this would build up to the impassable barrier he wanted, or if it would merely remain a sore obstacle in their way but eventually be bypassed and forgotten.

He did not believe it would be the only incident of its kind. There would be others as the Earthmen's stunned, blind acceptance gave way completely to sound, critical evaluation. And in any case there was one delegate who would never be the same again. No matter how he eventually rationalized it Dr. Forman K. Silvers would never feel quite the same about the Rykes as he did before they rejected his favorite piece of research.

Hockley arose early, eager but cautious, his senses open for further evidence of disaffection springing up. He joined the group of chemists once more for the morning lecture. The spirit of the group was markedly higher than when he first met with them. They had been inspired by what the Rykes had shown them, but in addition their own sense of judgment had been brought out of suspension.

The Ryke lecturer began inscribing on the board an enormous organic formula, using conventions of Earth chemistry for the benefit of his audience. He explained at some length a number of transformations which it was possible to make in the compound by means of high intensity fields.

Almost at once, one of the younger chemists named Dr. Carmen, was on his feet exclaiming excitedly that one of the transformation compounds was a chemical on which he had conducted an extensive research. He had produced enough to know that it had a multitude of intriguing properties, and now he was exuberant at the revelation of a method of producing it in quantity and also further transforming it.

At his sudden enthusiasm the lecturer's face took on what they had come to recognize as a very dour look. "That series of transformations has no interest for us," he said. "I merely indicated its existence to show one of the possibilities which should be avoided. Over here you see the direction in which we wish to go."

"But you never saw anything with properties like that!" Carmen protested. "It goes through an incredible series of at least three crystalline-liquid phase changes with an increase in pressure alone. But with proper control of heat it can be kept in the crystalline phase regardless of pressure. It is closely related to a drug series with anesthetic properties, and is almost sure to be valuable in—"

The Ryke lecturer cut him off sharply. "I have explained," he said, "the direction of transformation in which we are interested. Your concern is not with anything beyond the boundaries which our study has proven to be the direct path of research and study."

"Then I should abandon research on this series of chemicals?" Carmen asked with a show of outward meekness.

The Ryke nodded with pleasure at Carmen's submissiveness. "That is it precisely. We have been over this ground long ago. We know where the areas of profitable study lie. You will be told what to observe and what to ignore. How could you ever hope to make progress if you stopped to examine every alternate probability and possibility that appeared to you?" He shook his head vigorously and his plume vibrated with emotion.

"You must have a plan," he continued. "A goal. Study of the Universe cannot proceed in any random, erratic fashion. You must know what you want and then find out where to look for it."

Carmen sat down slowly. Hockley was sure the Ryke did not notice the tense bulge of the chemist's jaw muscles. Perhaps he would not have understood the significance if he had noticed.

*   *   *   *   *

Hockley was a trifle late in getting to the dining room at lunch time that day. By the time he did so the place was like a beehive. He was almost repelled by the furor of conversation circulating in the room as he entered.

He passed through slowly, searching for a table of his own. He paused a moment behind Dr. Carmen, who was declaiming in no mild terms his opinions of a system that would pre-select those areas of research which were to be entered and those which were not. He smiled a little as he caught the eye of one of the dozen chemists seated at the table, listening.

Moving on, he observed that Silvers had also cornered a half dozen or so of his colleagues in his own field and was in earnest conversation with them—in a considerably more restrained manner, however, than he had used the previous evening with Hockley, or than Carmen was using at the present time.

The entire room was abuzz with similar groups.

The senators had tried to mingle with the others in past days, always with more or less lack of success because they found themselves out of the conversation almost completely. Today they had no luck whatever. They were seated together at a couple of tables in a corner. None of them seemed to be paying attention to the food before them, but were glancing about, half-apprehensively, at their fellow diners—who were also paying no attention to food.

Hockley caught sight of his political colleagues and sensed their dismay. The field of disquietude seemed almost tangible in the air. The senators seemed half frightened by what they felt but could not understand.

Showalter's wild waving at the far corner of the room finally caught Hockley's eye and he moved toward the small table which the assistant had reserved for them. Showalter was upset, too, by the atmosphere within the room.

"What the devil is up?" he said. "Seems like everybody's on edge this morning. I never saw a bunch of guys so touchy. You'd think they woke up with snakes in their beds."

"Didn't you know?" said Hockley. "Haven't you been to any of the lectures this morning?"

"No. A couple of the senators were getting bored with all the scientific doings so I thought maybe I should try to entertain them. We took in what passes for such here, but it wasn't much better than the lectures as a show. Tell me what's up."

Briefly, Hockley described Silvers' upset of the day before and Carmen's experience that morning. Showalter let his glance rove over his fellow Earthmen, trying to catch snatches of the buzzing conversation at nearby tables.

"You think that's the kind of thing that's got them all going this morning?" he said.

Hockley nodded. "I caught enough of it passing through to know that's what it is. I gather that every group has run into the same kind of thing by now, the fencing off of broad areas where we have already tried to do research.

"After the first cloud of awe wore off, the first thing everyone wanted was an answer to his own pet line of research. Nine times out of ten it was something the Rykes told them to chuck down the drain. That advice doesn't sit so well—as you can plainly see."

Showalter drew back his gaze and stared for a long time at Hockley. "You knew this would happen. That's why you brought us here—"

"I had hopes of it. I was reasonably sure this was the way the Rykes operated."

Showalter remained thoughtful for a long time before he spoke again. "You've won your point, I suppose, as far as this group goes, but you can't hope to convince all of Earth by this. The Rykes will hold their offer open, and others will accept it on behalf of Earth.

"And what if it's we who are wrong, in the end? How can you be sure that this isn't the way the Rykes have made their tremendous speed—by not going down all the blind alleys that we rattle around in."

"I'm sure it *is* the way they have attained such speed of advancement."

"Then maybe we ought to go along, regardless of our own desires. Maybe we never did know how to do research!"

Hockley smiled across the table at his assistant. "You believe that, of course."

"I'm just talking," said Showalter irritably. "The thing gets more loopy every day. If you think you understand the Rykes I wish you would give out with what the score is. By the looks of most of these guys I would say they are getting ready to throttle the next Ryke they see instead of knuckle under to him."

"I hope you're right," said Hockley fervently. "I certainly hope you're right."

*   *   *   *   *

By evening there was increasing evidence that he was. Hockley passed up the afternoon lecture period and spent the time in the lounge doing some thinking of his own. He knew he couldn't push the group. Above all, he mustn't give way to any temptation to push them or say, "I told you so." Their present frustration was so deep that their antagonism could be turned almost indiscriminately in any direction, and he would be offering himself as a ready target if he were not careful.

On the other hand he had to be ready to take advantage of their disaffection and throw them a decisive challenge when they were ready for it. That might be tonight, or it might be another week. He wished for a sure way of knowing. As things turned out, however, the necessity of choosing the time was taken from him.

After dinner that night, when the group began to drift into the lounge, Silvers and Carmen and three of the other men came over to where Hockley sat. Silvers fumbled with the buttons of his coat as if preparing to make an address.

"We'd like to request," he said, "that is—we think we ought to get together. We'd like you to call a meeting, Hockley. Some of us have a few things we'd like to talk over."

Hockley nodded, his face impassive.

"The matter I mentioned to you the other night," said Silvers. "It's been happening to all the men. We think we ought to talk about it."

"Fine," said Hockley. "I've been thinking it would perhaps be a good idea. Pass the word around and let's get some chairs. We can convene in ten minutes."

The others nodded somberly and moved away with all the enthusiasm of preparing for a funeral. And maybe that's what it would be, Hockley thought—somebody's funeral. He hoped it would be the Rykes.

The room began filling almost at once, as if they had been expecting the call. In little more than five minutes it seemed that every member of the Earth delegation had assembled, leaving time to spare.

The senators still wore their looks of puzzlement and half-frightened anxiety, which had intensified if anything. There was no puzzlement on the faces of the scientists, however, only a set and determined expression that Hockley hardly dared interpret as meaning they had made up their minds. He had to have their verbal confirmation.

Informally, he thrust his hands in his pockets and sauntered to the front of the group.

"I have been asked to call a meeting," he said, "by certain members of the group who have something on their minds. They seem to feel we'd all be interested in what is troubling them. Since I have nothing in particular to say I'm simply going to turn the floor over to those of you who have. Dr. Silvers first approached me to call this discussion, so I shall ask him to lead off. Will you come to the front, Dr. Silvers?"

The mathematician rose as if wishing someone else would do the talking. He stood at one side of the group, halfway to the rear. "I can do all right from here," he said.

After a pause, as if coming to a momentous decision, he plunged into his complaint. "It appears that nearly all of us have encountered an aspect of the Ryke culture and character which was not anticipated when we first received their offer." Briefly, he related the details of the Ryke rejection of his research on the Legrandian Equations.

"We were told we were going to have all our questions answered, that the Ryke's science included all we could anticipate or hope to accomplish in the next few millenia. I swallowed that. We all did. It appears we were slightly in error. It begins to appear as if we are not going to find the intellectual paradise we anticipated."

He smiled wryly. "I'm sure none of you is more ready than I to admit he has been a fool. It appears that paradise, so-called, consists merely of a few selected gems which the Rykes consider particularly valuable, while the rest of the field goes untouched.

"I want to offer public apologies to Dr. Hockley, who saw and understood the situation as it actually existed, while the rest of us had our heads in the clouds. Exactly how he knew, I'm not sure, but he did, and very brilliantly chose the only way possible to convince us that what he knew was correct.

"I suggest we do our packing tonight, gentlemen. Let us return at once to our laboratories and spend the rest of our lives in some degree of atonement for being such fools as to fall for the line the Rykes tried to sell us."

Hockley's eyes were on the senators. At first there were white faces filled with incredulity as the mathematician proceeded. Then slowly this changed to sheer horror.

When Silvers finished, there was immediate bedlam. There was a clamor of voices from the scientists, most of whom seemed to be trying to affirm Silvers' position. This was offset by explosions of rage from the senatorial members of the group.

Hockley let it go, not even raising his hands for order until finally the racket died of its own accord as the eyes of the delegates came to rest upon him.

And then, before he could speak, Markham was on his feet. "This is absolutely moral treachery," he thundered. "I have never heard a more vicious revocation of a pledged word than I have heard this evening.

"You men are not alone concerned in this matter. For all practical purposes you are not concerned at all! And yet to take it upon yourselves to pass judgment in a matter that is the affair of the entire population of Earth—out of nothing more than sheer spite because the Rykes refuse recognition of your own childish projects! I have never heard a more incredible and infantile performance than you supposedly mature gentlemen of science are expressing this evening."

He glared defiantly at Hockley, who was again the center of attention moving carelessly to the center of the stage. "Anybody want to try to answer the Senator?" he asked casually.

Instantly, a score of men were on their feet, speaking simultaneously. They stopped abruptly, looking deferentially to their neighbors and at Hockley, inviting him to choose one of them to be spokesman.

"Maybe I ought to answer him myself," said Hockley, "since I predicted that this would occur, and that we ought to make a trial run before turning our collective gray matter over to the Rykes."

A chorus of approval and nodding heads gave him the go ahead.

"The Senator is quite right in saying that we few are not alone in our concern in this matter," he said. "But the Senator intends to imply a major difference between us scientists and the rest of mankind. This is his error.

"Every member of Mankind who is concerned about the Universe in which he lives, is a scientist. You need to understand what a scientist is—and you can say no more than that he is a human being trying to solve the problem of understanding his Universe, immediate or remote. He is concerned about the inanimate worlds, his own personality, his fellow men—and the interweaving relationships among all these factors. We professional scientists are no strange species, alien to our race. Our only difference is perhaps that we undertake *more* problems than does the average of our fellow men, and of a more complex kind. That is all.

"The essence of our science is a relentless personal yearning to know and understand the Universe. And in that, the scientist must not be forbidden to ask whatever question occurs to him. The moment we put any restraint upon our fields of inquiry, or set bounds to the realms of our mental aspirations, our science ceases to exist and becomes a mere opportunist technology."

Markham stood up, his face red with exasperation and rage. "No one is trying to limit you! Why is that so unfathomable to your minds? You are being offered a boundless expanse, and you continue to make inane complaints of limitations. The Rykes have been over all the territory you insist on exploring. They can tell you the number of pretty pebbles and empty shells that lie there. You are like children insistent upon exploring every shadowy corner and peering behind every useless bush on a walk through the forest.

"Such is to be expected of a child, but not of an adult, who is capable of taking the word of one who has been there before!"

"There are two things wrong with your argument," said Hockley. "First of all, there is no essential difference between the learning of a child who must indeed explore the dark corners and strange growths by which he passes—there is no difference between this and the probing of the scientist, who must explore the Universe with his own senses and with his own instruments, without taking another's word that there is nothing there worth seeing.

"Secondly, the Rykes themselves are badly in error in asserting that they have been along the way ahead of us. They have not. In all their fields of science they have limited themselves badly to one narrow field of probability. They have taken a narrow path stretching between magnificent vistas on either side of them, and have deliberately ignored all that was beyond the path and on the inviting side trails."

"Is there anything wrong with that?" demanded Markham. "If you undertake a journey you don't weave in and out of every possible path that leads in every direction opposed to your destination. You take the direct route. Or at least *ordinary* people do."

"Scientists do, too," said Hockley, "when they take a journey. Professional science is not a journey, however. It's an exploration.

"There is a great deal wrong with what the Rykes have done. They have assumed, and would have us likewise assume, that there is a certain very specific future toward which we are all moving. This future is built out of the discoveries they have made about the Universe. It is made of the system of mathematics they have developed, which exclude Dr. Silvers' cherished Legrandian Equations. It excludes the world in which exist Dr. Carmen's series of unique compounds.

"The Rykes have built a wonderful, workable world of serenity, beauty, scientific consistency, and economic adjustment. They have eliminated enormous amounts of chaos which Earthmen continue to suffer.

"But we do not want what the Rykes have obtained—if we have to pay their price for it."

"Then you are complete fools," said Markham. "Fortunately, you cannot and will not speak for all of Earth."

Hockley paced back and forth a half dozen steps, his eyes on the floor. "I think we do—and can—speak for all our people," he said. "Remember, I said that all men are scientists in the final analysis. I am very certain that no Earthman who truly understood the situation would want to face the future which the Rykes hold out to us."

"And why not?" demanded Markham.

"Because there are too many possible futures. We refuse to march down a single narrow trail to *the* golden future. That's what the Rykes would have us do. But they are wrong. It would be like taking a trip through a galaxy at speeds faster than light—and claiming to have seen the galaxy. What the Rykes have obtained is genuine and good, but what they have not obtained is perhaps far better and of greater worth."

"How can you know such an absurd thing?"

"We can't—not for sure," said Hockley. "Not until we go there and see for ourselves, step by step. But we aren't going to be confined to the Rykes' narrow trail. We are going on a broad path to take in as many byways as we can possibly find. We'll explore every probability we come to, and look behind every bush and under every pebble.

"We will move together, the thousands and the millions of us, simultaneously, interacting with one another, exchanging data. Most certainly, many will end up in blind alleys. Some will find data that seems the ultimate truth at one point and pure deception at another. Who can tell ahead of time which of these multiple paths we should take? Certainly not the Rykes, who have bypassed most of them!

"It doesn't matter that many paths lead to failure—not as long as we remain in communication with each other. In the end we will find the best possible future for us. But there is no *one* future, only a multitude of possible futures. We must have the right to build the one that best fits our own kind."

"Is that more important than achieving immediately a more peaceful, unified, and secure society?" said Markham.

"Infinitely more important!" said Hockley.

"It is fortunate at least, then, that you are in no position to implement these insane beliefs of yours. The Ryke program was offered to Earth, and it shall be accepted on behalf of Earth. You may be sure of a very poor hearing when you try to present these notions back home."

"You jump to conclusions, Senator," said Hockley with mild confidence. "Why do you suppose I proposed this trip if I did not believe I could do something about the situation? I assure you that we did not come just to see the sights."

Markham's jaw slacked and his face became white. "What do you mean? You haven't dared to try to alienate the Rykes—"

"I mean that there is a great deal we can do about the situation. Now that the sentiments of my colleagues parallel my own I'm sure they agree that we must effectively and finally spike any possibility of Earth's becoming involved in this Ryke nonsense."

"You wouldn't dare!—even if you could—"

"We can, and we dare," said Hockley. "When we return to Earth we shall have to report that the Rykes have refused to admit Earth to their program. We shall report that we made every effort to obtain an agreement with them, but it was in vain. If anyone wishes to verify the report, the Rykes themselves will say that this is quite true: they cannot possibly consider Earth as a participant. If you contend that an offer was once made, you will not find the Rykes offering much support since they will be very busily denying that we are remotely qualified."

"The Rykes are hardly ones to meekly submit to any idiotic plan of that kind."

"They can't help it—if we demonstrate that we *are* quite unqualified to participate."

"You—you—"

"It will not be difficult," said Hockley. "The Rykes have set up a perfect teacher-pupil situation, with all the false assumptions that go with it. There is at least one absolutely positive way to disintegrate such a situation. The testimony of several thousand years' failure of our various educational systems indicates that there are quite a variety of lesser ways also—

"Perhaps you are aware of the experiences and techniques commonly employed on Earth by white men in their efforts to educate the aborigine. The first procedure is to do away with the tribal medicine men, ignore their lore and learning. Get them to give up the magic words and their pots of foul smelling liquids, abandon their ritual dances and take up the white man's great wisdom.

"We have done this time after time, only to learn decades later that the natives once knew much of anesthetics and healing drugs, and had genuine powers to communicate in ways the white man can't duplicate.

"But once in a long while a group of aborigines show more spunk than the average. They refuse to give up their medicine men, their magic and their hard earned lore accumulated over generations and centuries. Instead of giving these things up they insist on the white man's learning these mysteries in preference to *his* nonsensical and ineffective magic. They completely frustrate the situation, and if they persist they finally destroy the white man as an educator. He is forced to conclude that the ignorant savages are unteachable.

"It is an infallible technique—and one that we shall employ. Dr. Silvers will undertake to teach his mathematical lecturer in the approaches to the Legrandian Equations. He will speculate long and noisily on the geometry which potentially lies in this mathematical system. Dr. Carmen will elucidate at great length on the properties of the chain of chemicals he has been advised to abandon.

"Each of us has at least one line of research the Rykes would have us give up. That is the very thing we shall insist on having investigated. We shall teach them these things and prove Earthmen to be an unlearned, unteachable band of aborigines who refuse to pursue the single path to glory and light, but insist on following every devious byway and searching every darkness that lies beside the path.

"It ought to do the trick. I estimate it should not be more than a week before we are on our way back home, labeled by the Rykes as utterly hopeless material for their enlightenment."

The senators seemed momentarily appalled and speechless, but they recovered shortly and had a considerable amount of high flown oratory to distribute on the subject. The scientists, however, were comparatively quiet, but on their faces was a subdued glee that Hockley had to admit was little short of fiendish. It was composed, he thought, of all the gloating anticipations of all the schoolboys who had ever put a thumbtack on the teacher's chair.

Hockley was somewhat off in his prediction. It was actually a mere five days after the beginning of the Earthmen's campaign that the Rykes gave them up and put them firmly aboard a vessel bound for home. The Rykes were apologetic but firm in admitting they had made a sorry mistake, that Earthmen would have to go their own hopeless way while the Rykes led the rest of the Universe toward enlightenment and glory.

Hockley, Showalter, and Silvers watched the planet drop away beneath them. Hockley could not help feeling sympathetic toward the Rykes. "I wonder what will happen," he said slowly, "when they crash headlong into an impassable barrier on that beautiful, straight road of theirs. I wonder if they'll ever have enough guts to turn aside?"

"I doubt it," said Showalter. "They'll probably curl up and call it a day."

Silvers shook his head as if to ward off an oppressive vision. "That shouldn't be allowed to happen," he said. "They've got too much. They've achieved too much, in spite of their limitations. I wonder if there isn't some way we could help them?"

Cubs of the Wolf

ILLUSTRATED BY ROGERS
ORIGINALLY PUBLISHED IN *ASTOUNDING SCIENCE FICTION*,
NOVEMBER 1955

*It may be that there is a weapon that, from the
viewpoint of the one it's used on, is worse than
lethal. You might say that death multiplies you by
zero; what would multiplication by minus one do?*

CUBS OF THE WOLF

In the spring the cherry blossoms are heavy in the air over
the campus of Solarian Institute of Science and Humanities. On
a small slope that rims the park area, Cameron Wilder lay on his
back squinting through the cloud of pink-white petals to the sky
beyond. Beside him, Joyce Farquhar drew her jacket closer with
an irritated gesture. It was still too cold to be sitting on the
grass, but Cameron didn't seem to notice it—or anything else,
Joyce thought.

"If you don't submit a subject for your thesis now," she said,
"you'll take another full six months getting your doctorate.
Sometimes I think you don't really want it!"

Cameron stirred. He shifted his squinting gaze from the sky
to Joyce and finally sat up. But he was staring ahead through
the trees again as he took his pipe from his pocket and began
filling it slowly.

"I *don't* want it if it's not going to mean anything after I get
it," he said belligerently. "I'm not going to do an investigation of
some silly subject like The Transience of Venusian Immigrants
in Relation to the Martian Polar Ice Cap Cycle. Solarian
sociologists are the butt of enough ridicule now. Do something
like that and for the rest of your life you get knocking of the
knees whenever anybody inquires about the specialty you
worked in and threatens to read your thesis."

"Nobody's asking you to do anything you don't want to. But
you picked the field of sociology to work in. Now I don't see why
you have to act such a purist that it takes months to find a
research project for your degree. Pick something—anything!—I
don't care what it is. But if you don't get a degree and an
appointment out of the next session I don't think we'll ever get
married—not ever."

Cameron removed his pipe from his mouth with a precise grip and considered it intently as it cupped in his hands. "I'm glad you mentioned marriage," he said. "I was just about to speak of it myself."

"Well, don't!" said Joyce. "After three years—Three years!"

He turned to face her and smiled for the first time. He liked to lead her along occasionally just to watch her explode, but he was not always sure when he had gone too far. Joyce had a mind like a snapping, random matching calculator while he operated more on a slow, carefully shaping analogue basis, knowing things were never quite what they seemed but trying to get as close an approximation of the true picture as possible.

"Will you marry me now?" he said.

The question did not seem to startle her. "No degree, no appointment—and no chance of getting one—we couldn't even get a license. I hope you aren't suggesting we try to get along without one, or on a forgery!"

Cameron shook his head. "No, darling, this is a perfectly bona fide proposal, complete with license, appointment, the works—what do you say?"

"I say this spring sun is too much for you." She touched the dark mass of his hair, warmed by the sun's rays, and put her head on his shoulder. She started to cry. "Don't tease me like that, Cameron. It seems like we've been waiting forever—and there's still forever ahead of us. You can't do anything you want to—"

Cameron put his arms about her, not caring if the whole Institute faculty leaned out the windows to watch. "That's why you should appreciate being about to marry such a resourceful fellow," he said more gently. And now he dropped all banter. "I've been thinking about how long it's been, too. That's why I decided to try to kill a couple of sparrows with one pebble."

Joyce sat up. "You aren't serious—?"

Cameron sucked on his pipe once more. "Ever hear of the Markovian Nucleus?" he said thoughtfully.

Joyce slowly nodded her head. "Oh, I think I've heard the name mentioned," she murmured, "but nothing more than that."

"I've asked for that as my research project."

"But that's clear out of the galaxy—in Transpace!"

"Yes, and obviously out of bounds for the ordinary graduate researcher. But because of the scholarship record I've been able to rack up here I took a chance on applying to the Corning Foundation for a grant. And they decided to take a chance on me after considerable and not entirely painless investigation. That's why you were followed around like a suspected Disloyalist for a month. My application included a provision for you to go along as my wife. Professor Fothergill notified me this morning that the grant had been awarded."

"Cam—" Joyce's voice was brittle now. "You aren't fooling me?"

He gathered her in his arms again. "You think I would fool about something like that, darling? In a week you'll be Mrs. C. Wilder, and as soon as school is out, on your way to the Markovian Nucleus. And besides, it took me almost as much work preparing the research prospectus as the average guy spends on his whole project!"

*   *   *   *   *

Sometimes Joyce Farquhar wished Cameron were a good deal different than he was. But then he wouldn't have been Cameron, and she wouldn't want to marry him, she supposed. And somehow, while he fell behind on the mid-stretch, he always managed to come in at the end with the rest of the field. Or just a little bit ahead of it.

Or a good deal ahead of it. As now. It took her a few moments to realize the magnitude of the coup he had actually pulled off. For weeks she had been depressed because he refused to use some trivial, breeze research to get his degree. He could have started it as much as a year ago, and they could have been married now if he'd set himself up a real cinch.

But now they were getting married anyway—and Cameron was getting the kind of research deal that would satisfy his frantic desire for integrity in a world where it counted for little, and his wish to contribute something genuine to the sociological understanding of sentient creatures.

Their marriage, as was customary, would be a cut and dried affair. A call to the license bureau, receipt of formal sanction in the mail—she supposed Cameron had already made application—and a little party with a few of their closest friends on the campus. She wished she had lived in the days when getting married was much easier to do, and something to make a fuss about.

She stirred and sat up, loosening the jacket as the sun came from behind a puff of cloud. "You could have told me about this a long time ago, couldn't you?" she said accusingly.

Cameron nodded. "I could have. But I didn't want to get false hopes aroused. I didn't have much hope the deal would actually go through, myself. I think Fothergill is pretty much responsible for it."

"Transpace—" Joyce said dreamily. "Tell me about the Markovian Nucleus. Why is it important enough for a big research study, anyway?"

"It's a case of a leopard who changed his spots," said Cameron. "And nobody knows how or why. The full title of the project is A Study of the Metamorphosis of the Markovian Nucleus."

"What happened? How are they any different from the way they used to be?"

"A hundred and fifty years ago the Markovians were the meanest, nastiest, orneriest specimens in the entire Council of Galactic Associates. The groups of worlds in one corner of their galaxy, which make up the Nucleus, controlled a military force that outweighed anything the Council could possibly bring to bear against them.

"With complete disregard of any scheme of interplanetary rules or order they harassed and attacked peaceful shipping and inoffensive cultures throughout a wide territory. They were something demanding the Council's military action. But the Council lacked the strength.

"For years the Council dragged on, debating and threatening ineffectively. But nothing was ever done. And then, so gradually it was hardly noticed, the harassments began to die down. The warlike posturing was abandoned by the Markovians. Within a period of about seventy or eighty years there was a complete about-face. They wound up as good Indians, peaceful, cooeperative and intelligent members of the Council."

"Didn't anybody ever find out why?" asked Joyce.

"No. Nobody *wanted* to find out. In the early years the worlds of the Council were hiding behind their collective hands hoping with all their might that the threat might go away if they kept their eyes closed long enough. And by some miracle of all miracles, when they parted their fingers for a scared glimpse, the threat *had* disappeared.

"When they could breathe a little more easily it seemed a foolish thing to bring out this old skeleton from the closet again, so a perpetual state of hush was established. Finally, the whole thing was practically forgotten except for a short paragraph in an occasional history text. But no politician or historian has ever dared publicly to question the mysterious why of the Markovian's about-face."

"Sociologists should have done it long ago," said Joyce.

"There was always the political pressure, of course," said Cameron. "But the real reason was simply our preoccupation with making bibliographies of each others' papers. It's going to take a lot of leg work, something in which our formal courses don't give us any basic training. Fothergill understands that— it's why he pushed me so hard with the Foundation. And Riley up there is capable of seeing it, too.

"I showed him that here was a complex of at least a hundred and ten major planets, inhabited by a fairly homogenous, civilized people, speaking from a technological point of view at least. And almost overnight some force changed the entire cultural posture. I made him see that identification of that force is of no small interest to us right now. If it operated once, it could operate again—and would its results be as happy a second time?

"Riley got the Foundation to kick through enough for you and me to make a start. A preliminary survey is about all it will amount to, actually, but if we show evidence of something tangible I'll get my degree, you'll get your basic certification— and we'll both return in charge of a full-scale inquiry with a staff big enough to really dig into things next year.

"Now—about this matter of marriage which you didn't want me to speak of—"

"Keep talking, Cam—you're doing wonderfully!"

*　　*　　*　　*　　*

They got married at once, even though there were several weeks of school which had to be finished before they could leave. Among their friends on the campus there were a good many whispered remarks about the insanity of Joyce and Cameron in planning such a fantastic excursion, but Joyce was certain there was as much envy as criticism in the eyes of her associates. It might be true when they asserted that every conceivable sociological factor or combination of factors could be found and analyzed right here in the Solar System, but a husband who could finagle a way to combine a honeymoon trip halfway across space with his graduate research thesis was a rare specimen. Joyce played her advantage for all it was worth.

Two weeks before departure time, however, Cameron was called to the office of Professor Fothergill. As he entered he found a third man present, wearing a uniform he recognized at once as belonging to the Council Secretariat.

"I'll wait outside," he said abruptly as Fothergill turned. "I got your message and came right over. I didn't know—"

"Sit down," said Fothergill. "Cameron, this is Mr. Ebbing, whose position you no doubt recognize. Mr. Ebbing, Mr. Wilder."

The men shook hands and took seats across from each other. Fothergill sat between them at the polished table. "The Council, it seems, has developed an interest in your proposed research among the Markovians," he said. "I'll let Mr. Ebbing tell you about it."

Cameron felt a sinking anticipation within him as he turned to the secretary. Surely the Council wasn't going to actively oppose the investigation after so long a time!

The secretary coughed and shuffled the papers he drew from his case. "It's not actually the Council's interest," he said, and Cameron was immediately relieved. "But I have been asked by the Markovian Nucleus, through their representative, to suggest that they would like to save you the long and unnecessary trip. He offers to co-operate to the fullest degree by causing all necessary materials to be transferred to your site of study right here. He feels that this is the least they can do since so much interest appears to exist in the Nucleus."

Cameron stared at the secretary, trying to discern what the man's own attitude might be, but Ebbing gave no sign of playing it any way but straight.

"It sounds like a polite invitation to stay home and mind our own business," said Cameron finally. "They don't want company."

The secretary's expression changed to acknowledgment of the correct appraisal. "They don't want any investigation into the Metamorphosis of the Markovian Nucleus. There is no such thing. It is entirely a myth."

"Says the Markovians—!"

Ebbing nodded. "Says the Markovians. Other worlds, both within and without the Council have persisted in spreading tales and rumors about the Markovians for a long time. They don't like it. They are willing to co-operate in having a correct analysis of their culture published, but they don't want any more of these infamous rumors circulated."

"Then why aren't they willing to promote such an investigation? This would be their big chance—if their ridiculous position were true!"

"They *are* willing. I've told you the representative has offered to send you all needed material showing the status of their culture."

Cameron looked at the secretary for a long time before speaking again. "What's your position?" he asked finally. "Are we being ordered off the investigation?"

"The Markovian representative doesn't want to go to quite that extreme. He knows that, too, would react unfavorably towards his people. Here's his point: So far, he's blocked news of your proposed research getting to his home worlds. But he knows that if you do carry it out in the manner you propose it is going to make a lot of the home folks mighty unhappy and they'll demand to know why he didn't stop it. So he's trying to satisfy both sides at once."

"Why will the people in the Nucleus be made unhappy by our coming?"

"Because you'll go there trying to track down the basis for the rumors that defame the Markovian character. You'll bring forcibly to their attention the fact that the rest of the Universe believes the Markovians are basically a bunch of pirates."

"And the Markovians don't like to hear these things?"

"Definitely not."

"So you tell me the research is not being forbidden, but that the Markovians won't like it. Suppose I tell you, then, I'm not going to give up short of an order from the Council itself. But I am willing to camouflage the investigation if necessary. I'll make no open mention of what outside opinion says of the Markovians. I'll simply make a study of their history and character as it becomes available to me."

Ebbing nodded slowly, his eyes fixed on Cameron's face. "I would say that would be eminently satisfactory," he said. "I will inform the representative of your decision."

Then his face became more severe. "The Council will be pleased to learn of your willingness to be discreet. I wonder if you understand that the Foundation came to us upon receipt of your application, for official clearance of the project. It coincided quite fortuitously with the plans of the Council itself. For a long time we have been concerned with the lack of information regarding the Markovian situation and have been at a loss as to how to improve our situation.

"Your proposed investigation seemed the answer, but we anticipated the Markovian objection and had to make certain you would co-operate to his satisfaction. I believe this will do it."

"Why is the Council concerned?" said Cameron. "Have the Markovians changed their attitude in any way?"

"No—but the rest of us remember, even though we don't speak of it, that the Nucleus was never punished for its depredations, nor was it ever defeated. Its strength is as great as ever in proportion to the other Council worlds.

"What are the chances and potentialities of the Nucleus worlds ever again becoming the marauders they once were? That is the question which we feel must be answered. Without knowing, we are sitting on a powder keg in which the fuse may or may not be lighted. Will you bring us back the answer we need?"

Cameron felt a sudden grimness which had not been present before. "I'll do all I can," he said soberly. "If the information is there I'll bring it back."

*   *   *   *   *

After the secretary had gone and Fothergill turned from the door to rejoin him Cameron sat in faintly shocked consideration of the Council's unexpected support. It took his research out of the realm of the purely sociological and projected it into politics and diplomacy. He was pleased by their confidence, but not cheered by the added responsibility.

"That's a lucky break," said Fothergill enthusiastically, "and I'm beginning to suspect you may be rather badly in need of all the breaks you can get once you land among the Markovians. Don't forget for a single minute that you are dealing with the sons and grandsons of genuine pirates."

The professor sat down again. "There's one other little item of interest I turned up the other day. You should know about it before you leave. The Markovian Nucleus is somewhat of a hotbed of Ids."

"Ids—you mean the Idealists—?"

Fothergill nodded. "Know anything about them?"

"Not much, except that they are a sort of parasitic group, living usually in a servant relationship to other races on terran-type worlds. As I recall, even they claim that they do not know the planet or even the galaxy of their origin, because they have been wanderers for so many generations among alien races. Perhaps it would be a good idea to make a study of them, too—I don't know that a thorough one has ever been made."

"That's what I wanted to warn you about," said Fothergill, smiling. "Stick to one subject at a time. The Ids *would* make a nice research project in themselves, and maybe you can get around to it eventually. But leave them alone for the present and don't become distracted from your basic project among the Markovians. The policy of the Corning Foundation is to demand something very definite in return for the money they lay on the line. You won't get to go back next year unless you produce. That's why I don't want you to get sidetracked in any way."

II

Cameron admitted to himself that he was getting more edgy as the day of departure approached, but he tried to keep Joyce from seeing it. He was worried about the possible development of further opposition now that the Markovian had expressed his displeasure, and he was worried about their reception once they reached the Nucleus. He wondered why they had not seen in advance that it would be an obvious blunder to let the Markovians be aware of their real purpose. It didn't even require a pirate ancestry to make groups unappreciative about resurrection of their family skeletons.

But no other hindrance appeared, and on the evening before their departure Fothergill called that word had been received from Ebbing stating the Markovian representative had approved the visit now that Cameron had expressed a change in his objectives. Their coming had been announced to the Markovian people and the way prepared for an official welcome.

Cameron was pleased by the change of attitude. He was hit for the first time, however, by the full force of the fact that he was taking his bride to a pirate center which the Council had never overthrown and which was active only moments ago, culturally speaking.

If any kind of trouble should develop the Council would be almost impotent in offering them assistance. On the face of it, there was no reason to expect trouble. But the peculiarly oblique opposition of the Markovian delegate in the Council continued to make him uneasy.

His tentative suggestion that he would feel better if he knew she were safe on Earth brought a blistering response from Joyce, which left him with no doubts about carrying out his original plans.

And then, as the last of their packing was completed and they were ready to call it a day, the phone buzzed. Cameron hesitated, determined to let it go unanswered, then punched the button irritably on audio only.

Instead of the caller, he heard the voice of the operator. "One moment please. Interstellar, Transpace, printed. Please connect visio."

It was like a shock, he thought afterwards. There was no one he knew who could be making such a call to him. But automatically he did as directed. Joyce had come up and was peering over his shoulder now. The screen fluttered for a moment with polychrome colors and cleared. The message, printed for English translation, stood out sharply. Joyce and Cameron exclaimed simultaneously at the titling. It was from Premier Jargla, Executive Head of the Markovian Government.

"To Wilder, Cameron and Joyce," it read, "greetings and appreciation for your proposed visit to the Markovian Nucleus for study of our history and customs. We have not been before so honored. We feel, however, that it is an imposition on your Foundation and on you personally to require that you make the long journey to the Nucleus for this purpose alone. While we would be honored to entertain you—"

It was the same proposition as Ebbing had reported the delegate offered. Only this time it was from the head of the Markovian government himself.

They sat up nearly all the rest of the night considering this new development. "Maybe you shouldn't go, after all," said Joyce once. "Maybe this is something that needs bigger handling than we can possibly give it."

Cameron shook his head. "*I've* got to go. They haven't closed the door and said we can't come. If I backed out before they did, I'd be known the rest of my life as the guy who was *going* to crack the Markovian problem. But I'd much rather you—"

"No! If you're going, so am I."

*   *   *   *   *

They consulted again with Fothergill and finally drafted as polite a reply as possible, explaining they were newly married, desired to make the trip a honeymoon excursion primarily and conduct an investigation into Markovian culture to prevent the waste of the wonderful opportunity their visit would afford them.

An hour before takeoff a polite acknowledgment came back from the Nucleus assuring them a warm welcome and congratulating them on their marriage. They went at once to the spaceport and took over their stateroom. "Before anything else happens to try to pull us off this investigation," Cameron said.

The trip would be a long one, involving more than two months subjective time, because no express runs moved any distance at all in the direction of the Nucleus. It was necessary to transfer three times, with days of waiting between ships on planets whose surface conditions permitted exploration only in cumbersome suits that could not be worn for more than short periods. Most of the waiting time was spent in the visitors' chambers at the landing fields.

CAMERON

These seemed to grow progressively worse. The last one could not maintain a gravity below 2G, and the minimum temperature available was 104 degrees. There was a three-day wait here and Joyce spent most of it lying on the bed, under the breeze of a fan which seemed to have required a special dispensation of the governing body to obtain.

Cameron, however, was unwilling to spend his time this way in spite of the discomfort imposed by any kind of activity. Humidity was a physical factor which seemed to have gone undiscovered by the inhabitants of the planet they were on. He was sure it was constantly maintained within a fractional per cent of one hundred as he donned a clean pair of trunks and staggered miserably along the corridor toward a window that gave a limited view of the city about them.

That was when he discovered that they were to be accompanied on the remainder of the journey by a Markovian citizen and his Id servant.

The visitors' chamber in which these semi-terran conditions were supplied consisted of only three suites. The other two had been empty when Cameron and Joyce arrived the night before. Now a Markovian Id occupied a seat by the window. He glanced up with warm friendliness and invited Cameron to join him.

Cameron hesitated, undecided for a moment whether to return to his suite for the portable semantic translator used in his profession at times like this. He always felt there was something decidedly unprofessional about resorting to their use and had spent many hours trying to master Markovian before leaving. He understood the Id well enough and decided to see if he could get along without the translator.

"Thanks," he said, taking a seat. "I don't suppose there's much else to do except look at the scenery here."

The Id showed obvious surprise that Cameron spoke the language without use of an instrument. His look of pleasure increased. "It is not often we find one of your race who has taken the trouble to make himself communicable with us. You must be expecting to make a long stay?"

Cameron's sense of caution returned as he remembered the previous results of indiscreet announcement of his purpose. He wiped the stream of sweat from his face and neck and took a good look at the Id.

*   *   *   *   *

The Idealists were of an anthropomorphic race, dark-skinned like the terran Indian. Very few of them had ever appeared on Earth, however, and this was actually Cameron's first view of one in the flesh. He knew something of their reputation and characteristics from very brief study at the Institute—but no one really knew very much of the Ids as far as Earthmen were concerned. The warning of Fothergill to keep to the main line of his research sank to the bottom of his mind as he leaned toward the stranger with a fresh sense of excitement inside him.

"I have never felt you could understand another man unless you spoke his language," he said in his not too stumbling Markovian.

The Id, like himself, was dressed in the briefest of garments and perspiration poured from the dark skin as he nodded. "You speak sounder wisdom than one usually meets in a stranger," he said. "May I introduce myself: Sal Karone, servant of the Master Dalls Ret Marthasa?"

Cameron introduced himself and cautiously explained that he and Joyce were on their honeymoon, but had a side interest in the history and customs of the Markovian Nucleus. "My people know so little about you," he said, "it would be a great privilege to be able to take back information that would increase our mutual understanding."

"All that the Idealists have belongs to every man and every race," said Sal Karone solemnly. "What we can give you may be had for the asking. But I would give you a word of warning about my Masters."

Cameron felt the flesh of his back tingle with sudden chill as the eyes of the Id turned full upon him.

"Do not try to find out the hidden things of the Masters. That is what you have come for, is it not, Cameron Wilder? That is why you have taken so much trouble to learn the language which we speak. I say do not inquire of the things about which they do not wish to speak. My Masters are a people who cannot yet be understood by the men of other worlds. In time there will be understanding, but that time is not yet. You will only bring disaster and disappointment upon us and yourselves by attempting to hasten that time."

"I assure you I have no intention of prying," said Cameron haltingly. He fumbled for the right Markovian words. "You have misunderstood—We come only in friendship and with no intention of disturbing—"

The Id nodded sagely. "So many crises are originated by good intentions. But I am sure that now you understand the feelings of my Masters in these things that you will be concerned only with your own enjoyment while in the Nucleus. And do come to the centers of the Idealists, for there is much we can show you, and our willingness has no limits."

For a moment it was impossible for Cameron to remember that he was dealing with a mere servant of the Markovians. The Id's words were so incisive and his manner so commanding that it seemed he must be speaking in his own right.

And then his manner changed. His boldness vanished and he spoke obsequiously. "You will forgive me," he said, "but this is a matter concerning which there is much feeling."

*   *   *   *   *

Cameron Wilder was more than willing to agree with this sentiment. As he returned to his own quarters he debated telling Joyce of his encounter with the Id, deciding finally that he'd have to mention it since they'd all be traveling together, but omitting the Id's repetition of the previous warnings.

He did not meet the Markovian, nor did he encounter the Id again in the waiting quarters. It was not until they had embarked on the last leg of the journey and had been aboard the vessel for half a day that they met a second time.

The ship was not a Markovian or a terran-type vessel of any kind. Another week's wait would have been required for one of those. As it was, their quarters were not too uncomfortable although very limited. The bulk of the vessel was designed for crew and passengers very much unlike Terran or Markovian, and only a few suites were provided for accommodation of such races.

This threw the travelers to the Nucleus in close association again. Their suites opened to a common lounge deck and when Cameron and Joyce went out they found Sal Karone and the Markovian, Marthasa, already there.

The Id was on his feet instantly. With a sharp bow he introduced the newcomers to his Master. Dells Marthasa stood and extended a hand with a smile. "I believe that is your greeting on Earth, is it not?" he said.

"You must be familiar with our home world," said Cameron, returning the handshake.

"Only a little, through my studies," said the Markovian. "Enough to make me want to hear much more. Please join us. Since my *sargh* told me we would be traveling together I have looked forward to your company."

The term, *sargh*, as Cameron learned shortly was applied to all Ids attached to Markovians. It had a connotation somewhere between servant and companion. Sal Karone remained in the background, but there was no servility in his manner. His eyes remained respectfully—almost fondly; that was the right word, Cameron thought curiously—on Marthasa.

While the Id was slender in build, the Markovian was taller and bulkier. His complexion was also dark, but not quite so much so as the Id's. He was dressed in loose, highly colored attire that gave Cameron an impression of an Oriental potentate of his own world.

But somehow there was a quality in Marthasa's manner that was jarring. It would have been less so if the Markovian had been less anthropomorphic in form and feature, but Cameron found it difficult to think of him as anything but a fellow man.

A man of arrogance and ill manners, and completely unaware that he was so.

It was apparent in his gestures and in the negligence with which he leaned back and surveyed his companions. "You'll be surprised when you see the Nucleus," he said. "We sometimes hear of rumors circulated among Council worlds that Markovian culture is rather backward."

"I've never heard anything of that kind," said Cameron. "In fact we've heard almost nothing at all of the Nucleus. That's why we decided to come."

"I'm sure we can make you glad you did. Don't you think so, Karone?"

The face of the Id was very sober as he nodded solemnly and said, "Indeed, Master." His burning eyes were boring directly into Cameron's own.

"I want to hear about your people, about Earth," said Marthasa. "Tell me what you would like to see and do while you're in the Nucleus."

While Joyce answered, explaining they hardly knew what there was to be seen, Cameron's attention was fixed by the problem of the strange relationship between the two men—the two races. In the face of the Id there seemed a serenity, a dignity that the Markovian would never know. Why had the Ids failed to lift themselves out of servility to a state of independence, he wondered?

Joyce explained the story about their honeymoon trip and built their interest in Markovian culture as casual indeed. As she went on, Marthasa seemed to be struck by a sudden thought.

"I insist that you make your headquarters with me during your stay," he said. "I can see that you learn everything possible about the Nucleus while you are here. My son is a Chief

Historian at our largest research library and my daughter has the post of Assistant Curator at our Museum of Science and Culture. You will never have a better opportunity to examine the culture of the Nucleus!"

Cameron winced inwardly at the thought of Marthasa's companionship during their whole stay, and yet the Markovian's statement might be perfectly true—there would be no better opportunity to make their study.

"We have an official note of welcome from your Executive Head, Premier Jargla," he said. "While we would be very happy to accept your invitation, it may be that he has different plans for our reception."

Marthasa waved a hand. "I shall arrange for my appointment as your official host. Consider it agreed upon!"

It was agreed. But Joyce was not as optimistic as Cameron in regarding it an aid to their study. "If they have a general aversion to talking about their pirate ancestry, Marthasa is just the boy to put us off the track," she said. "If he gets a clue to what we really want to know, he'll keep us busy looking at everything else until we give up and go home."

Cameron leaned back in the deep chair with his hands behind his head. "It's not too hard to imagine Marthasa's great-great-grandfather running down vessels in space and pillaging helpless cities on other planets. The veneer of civilization on him doesn't look very thick."

"It's not hard to imagine Marthasa doing it," said Joyce. "A scimitar between his teeth would be completely in character!"

"If all goes well, you will probably see just that—figuratively speaking, of course. Where a cultural shift has been so great as this one you are certain to see evidence of both levels in conflict with one another. It's like a geologic fault line. Once we learn enough about the current mores the anomalies will stand out in full view. That's what we want to watch for."

"One thing that's out of character right now is his offer of assistance through his son, the Chief Historian," said Joyce. "That doesn't check with the previous invitations to stay home. Once they let us have access to their historical records we'll have them pegged."

"We haven't got it yet," said Cameron. "We can't be sure just what they'll let us see. But for my money I'd just as soon tackle the question of the Ids. Sal Karone is twice the man Marthasa is, yet he acts like he has no will of his own when the Markovian is around."

"The Roman-slave relationship," said Joyce. "The Markovians probably conquered a large community of the Ids in their pirate days and brought them here as slaves. And I'll bet they are very much aware that the Ids are the better men. Marthasa knows it. That's why he has to put on a show in front of Sal Karone. He's the old Roman merchant struggling to keep up his conviction of superiority before the Greek scholar slave."

"The Ids aren't supposed to be slaves. According to the little that's known they are completely free. I'm going to get Marthasa's version of it, anyway. Fothergill and the Foundation can't object to that much investigation of the Ids."

He found the Markovian completely willing to talk about his *sargh*. On the last day of the voyage they managed to be alone for a time without the presence of Sal Karone.

Marthasa shook his head in answer to Cameron's question. "No, the *sargh* is not a slave—not in the sense I believe you mean it. None of the Ids are. It's a matter of religion with them to be attached to us the way they are. They have some incomprehensible belief that their existence is of no value unless they are serving their fellow beings. Since that means *all* of them they can't be satisfied by serving each other so they have to pick on some other race.

"I don't recall when they first showed up in the Nucleus, but it's been many generations ago. There've been Ids in my family for a half dozen generations anyway."

"They had space flight, so they came under their own power?" Cameron asked incredulously.

"No. Nothing like that. You can't imagine *them* building spaceships can you? They migrated at first as lowest-class passengers on the commercial lines. Nobody knows just where they came from. They don't even know their home worlds. At first we tried to persuade them to go somewhere else, but then we saw how useful they could be with their fanatic belief in servitude.

"At present there is probably no family in the Nucleus that doesn't have at least one Id *sargh*. Many of us have one for every member of the family." Marthasa paused. The tone of his voice changed. "When you've had one almost all your life as I've had Sal Karone it—well, it does something to you."

"What do you mean?" Cameron asked cautiously.

"Consider the situation from Sal Karone's point of view. He has no life whatever that is his own. His whole purpose is to give me companionship and satisfy my requirements. And I don't have to force him in any way. It's all voluntary. He's free to leave, even, any time he wants to. But I'm certain he never will."

"Why do you feel so sure of this?"

"It's hard to explain. I feel as if I've become so much a part of him that he couldn't survive alone any more. He's the one who's made it that way, not me. I have become indispensable to his existence. That's the way I explain it to myself. Most of my friends agree that this is about right."

"It's rather difficult to understand a relationship like that— unless you put it in terms I am familiar with on Earth."

"Yes—? What would it be called among your people?"

"When a man so devotes his life to another we say it is because of love."

Marthasa considered the word. "You would be wrong," he said. "It is just that in some way we have become indispensable to the Ids. They're parasites, if you want to put it that way. But they provide us a relationship we can get nowhere else, and that does us a great deal of good. That's what I meant when I said it does something to us."

"What about the Id's own culture? Haven't they any community ties among themselves, or do they ignore their own kind?"

"We've never investigated very much. I suppose some of our scholars know the answer to that, but the rest of us don't. The Ids have communities, all right. Not all of them are in service as *sarghs* at one time. They have little groups and communities on the outskirts of our cities, but they don't amount to much. As a race they are simply inferior. They don't have the capacity for a strong culture of their own, so they can't exist independently and build a social structure like other people. It's this religion of theirs that does it. They won't let go of it, and as long as they hang onto it they can't stand on their own feet. But you don't need to feel sorry for them. We treat them all right."

"Of course—didn't mean to imply anything else," said Cameron. "Do you know if there are other Id groups serving in other galaxies?"

"Must be thousands of them altogether. Out beyond the Nucleus, away from your galaxy, you can't find a planet anywhere that isn't using the Ids. It's a wonderful setup. The Ids get what they want, and we get *sarghs* with nothing like the slave relationship you had in mind. With slaves there's rebellion, constant need of watchfulness, and no genuine companionship. A *sargh* is different. He can be a man's friend."

III

They came out of the darkness of Transpace that evening and the stars returned in the glory of a million closely gathered suns. The Markovian Nucleus lay in a galaxy of tightly packed stars that made bright the nights of all their planets. It was a spectacle for Cameron, who had traveled but little away from the Solar System, and for Joyce who had never traveled at all.

Marthasa and Sal Karone were with them in the lounge watching the screens as the ship changed drives. The Markovian squinted a moment and pointed to a minor dot near the corner of the view. "That's our destination. Another six hours and you can set foot on the best planet in the whole Universe!"

If it had been mere enthusiasm, Cameron could have taken it with tolerant understanding. But Marthasa's smugness and arrogance had not deserted him once since the beginning of this leg of the trip. Objectively, as a cultural facet to be examined, it was interesting, but Cameron agreed with Joyce that it was going to be difficult to live with.

The unsolved puzzle, however, was Sal Karone. It was obvious that the Id was sensitive to the gauche ways of the Master, yet his equally obvious devotion was unwavering.

Marthasa had sent word ahead to the government that he desired the Terrans to be his guests. Evidently he was a person of influence for assent was returned immediately.

His planet was a colorful world, banded by huge, golden deserts and pinkish seas. The dense vegetation of the habitable areas was blue with only a scattered touch of green. Cameron wondered about the chemistry involved.

The landing was made at a port that bordered a sea. The four of them were the only ones disembarking, and before the car that met them had reached the edge of the city the ship was gone again.

A pirates' lair, Cameron thought, without the slightest touch of amusement. The field looked very old, and from it he could imagine raiders had once taken off to harass distant shipping and do wanton destruction of cities and peoples on innocent worlds.

He watched the face of Marthasa as they rode through the city. There was a kind of Roman splendor in what they saw, and there was a crude Roman pride in the Markovian who was their host. The arrogance, that was not far from cruelty, could take such pride in the sweep of spaceships embarking on missions of murder and plunder.

And yet all this barbarism had been put aside. Only the arrogance remained, expressed in Marthasa's tone as he called their attention to the features of the city and landscape through which they passed. It wasn't pleasing particularly to Terran tastes, but Cameron guessed that it represented a considerable accomplishment to the Markovians. Stone appeared to be the chief building material, and, while the craftsmanship was exact, the lines of the structures lacked the grace of the Greek and Roman monuments of which Cameron was reminded.

They came at last to the house of Marthasa. There was no doubt now that he was a man of wealth or importance—probably both. He occupied a vast, villa-like structure set on a low hill overlooking the city. It was a place of obvious luxury in the economic scale of the Markovians.

They were assigned spacious quarters overlooking a garden of incredible colors beyond the transparent wall facing it. Sal Karone was also assigned duties as their personal attendant, which Cameron grasped intuitively was a gesture of supreme honor among the Markovians. He thanked Marthasa profusely for this courtesy.

After getting unpacked they were shown through the house and grounds and met Marthasa's family. His wife was a woman of considerable beauty even by Terran standards, but there was a sharpness in her manner and a sense of coldness in the small black eyes that repelled Cameron and Joyce even as the thoughtless actions of Marthasa had done.

Cameron looked carefully for the same qualities in the three smaller children who were at home, and found them easily. In none of them was there the aura of serenity possessed by the Id servants.

When they were finally alone that night Cameron sat down to make some notes on their observations up to date. "The fault line I mentioned is so obvious you can't miss it," he said to Joyce. "It's as if they're living one kind of life because they think it's the thing to do, but all their thoughts and feelings are being drawn invisibly in another direction—and they're half ashamed of it."

"Maybe the Ids have something to do with it. Remember Marthasa's statement that the relationship of the *sarghs* does something to the Markovians? If we found out exactly what that something is, we might have the answer."

Cameron shook his head. "I've tried to fit it together that way, too, but it just doesn't add up. The basic premise of the Ids is asceticism and there never was any strength in that idea. Marthasa is probably right in his estimate of the Ids. They have achieved an internal serenity but only through compensating their basic weakness with the crude strength of the Markovians and other races to which they cling. They haven't the strength to build a civilization of their own. Certainly they haven't got the power to influence the whole Nucleus. No—we'll have to look a good deal farther than the Ids before we find the answer. I'm convinced of that, even though I'd like to find out exactly what makes *them* tick. Maybe next trip—"

*   *   *   *   *

The following days were spent in almost profitless activity as far as their basic purpose in being in the Nucleus was concerned. Marthasa and his wife took them on long tours through the city and into the scenic areas of the continent. They promised trips over the whole planet and to other worlds of the Nucleus. There seemed no end to the sight-seeing that was proposed for them to do.

Cameron improved his facility with the language, and Joyce was beginning to get along without the translator. They were introduced to a considerable number of other Markovians, including the official representative of Premier Jargla. This gave them added contact with the Markovian character, but Marthasa and his family seemed so typical of the race that scarcely anything new was learned from the others.

At no time was anything hinted in reference to the original reluctance to have the Terrans visit the Nucleus. All possible courtesy was shown them now, and Cameron dared not mention the invitations to stay home. He felt the situation was as penetrable as a thick wall of sponge rubber backed by a ten-foot foundation of steel.

After three weeks of this, however, he cautiously broached the subject of meeting the son and daughter of Marthasa in regard to visiting the library and museum. He had met each of them just once and found them rather cool to his presence. He had not dared express his interest in their specialties at that time.

Marthasa was favorable and apologetic, however. "I have intended to arrange it," he said. "There have been so many other things to do that I have neglected your interest in these things. We won't neglect it any longer.

Suppose we make an appointment for this afternoon? Zlenon will be able to give you his personal attention."

Zlenon was Marthasa's son, who held the position of Chief Historian at the research library. He was more slender and darker than his father, and lacking in his volubility and glad-handedness.

He greeted Cameron's request with a tolerant smile. "You have to be quite specific, Mr. Wilder, when you say you would like to know about the history of the Markovian Nucleus. You understand the Nucleus consists of over a hundred worlds and has a composite history extending back more than thirty thousand of your years in very minute detail."

Cameron countered with a helpless shrug and smile. "I'm afraid I'll have to depend on your good nature to guide me through such a mass. I don't intend to become a student of Markovian history, of course, but perhaps you have adequate summaries with which a stranger could start. Going backward, let us say, for perhaps two or three hundred Terran years?"

"Of course—some very excellent ones are available—" He moved toward the reading table nearby and began punching a selection of buttons.

As Cameron and Joyce moved to follow, Marthasa waved a hand expansively and started out the other way. "I can see you're going to be set for a while. I'll just leave you here, and send the car back after I reach the house. Don't be late for dinner."

They nodded and smiled and turned to Zlenon. The Markovian was watching them with pin-point eyes. "I wondered if there was any *particular* problem in which you might be interested," he said calmly. "If there is—?"

Cameron shook his head hastily. "No—certainly not. Just general information—"

The Historian turned his attention to the table and began explaining its use to the Terrans, showing how they could obtain recording of any specific material they wished to choose. It would appear in either printed or pictorial form or could be had on audio if they wanted it. Once he was certain they could make their own selections he left them to their study.

"This is the best break we could possibly have hoped for," Joyce whispered as Zlenon disappeared from their sight. "We can get anything we want in the whole library if I understand the operation of this gadget the way I think I do."

"That's the way it looks to me," Cameron answered. "But don't get your hopes too high. There must be a catch in it somewhere, the way they were trying to shoo us away from coming here."

*   *   *   *   *

They punched the buttons for the history of the planet they were on, scanning slowly from the present to earlier years. There were endless accountings of trading and commercial treaties between members of the Nucleus as shifts of economic balance occurred. There were stories of explorations and benevolent contacts with races on the outer worlds. Details of their most outstanding scientific discoveries, which seemed to come with profligate rapidity—

Cameron whipped back through the pages of the histories, searching only for a single item, one clue to the swift evolution from barbarism to peaceful co-operation. After an hour he was in the middle of that critical period when the Council despaired of its inability to cope with the Markovian menace.

But the stories of commerce and invention and far-flung exchange with other peoples continued. Nowhere was there any reference to the violence of the period. They went back two hundred—five hundred years—beyond the time when Council members first made contact with the Nucleus.

There was nothing.

Cameron sat back in complete puzzlement as it became apparent that it was useless to go back further. "The normal thing would be for them to brag all over the place about their great conquests. Even races who become comparatively civilized citizens ordinarily let themselves go when it comes to history. If they've had a long record of conquest and bloodshed, they say so with plenty of chest pounding. Of course, it's padded out to reflect their righteous conquest over tyranny, but it's always there in *some* form.

"But nothing up to now has been normal about the development of the Markovian problem and this really tops it off—the complete omission of any reference to their armed conquests."

"Maybe this planet didn't participate very much. Perhaps only a small number of the Nucleus worlds were responsible for it," said Joyce.

Cameron shook his head. "No. The Council records show that the Nucleus as a unit was responsible, and that virtually all the worlds are specifically mentioned. And even if this one had been out of it completely you could still expect references to it because there was constant interchange with most of the other planets. We can try another one, though—"

They tried one more, then a half dozen in quick scanning. They swept through a summarization of the Nucleus as a whole during that critical period.

There was nothing to show that the Markovians had ever been anything but peace-loving citizens intent on pursuit of science, commerce, and the arts.

"This could have been rigged for our special benefit," said Joyce thoughtfully as they ended the day's futile search. "They didn't want to apply enough pressure to keep us from coming, but they did want to make sure we wouldn't find out anything about their past."

Cameron shook his head slowly. "It couldn't have been done in the time they've had. Simply cutting out what they didn't want to show us wouldn't have done it. There's too much cross reference to all periods involved. It's a complete phony, but it's not something done on the spur of the moment just for our benefit. It's too good for that."

"Maybe they've had it for a *long* time—just in case somebody like us should come along."

"It's possible, but I don't think that's right either," said Cameron. "I can't give you any reason for thinking so—except the phoniness goes deeper than merely deceiving an investigator. Somehow I have the feeling that the Markovians are even deceiving themselves!"

*   *   *   *   *

They left the building and took the car back to the house of Marthasa without seeing Zlenon again. Their Markovian host was waiting. Cameron thought he sensed a trace of tension in Marthasa that wasn't there before as he led them to seats in the garden.

"We don't like to boast about the Nucleus," he said with his customary volubility, "but we have to admit we are proud of our science and technology. Few civilizations in the Universe can match it. That's not to disparage the fine accomplishments of the Terrans, you understand, but it's only *natural* that out here on these older worlds—"

They listened half attentively, trying in their imaginations to pierce the armor he used to defend so frantically the thing the Markovians did not want the outer worlds to know anything about.

The talk went on during mealtime. Marthasa's wife caught the spirit of it and they both regaled the Terrans with accounts of the grandeur of Markovian exploits. Cameron grew more and more depressed by it, and as they retired to their rooms early he began to realize how absolutely complete was the impasse into which they had been driven.

"They've let us in," he said to Joyce. "They've shown us the history they've written of themselves. There's no way in the Universe we can stand up and boldly challenge that history and call them the liars we know they are."

"But they must know of the histories written on other Council worlds about their doings," said Joyce. "Maybe we could reach a point where we could at least ask about them. Ask how it is that other histories show that a hundred and twenty years ago a fleet of Markovian ships swept unexpectedly out of space and looted and decimated the planet Lakcaine VI. Ask why the Markovian history says only that the Nucleus concluded six new commercial treaties to the benefit of all worlds concerned in that period, without any mention of Lakcaine VI."

"When you start asking questions like that you've got to be ready to run. And if it fizzles out you've lost all chance of coming back for a second try. That could fizzle out because they simply deny the validity of all history outside their own."

"Then we might as well pack and go home if you're not going to challenge any of this stuff they hand out. We won't find the answer by standing around and taking *their* word on everything."

"I forgot to tell you one thing," Cameron said slowly. "We may not have to take their word for it. Someone else here knows the truth of the situation, also."

"Who?"

"The Ids." He told her then of the warning Sal Karone had given him aboard the ship on the way to the Nucleus, the statement that "My Masters are a people who cannot yet be understood by the men of other worlds."

"The Ids know what the Markovians are and what they are trying to hide. I had almost overlooked that simple fact."

"But you can't go out and challenge them to tell the truth any more than you can the Markovians!" Joyce protested. "Because Sal Karone went out of his way to warn you doesn't mean he's going to get real buddy-buddy and tell you everything you want to know."

"No, of course not. But there's one little difference between him and the Markovians. He has admitted openly that he knows why we're here. None of the Markovians have done that yet. We don't have to challenge him because there already exists the tacit understanding that something is decidedly phony.

"And besides, he invited us to come and visit the Id communities outside the city. I think that's an invitation we should accept just as soon as possible."

IV

Sal Karone had not repeated his invitation that the Terrans visit the Id communities, but he showed no adverse reaction when Cameron said they would like to take him up on his previous offer.

"You will be very welcome," he said. A soft smile lightened his features. "I will notify my leaders you will come."

With a start, Cameron realized that the existence of any kind of community probably implied leaders, but he had ignored this in view of Marthasa's insistence that the Ids had no culture of their own. He wondered just how untrue that assertion might be.

For the first time, he sensed genuine disapproval in the attitude of Marthasa when he mentioned plans to go with Sal Karone to the Id centers. "There's nothing out there you'd want to see," the Markovian said. "Their village is only a group of crude huts in the forest. It'll be a waste of your time to go out there when there's so much else we could show you."

"Sal Karone suggested the visit before we arrived," said Cameron. "He'd be hurt if we turned him down. Perhaps just to satisfy him—"

Angry indecision hid behind Marthasa's eyes. "Well—maybe that makes it different," he said finally. "We try to do everything possible to make the Ids happy. It's up to you if you want to waste your time on the visit."

"I think I do. Sal Karone has been very attentive and pleasant to us. It's a small favor in return."

*   *   *   *   *

Early in the morning, two days later, they left with Sal Karone directing them to the Idealist center. They discovered that the term, at the edge of the city, was a mere euphemism. It was a long two-hour trip at the high speed of which the Markovian cars were capable.

The city itself vanished, and a thickly wooded area took its place during the last half of the journey, reminding them of the few remote, peaceful forests of Earth. Then, as the car slowed, they left the highway for a rough trail that led for a number of miles back into the forest. They came at last into a clearing circled by rough wooden dwellings possessing all the appearance of crude, primitive existence on little more than a subsistence level.

"This is the village of our Chief," said Sal Karone. "He will be pleased to explain all you may wish to know about the Idealist Way."

Cameron was shocked almost beyond speech by his first sight of the clearing. He had tried to prepare for the worst, but he had told himself that the Markovian's estimate of the Ids could not be true. Now he was forced to admit that it was. In contact with all the skills of their Masters, which they would certainly be permitted to learn if they wanted to, the Ids chose primitive squalor when they were on their own.

Their serenity could be little more than the serenity of the savage who has no wants or goals and is content to merely serve those whose ambitions are greater. It was the serenity and peacefulness of death. The Ids had died—as a race—long ago. The Markovians were loud, boastful, and obnoxious, but that could be discounted as the awkwardness of youth in a race that would perhaps be very great in the Universe at a time when the Ids were wholly forgotten.

Cameron felt depressed by the sight. He began to doubt the wisdom of his coming here in hope of finding an answer to the Markovian deception. The warning of Sal Karone on shipboard seemed now like nothing more than a half ignorant demonstration of loyalty toward the Markovian Masters. Possibly there had been some talk which the Id had overheard and he had taken it upon himself to warn the Terrans—knowing perhaps nothing of the matter which the Markovians were reluctant to expose.

If he could have done so gracefully, Cameron felt he would have turned and gone back without bothering with the interview. His curiosity about the Ids themselves had all but vanished. The answer to their situation was obvious. And he had maintained such high hope that somehow his expectation in them would be fulfilled during this visit.

There was a satisfying cleanliness apparent in everything as Sal Karone led them to the largest of the buildings. Joyce seemed to be enjoying herself as she surveyed the surroundings with an interest Cameron had lost.

As they entered the doorway a thin, straight old man with a white beard arose from a chair and approached them in greeting. The ancient, conventional, patriarchal order, Cameron thought. He could see the whole setup in a nutshell right now. Squalid communities like this where the too-old and the too-young were nurtured on the calcified traditions to which nothing was ever added. The able serving in the homes of the Markovians, providing sustenance for themselves and those who depended on them. The Markovians were generous indeed in not referring to the Ids as slaves. There was little else they could ever be called.

The Chief was addressed as Venor by Sal Karone, who introduced them. "It is kind of you to include our village in your visit to the Nucleus," said Venor. "There are many more spectacular things to see."

"There is often greatest wisdom in the least spectacular," said Cameron, trying to sound like a sage. "Sal Karone was kind enough to invite us to your center and said there was much you could show us."

"The things of the soul are not possible to *show*," said Venor gently. "We wish there were time that we might teach you some of the great things our people have learned in their long wanderings. I am told that your profession and your purpose in being here is the study of races and their actions and the things they have learned."

With a start, Cameron came to greater attention. He was certain he had never given any such information in the presence of Sal Karone or Marthasa. Yet even Venor knew he was a sociologist! Here was the first knowledge that must lie behind the evidence of the undercurrent of objections of the Markovian representative in the Council and Premier Jargla.

And this primitive patriarch was in possession of it.

Relations between the individuals of this planet were something far more complex than Cameron had assumed. He hesitated a moment before speaking. Just why had this bait been so innocently thrown to him? Marthasa had never mentioned it. Yet had the Markovians asked for an attempt to get an admission from him for their own purposes? And what purposes—?

He abandoned caution, and nodded. "Yes, that is the thing I am interested in. I had hoped to study the history and ways of the Markovians. As Sal Karone has told me, they don't want strangers to make such a study. You are perhaps not so unwilling to be known—?"

"We wish the entire Universe might know of us and be as we are."

"You hardly make that possible, subjugating your identity so completely to that of another race. The worlds will never know of you unless you become strong and unified as a people and obtain a name of your own."

"Our name is known," said Venor. "We are the Idealists. You will not find many worlds on which we are unknown, and they call us the ones who serve. Even on your world you have the saying of a philosopher who taught that any who would be master should become the servant of all. Your people once understood it."

"Not as a literal undertaking," said Cameron. "You can't submerge your entire racial identity as you have done. That is not what the saying meant."

"To us it does," said Venor solemnly. "We would master the Universe—and therefore we must serve it. That is the core of the law of the Idealists."

*   *   *   *   *

Cameron let his gaze scan through the window to the small clearing in the thick forest, to the circle of wooden houses. *We would master the Universe*—he restrained a smile.

"You cannot believe this," said Venor, "because you have never understood the mark of the servant or the mark of the master. How often is there difficulty in distinguishing one from the other!"

And how often do the illusions of the mind ease the privations of the body, Cameron thought. So that was the source of the Idealist serenity. Wherever they went they considered themselves the masters through service—and conversely, those they served became the slaves, he supposed. It was a pleasant, easy philosophy that hurt no one. Except the ones who believed it. They died the moment they accepted it, for all initiative and desire were gone.

"The master is he who guides the destiny of a man or a race," said Venor almost in meditation. "He is not the man who gathers or disperses the wealth, or who builds the cities and the ships to the stars. The master is he who teaches what must be done with these things and how a people shall expend their lives."

"And the Markovians do this, in obedience to you?" said Cameron whimsically.

"Wherever my people are," answered Venor, "strife ceases and peace comes. Who can do this is master of worlds."

There was a strange solemnity about the voice and figure of the old Idealist that checked the sense of ridiculousness in Cameron. It seemed somehow strangely moving.

"You believe the worlds are better," he asked gently, "just because you are there?"

"Yes," said Venor, "because we are there."

There was a pathos about it that fired Cameron's anger. On scores of worlds there were primitive groups like this one, blinding themselves with a glory that didn't exist, in the grip of ancient, meaningless traditions. The younger ones—like Sal

Karone—were intelligent, worth salvaging, but they could never be lifted out of this mire of false belief unless they could be shown how empty it was.

"Nothing you have said explains the mystery of how this great thing is accomplished," said Cameron almost angrily. "Even if we wanted to believe it were true, it is still as utterly incomprehensible as before we came."

"There is a saying among us," said Venor kindly. "Translated into your tongue it would be: How was the wild dog tamed, and a saddle put upon the fierce stallion?"

*   *   *   *   *

Stubbornly, then, Venor would say no more about the philosophy of the Idealists. He spoke freely of the many other worlds upon which the Idealists lived and served, and he affirmed the tradition that they did not even know the place of their origin, the planet that might have been their home world.

He was evasive, however, when Cameron asked when the first contact was made between his people and the Markovians. There was something that the Ids, too, were holding back, the sociologist thought, and there was no apparent reason for it.

Recklessly, he decided nothing could be lost by attempting to blast for it. "Why have the Markovians consistently lied to us?" he said. "They've given us their history—and if your people know the feelings of other worlds they know this history is a lie. Only a few generations ago the Markovians pirated and plundered these worlds, and now they pose as little tin gods with a silver halo. Why?"

Sal Karone stood by with a look of horror on his face, but Venor made no sign of alarm at this forbidden question. He merely inclined his held slowly and repeated, "How was the wild dog tamed, and a saddle put upon the fierce stallion?"

*   *   *   *   *

That was the end of the interview. The Ids insisted, however, that he inspect the rest of the village and they personally guided the Terrans on the tour. Cameron's trained eye took in at a glance, however, the evidence supporting his previous conclusion. The artifacts and buildings demonstrated a primitive forest culture. The other individuals he saw were almost entirely the old and very young—the ones unsuitable as servants to the Markovians. Venor explained that family life among them paralleled in general that of the Masters. Whole Idealist families lived and served as units in the Markovian household. Exceptions existed in the case of Sal Karone and others of his age who were separated from their families and had not yet begun their own.

As they returned to the car Venor took their hands. He pressed Cameron's warmly and looked into his eyes with deep sincerity. "You have made us glad by your presence," he said. "And when the time comes for you to return, we shall repay all the pleasure you have given us."

"I'm afraid we won't be able to do that," said Cameron. "We appreciate your hospitality, but I'm sure time will not permit us to visit you again, as much as we'd like to." In the past few minutes he had reached the conclusion that further research on this whole planet was futile. The best thing they could do was go somewhere else in the Nucleus and make a fresh start.

Venor shook his head, smiling. "We will see each other again, Joyce and Cameron. I feel that the day will be very soon."

It was senseless to let himself be irritated by the senile patriarch who spoke out of a world of illusion but Cameron could not help feeling nettled as he started back to the city. Somehow it seemed impossible to regard Venor as merely a specimen for sociological research. The Chief of the Idealists reached out of his unreal world and made his contact with the Terrans a personal thing—almost as if he had spent all his life waiting for their coming. There was a sense of intimacy against which Cameron rebelled, and yet it was not an unpleasant thing.

Cameron's mind oscillated between the annoyance of Venor's calm assertion that they would be back shortly, and the nonsense of the Id belief that they controlled the civilizations in which they were servants. How was the wild dog tamed, and a saddle put upon the fierce stallion?

He smiled faintly to himself, wondering if the Markovians were fully aware that the Ids regarded them as tamed dogs and saddled stallions. They couldn't help knowing, of course, but it was hard to imagine Marthasa and his wife being very much amused by such an estimate. The situation would be intolerable, however, if it were met by anything except amusement. It might be a mildly explosive subject, but he was going to find out about that one small item before moving on, anyway, Cameron decided.

*   *   *   *   *

Sal Karone was strangely silent during the whole of the return trip. He offered no comments and made only brief, noncommittal replies to questions about the country through which they passed. He seemed depressed by the results of their visit. Probably because the violation of his warning to not question the lives of the Markovians. It was a curious evidence of their completely unreal, proprietary attitude in respect to their Masters. They'd have to investigate Marthasa's response as thoroughly as possible. There seemed to be no taboo on discussion of the Ids with him.

His annoyance at their acceptance of the invitation to the Id village appeared to have vanished as he greeted them upon their return. "We delayed eating, thinking you'd be back in time. If you'll join us in the dining room as soon as you're ready—?"

The villa of Marthasa seemed different after the day's experience with the Ids, although Cameron was certain nothing had changed either in a physical way or in their relations with the Markovians. It was as if his senses had been somehow sharpened to detect an undercurrent of feeling of which he had previously been unaware. Glancing at Joyce, he sensed she felt the same.

"I have the feeling that we missed something," she said, as they changed clothes to join Marthasa and his wife. "There was something Venor wanted us to know and wouldn't say. I would almost like to go back there again before we go away."

Cameron was surprised at his own annoyance with Joyce's statement. It reflected the impressions in his own mind which he was trying to ignore. "Nonsense," he said. "There's no use trying to read great profundity in the words of an old patriarch of the woods. He's nothing except what he appears to be."

The Markovians talked easily of Venor and the rest of the Ids. "We have tried to get him to join us in the city," said

Marthasa as the meal began, "but he won't hear of it. It seems to give him a sense of importance to live out there alone with his retinue and have the other Ids come to him with their problems. He's a kind of arbiter and patriarch to all of them for many miles around."

While Marthasa talked Cameron tried to bring his awareness of all the varied facets of the problem together and see it whole, as he now understood it. The Markovians, a vast pirate community, had voluntarily abandoned freebooting for reasons yet to be discovered. They had turned their backs upon it so forcibly that they hid even the history of their depredations. And one of their last acts must have been the capture of a large colony of Idealists who were forced into servitude. Now the Ids compensated their enslavement by the religious belief that service made them masters over the ex-pirates, convincing themselves that *they* had changed the Markovians, taming them like wild dogs, saddling them as fierce stallions—

Cameron wondered if he dared, and then dismissed the thought that there could be any risk. It was too ridiculous!

$$*\qquad*\qquad*\qquad*\qquad*$$

There was even a half-malicious smile on his lips as he broke into Marthasa's conversation. "One of the things that made me very curious today," he said, "was the general reaction of your people to the Idealist illusion that they have *tamed* you—as expressed in their aphorism about how was the wild dog—?"

He never finished. Across the table the faces of the Markovians had frozen in sudden bitterness. The shield of friendliness vanished under the cold glare from their eyes.

Marthasa's lips seemed to curl as he whispered, "So you came like all the rest! And we wanted so much to believe you were honest. A study! A chance to find material for lies about the Nucleus to spread among all the Council worlds."

He continued almost sadly, "You will be confined to your quarters until transfer authorities can arrange for your return to Earth. And you may be sure that never again will such a scheme get one of your kind into the Nucleus again."

But there was no hint of sadness in his wife's face. She glared coldly. "I said they should never had been permitted to come!"

Cameron rose in sudden bewildered protest. "I assure you we have no intention—" he began.

And then he stopped. In one moment of incredible clarity while they stood there, eyes locked in bitter stares, he understood. He knew the myth was not a myth. It was cold, unbelievable reality. The Ids *had* tamed the Markovians.

In a moment of fear he wondered if it were anything more than a thin shell that could be shattered by a whisper from a stupid dabbler in cultures, who really knew nothing at all about the profession to which he pretended.

V

As if upon some secret signal Sal Karone appeared from the serving room at their left.

"Our visitors are no longer our guests," Marthasa said sharply with accusing eyes still upon Cameron. "They will remain in their rooms until time for deportation.

"I trust it will not be necessary to use force," he said directly to Cameron.

"Of course not. But won't you let me explain—won't you even allow an apology for breaking a taboo we did not understand?"

"Is it not taboo among all civilized peoples, including your own, to invent and spread lies about those who wish you only well?"

It was useless to argue, Cameron saw. He turned, taking Joyce's arm, and allowed Sal Karone to lead them back to their rooms. As they paused at the doorway the Id spoke without expression on his dark face. "This is not a good thing, Cameron Wilder. It would have been best for you to have considered my warning."

He turned and stepped away, locking the door behind him.

Joyce slumped on the bed in dejection. "This is a fine fix we've got ourselves into, being declared *persona non grata* before we even get a good start! They'll remember *that* back home when A Study of the Metamorphosis of the Markovian Nucleus is mentioned in professional circles!"

"Don't rub it in," Cameron said, half angrily. "How was I to know that was such a vicious taboo? It can't be any secret to the Markovians that the Ids look upon them as tamed. Why should they get their hackles up because *I* mentioned it?"

"All I know is we're washed up as of now. What do we do when we get back home?"

Cameron stood with his back to her, looking through the windows to the garden beyond. "I'm not thinking of that," he said. "Can't you see we haven't failed? We've almost got it—the thing we came to find. We *knew* why the Markovians suddenly became good Indians. The Ids actually did tame them. We've got to find out how such an apparently impossible thing could be done."

"Do you really believe that's what happened?" asked Joyce.

Cameron nodded. "It's the only thing there is to believe. If it weren't true, Marthasa and his wife would have laughed it off as nonsense. Getting all huffy and talking about deportation for cooking up lies is the best proof you could ask for that we hit pay dirt. Don't ask me how I think the Ids could do it. *That's* what I'm going to find out."

"How?"

"I don't know."

But he did have an idea that if he could somehow get word to the old Id chieftain help could be had. He knew he was straining to believe things he wanted to believe, yet it seemed as if this were almost the very thing Venor had tried to convey the day before but had left unspoken.

There was only one possibility of establishing contact, however, and that was through Sal Karone. A remote chance indeed, Cameron thought, in view of the relationship between the Markovian and his *sargh*. As a last resort it was worth trying, however.

It looked as if they would not have even this chance as the evening grew darker. Cameron kept watch through the windows in the hope of signaling Sal Karone in case he should appear. They hoped he might come to the room for a final check of their needs for the night as he usually did.

But he did not appear.

*   *   *   *   *

Cameron finally went to bed after Joyce was long asleep. He turned restlessly, beating his mind with increasing wonder as to how it could be so incredibly true that the Idealists were the actual masters of the Nucleus. That they had somehow tamed the murderous, piratical Markovians. He couldn't have known this was it!

One thing he could understood, however, was the Markovians reluctance to have visitors—and their careful watch over them. Marthasa had been more than a host, he thought. He was a guard as well, trying to keep the Terrans from discovering the unpleasant reality concerning the influence of the Ids. He had slipped in allowing the visit to Venor.

At dawn there was the sound of their door opening and Cameron whirled from his dressing, hopeful it might be Sal Karone. It was Marthasa, however, grim and distant. "I have obtained word that your deportation can be accomplished today. Premier Jargla has been informed and concurs. The Council has been notified and offers no protestations. You will ready yourselves before the evening hour."

He slammed the door behind him. Joyce turned down the covers in the other room and sat up. "I wonder if he isn't even going to feed us today?"

Cameron made no answer. He finished dressing hurriedly and kept a frantic watch for any sign of Sal Karone.

At last there was a knock on the door and the Id appeared with breakfast on a cart. Cameron exhaled with relief that it was not one of the other *sarghs* in the household.

Sal Karone eyed them impassively as he wheeled in and arranged the food on the table by a window. Cameron watched, estimating his chances.

"Your Chief, Venor, was very kind to us yesterday," he said quietly. "Our biggest regret in leaving is that our conversation with him must go unfinished."

Sal Karone paused. "Were there things you had yet to say to him?" he asked.

"No—there were things Venor wanted to tell us. You heard him. He wanted us to come back. It is completely impossible for us to see him again before we go?"

Sal Karone straightened and set the utensils on the table. "No, it is not impossible. I have been instructed to bring you back to the village if it should be your request."

Cameron felt a surge of eager excitement within him. "When? Our deportation is scheduled for today. How can we get there? How can we avoid Marthasa and the Markovians?"

"Stand very quietly," said Sal Karone, that sense of power and command in his voice and bearing as Cameron had seen it once before aboard the spaceship. "Now," he said. "Close your eyes."

There was a sudden wrenching twist as if two solid surfaces had slammed them from front and back, and a third force had thrust them sideways.

They opened their eyes in the wooden house of Venor, in the village of the Idealists.

*   *   *   *   *

"We owe you apologies," said Venor. "We hope you are not harmed in any way."

Cameron stared around uncertainly. Joyce clutched his hand. "How did we—?" Cameron stammered.

"Teleportation is the descriptive term in your language, I believe," said Venor. "It was rather urgent that you come without further delay so we resorted to it. Nothing else would do in the face of Marthasa's action. Sit down if you will, please. If you wish to rest or eat, your quarters are ready."

"Our quarters—! Then you *did* expect us back. You knew this was going to happen exactly as it has!"

"Yes, I knew," said Venor quietly. "I planned it this way when word first came to us of your visit."

"I think we are entitled to explanations," Cameron said at last. "We seem to have been pieces in a game we knew nothing about."

And it had taken this long for the full impact of Venor's admission of teleportation to hit him. He closed his eyes in a moment's reaction of fright. He didn't want to believe it—and knew he must. These Idealists—who could master galaxies and tame the wild Markovians—was there anything they could not do?

"Not a game," Venor protested. "We planned this because we wanted you to see what you have seen. We wanted a man of Earth to know what we have done."

"But don't the Markovians realize the foolishness of deporting us because we stumbled onto the relationship between you and them? And if you are in control how can they issue such an order—unless you want it?"

"Our relationship is more complex than that. There are different levels of control. We operate the one that brought you here—" He let Cameron consider the implication of the unfinished statement.

Then he continued, "To understand the Markovians' reason for deporting you, consider that on Earth men have tamed wolves and made faithful, loyal dogs who can be trusted. Dogs who have forever lost the knowledge their ancestors were fierce marauders ready to rip and tear the flesh of any man or beast that came their way.

"Consider the dogs only a generation or two from the vicious wolves who were their forebears. The old urges have not entirely died, yet they want to know man's affection and trust. Could you remind them of what their kind once was without stirring up torment within them?

"So it is with the Markovians. They are peaceful and creative, but only a few generations behind them are pirates who were not fit to sit in the Councils of civilized beings. They have no tradition of culture to support them. It knocks the props out from under them, so to speak, to have it known what lies behind them. They cannot be friends with such a man. They cannot even endure the knowledge among themselves."

"Then I was right!" Cameron exclaimed. "Their phony history *was* set up to deceive their own people as well as others."

"Yes. The dog would destroy all evidence of his wolf ancestry. It has been an enormous project, but the people of the Nucleus have been at it a long time. They have concocted a consistent history which leaves out all evidence of their predatory ancestry. The items of reality which were possible to leave have been retained. The gaps between have been bridged by fictionized accounts of glorious undertakings and discoveries. Most of the Markovian science has been taken from other cultures, but now their history boasts of heroes and discoverers who never lived and who were responsible for all the great science they enjoy."

"But nothing stable can be built upon such an unhealthy foundation of self-deception!" Cameron protested.

"It is not unhealthy—not at the present moment," said Venor. "The time will come when it, too, will be thrust aside and a tremendous effort of scholarship will extract the elements of truth and find that which was suppressed. But the Markovians themselves will do it—a generation of them who can afford to laugh at the fears and fantasies of their ancestors."

"This tells us nothing of how you were able to make a creative people out of a race of pirate marauders," said Cameron.

"I gave you the key," said Venor. "It was one used long ago by your own people before it was abandoned.

"How was the savage wolf tamed to become the loyal, friendly dog? Did ancient man try to exterminate the wolves that came to his caves and carried off his young? Perhaps he tried. But he learned, perhaps accidentally, another way of conquest. He found the wolf's cubs, and learned to love them. He brought the cubs home and cared for them tenderly and his own children played with them and fed them and loved them.

"It took time, but eventually there were no more wild wolves to trouble man, because he had discovered a great friend, the dog. And man plus dog could handle wolf with ease. Dog forgot in time what his forebears were and became willing to defend man against his own kind—because man loved him.

"It happened again and again. Agricultural man hated the wild horse that ate his grain and trampled his fields. But he learned to love the horse, too, after a while. Again—no more wild horses."

"But you can't take a predatory, savage pirate and love him into decency!" Cameron protested.

"No," Venor agreed. "It is too difficult ordinarily at that level, and wasteful of time and resources. But I didn't say that is what happened. You don't tame a wolf by loving it, but the *cubs*—yes. And even pirates have cubs, who are susceptible to being loved.

"The first weapon was hate. But after learning the futility of it, sentient creatures discovered another, the succeeding evolutionary emotion. It is pure savagery in its destructive power, a thousand times more effective in annihilating the enemy.

"You've thought 'Love thy enemy' was a soft, gentle, futile doctrine! Actually, instead of merely killing the enemy it twists his personality, destroys his identity. He continues to live, but he has lost his integrity as an entity. The wolf cub never becomes an adult wolf. He becomes Dog.

"It is not a doctrine of weakness, but the ultimate weapon of destruction. It can be used to induce any orientation desired in the mind of the enemy. He'll do everything you want him to—because he has your love."

*　　*　　*　　*　　*

"How did you apply that to the Markovians?" asked Joyce in almost a whisper.

"It was one of the most difficult programs we have ever undertaken," said Venor. "There were comparatively few of us and such a tremendous population of Markovians. We had predicted long ago, even before the organization of the Council, the situation would grow critical and dangerous. By the time the Council awoke to the fact and started its futile debates we had made a strong beginning.

"We arranged to be in the path of a Markovian attack on one of the worlds where our work was completed. The Markovians were only too happy to take us into slavery and use us as victims in their brutal sports."

"You didn't deliberately fall into a trap where you allowed yourselves to be killed and tortured by them?" exclaimed Cameron.

Venor smiled. "The Markovians thought we did. We could hardly do that, of course. Our numbers were so small compared with theirs that we wouldn't have lasted very long. And, obviously, it would have been plain stupid. There is one key that must not be forgotten: An effective use of love requires an absolute superiority on the levels attainable by the individual to be tamed. So, in this case, we had to have power to keep the Markovians from slaughtering us or we would have been unable to accomplish our purpose.

"Teleportation is of obvious use here. Likewise, psychosomatic controls that can handle any ordinary wound we might permit them to inflict. We gave them the illusion of slaughtering and torturing us, but our numbers did not dwindle."

"Why did you give them such an illusion?" Joyce asked. "And you say you *permitted* them to inflict wounds—?"

Venor nodded. "We were in their households, you see, employed as slaves and assigned the care of their young. The cubs of the wolf were given into our hands to love—and to tame.

"These Markovian children were witnesses to the supposed torture and killing of those who loved them. It was a tremendous psychic impact and served to drive their influence toward the side of the slaves. And even the adults slowly recognized the net loss to them of doing away with servants so skilled and useful in household tasks and caring for the young. The games and brutality vanished spontaneously within a short time. Markovians, young and old, simply didn't want them any longer.

"During the maturity of that first generation of young on whom we expended our love our position became more secure. These were no longer wolves. They had become dogs, loyal to those who had loved them, and we could use them now against their own kind. Influences to abandon piracy against other peoples began to spread throughout the Nucleus.

"Today the Markovians are no longer a threat capable of holding the Council worlds in helpless fear. They long ago ceased their depredations. Their internal stability is rising and is almost at the point where we shall be able to leave them. Our work here is about finished."

"Surely all this was unnecessary!" Joyce said. "With your powers of teleportation and other psionic abilities you must possess it should have been easy for you to *control* the Markovians directly, force them to cease their piracy—"

"Of course," said Venor. "That would have been so much easier for us. And so futile. The Markovians would have learned nothing through being taken over by us and operated externally. They would have remained the same. But it was our desire to change them, teach them, accomplish genuine learning within them. It is always longer and more difficult this way. The results, however, are more lasting!"

"*Who* are you people—*what* are you?" Cameron said with sudden intensity. "You have teleportation—and how many other unknown psychic powers? You have forced us to believe you can tame such a vicious world as the Markovian Nucleus once was.

"But where is there a life of your own? With all your powers you must live at the whim of other cultures. Where is *your* culture? Where is your own purpose? In spite of all you have, your life is a parasitical one."

Venor smiled gently. "Is not the parent—or the teacher—the servant of the child?" he said. "Has it not always been so if a species is to rise very far in its conquest of the Universe?

"But this does not mean that the parent or teacher has no life of his own. You ask where is our culture? The culture of *all* worlds is ours. We don't have great cities and vast fleets. The wolf cubs build these for us. They carry us across space and shelter us in their cities.

"Our own energies are expended in a thousand other and more profitable ways. We have sought and learned a few of the secrets of life and mind. With these we can move as you were moved, when we choose to do so. From where I sit I can speak with any of our kind on this planet or any world of the entire Nucleus. And a few of us, united in the effort, can touch those in distant galaxies.

"What culture would you have us acquire, that we do not have?" Venor finished.

*   *   *   *   *

Without answer, Cameron arose and strode slowly to the window, his back to the room. He looked out upon the rude wooden huts and the towering forest beyond. He tried to tell himself it was all a lie. Such things couldn't be. But he could feel it now with increasing strength, as if all his senses were quickening—the benign aura, the indefinable wash of power that seemed to lap at the edge of his mind.

Out of the corner of his eye he could see Joyce's face, almost radiant as she, too, sensed it here in the presence of the Ids.

Love, as a genuine power, had been taught by every Terran philosopher of any social worth. But it had never really been tried. Not in the way the Ids understood it. Cameron felt he could only guess at the terrible discipline of mind it required to use it as they did. The analogy of the wolf cubs was all very well, and man had learned to go that far. But there is a difference when your own kind is involved, he thought.

Perhaps it was out of sheer fear of each other that men continued to try to sway with hate, the most primitive of all their weapons.

It's easy to hate, he thought. Love is hard, and because it is, the tough humans who can't achieve it and have the patience to manipulate it must scorn it. The truly weak ones, they're incapable of the stern and brutal self-discipline required of one who loves his enemy.

But men had known how. Back in the caves they had known how to conquer the wolf and the wild horse. Where had they lost it?

The vision of the buildings and the forest with its eternal peace was still in his eyes. What else could you want, with the whole Universe in the palm of your hand?

He turned sharply. "You tricked us into betraying ourselves to Marthasa, and you said that you planned it this way when you first heard of our coming. But you have not yet said why. Why did you want us to see what you had done?"

"You needed to have evidence from the Markovians themselves," said Venor. "That is why I led you to the point where the admission would be forced from them. The problem you came to solve is now answered, is it not? Is there anything to prevent you returning to Earth and writing a successful paper on the mystery of the Markovians?"

"You know very well there is," said Cameron with the sudden sense that Venor was laughing gently at him. "Who on Earth would believe what you have told me—that a handful of meek, subservient Ids had conquered the mighty Markovian Nucleus?"

He paused, looking at Joyce who returned his intense gaze.

"Is that all?" said Venor finally.

"No that is not all. After taking us to the heights and showing us everything that lies beyond, are you simply going to turn us away empty-handed?"

"What would you have us give you?"

"This," said Cameron, gesturing with his hand to include the circle of all of them, and the community beyond the window. "We want what you have discovered. Is your circle a closed one—or can you admit those who would learn of your ways but are not of your race?"

Venor's smile broadened as he arose and stepped toward them, and they felt the warm wave of acceptance from his mind even before he spoke. "This is what we brought you here to receive," he said. "But you had to ask for yourselves. We wanted men of Earth in our ranks. There are many races and many worlds who make up the Idealists. That is why it is said that the Ids do not know the home world from which they originally came. It is true, they do not. We are citizens of the Universe.

"But we have never been represented by a native of Earth, which needs us badly. Will you join us, Terrans?"

Human Error

ILLUSTRATED BY PAUL ORBIN
ORIGINALLY PUBLISHED IN *IF WORLDS OF SCIENCE FICTION*, APRIL 1956

The government was spending a billion dollars to convince the human race that men ought to be ashamed to be men— instead of errorless, cybernetics machines. But they forgot that an errorless man is a dead man....

HUMAN ERROR

During its three years' existence, the first Wheel was probably the subject of more amateur astronomical observations than any other single object in the heavens. Over three hundred reports came in when a call was issued for witnesses to the accident that destroyed the space station.

It was fortunately on the night side of Earth at the time, and in a position of bright illumination by the sun. Two of the observers had movie cameras attached to their ten-inch mirrors. The film in one of these was inadequate, but the other carried a complete record of the incident from the moment of the *Griseda's* first approach, through the pilot's fumbling attempt to correct course, and the final collision.

The scene was lost for a few seconds as the wreckage drifted out of the field. The observer had been watching through a small pilot scope, however, and had wits enough to pan by hand so that he got most of the remaining fall that was visible above his horizon as the locked remnants of the Wheel and the *Griseda* began their slow, spiral course to Earth.

By the time this scene was finished, word of the disaster was already flashing to Government centers. Joe McCauley, radio operator aboard the Wheel, had been talking with Ed Harris on the *Griseda*. As a matter of routine, all their conversation was taped, and some of this was recovered from the crash and played back at the investigation.

"—and get this," Ed was saying, "my kid had his fifth birthday just last week, and I've got him working through quadratic equations already. You've got to go some to beat that one."

"Doesn't mean a thing," said Joe. "You know how these infant brain boxes burn out. Better take him fishing and forget that stuff for a while. Hey—what the devil's going on? You got a truck driver in the control room? I just saw you out the port and it looks like you're right on top of us!"

"Jeez, I dunno. It's been like that ever since we cleared Lunaport. Sometimes I think this guy Cummins trained in a truck the way he—Hell, he's comin' up on the wrong side of the Wheel! I relayed the orders to go to the east turret. Acknowledged them himself—"

"Ed! I can see you outside the port—we're going to hit!"

The words were ripped by the shattering, grinding roar of colliding metal. Then a moment later the blast of an exploding fuel tank.

"Ed!"

"Joe—yeah, I'm here. Lights gone. Emergency power still on. Take the emergency band if you've still got a rig. I'll stand by—"

Joe switched over without comment and called Space Command Base on the emergency channel, which was always monitored. "Wheel just rammed by *Griseda*," he said. "Possible loss of orbital velocity. Extent of damage unknown."

Lieutenant James, on duty at the Base, had just returned from a three day leave and was scarcely settled in the routine of his post once more. He glanced automatically at the radar tracking screen and his face paled at the sight of the irregular figure there, slightly out of the centering circle. It was no gag.

"You're dropping," he said. "Orbital velocity must be down. Can you correct?"

"I haven't been able to contact the bridge," said Joe. "Alert all Command and have crash point computed. Stand by."

It developed that the bridge was entirely gone, along with a full thirty percent of the station. Captain West had been spared, however, being on inspection in the other sector of the station. He came on at once as Joe McCauley managed to get the communication lines repatched.

"Emergency red!" he called. "All stations report!"

One by one, the surviving crew chiefs reported conditions in their sectors. And when they were finished, they all knew their chance of survival was microscopic. Captain West ordered: "Communicate with Base. Request plotting of crash point."

"Done, sir," Joe answered.

"Command post will be established in the radio room. Emergency steering procedure will be started on command. Man all taxi craft."

It was all on the tapes that were salvaged. Everything was done that desperate men could humanly do.

*   *   *   *   *

At Base, its Commander, General Oglethorpe, was in the communications and tracking room by the time Joe McCauley had established contact with Captain West.

He picked up the mike at the table. "Plug me in to the station," he commanded the Lieutenant.

He got Joe first, but the radio operator put Captain West on as soon as he arrived in the radio room. "Hello, Frank," said General Oglethorpe in a quiet voice.

"Yes, Jack—" Captain West answered. "I'm glad you're there. Does it look pretty bad?"

"Orbital velocity is down two percent. You've been falling for eight minutes."

"That's pretty bad. I've got all steering stations manned, but only thirty percent of them are still operable. We're using the taxis to give a push too. But we haven't been able to dislodge the *Griseda*. Its inertia takes almost half our available energy."

"Couldn't you get a blast from the *Griseda's* tubes to put you in orbit?"

"Adler's got a crew out there working on it. But his controls are gone, besides his fuel tanks being opened. And even if we could get their rockets operating it's doubtful we could get the right direction of thrust. Our hope is in our own rockets, and in breaking the ship away from the station."

But the closer the massed wreckage dropped toward Earth, the higher were its requirements for orbital velocity. While the crews worked at their desperate tasks General Oglethorpe sat with his eyes on the tracking scope, and the voice of his friend in his ear. He listened to Captain West's measured commands to the men in the station and to those working to free the ship. General Oglethorpe heard the repeated reports of failure to free the *Griseda*. He listened to West's orders to transfer fuel from the ship to the station as the latter's supply ran low. He watched the continued deviation of the spot on the tracking scope.

Then he turned as a lieutenant came up behind him with a sheet of calculations. "Present rate of fall indicates a crash point in the San Francisco Bay region, sir."

The General gripped the paper, his face tightening. West said, "Did I hear correctly, Jack? The San Francisco area?"

"Yes."

"We'll have to try to keep it from happening there. I'll order the rockets shut off now. We'll save enough fuel to try to do some last minute steering as we approach Earth."

"No!" General Oglethorpe cried. "Use it now! Its effect will be the same as later. Blow the chambers apart! Get back in orbit!"

"We can't make it," West said quietly. "We've gained forward velocity, but I'll bet your computers will show us better than four percent below requirements at this orbit. Spot our crash as accurately as possible on free fall from our present position. We'll save remaining fuel for last minute steering in case we're near a city."

The General was silent then as he heard the responses come back from the men who manned the rockets and who knew that with the closing of their fuel valves their own lives had also come to an end.

"We'll want testimony account for the investigation," Oglethorpe said finally. "Get the responsible officers on the circuit—but you first, Frank—"

There was a moment of silence before Captain Frank West began speaking in changed tones. "What is there to say?" he asked, finally. "You won't need to hold an investigation. I can tell you all you need to know—all you'll ever find out at least,—right now. Your decision will be the same one so many hundreds and thousands of investigating boards have made in the past: Pilot Error.

"*Human* error! That's what killed the first Wheel, and the *Griseda*. I don't know why it happened. Adler doesn't. Neither does any other man up here with us. Those who were with Cummins in the control room are dead, but they didn't know any more than we do.

"We spent a million dollars training that man, Cummins. We believed he was the best we could produce. We measured his reflexes and his intelligence and his blood composition until we thought we knew the function and capability of every molecule in his body. And then, in just one split second, he makes the decision of a moron, fumbling when he needed to be precise."

"Just what did he do?" Oglethorpe asked gently.

"Our customary approach is to the west turret. This time he had been ordered to go to the east side because of repairs on the other end of the hub. Cummins had seen and acknowledged the orders. Apparently, they slipped his mind during approach to the Wheel and he came up on the west side. Then he remembered and tried to correct his position.

"Everything must have gone wrong then. The decision was a blunder to begin with. Wrong approach, yes. But it was suicide to attempt such a detailed maneuver that close to the station. He used his side jets and slammed the *Griseda* into the Wheel at a forty-five degree angle, locking the ship in the wreckage of the rim and in the girders of the spokes."

"Was there any previous indication of instability in the pilot that you know of? We'll get a better answer on that from Adler, but we need to know if you were aware of anything."

"The answer is no! Cummins was checked out before the start of the flight just three days ago. He was all right as far as any of our means of evaluation go. As right as any man will ever be—

"Jack, listen to me. Remember when we were back at White Sands and talked of the days when there would be a Wheel up here, and ships taking off for the Moon and for Mars?"

"I remember," said General Oglethorpe softly.

"Well, we've got a piece of that dream. But there'll never be any more, and what we've got is going to go smash unless we correct the one weakness we've never tackled properly. You'll fail again and again as long as men like Cummins can destroy twenty years' work and billions of dollars worth of engineering construction. One man's stupid, moronic error, and all of this goes to destruction, just as if it had never been.

"On the ground, a plane crashes—the board puts it down as pilot error and planes go on flying. You can't do that out here! The cost is too great. It's a sheer gamble putting this mountain of machinery and effort into the hands of men we can never be sure of. You think you know them; you do everything possible to find out about them. But you just don't *know*.

"We've solved every other technical problem that has stood in our way. Why haven't we solved this one? We've learned how to make a machine that will perform in a predictable manner, and when it fails to do so we can provide adequate feedback alarms and correctors, and we can find the cause of error.

"With a man, we can do nothing. We have to accept him, in the final analysis, on little more than faith.

"A couple of hundred men are going to die because of a human error. Give us a monument! Find out why men make errors. Produce a means of keeping them from it. Do that, and our deaths will be a small price to pay!"

*   *   *   *   *

These were the words of a dead man. They were heard again and again in the committee rooms and investigation chambers. They were printed and broadcast around the world, and they enabled General Oglethorpe to do the thing that became a burning crusade with him.

He would probably have failed in his effort if those words hadn't been spoken by a dying man while a shrieking, white-hot mass plunged through the atmosphere to land, finally, in the waters of the Pacific.

The wreckage missed the city of San Francisco without the necessity of guidance by the rocket fuel so preciously hoarded by West. The Wheel and the *Griseda* were doomed the moment the pilot, Cummins, decided to shift the position of the ship with respect to the station.

*   *   *   *   *

In the anteroom of the Base Commander's office, Dr. Paul Medick rubbed the palms of his hands against his trouser legs when the secretary wasn't watching, and licked the dryness that burned the membrane of his lips.

The secretary remembered him. She probably had been the one to make out his severance papers and knew all about Oglethorpe's firing him.

Now she was no doubt wondering about the General's calling him back after that bitter occasion—just as Paul himself was wondering.

But he was pretty sure he knew. If he were right it was the opportunity of a lifetime, and he couldn't afford to muff it.

The girl turned at the sound of a buzz on the intercom. She smiled and said, "You may go in now."

"Thanks." He stood up and told his nerves to quit remembering the last time he passed through the door he was now entering. General Oglethorpe was nobody but the Base Commander, and if Paul Medick got thrown out once more he would be no worse off than he now was.

Oglethorpe looked up, a grim trace of a smile at the corners of his mouth. He shook hands and indicated a chair by the desk, resuming his own seat behind it. "You know why I called you—in spite of our past differences."

Paul hesitated. He didn't want to show his anxiety—and hopefulness—He weighed the answers that might be expected of him, and said, "It's this crash thing—and the appeal of Captain West?"

"Would there be anything else?"

"I'm flattered that you thought of me."

"There's nothing personal involved, believe me! I'd a thousand times rather have called somebody else—anybody else—but there's nobody that can do the job you can."

"Thanks."

"Don't bother thanking me. I expect there'll still be a great deal of difference between us about the basic goals of this project. But once we start I don't want to have to fire you again."

"Just what is the nature of this project," said Paul, "its goals? Fill me in on the details."

"There are no details—beyond what you've read and heard—you're going to provide them. The objective is to find a kind of man that will keep the Frank Wests of the future from dying, as those men aboard the Wheel did."

"What kind of man do you expect that to be?" Paul asked.

"One who will eliminate, for all time, the damning verdict that has been handed down in tens of thousands of investigations of accident and disaster: *human error.*

"We're going to find a kind of man who can be depended on to function without error. One who can undertake a complicated task of known procedure and perform it an infinite number of times, if necessary, without a single deviation from standard."

Paul Medick regarded the General through narrowed eyes. In spite of his almost agonizing desire to possess the appointment to head up this Project he had to have a clear understanding with Oglethorpe now. He had to risk his chances, if necessary, to make himself absolutely clear.

He said, "For untold thousands of years the human race has spent its best efforts to reach the goal of perfection without achieving it. Now you propose to assemble all the money in the world, and all the brains and say: give us a perfect man! The United States Space Command demands him!"

"Exactly." General Oglethorpe's face hardened as he returned Paul's steady gaze. "No other technical problem has been able to stand before such an attack. There is no reason why this one should. And the problem *must* be solved, or we're going to have to abandon space just as we stand on the frontier, getting our first real glimpse of it."

"Your world is such a simple, uncomplicated place, General," said Paul slowly. "You want a man with two heads, four arms, and a tail? Order it! Coming up!

"That's the way you operated when I set up your basic personnel program five years ago. It didn't work then; it won't work now."

The General's face darkened. "It *will* work. Because it has to. Men are going to the stars—because they have to. And they're going to change themselves to whatever form or shape or ability is required by that goal. They've done everything else they've ever set themselves to do—life came up out of the sea because it had courage. Men left their caves and struck out across the plains and seas, and took up the whole Earth and made it what it is—because they had courage.

"But to go to space, courage is not enough. We need a new kind of man that we've never seen before. He's a man of iron, who's forgotten he was ever flesh and blood. He's a machine, who can perform over and over the same kind of complicated procedure and never make an error. He's more reliable and endurable than the best machines we've ever made.

"I don't know where we'll find him, but he can be found, and you *will* do it, because you believe, as I do, that Man's frontier must not be closed. And because, in spite of your cynicism, you still understand the meaning of duty to your society and your race. There is no possibility of your refusal, so I have taken steps already to make your appointment official."

"You must also have prepared yourself," said Paul, "to accept me with the basic philosophy that must guide me in this matter. And my philosophy is that this Project *must* fail. It has no possibility of success. The man you seek does not exist. An errorless man would be a dead man.

"Any living man is going to make errors. That's the process of learning: make an approach, correct for error, approach again, correct once more. It's the only way there is to learn."

The General inhaled deeply and hesitated. "I know nothing about that," he said finally. "You know what I want. Even if what you say were partially true, there remains no reason why that which has been learned cannot be performed without error. I may have to put up with it, but you'll save yourself and all of us a lot of time if you don't spend three months digging up reasons why the Project can't succeed."

He stood up as if everything had been said that could possibly be said. "Let's go and have a look at your laboratory quarters."

*   *   *   *   *

In the hot sunlight of the Southwest desert, they walked across the yard from the administration building to a large laboratory which had been cleared to the bare floor and walls. Paul felt a sense of instability returning. But only for an instant. He'd all but insulted the General and told him he had no intention of producing the iron superman the Space Command contemplated. And still he had not been thrown out. They must want him very badly, indeed!

He had no qualms of conscience about taking the post now. General Oglethorpe had been forewarned and knew what Paul Medick's hopes and intentions were.

"You can build your staff as big as you need it," the General was saying. "This Project has crash priority over everything else.

We've got the machines to go to space. The machines need the men.

"You can have anybody you want and do anything you like to them. We hope you can put them back together again in reasonable shape, but that doesn't matter too much."

Paul turned about the bare room that would serve adequately as office space. "All right," he said. "Consider Project Superman begun. Remember, I have no hope of finding a solution in an errorless human being. I'll find whatever answer there is to be found. If you have any objections to my working of those terms, say so now. I don't intend to get fired again with a Project in the middle of its course."

"You won't be. You'll find the way to give us what we need. I want you to come down to the other end of the building and meet a man who will be working closely with you."

There had been sounds of activity in the distance, and General Oglethorpe led Paul towards them. They entered a large area in which instrumental equipment was being set up. A tall, thin, dark-haired man came up as they entered.

"Dr. Nat Holt," said the General, "instrument and electronics expert. This is Dr. Medick, the country's foremost man in psychology and psychometric analysis.

"Dr. Holt will be your instrument man. He will design and build whatever special equipment your researches call for. Let me know soon what you'll need in the way of furniture and assistants."

He left them standing in the nearly bare room. Through the window they watched his stiff form march back to his own office.

Nat Holt shifted position and grinned at Paul. "I may as well tell you that the General has briefed me thoroughly on what he considered your probable reaction to the Project. I'm just curious enough to want to know if he was right."

"The General and I understand each other—I think," said Paul. "He knows I'm contemptuous of his approach to a problem of human behavior by ordering it solved. But he knows I'll take his money and spend it on the biggest, deepest investigation of human behavior via psychometrical analysis that has ever been conducted."

"It ought to be enough to buy gold fringed couches for all the analysts in the country."

Paul raised his brows. "If it's that way with you, then why are you joining me?" he asked.

"Because I have a stake in this, too! I want to see the problem solved just as much as the General does. And I think it *can* be solved. But not this way!

"There's only one way to produce men of superior abilities. The method of adequate training. Hard, brutal discipline and training of oneself. I'm going to convince Oglethorpe of it after he's seen the failure you intend to produce for him."

"That shouldn't be hard," said Paul. "It's the General's own view. The Project is simply to implement that view.

"But let's not have any misunderstanding about my intentions. I expect to give honest value in research for every dollar spent. I expect to turn up data that will go a long way toward providing better spacemen for the Command—and to give Captain West the monument he asked for!"

*   *   *   *   *

Alone in his hotel room that night, Paul stood at the window overlooking the desert. Beyond the distant hills a faint glow in the sky marked the location of Space Command Base. He regarded it, and considered the enormity of the thing that was being brewed for the world in that isolated outpost. Now the chance was his to prove that manhood was a quality to be proud of, that machines could be built and junked and built again, but that a man's life was unique in the universe and could never be replaced once it was crushed.

For years he'd struggled to probe the basic nature of Man and find out what divorces him from the merely mechanical. He'd known there would probably never be enough money to reach his goal. And then Oglethorpe had come, offering him all the money in the world to reach a nebulous objective that Space Command did not know was unobtainable.

Somebody was going to spend that money. With clear conscience, Paul rationalized that it might as well be him. He'd see that the country got value for what it spent, even if this was not quite what the Space Command expected.

Nat Holt was going to be a most difficult obstacle. Paul wished the General had let him pick his own technical director, but obviously the two men understood each other. In their separate fields, they were alike in their approach to human performance. Whip a man into line, make him come to heel like a reluctant hound. Beat him, shape him, twist him to the form you want him to bear.

Discipline him. That was the magic word, the answer to all things.

Paul turned from the window in revulsion, drawing the curtains on the skyglow of the Base.

Human error!

When would Man cease to indulge in this most monumental of all errors? When would he cease to regard himself and his fellows as brute creatures to be beaten into line?

He had to find the right answer before Oglethorpe and his kind found some flimsy validation for the one they had already chosen long ago.

He stood up and glanced at the clock, deciding he wanted dinner, after all. Tomorrow he'd wire Betty and the kids to get packed and be on their way. No—he'd phone tonight. She had a right to know immediately the outcome of his interview.

The dining room was almost empty. He ordered absently and clipped the speaker of his small personal radio behind his ear while waiting. He seldom used it, but here in the desert was a sense of isolation that made him seize almost compulsively upon any contact with the bright, distant world. The music was dull, and the news uninspiring. He was about to turn it off when his order arrived.

The wine was very bad; the steak, however, was good, so Paul considered it about even. His finger touched the radio switch once more. The newscaster's voice changed its tone of pounding urgency. "Repercussions of the recent crash of the world's first space station are still being heard," he said. "Murmurs of protest against construction of a new Wheel are rising in many quarters. Today they approach the proportions of a roar.

"The influential New England Times states that it is 'unqualifiedly opposed' to any restoration of the Wheel. 'In its three years' existence the structure proved beyond any question of doubt its utter lack of utility. Now its fall to Earth demonstrates the menace constituted by its presence over every city on the face of the globe.'

"Senator Elbert echoes these sentiments. 'It was utter folly in the first place to spend billions of dollars to construct this Sword of Damocles in the sky of all the world. I propose that our Government go on record denying any further intention to rebuild such a threat to the peace and well-being of nations who stand now on the threshold of understanding and friendliness which they have sought for so long.'"

Paul switched it off. He remembered the hours of world-wide tension while the Wheel was falling toward the city of San Francisco. In panic, the whole population of the Bay Area attempted evacuation, but there wasn't time. The bridges became clogged with traffic, and some hysterical drivers left their cars and jumped to the waters below.

As the wreckage neared Earth, the computers narrowed their circle of error until it was certain at last that the city would not be struck. But the damage was done. The fear remained, and now was congealing in angry determination that another Wheel would not be built.

Paul finished his meal, wondering what effect this would have on the plans to build a new Wheel—and on Project Superman. Maybe Congress would react in anger that would cut off all appropriations to the Project.

He wondered, in sudden weariness, if this would not be an unmixed blessing, after all.

*   *   *   *   *

The next three days were spent in telephone and telegraph communication with members of his profession as he proceeded to recruit a staff.

On Friday, Betty arrived with the kids. By the end of the following week, laboratory furniture had been installed and the first trickle of potential staff members was coming in to see what Superman was all about. Nat, too, had been busy forming his own staff and setting up basic equipment.

Paul had the feeling that they were opposing camps setting up on the same site of exploration. He tried to tell himself it was completely irrational, until Nat approached him a few days later.

"Quite a crew you're getting in here," the technician said. "You'll have to take Oglethorpe up on his offer of new buildings if you expect to find couch space for all your boys."

"That's what you're here for," Paul suggested mildly, "to do away with couches."

"Right." Nat nodded. "Anything a couch can do, a meter can do twice as efficiently."

"Sometimes both are necessary. You forget my specialty is psychometry."

"No, I'm not forgetting," said Nat. "But that's what makes it so hard for me to figure out. You're attempting to span two completely incompatible fields: science and humanities. Man behaves either as a machine or as a creature of unstable emotion. To function as one you have to suppress the other."

"Splitting Man in two has never produced an answer to anything. It has been tried even longer than couches—and with far less result."

"I'll make you a small side bet. We're going to have to work together on Superman, and coordinate all our procedures and results. But I'll bet the final answer turns up on the side of a completely mechanistic man, shorn of all other responses and motivations."

"I'll take that!" Paul said with a grim smile. "I don't know how much of an answer we'll find, but I know *that* won't be it!"

"Let's say a small celebration feed for the whole crew when Superman is completed. Nothing chintzy, either!"

They shook on it. And afterward Paul was glad the incident had occurred. It left no doubt about the direction Nat Holt would be traveling in his work.

*   *   *   *   *

Four weeks to the day, from the time Paul had stepped into Oglethorpe's office, he called the first meeting of his staff leaders. Invitations to the General and to Nat Holt were deliberately omitted. He wanted this first get together to be a family affair.

He felt just a little shaky in the knees as he got up before that group for the first time.

"I won't repeat what you already know," Paul said carefully. "You all know the background events that produced Project Superman.

"I am sure that each of you has also caught the two basic errors that have been assumed by the Space Command, first, that an errorless man is possible, and second, that genuine scientific discovery can be secured wholly upon command. General Oglethorpe recognizes that we consider these assumptions erroneous, but he also knows that our professional integrity demands that we pursue vigorously a course which he believes will result in success.

"We recognize, too, that we are not here to invent or produce anything that does not already exist. But, in a sense, our superiors and some of our co-workers expect us to do exactly that.

"We can agree, however, that most of Man's potential still remains to be discovered. And for us, who have hoped for a means of understanding that potential, this Project is the fulfillment of dreams. If we fail to take full advantage of it, we will win the condemnation of our profession for a century to come.

"Space Command has already concluded that a man can be stripped of his humanity and driven to an utterly mechanistic state with the robotic responses of a machine. Let there be no mistake about it: we have been brought here to validate that conclusion.

"We will validate it by default, so to speak, unless we can produce a clean-cut analysis and demonstrations of the thing that most of us believe: that the essence of Man is more than a piece of machinery or a collection of bio-chemical reactions.

"Our science of mind and Man is on trial. If we fail, we give consent to a doctrine that will spread from space technology to all the rest of our society, and bind Man in an iron mold that will not be broken for generations. While we have been hired and will ostensibly work at the task of developing an errorless man, our basic purpose must be to validate the humanity of Man!"

He waited for their reaction. Outside, far across the open desert at the station, a rocket screamed into the air. They waited until the sound died away.

Professor Barker stood up. "There is scarcely a human being who has not by now read or heard the words of Captain West's appeal. They will be looking for the day when there will come marching from our laboratories, like a robot, the errorless man he asked for.

"Do you mean we have to fight the stated objectives of this Project? Can we not discover sufficient understanding to establish some method of training which will accomplish, in another way, the things the Space Command needs?"

"We are not fighting the Space Command's desire for more adequate men for its ships," said Paul. "We are fighting only against the false conclusions they have already formed concerning the nature of such men.

"We must solve the problem of human error. We know its purpose in the learning process. We must discover the reason for its existence in a *learned* process. We have to find out what training actually means.

"We have to ask how we know when an error has been made. It is obvious, of course, when a spaceship rams a fixed orbit station. But what of the subtler situations, where results are less dramatic, or are postponed for a long time—?

"The primary thing to remember at this point is that our basic goal is to prevent any false confirmation of the dogma that Man is no more than a badly functioning machine, which will gain value when he has been tinkered with sufficiently so that he can slip in beside the gears and vacuum tubes and be indistinguishable from them. And to reach this goal we must discover his true nature."

*　　*　　*　　*　　*

It was two weeks later that General Oglethorpe made his first visit since Superman got under way. The soldier's face seemed more deeply lined and his eyes more tired than Paul remembered seeing them before.

"You seem to have things well in hand," he said. "How soon can you give us some tangible results?"

"Results! We've just started housekeeping. In a year, maybe two, we'll have an idea where to begin a concentrated search for what you want to know."

The General shook his head slowly, his eyes remaining on Paul's face. "You aren't going to have anything like a year. You haven't got time to run down one line of research and then another. Run them all at once—a thousand of them if you want to. Why do you think you've got the budget you have!"

"Some things," said Paul, "like threading a needle—or analysing a human being—don't go much faster when a thousand men work at it than when there's only one."

"They do when there're a thousand needles to thread—or brains to pick. And that's what we're up against here. We need a volume of the kind of men we've been talking about, and we need them quick!"

"We have to find out how to get the first one."

"And you haven't got as much time now as we thought you had when Superman began. They're trying to close us up.

"We hadn't planned to build another Wheel right away, not until some refinements of design had been worked out, and we had some results from Superman.

"Now, all that's been scrapped. We've received orders from Washington that erection of a second Wheel is to begin at once, using the plans of the first one. Fabrication of structures is already under way."

"I don't understand," said Paul.

"If we don't get another one up there within a matter of weeks, this hysterical opposition among the public is liable to prevent us ever getting one there again. We have to act while we still have authority, before the crackpots persuade Congress to take it away. And by the time it's built, I want some men to put in it. Men who can be trusted to not jeopardize it the moment they put their clumsy feet aboard. I want them, Medick, and I intend to have them. That's by way of an order!"

The General rose, but Paul remained seated. "You can't get them that way, and you know it," the latter said. "We'll do all we can, as I've told you before."

"I think you'll do considerably more, now. That was quite a talk you delivered to your boys a couple of weeks ago. We will 'ostensibly work at the task of developing an errorless man', is the way I believe you put it. You're going to do a lot more than ostensibly work at it, Medick. Just how much do you think you can get away with?"

Paul remained motionless in the chair. Only his lips moved. "So you had a report on our little meeting? I hope it was complete enough to give you the rest of the things I said, that my basic purpose was not to produce human robots, but to validate the humanity of man."

Oglethorpe leaned closer, his fists resting on the top of the desk. "The humanity of man be damned! I told you before we want men who've forgotten they were ever human, men of metal and electrons. If I didn't think you were the man who could do it—probably the *only* man in the whole country—you wouldn't last here another minute. But you *can* do it, and you're going to.

"Your little lecture was enough to ruin your career in any place you try to run to, if you undermine Superman. Who do you suppose would trust you with any kind of research after that expression of intent to sabotage the Project your Government entrusted you with, and which you agreed to carry out?

"You're finished, Medick, washed up completely in your own profession, unless you give me what I've asked for! I won't take promises any more. The only assurance you can give me from here on out is results! I want those men, and I want them damn fast!"

*   *   *   *   *

Professor Barker listened attentively as Paul sat across from him in the administration office and reported Oglethorpe's visit and demands.

"We're caught in a squeeze, and we've got to push both ways," Paul said. "If the Base goes down, Superman goes with it, and we've lost an opportunity that will never come again in our lifetimes. So we've got to do two things: We've got to give active support to the rebuilding of the Wheel, and we've got to develop some kind of show that will convince Oglethorpe that Superman is giving him what he wants. It will mean detouring our basic objectives, but it's necessary in order to have a project at all. I'd like you to take charge of it."

"It'll be a waste of time," Barker said slowly. "I wonder if we'll ever get back on the track."

"We'll have to gamble on it," said Paul. "I don't want you to feel I'm deliberately pushing you up a blind alley, but I think you're the best man for bringing up something we can sell Oglethorpe—while we try to do some real research on some honest goals."

"We can follow the usual lines of so-called training—brute conditioning through shock and fear and pain and discomfort. Most of the men here are already well anaesthetized in that respect. Their breakdown level is high."

"Cummins' was the highest," said Paul, "and he cracked. But work along those lines anyway. Maybe we can find a way to thicken the conditioning armor. At the same time let's push a genuine investigation into the nature of error as hard as we can. For the moment we'll forget broader objectives, until we know the Project is safe."

Barker agreed reluctantly, feeling that they would end up as mere personnel counselors before long. As soon as he left, Paul called Oglethorpe.

"I've got a suggestion," he said. "Let's not get on the defensive about this thing. Why don't you propose a Senatorial investigation of Space Command?"

"Are you crazy? Why would we want to have them come out here and pick our bones to pieces before making final burial?"

"We've got a story to tell them—remember? We've got Superman, that's going to produce for the first time in the world's history a man adequate to go into the dangers of space. And there's that little story of yours about courage. I think that would go over with them. We'd be out in front if we took the initiative in this instead of just waiting until it rolled over us."

There was a long pause before Oglethorpe spoke again. "I wonder just what you're trying to do," he said finally. "I know you don't mean a word of what you're saying at all—"

"But I do mean it," Paul said earnestly. "I want Superman saved; you want the Wheel. It amounts to the same thing."

"You could be right. You might even be telling the truth. I'll give it some thought."

*　　*　　*　　*　　*

The officer in charge of the rocket crews and the take-off stand was a young engineer-soldier named Harper. Paul had met him during the first week at Base. His endorsement of Project Superman was enthusiastic.

After talking with Oglethorpe, Paul took a jeep over to the stand and located Harper. The engineer was overseeing the fueling process on a big rocket.

"Doc Medick!" Harper exclaimed. "How's your crew of head shrinkers coming along? We're just about ready for your new breed of pilots."

"What do you mean?"

"This is the nucleus ship. She's going out in orbit tonight with the first batch of supplies and instruments to get ready for the new Wheel. We're going to need your men awfully fast."

"That's what I came to talk about. Can you spare a few minutes?"

"Sure." Harper led him to the office, where the whining of fueling pumps was silenced. "What can we do for you?"

"I wanted to ask about Cummins. You knew him pretty well, didn't you?"

"Buddies. Just like that." Harper crossed his fingers.

"What went wrong, do you think? I know it's all been hashed over in the investigations, but I'd like your personal feelings about him."

Harper's face sobered and he looked away a moment. "Cummins was as good a guy as they come," he said. "But in a pinch he was just a weak sister. That doesn't mean he didn't have a lot on the ball," Harper added defensively. "He was a better pilot than most of us ever will be, but he was just human like the rest of us."

"What do you mean, 'human'?"

"Weak, soft, failure when the going gets rough—everything we have to be on guard against every minute we're alive."

"I take it you don't think much of human beings, as such."

Harper leaned forward earnestly. "Listen, Doc, when you've been around ships as long as I have, you'll know what Captain West really meant. The weakest link in any technological development has always been the men involved with its operation. In space flight our weakness is pilots and technicians.

Set a machine on course and it'll go until it breaks down—and flash you a warning before it fails. With a man, you never know when he's going to fail, and you have to be on guard against *his* breakdown every minute because he won't give any warning.

"Think what it's like to be in our shoes! We take the controls of a few hundred million dollars worth of machinery, and we know that every last man of us is booby-trapped with some weakness that can break out in a critical moment and destroy everything. We fight against it; we struggle to hold it in and act like responsible instruments. And we grow to hate ourselves because of the weak things that we are.

"Cummins was like that. He fought himself every waking hour, knowing that he had a weakness of becoming confused in a tight spot. Oh, it was nothing that even showed up on the tests, and he was the best man of any of us on the Base. But he knew it was there, just as we all know our closets bulge with skeletons that we try to keep from breaking out."

"Do you fight yourself the way Cummins did?" Paul asked.

"Sure."

"What would happen if you pulled a blunder that wrecked that ship out there on the stand."

"I'd have had it, that's all. I'd never get within ten miles of a rocket base again as long as I lived. And there wouldn't be much worth living for—"

"It would be pretty wonderful to feel you weren't constantly on the verge of some disastrous blunder, wouldn't it?"

"It would be a rocket man's idea of heaven to handle these ships with that kind of a feeling inside him."

"We're about ready to begin running tests on Superman, and I'd like you to be the first to help us out. Can you arrange it?"

"We're tied up like a ball of string on getting the nucleus ship in orbit. I know Oglethorpe gave orders we were to jump when you called, but I'll have to check on replacements for those of us you take. What kind of test are you going to run on me?"

"I want to find out how long it takes you to make a serious error, and what happens to you when you do!"

*　　*　　*　　*　　*

Arrangements were made for initiating this series of tests two days later. Paul had designed them, and Nat Holt's crew had built the equipment.

But before they were started, Paul grew increasingly aware of the clamor and public agitation against the Wheel. Instead of dying out after a small spurt of anger, it was accumulating momentum in every corner of the nation.

A rabble rouser named Morgan in the middle-west had proposed a motor caravan to Space Command Base, where the participants would go on a sit-down strike until assurance was given that no Wheel would be built again. And on the heels of this came the demand by an increasing number of Senators for a full investigation of the Base.

Paul met Barker after seeing the newscast of Morgan's revivalist type appeal for a caravan of protest against the Base. "This looks like it could get to be something that would be hard to handle," Barker said. "It doesn't seem reasonable that the near-crash of the first Wheel at San Francisco could be responsible for all this commotion."

"I don't think it is," Paul answered reflectively. "The sinking of a big ocean liner doesn't produce hysterical demands that no more ships be built. The crash of an airship with a hundred people aboard is accepted for what it is, without this kind of reaction. I think these broadcasts and write-ups of Captain West's appeal have sunk in deeper than Oglethorpe or anyone else ever intended.

"For a long time there has been building up a sense of man's inferiority to his machines. Now this incident of the Wheel and the world-wide broadcast of West's final words have triggered that inferiority into a genuine fear. They're afraid to have another Wheel up there over their heads. They're afraid that no man is capable of mastering such a piece of machinery."

Not only the public was infected with this fear, but the very men on whom the operation of the ships depended. Harper was right, Paul thought, as he reached his own office again. It must be terrible to be in their shoes, fighting constantly the conviction that they were poor miserable creatures hardly fit to polish the shining hulls of their creations!

They were trained in the best of military traditions, crushing their weaknesses by sheer force. And they had concluded their own breakdown was inevitable, in spite of their training and traditions. How could such men even hope for the stars!

But where was the flaw in it all? If the answer was not in men who were more nearly like their own machines, where was it?

They needed a year or two to even approach the problem properly, and some kind of answer was demanded within weeks!

Oglethorpe came to the laboratory the morning Harper was to begin his test runs. "We're going on a complete crash-priority basis, with round-the-clock shifts," he said. "It's been a toss-up whether to close Superman and put everything we had on the new Wheel, or leave it open in the hope of getting something out of it.

"For the time being I'm leaving it open, but remember that every hour Harper or one of his men spends here is an hour away from the job on the Wheel.

"We didn't need your suggestion about an investigation. Plenty of other people thought of it first. The Senators will be here in four or five days. You're going to talk to them. You're going to tell them what you proposed to tell them."

"Of course. And what are you going to do about Morgan's cavalcade?"

Oglethorpe spat out an exclamation. "We'll set up barricades that they'd better not cross within ten miles of Base!"

"That won't help," Paul warned. "I think you'd better let me prepare something for them, too."

"Forget them! Take care of the Senators and the Project and you'll be doing enough."

Harper arrived shortly, nervous in spite of his attempt to appear composed. But he was put at ease when they took him to the laboratory of complex testing equipment assembled by Nat Holt.

Paul indicated a seat in the middle of the mass of equipment. "As near as we've been able to make it," he said, "this simulates the landing procedure of a rocket craft. There are a hundred and thirty-five distinct actions, observations and judgements involved. A taped voice will lead you through the sequence, asking you to press buttons and make adjustments to indicate your observations and responses. When you can do all this to your satisfaction, you will turn off the tape and continue for as many cycles as you can."

"How long? A man could do that for a month, provided he didn't have to sleep."

"I think you'll be a little surprised. You will continue until your accumulation of errors becomes so great that the entire procedure collapses."

"It still looks like a kid's game to me," Harper said confidently. "Let's get started."

Carefully, they fitted the multiple electrodes of the electro-encephalograph recorder to his skull. The tape instructor was turned on, and Harper began the first cycle.

Behind the one-way glass of the observation room, Paul sat with Nat Holt and Professor Barker and two assistants, watching. The rocket engineer began jauntily, contemptuous of the simple actions required of him, impatient to have it over with and get back to his duties at the take-off stand.

The instructions coming over the speaker had some variations from the normal handling of a ship, including the items necessary to record observations and responses. Harper listened to these for a half dozen cycles. Then, confident that he could breeze through the procedure for the rest of the day if he had to, he switched off the tape and settled back to take it easy.

One by one, he watched the meters, noted their information, made the proper adjustments, added compensations, waited for results, checked and re-checked—

"He'll go a long time," said Nat Holt confidently. "He's had top training. If it breaks down, we may find out a few things."

"Cummins had top-drawer training, too," Paul said. "His break point seemed to have no adequate antecedents. I don't think we're going to find Harper holding out very long."

After an hour, the attitude of contempt had left Harper's face, and he was proceeding with obvious boredom. He had made no error yet, but there was evident a faint trace of anxiety as he concentrated on the instruments and levers.

At two hours and a half Harper reached for a button and withdrew his hand in abrupt hesitation. Then it darted out again and pressed decisively. At three hours he was making two such hesitations every cycle.

"Not so good," Barker commented. "Not for a man who battles himself the way Harper does."

Nat Holt remained silent, watching critically the wavering dials and graphs showing the engineer's physical condition and reaction.

At four and a half hours, Harper's hand reached for a lever in the center of the board. But it didn't get more than a third of the way. In mid-air it froze, as if paralysis had suddenly struck it. Harper regarded it in seeming dumb astonishment. His face grew red, and sweat broke out upon his forehead as if from the physical exertion of trying to put his hand to the lever.

Paul grabbed a microphone and switched it on. "Touch the lever," he commanded. "Draw it toward you."

Harper looked around as if in panic, but he completed the motion. He sat staring at the panels for a full two minutes while alarm eyes went from green to yellow to red.

"Alarm red!" Paul exclaimed into the microphone. "Correct course!"

Harper turned and glared about with hate in his eyes as if to find the source of the sound. He began tearing at the wires and contacts fastened to his head and body. "To hell with the course!" he cried. "I'm getting out of here!"

He hurled the wiring harness at the panels. Then, he stood in a moment's further paralysis and slumped finally into the chair. He put his arms and head down on the instrument desk and began sobbing deeply.

Paul put away the microphone and moved to the door. "That's the end of that," he said. "I hope our record is good. Harper might not like to go through that again."

Nat Holt was still staring through the window at the sobbing engineer. "I don't understand," he murmured. "What made him break down like that for no reason at all?"

* * * * *

One by one, the top engineers of the Base went through the breakdown test. Some broke down with an emotional storm as Harper had, others simply ended in a swirl of confusion that put lights flashing all over the panels. But all of them had a breaking point of some kind that could be measured in a small number of hours.

The test was a stab in the dark. It was based on an old and well-known principle that repeated tactile contact under command will break down the motor responses of the body in a matter of hours. Paul did not know whether it would actually provide a fertile lead to the problem of error or not, but it seemed the closest possible approach at present.

Nat Holt, however, was astonished at the reaction of the men. He insisted on trying it himself, determined that he would not break down no matter what happened. He lasted six hours before the panel lit up like a Christmas tree.

He subjected the resulting curves to an analyzer, and to his own he gave the most detailed attention. At the end of a full week of study on it, he called Paul with an excitement he could not suppress in his voice.

"It looks like you owe that dinner," he said. "We've got what we were looking for!"

"What are you talking about?" Paul demanded.

"We've got proof that a human being is nothing more nor less than a simple cybernetic gadget. It's a laugh—people trying to build a mechanical man all these years. That's the only kind there is!"

"You still aren't making sense."

"Come on over and see for yourself."

Puzzled and irritated, Paul left his office and went down to the analyzer laboratory. There he found Holt and his staff in a buzz of excitement.

The multiple recorder sheets were laid out on long tables, being studied intensely. Paul followed Holt to one series that was separated from the rest.

"We didn't know we had anything at first," said Holt. "The pulse was so low in amplitude that it was hard to pick out of the noise, but the analyzer showed it was consistently present under certain conditions of the subject."

"What conditions?" said Paul.

"At the exact moment of committing an error! I should say it occurs between the moment of making the decision to carry out an erroneous act and the triggering of the motor impulse that executes it."

Paul frowned. "How can you be sure it doesn't occur at any other time as well?"

"Because we've run every set of charts through the analyzer and this particular impulse comes out no other place."

"It looks very interesting," Paul said. "But why did you say you've got proof that a human being is nothing but a cybernetic gadget? I don't see what this has got to do with it."

"I didn't give you quite all the story," Holt said smugly. "I should have said that the pulse occurred every time there was an *intent* to perform an error. Sometimes that intent was not carried out."

"I don't understand."

"That pulse is nothing more nor less than a feedback pulse indicating that an action matrix has been set up which is in non-conformity with the previously chosen pattern of learning or intent. It's a feedback alarm carrying the information that an error will result if the proposed action is carried out. When the feedback is successfully returned to the action matrix a change is made until there is no feedback and a correct action is taken. When the feedback is blocked or ignored, an error results. It's as simple as that! Your complex human being is nothing but a fairly elaborate cybernetic machine operating wholly on feedback principles. The only time he fails and breaks down is when he ceases to act like the cybernetic machine that he is!"

*   *   *   *   *

Holt's eyes shone triumphantly as he patted the long strips of paper on the table. Paul followed the motion of his hand and remained staring at the graphs in a kind of stunned recognition. There must be some mistake, there *had* to be. Holt's interpretation was wrong, even if the data were correct. Man, a feedback response mechanism—! If that were true a vacuum tube structure could eventually be devised to do *anything* a man could do.

"I think we'll hold off on that dinner a while yet," Paul said. "The data are interesting and, I'm sure, important—but I can hardly agree with your conclusions." Inwardly, he cursed the stiltedness he felt creeping into his voice, and his irrational resentment of Holt's continued smug grin.

"Take all the time you want," Holt said, "but when you're through you'll come up with the same answers I've got. Man is a machine and nothing else. Our only job now is to discover why the feedback sometimes fails, and to set it back on the job."

Paul took the recordings and the analyzer graphs back to his own office.

He called Barker and showed the older man what Holt had found out. "If this is true," he said, "we don't need to worry about validating Space Command's pre-chosen conclusions. It has already been done."

Dr. Barker looked puzzled and a little frightened as he sat down at the desk to examine the charts. After an hour, he looked up. "It's true," he said. "There's no escaping the fact. Look what we have here—" He pointed to a corresponding sector of the six charts he'd lined up.

"After the first feedback impulse, there was no attempt to correct," he said, "or, rather, there was a deliberate effort to suppress the feedback. This created a second, larger feedback, which, in turn resulted in increased suppression and a simultaneous enlargement of the error. The result was a hunting effect in increasingly large amplitude, like the needle of an autosyn indicator with undamped positive feedback.

"Now, here's another one with the opposite effect. In this case the hunting shows diminishing amplitude as correction of the effort results from application of the feedback pulses. One pulse is not sufficient, but they are applied in decreasing force as the intent is brought into alignment with the learned pattern. A purely mechanical response!"

Paul turned from the window through which he had been staring toward the launchers. "Then Space Command is perfectly right," he said bitterly. "We *can* give them their errorless, mechanical men—just as soon as we find ways of correcting the blockage of the feedback pulses!"

Barker leaned back in his chair and folded his hands across his moderate paunch. "I'm afraid that's right. We've been wrong all along in bucking the mechanical concept of Man. The technologists saw it long ago in a sort of intuitive way, but they couldn't prove it. Now, they can!"

"And the soul of Man is nothing but a feedback impulse!"

Barker sighed heavily. "What else, Paul?"

*   *   *   *   *

Morgan's Caravan appeared that evening and camped at the ten-mile limit imposed by the military police guards. They posted their signs of protest and began their picket lines. Oglethorpe sent out his sound trucks to try to scare them away, but they wouldn't scare.

Paul watched at home the broadcast of the scene, but the fate of the Base and the Wheel had almost ceased to concern him. He told Betty of the discovery Holt had made on Superman.

"It leaves nothing to account for the most valued acts of Man," he said. "It can't account for creativeness, because a cybernetic device cannot create; it can only follow a pattern. So where is the poetry, the art, the scientific invention if this is the essence of Man? It can't be, yet there's no way of getting around this thing."

"Where does the pattern come from?" asked Betty. "Isn't that the created thing which the cybernetic system tries to follow?"

Paul shook his head. "The pattern we're talking about is no more than a response to stimuli, a purely mechanical thing also. Holt claims this is all there ever is, that what we call art, poetry, music inspiration, and intuition are nothing more than the results of badly functioning cybernetic systems. The more or less irrational results of errors in accommodating to the real world. We find pleasure in them because they tend to excuse our badly malfunctioning circuits.

"The ideal race of Man would be devoid of all this, a smoothly operating group of individuals unperturbed by emotional or artistic responses, completely capable of solving any problem in a purely cybernetic manner."

"And do you agree with it?" Betty asked.

"There's nothing else I can do! The evidence is there." He laughed shortly and moved to the window where he could see the nearby camp of Morgan's Caravan. "Human development has moved—is moving—in a completely different direction from anything I ever dreamed. Oglethorpe's iron-hard, emotionless machine-men are the only ones who'll get there. The rest of us who can't match the pace of a technological society will be shucked off as the waste part in the development of a species meant to inhabit galaxies instead of a single world."

"If I had ever wondered how you'd sound when you were completely out of your mind I'd have the answer now," said Betty.

In the morning he turned over to one of the units the task of further identifying and analyzing the feedback impulse they had discovered. In the middle of this he was called to Oglethorpe's office. The investigating Senators had arrived.

They were favorably impressed by the day-long tour that General Oglethorpe provided for them around the entire Base. But they found in Paul's announcement the strongest single factor in favor of permitting Space Command to continue with its work.

"We know now," he said, "and this is something I haven't even had time to present to General Oglethorpe—we know that a completely mechanical man is possible."

The General's eyes narrowed as Paul's flat statement continued. "We know that it is possible to have men at the helm of our ships, who are incapable of error. We have hopes of producing them within a very short time if Project Superman is allowed to continue. And when this is done, there is no technical goal we cannot reach."

This was the thing the Senators had come to find out, and they were satisfied. "But the public has got to be reassured of this," Senator Hart said. "We need to get this mob away from your gates for one thing. The news programs keep them constantly before the public eye and the whole country is stirred up."

"We'll take care of it at once," General Oglethorpe said. "As Dr. Medick has indicated, this discovery is so new that even I had not been informed of it. Morgan's mob will go away as soon as they hear the news. And that, in turn, will reassure the entire country. We can arrange for a broadcast by Dr. Medick to the whole nation."

Paul was swept along as arrangements were made to make a statement to Morgan and his group camped outside the Base, to the press, and to the public in general.

Oglethorpe cornered him after the meeting with the Committee. "This is on the level," he said, "not something you cooked up on the spur of the moment?"

"It's on the level," said Paul. "You were right all along."

When he returned to his office an urgent message from Barker awaited him. He hurried down to the testing laboratory, where the older man greeted him in excitement and anxiety.

"It looks like we've got something by the tail and can't let go of it. Come in and have a look."

Paul followed him and found Captain Harper in an observation room, writhing on a cot in a storm of tears and emotional fury. He beat against the walls and the floor with his fists as his sobbing continued beyond control.

"What happened to him?" Paul demanded.

"We have three others in the same condition," said Barker. "We tried to determine the effect of a pure feedback impulse, and fed it back to each of them in amplified form as we found it on their charts. This is what happened. I'm afraid we may have cost them their sanity, and we don't know why."

"How could their own feedback do such a thing to them?" he asked in wonder. "What part of the chart did you take it from?"

"We used the impulse that didn't get through, the one that was blocked so that error resulted. Apparently this is the alternative to error." He nodded toward the writhing, sobbing man. "Harper reached a point where he *had* to fail or else be subject to this psychic storm."

Paul ran his long, bony fingers through his hair. "This makes less sense than ever! If that's true, then we've got to take back what we've told Oglethorpe. His errorless man isn't possible, after all."

"I don't know." Barker shook his head thoughtfully. "Evidently the production of error is a protection against the admission of this intolerable feedback impulse. But the question remains: why is it intolerable, and why does it become so after numerous other feedback impulses have been passed?

"Yesterday we thought we had it all wrapped up. Now it's blown open wider than ever before!"

*   *   *   *   *

Oglethorpe's public relations man prepared a statement to the effect that further danger from pilot error in rocket ships and the second Wheel could be considered as completely eliminated with the new training processes that would make men incapable of technical errors.

Paul knew it was as ineffectual as the average Government release, but he made no protest in his concern for Harper and the three other men. He signed the statement automatically.

He was presented the following day, however, with arrangements to give it personally to the members of Morgan's Caravan from the top of one of the sound trucks. He did protest then that any flunky on the Base could read it to the crowd as well as he. But Oglethorpe insisted he do it personally.

With official pompousness the big, olive-green truck rolled out from the Base. Paul rode beside the driver and Metcalf, the public relations man. He'd not told Oglethorpe about their latest development. If this psychic reaction to feedback proved an impenetrable barrier there'd be time enough to give Space Command the bad news. In the meantime a Wheel would be built, the public would be mollified, and Superman would continue on—to what unknown ends Paul didn't know.

The massed camp of the fanatic followers of Morgan appeared in the distance like a discarded rag on either side of the road. Then as they approached it broke into individual knots of sand-scoured, unwashed people clustered about their tents. Morgan hadn't given much thought to adequate facilities before leading them out here.

The truck rolled to a halt in the center of the camp. Morgan himself, a long, lanky figure in a dusty black suit, came at the head of a group of his people to meet them. "I hope you have the news we are waiting for," he said cordially.

"We have a statement," said Metcalf. "Dr. Medick here, who has made an important discovery that will enable all of you to return to your homes, will read it to you."

Paul could have stayed in the cab, but he preferred to climb to the platform atop the truck to get a look at the crowd Morgan had assembled. He hesitated a moment with the paper in his hands, then took up the mike and read the statement Metcalf had prepared. "The United States Space Command wishes to announce that—"

It fell utterly flat on completely non-understanding ears. Paul looked over the mass of faces and knew it had failed. Something far more than this was needed. A little feedback, he thought grimly. A little feedback of the idiocy of their present situation to correct their course and return it to normalcy.

"Five hundred years ago there might have been a crowd of people just like you," he said suddenly in low tones. "There was a harbor, and some small ships, and a man who believed he could sail them over the edge of the world. On the shore were people who thought he was a fool and a blasphemer, and a few who thought he was right—or at least hoped he was.

"Five hundred years ago was the beginning of a new freedom from the prison of a tiny, constricted world. Today, another freedom waits our successful conquest of space. And whenever a freedom has been won there have been more who jeered against it than have cheered for it. You are today making a choice—"

He talked for ten minutes, and when he was through he knew that he'd accomplished his goal. Even before the sound truck pulled out, the cars of the Caravan were breaking away from the mass and disappearing in the distance.

"Nice job," Metcalf congratulated, as if he'd been responsible for it himself.

"Just a little feedback in the right place—" murmured Paul absently.

"Feedback? What's that—new kind of propaganda technique—?"

"Yeah, you might call it that. How could a guy have been so *blind*—?" he said fiercely, more to himself than to his companions.

He hurried to the laboratory as soon as the truck got him back to Base. He rounded up Barker and Nat Holt and a dozen of his other top men. "The answer's been under our noses all the time," he said. "We've been too busy fighting each other for the sake of our own preconceived notions to have seen it!"

"What are you talking about?" Holt demanded.

"Feedback. Can't you guess what it is?"

"No."

"Are you willing to let us give you a small dose—something less than the level given Harper and his men—and then tell us what you find out about it?"

Nat Holt looked hesitant. "If you think you know what you're talking about. There's no point in my getting in a condition like Harper's."

"We'll pull you out before you get anywhere near that far."

Still dubious, he took a seat amid the mass of pulse generating equipment and electro-encephalograph recorders. A single pair of feedback terminals were fitted to his skull. The generator was set to duplicate his own feedback impulse taken from a moment of failure.

Paul switched on the circuits and advanced the controls carefully. A look of pain and regret crossed Holt's face. He cried out with a whimper. "Turn it off!"

"A second more—," Paul said. He advanced the control a hair and waited. The technologist began to cry suddenly in a low, sobbing voice.

Paul cut the switch.

For a moment Holt continued to slump in the chair, his shoulders jerking. Then he looked up, half-bewildered, half-furious. "What did you do to me?" he demanded.

"You did it to yourself," Paul reminded him. "That's your own feedback pulse just beefed up a little, remember. How did it feel?"

"Terrible! No wonder a guy dodges that. It's enough to make him wreck a space station to avoid the full blast of it."

"What would you call it?"

"I don't know—," Holt hesitated. "Grief, maybe. Regret—anxiety. But regret, mostly, I guess."

"That's your feedback," Paul said as he removed the terminals and turned to the others. "These feedback pulses we've isolated are nothing but stabs of pure emotion."

He turned with a faint smile to Holt. "You and Harper and the rest of the iron-bowelled boys were so convinced that the pure mechanical man would be utterly devoid of all emotional responses and content! And I was so sure that a warm, responsive, emotional human being could never respond like a cold machine!

"And we were both utterly wrong. The human being does both. He operates on true cybernetic principles. But the content of his feedback control pulses is sheer emotion!

"A small error, a stab of regret. It's repeated, magnified, or diminished until the action gets back on the track that brings predicted results. Ignored, the error builds up until the whole structure goes smash.

"And we're *taught* to ignore it! It's the noble, brave and manly thing to ignore the human feelings that surge through us. Be steel, be glass, be electrons—anything but a responsive, emotional human being! That's the way to be a superman! We've tried to find the way to perfection and have fought tooth and nail against the only means of achieving it."

Barker's face was glowing with excitement and Holt seemed to be remembering something afar off. "That *was* it," he breathed softly. "I can feel it now—the way it was as I began to get jittery and make mistakes in the test procedures. I seemed to fight something within myself—something I thought was making me do it wrong. But it wasn't that, at all. I was fighting against the emotional feedback the errors were throwing at me."

"Right," said Paul. "And your iron-hard, errorless Superman is going to be the most emotionally sensitive creature you can produce."

"How did you catch on to this?" Barker asked.

"We should have seen it in Harper. He's the original iron-man. He's bottled up and fought his emotions all his life. A concentrated dose of his own feedback simply shattered the dam.

"But I didn't get it until I watched Morgan's mob reacting to the purely rational explanation Metcalf prepared to convince them they should go home. They were on a wrong tack and needed a generous amount of the right feedback to get them back where they belonged. The cold, logical approach was a dud. What does it take to move an intractible mob? Emotion—based on the projected consequences of what they're doing. A perfect feedback setup when correctly applied. And it worked."

Holt shuddered faintly and moved away from the chair he had sat in to experience his own feedback. "I'm not quite sure who owes who that dinner," he said to Paul. "But I think somebody does."

"We'll split it," Paul said. And then he was silent as they listened to the departure of another cargo ship carrying parts of the second Wheel to the thousand-mile orbit.

He smiled to himself. Ye of little faith!—he thought. Frightened about the true nature of a race that had come through three billion years of the kind of torment that Man had survived!

Man had everything that was needed to go to the stars or anywhere else he might want to go. He was safe. Man could never be turned into a robot. The basic mechanisms of his humanity were so interwoven with the structure of his being that they could never be separated.

But they hadn't come very far, Paul knew. They had opened only a small crack in a door that had been irrationally closed from the beginning of time. They had to know fully why that door had never been opened before. And beyond it might lie a thousand others just as tightly closed and closely guarded.

Yet they had reached a starting point, at last. Project Superman could get about its business of preparing men for the stars.

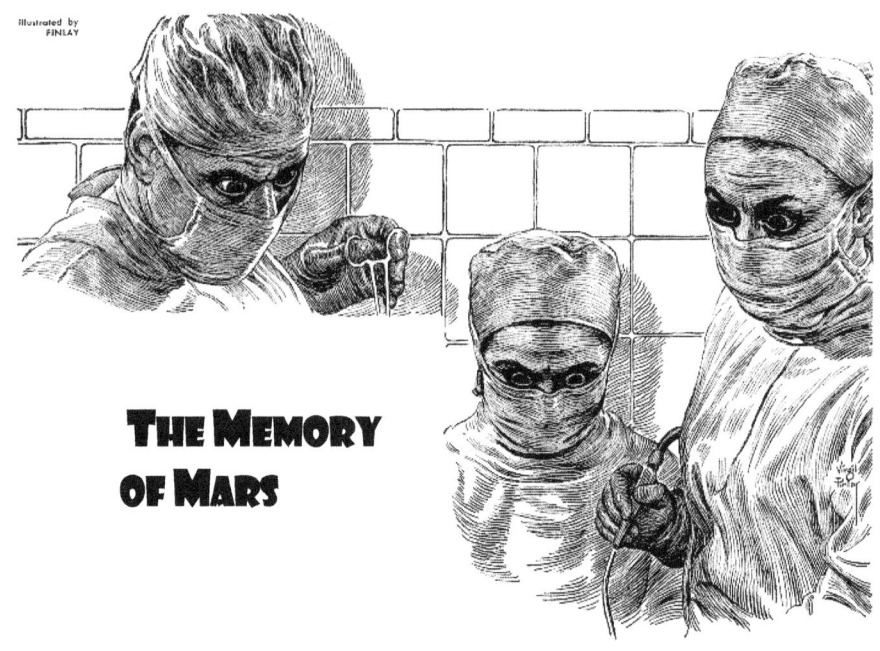

Illustrated by
FINLAY

THE MEMORY
OF MARS

ILLUSTRATED BY FINLAY
ORIGINALLY PUBLISHED IN *AMAZING STORIES*,
DECEMBER 1961

"As soon as I'm well we'll go to Mars for a vacation again," Alice would say. But now she was dead, and the surgeons said she was not even human. In his misery, Hastings knew two things: he loved his wife; but they had never been off Earth!

THE MEMORY OF MARS

A reporter should be objective even about a hospital. It's his business to stir others' emotions and not let his own be stirred. But that was no good, Mel Hastings told himself. No good at all when it was Alice who was here somewhere, balanced uncertainly between life and death.

Alice had been in Surgery far too long. Something had gone wrong. He was sure of it. He glanced at his watch. It would soon be dawn outside. To Mel Hastings this marked a significant and irrevocable passage of time. If Alice were to emerge safe and whole from the white cavern of Surgery she would have done so now.

Mel sank deeper in the heavy chair, feeling a quietness within himself as if the slow creep of death were touching him also. There was a sudden far distant roar and through the window he saw a streak of brightness in the sky. That would be the tourist ship, the Martian Princess, he remembered.

That was the last thing Alice had said before they took her away from him. "As soon as I'm well again we'll go to Mars for a vacation again, and then you'll remember. It's so beautiful there. We had so much fun—"

Funny, wonderful little Alice—and her strange delusion that she still clung to, that they had taken a Martian vacation in the first year of their marriage. It had started about a year ago, and nothing he could say would shake it. Neither of them had ever been to space.

He wished now he had taken her. It would have been worth it, no matter what its personal cost. He had never told her about the phobia that had plagued him all his life, the fear of outer space that made him break out in a cold sweat just to think of it—nor of the nightmare that came again and again, ever since he was a little boy.

There must have been some way to lick this thing—to give her that vacation on Mars that she had wanted so much.

Now it was too late. He knew it was too late.

*   *   *   *   *

The white doors opened, and Dr. Winters emerged slowly. He looked at Mel Hastings a long time as if trying to remember who the reporter was. "I must see you—in my office," he said finally.

Mel stared back in numb recognition. "She's dead," he said.

Dr. Winters nodded slowly as if in surprise and wonder that Mel had divined this fact. "I must see you in my office," he repeated.

Mel watched his retreating figure. There seemed no point in following. Dr. Winters had said all that need be said. Far down the corridor the Doctor turned and stood patiently as if understanding why Mel had not followed, but determined to wait until he did. The reporter stirred and rose from the chair, his legs withering beneath him. The figure of Dr. Winters grew larger as he approached. The morning clatter of the hospital seemed an ear-torturing shrillness. The door of the office closed and shut it out.

"She is dead." Dr. Winters sat behind the desk and folded and unfolded his hands. He did not look at Mel. "We did everything we could, Mr. Hastings. Her injuries from the accident were comparatively minor—" He hesitated, then went on. "In normal circumstances there would have been no question—her injuries could have been repaired."

"What do you mean, 'In normal circumstances—'?"

Dr. Winters turned his face away from Mel for a moment as if to avoid some pain beyond endurance. He passed a weary hand across his forehead and eyes and held it there a moment before speaking. Then he faced Mel again. "The woman you brought in here last night—your wife—is completely un-normal in her internal structure. Her internal organs cannot even be identified. She is like a being of some other species. She is not— she is simply not human, Mr. Hastings."

Mel stared at him, trying to grasp the meaning of the words. Meaning would not come. He uttered a short, hysterical laugh that was like a bark. "You're crazy, Doc. You've completely flipped your lid!"

Dr. Winters nodded. "For hours during the night I was in agreement with that opinion. When I first observed your wife's condition I was convinced I was utterly insane. I called in six other men to verify my observation. All of them were as stupefied as I by what we saw. Organs that had no place in a human structure. Evidence of a chemistry that existed in no living being we had ever seen before—"

The Doctor's words rolled over him like a roaring surf, burying, smothering, destroying—

"I want to see." Mel's voice was like a hollow cough from far away. "I think you're crazy. I think you're hiding some mistake you made yourself. You killed Alice in a simple little operation, and now you're trying to get out of it with some crazy story that nobody on earth would ever believe!"

"I want you to see," said Dr. Winters, rising slowly. "That's why I called you in here, Mr. Hastings."

*   *   *   *   *

Mel trailed him down the long corridor again. No words were spoken between them. Mel felt as if nothing were real anymore.

They went through the white doors of Surgery and through the inner doors. Then they entered a white, silent—cold—room beyond.

In the glare of icy white lights a single sheeted figure rested on a table. Mel suddenly didn't want to see. But Dr. Winters was drawing back the cover. He exposed the face, the beloved features of Alice Hastings. Mel cried out her name and moved toward the table. There was nothing in her face to suggest she was not simply sleeping, her hair disarrayed, her face composed and relaxed as he had seen her hundreds of times.

"Can you stand to witness this?" asked Dr. Winters anxiously. "Shall I get you a sedative?"

Mel shook his head numbly. "No—show me ..."

The great, fresh wound extended diagonally across the abdomen and branched up beneath the heart. The Doctor grasped a pair of small scissors and swiftly clipped the temporary sutures. With forceps and retractors he spread open the massive incision.

Mel closed his eyes against the sickness that seized him.

"Gangrene!" he said. "She's full of gangrene!"

Below the skin, the surface layers of fatty tissue, the substance of the tissue changed from the dark red of the wounded tissue to a dark and greenish hue that spoke of deadly decay.

But Dr. Winters was shaking his head. "No. It's not gangrene. That's the way we found the tissue. That appears to be its—normal condition, if you will."

Mel stared without believing, without comprehending.

Dr. Winters probed the wound open further. "We should see the stomach here," he said. "What is here where the stomach should be I cannot tell you. There is no name for this organ. The intestinal tract should lie here. Instead, there is only this homogeneous mass of greenish, gelatinous material. Other organs, hardly differentiated from this mass, appear where the liver, the pancreas, the spleen should be."

Mel was hearing his voice as if from some far distance or in a dream.

"There are lungs—of a sort," the Doctor went on. "She was certainly capable of breathing. And there's a greatly modified circulatory system, two of them, it appears. One circulates a blood substance in the outer layers of tissue that is almost normal. The other circulates a liquid that gives the remainder of the organs their greenish hue. But how circulation takes place we do not know. She has no heart."

*　　*　　*　　*　　*

Mel Hastings burst out in hysterical laughter. "Now I know you're crazy Doc! My tender, loving Alice with no heart! She used to tell me, 'I haven't got any brains. I wouldn't have married a dumb reporter if I did. But so I've got a heart and that's what fell in love with you—my heart, not my brains.' She loved me, can't you understand that?"

Dr. Winters was slowly drawing him away. "I understand. Of course I understand. Come with me now, Mr. Hastings, and lie down for a little while. I'll get you something to help take away the shock."

Mel permitted himself to be led away to a small room nearby. He drank the liquid the Doctor brought, but he refused to lie down.

"You've shown me," he said with dull finality. "But I don't care what the explanation is. I knew Alice. She was human all right, more so than either you or I. She was completely normal, I tell you—all except for this idea she had the last year or so that we'd gone together on a vacation to Mars at one time."

"That wasn't true?"

"No. Neither of us had ever been out in space."

"How well did you know your wife before you married her?"

Mel smiled in faint reminiscence. "We grew up together, went to the same grade school and high school. It seems like there was never a time when Alice and I didn't know each other. Our folks lived next door for years."

"Was she a member of a large family?"

"She had an older brother and sister and two younger sisters."

"What were her parents like?"

"They're still living. Her father runs an implement store. It's a farm community where they live. Wonderful people. Alice was just like them."

Dr. Winters was silent before he went on. "I have subjected you to this mental torture for just one reason, Mr. Hastings. If it has been a matter of any less importance I would not have told you the details of your wife's condition, much less asking you to look at her. But this is such an enormous scientific mystery that I must ask your cooperation in helping to solve it. I want your permission to preserve and dissect the body of your wife for the cause of science."

Mel looked at the Doctor in sudden sharp antagonism. "Not even give her a burial? Let her be put away in bottles, like—like a—"

"Please don't upset yourself any more than necessary. But I do beg that you consider what I've just proposed. Surely a moment's reflection will show you that this is no more barbaric than our other customs regarding our dead.

"But even this is beside the point. The girl, Alice, whom you married is like a normal human being in every apparent external respect, yet the organs which gave her life and enabled her to function are like nothing encountered before in human experience. It is imperative that we understand the meaning of this. It is yours to say whether or not we shall have this opportunity."

Mel started to speak again, but the words wouldn't come out.

"Time is critical," said Dr. Winters, "but I don't want to force you to an instantaneous answer. Take thirty minutes to think about it. Within that time, additional means of preservation must be taken. I regret that I must be in such haste, but I urge that your answer be yes."

Dr. Winters moved towards the door, but Mel gestured for him to remain.

"I want to see her again," Mel said.

"There is no need. You have been tortured enough. Remember your wife as you have known her all her life, not as you saw her a moment ago."

"If you want my answer let me see her again."

*   *   *

Dr. Winters led the way silently back to the cold room. Mel drew down the cover only far enough to expose the face of Alice. There was no mistake. Somehow he had been hoping that all this would turn out to be some monstrous error. But there was no error.

Would she want me to do what the Doctor has asked? he thought. She wouldn't care. She would probably think it a very huge joke that she had been born with innards that made her different from everybody else. She would be amused by the profound probings and mutterings of the learned doctors trying to find an explanation for something that had no explanation.

Mel drew the sheet tenderly over her face.

"You can do as you wish," he said to Dr. Winters. "It makes no difference to us—to either of us."

*   *   *   *   *

The sedative Dr. Winters had given him, plus his own exhaustion, drove Mel to sleep for a few hours during the afternoon, but by evening he was awake again and knew that a night of sleeplessness lay ahead of him. He couldn't stand to spend it in the house, with all its fresh reminders of Alice.

He walked out into the street as it began to get dark. Walking was easy; almost no one did it any more. The rush of private and commercial cars swarmed overhead and rumbled in the ground beneath. He was an isolated anachronism walking silently at the edge of the great city.

He was sick of it. He would have liked to have turned his back on the city and left it forever. Alice had felt the same. But there was nowhere to go. News reporting was the only thing he knew, and news occurred only in the great, ugly cities of the world. The farmlands, such as he and Alice had known when they were young, produced nothing of interest to the satiated denizens of the towns and cities. Nothing except food, and much of this was now being produced by great factories that synthesized protein and carbohydrates. When fats could be synthesized the day of the farmer would be over.

He wondered if there weren't some way out of it now. With Alice gone there was only himself, and his needs were few. He didn't know, but suddenly he wanted very much to see it all again. And, besides, he had to tell her folks.

*   *   *   *   *

The ancient surface bus reached Central Valley at noon the next day. It all looked very much as it had the last time Mel had seen it and it looked very good indeed. The vast, open lands; the immense ripe fields.

The bus passed the high school where Mel and Alice had attended classes together. He half expected to see her running across the campus lawn to meet him. In the middle of town he got off the bus and there were Alice's mother and father.

They were dry-eyed now but white and numb with shock. George Dalby took his hand and pumped it heavily. "We can't realize it, Mel. We just can't believe Alice is gone."

His wife put her arms around Mel and struggled with her tears again. "You didn't say anything about the funeral. When will it be?"

Mel swallowed hard, fighting the one lie he had to tell. He almost wondered now why he had agreed to Dr. Winters' request. "Alice—always wanted to do all the good she could in the world," he said. "She figured that she could be of some use even after she was gone. So she made an agreement with the research hospital that they could have her body after she died."

It took a moment for her mother to grasp the meaning. Then she cried out, "We can't even bury her?"

"We should have a memorial service, right here at home where all her friends are," said Mel.

George Dalby nodded in his grief. "That was just like Alice," he said. "Always wanting to do something for somebody else—"

And it was true, Mel thought. If Alice had supposed she was not going to live any longer she would probably have thought of the idea, herself. Her parents were easily reconciled.

They took him out to the old familiar house and gave him the room where he and Alice had spent the first days of their marriage.

*   *   *   *   *

When it was night and the lights were out he felt able to sleep naturally for the first time since Alice's accident. She seemed not far away here in this old familiar house.

In memory, she was not, for Mel was convinced he could remember the details of his every association with her. He first became conscious of her existence one day when they were in the third grade. At the beginning of each school year the younger pupils went through a course of weighing, inspection, knee tapping, and cavity counting. Mel had come in late for his examination that year and barged into the wrong room. A shower of little-girl squeals had greeted him as the teacher told him kindly where the boy's examination room was.

But he remembered most vividly Alice Dalby standing in the middle of the room, her blouse off but held protectingly in front of her as she jumped up and down in rage and pointed a finger at him. "You get out of here, Melvin Hastings! You're not a nice boy at all!"

Face red, he had hastily retreated as the teacher assured Alice and the rest of the girls that he had made a simple mistake. But how angry Alice had been! It was a week before she would speak to him.

He smiled and sank back deeply into the pillow. He remembered how proud he had been when old Doc Collins, who came out to do the honors every Fall, had told him there wasn't a thing wrong with him and that if he continued to drink his milk regularly he'd grow up to be a football player. He could still hear Doc's words whistling through his teeth and feel the coldness of the stethoscope on his chest.

Suddenly, he sat upright in bed in the darkness.

Stethoscope!

They had tapped and inspected and listened to Alice that day, and all the other examination days.

If Doc Collins had been unable to find a heartbeat in her he'd have fainted—and spread the news all over town!

Mel got up and stood at the window, his heart pounding. Old Doc Collins was gone, but the medical records of those school examinations might still be around somewhere. He didn't know what he expected to prove, but surely those records would not tell the same story Dr. Winters had told.

It took him nearly all the next day. The grade school principal agreed to help him check through the dusty attic of the school, where ancient records and papers were tumbled about and burst from their cardboard boxes.

Then Paul Ames, the school board secretary, took Mel down to the District Office and offered to help look for the records. The old building was stifling hot and dusty with summer disuse. But down in the cool, cobwebbed basement they found it.... Alice's records from the third grade on up through the ninth. On every one: heart, o.k.; lungs, normal. Pulse and blood pressure readings were on each chart.

"I'd like to take these," said Mel. "Her doctor in town—he wants to write some kind of paper on her case and would like all the past medical history he can get."

Paul Ames frowned thoughtfully. "I'm not allowed to give District property away. But they should have been thrown out a long time ago—take 'em and don't tell anybody I let you have 'em."

"Thanks. Thanks a lot," Mel said.

And when she was fourteen or fifteen her appendix had been removed. A Dr. Brown had performed the operation, Mel remembered. He had taken over from Collins.

"Sure, he's still here," Paul Ames said. "Same office old Doc Collins used. You'll probably find him there right now."

Dr. Brown remembered. He didn't remember the details of the appendectomy, but he still had records that showed a completely normal operation.

"I wonder if I could get a copy of that record and have you sign it," Mel said. He explained about the interest of Dr. Winters in her case without revealing the actual circumstances.

"Glad to," said Dr. Brown. "I just wish things hadn't turned out the way they have. One of the loveliest girls that ever grew up here, Alice."

*   *   *

The special memorial service was held in the old community church on Sunday afternoon. It was like the drawing of a curtain across a portion of Mel's life, and he knew that curtain would never open again.

He took a bus leaving town soon after the service.

There was one final bit of evidence, and he wondered all the way back to town why he had not thought of it first. Alice's pregnancy had ended in miscarriage, and there had never been another.

But X-rays had been taken to try to find the cause of Alice's difficulty. If they showed that Alice was normal within the past two years—

*   *   *   *   *

Dr. Winters was mildly surprised to see Mel again. He invited the reporter in to his office and offered him a chair. "I suppose you have come to inquire about our findings regarding your wife."

"Yes—if you've found anything," said Mel. "I've got a couple of things to show you."

"We've found little more than we knew the night of her death. We have completed the dissection of the body. A minute analysis of each organ is now under way, and chemical tests of the body's substances are being made. We found that differences in the skeletal structure were almost as great as those in the fleshy tissues. We find no relationship between these structures and those of any other species—human or animal—that we have ever found."

"And yet Alice was not always like that," said Mel.

Dr. Winters looked at him sharply. "How do you know that?"

Mel extended the medical records he had obtained in Central Valley. Dr. Winters picked them up and examined them for a long time while Mel watched silently.

Finally, Dr. Winters put the records down with a sigh. "This seems to make the problem even more complex than it was."

"There are X-rays, too," said Mel. "Alice had pelvic X-rays only a little over two years ago. I tried to get them, but the doctor said you'd have to request them. They should be absolute proof that Alice was different then."

"Tell me who has them and I'll send for them at once."

An hour later Dr. Winters shook his head in disbelief as he turned off the light box and removed the X-ray photograph. "It's impossible to believe that these were taken of your wife, but they corroborate the evidence of the other medical records. They show a perfectly normal structure."

The two men remained silent across the desk, each reluctant to express his confused thoughts. Dr. Winters finally broke the silence. "It must be, Mr. Hastings," he said, "—it must be that this woman—this utterly alien person—is simply not your wife, Alice. Somehow, somewhere, there must be a mistake in identity, a substitution of similar individuals."

"She was not out of my sight," said Mel. "Everything was completely normal when I came home that night. Nothing was out of place. We went out to a show. Then, on the way home, the accident occurred. There could have been no substitution—except right here in the hospital. But I know it was Alice I saw. That's why I made you let me see her again—to make sure."

"But the evidence you have brought me proves otherwise. These medical records, these X-rays prove that the girl, Alice, whom you married, was quite normal. It is utterly impossible that she could have metamorphosed into the person on whom we operated."

Mel stared at the reflection of the sky in the polished desk top. "I don't know the answer," he said. "It must not be Alice. But if that's the case, where is Alice?"

"That might even be a matter for the police," said Dr. Winters. "There are many things yet to be learned about this mystery."

"There's one thing more," said Mel. "Fingerprints. When we first came here Alice got a job where she had to have her fingerprints taken."

"Excellent!" Dr. Winters exclaimed. "That should give us our final proof!"

It took the rest of the afternoon to get the fingerprint record and make a comparison. Dr. Winters called Mel at home to give him the report. There was no question. The fingerprints were identical. The corpse was that of Alice Hastings.

* * * *

The nightmare came again that night. Worse than Mel could ever remember it. As always, it was a dream of space, black empty space, and he was floating alone in the immense depths of it. There was no direction. He was caught in a whirlpool of vertigo from which he reached out with agonized yearning for some solidarity to cling to.

There was only space.

After a time he was no longer alone.

He could not see them, but he knew they were out there. The searchers. He did not know why he had to flee or why they sought him, but he knew they must never overtake him, or all would be lost.

Somehow he found a way to propel himself through empty space. The searchers were growing points of light in the far distance. They gave him a sense of direction. His being, his existence, his universe of meaning and understanding depended on the success of his flight from the searchers. Faster, through the wild black depths of space—

He never knew whether he escaped or not. Always he awoke in a tangle of bedclothes, bathed in sweat, whimpering in fear. For a long time Alice had been there to touch his hand when he awoke. But Alice was gone now and he was so weary of the night pursuit. Sometimes he wished it would end with the searchers—whoever they were—catching up with him and doing what they intended to do. Then maybe there would be no more nightmare. Maybe there would be no more Mel Hastings, he thought. And that wouldn't be so bad, either.

He tossed sleeplessly the rest of the night and got up at dawn feeling as if he had not been to bed at all. He would take one day more, and then get back to the News Bureau. He'd take this day to do what couldn't be put off any longer—the collecting and disposition of Alice's personal belongings.

*   *   *   *   *

He shaved, bathed and dressed, then began emptying the drawers, one by one. There were many souvenirs, mementos. She was always collecting these. Her bottom drawer was full of stuff that he'd glimpsed only occasionally.

In the second layer of junk in the drawer he came across the brochure on Martian vacations. It must have been one of the dreams of her life, he thought. She'd wanted it so much that she'd almost come to believe that it was real. He turned the pages of the smooth, glossy brochure. Its cover bore the picture of the great Martian Princess and the blazoned emblem of Connemorra Space Lines. Inside were glistening photos of the plush interior of the great vacation liner, and pictures of the domed cities of Mars where Earthmen played more than they worked. Mars had become the great resort center of Earth.

Mel closed the book and glanced again at the Connemorra name. Only one man had ever amassed the resources necessary to operate a private space line. Jim Connemorra had done it; no one knew quite how. But he operated now out of both hemispheres with a space line that ignored freight and dealt only in passenger business. He made money, on a scale that no government-operated line had yet been able to approach.

Mel sank down to the floor, continuing to shift through the other things in the drawer.

His hand stopped. He remained motionless as recognition showered sudden frantic questions in his mind. There lay a ticket envelope marked Connemorra Lines.

The envelope was empty when he looked inside, and there was no name on it. But it was worn. As if it might have been carried to Mars and back.

In sudden frenzy he began examining each article and laying it in a careless pile on the floor. He recognized a pair of idiotic Martian dolls. He found a tourist map of the ruined cities of Mars. He found a menu from the Red Sands Hotel.

And below all these there was a picture album. Alice at the Red Sands. Alice at the Phobos Oasis. Alice at the Darnella Ruins. He turned the pages of the album with numb fingers. Alice in a dozen Martian settings. Some of them were dated. About two years ago. They had gone together, Alice had said, but there was no evidence of Mel's presence on any such trip.

But it was equally impossible that Alice had made the trip, yet here was proof. Proof that swept him up in a doubting of his own senses. How could such a thing have taken place? Had he actually made such a trip and been stripped of the memory by some amnesia? Maybe he had forced himself to go with her and the power of his lifelong phobia had wiped it from his memory.

And what did it all have to do—if anything—with the unbelievable thing Dr. Winters had found about Alice?

Overcome with grief and exhaustion he sat fingering the mementos aimlessly while he stared at the pictures and the ticket envelope and the souvenirs.

*   *   *   *   *

Dr. Winters spoke a little more sharply than he intended. "I don't think anything is going to be solved by a wild-goose chase to Mars. It's going to cost you a great deal of money, and there isn't a single positive lead to any solution."

"It's the only possible explanation." Mel persisted. "Something happened on Mars to change her from what she once was to—what you saw on your operating table."

"And you are hoping that in some desperate way you will find there was a switch of personalities—that there may be a ghost of a chance of finding Alice still alive."

Mel bit his lip. He was scarcely willing to admit such a hope but it was the foundation of his decision. "I've got to do what I can," he said. "I must take the chance. The uncertainty will torment me all my life if I don't."

Dr. Winters shook his head. "I still wish I could persuade you against it. You will find only disappointment."

"My mind is made up. Will you help me or not?"

"What can I do?"

"I can't go into space unless I can find some way of lifting, even temporarily, this phobia that nearly drives me crazy at the thought of going out there. Isn't there a drug, a hypnotic method, or something to help a thing like this?"

"This isn't my field," said Dr. Winters. "But I suspect that the cause of your trouble cannot be suppressed. It will have to be lifted. Psycho-recovery is the only way to accomplish that. I can recommend a number of good men. This, too, is very expensive."

"I should have done it for Alice—long ago," said Mel.

*   *   *   *   *

Dr. Martin, the psychiatrist, was deeply interested in Mel's problem. "It sounds as if it is based on some early trauma, which has long since been wiped from your conscious memory. Recovery may be easy or difficult, depending on how much suppression of the original event has taken place."

"I don't even care what the original event was," said Mel, "if you rid me of this overwhelming fear of space. Dr. Winters said he thought recovery would be required."

"He is right. No matter how much overlay you pile on top of such a phobia to suppress it, it will continue to haunt you. We can make a trial run to analyze the situation, and then we can better predict the chance of ultimate success."

As a reporter, Mel Hastings had had vague encounters with the subject of psycho-recovery, but he knew little of the details about it. He knew it involved some kind of a machine that could tap the very depths of the human mind and drag out the hidden debris accumulated in mental basements and attics. But such things had always given him the willies. He steered clear of them.

When Dr. Martin first introduced him into the psycho-recovery room his resolution almost vanished. It looked more like a complex electronic laboratory than anything else. A half dozen operators and assistants in nurses' uniforms stood by.

"If you will recline here—," Dr. Martin was saying.

Mel felt as if he were being prepared for some inhuman biological experiment. A cage of terminals was fitted to his head and a thousand small electrodes adjusted to contact with his skull. The faint hum of equipment supported the small surge of apprehension within him.

After half an hour the preparations were complete. The level of lights in the room was lowered. He could sense the operators at their panels and see dimly the figure of Dr. Martin seated near him.

"Try to recall as vividly as possible your last experience with this nightmare you have described. We will try to lock on to that and follow it on down."

This was the last thing in the world Mel wanted to do. He lay in agonized indecision, remembering that he had dreamed only a short time ago, but fighting off the actual recollection of the dream.

"Let yourself go," Dr. Martin said kindly. "Don't fight it—"

A fragment of his mind let down its guard for a brief instant. It was like touching the surface of a whirlpool. He was sucked into the sweeping depths of the dream. He sensed that he cried out in terror as he plunged. But there was no one to hear. He was alone in space.

Fear wrapped him like black, clammy fur. He felt the utter futility of even being afraid. He would simply remain as he was, and soon he would cease to be.

But they were coming again. He sensed, rather than saw them. The searchers. And his fear of them was greater than his fear of space alone. He moved. Somehow he moved, driving headlong through great vastness while the pinpoints of light grew behind him.

"Very satisfactory," Dr. Martin was saying. "An extremely satisfactory probe."

His voice came through to Mel as from beyond vast barriers of time and space. Mel felt the thick sweat that covered his body. Weakness throbbed in his muscles.

"It gives us a very solid anchor point," Dr. Martin said. "From here I think we run back to the beginning of the experience and unearth the whole thing. Are you ready, Mr. Hastings?"

Mel felt too weak to nod. "Let 'er rip!" he muttered weakly.

*   *   *   *   *

The day was warm and sunny. He and Alice had arrived early at the spaceport to enjoy the holiday excitement preceding the takeoff. It was something they had both dreamed of since they were kids—a vacation in the fabulous domed cities and ruins of Mars.

Alice was awed by her first close view of the magnificent ship lying in its water berth that opened to Lake Michigan. "It's *huge*—how can such an enormous ship ever get off the Earth?"

Mel laughed. "Let's not worry about that. We know it does. That's all that matters." But he could not help being impressed, too, by the enormous size and the graceful lines of the luxury ship. Unlike Alice, he was not seeing it at close range for the first time. He had met the ship scores of times in his reporting job, interviewing famous and well-known personages as they departed or arrived from the fabulous playgrounds of Mars.

"If you look carefully," Mel pointed out, "you'll see a lot of faces that make news when they come and go."

Alice's face glowed as she clung to Mel's arm and recognized some of the famous citizens who would be their fellow passengers. "This is going to be the most fun we've ever had in our lives, darling."

"Like a barrel of monkeys," Mel said casually, enjoying the bubbling excitement that was in Alice.

The ship was so completely stabilized that the passengers did not even have to sit down during takeoff. They crowded the ports to watch the land and the water shoot past as the ship skimmed half the length of Lake Michigan in its takeoff run. As it bore into the upper atmosphere on an ever-increasing angle of climb, its own artificial gravity system took over and gave the illusion of horizontal flight with the Earth receding slowly behind.

Mel and Alice wandered through the salons and along the spacious decks as if in some fairyland-come-true. All sense of time seemed to vanish and they floated with the great ship in timeless, endless space.

He wasn't quite certain when he first became aware of his own sense of disquietude. It seemed to result from a change in the members of the crew. On the morning of the third day they ceased their universal and uninterrupted concern for their passengers' entertainment and enjoyment.

Most of the passengers seemed to have taken no note of it. Mel commented to Alice. She laughed at him. "What do you expect? They've spent two full days showing us the ship and teaching us to play all the games aboard. You don't expect them to play nurse to us during the whole trip, do you?"

It sounded reasonable. "I suppose so," said Mel dubiously. "But just what *are* they doing? They all seem to be in such a hurry to get somewhere this morning."

"Well, they must have some duties to perform in connection with running the ship."

Mel shook his head in doubt.

*   *   *   *   *

Alice joined him in wandering about the decks, kibitzing on the games of the other passengers, and watching the stars and galaxies on the telescopic screens. It was on one of these that they first saw the shadow out in space. Small at first, the black shadow crossed a single star and made it wink. That was what caught Mel's attention, a winking star in the dead night of space.

When he was sure, he called Alice's attention to it. "There's something moving out there." By now it had shape, like a tiny black bullet.

"Where? I don't see anything."

"It's crossing that patch of stars. Watch, and you can see it blot them out as it moves."

"It's another ship!" Alice exclaimed. "That's exciting! To think we're passing another ship in all this great emptiness of space! I wonder where it's coming from?"

"And where it's going to."

They watched its slow, precise movement across the stars. After several minutes a steward passed by. Mel hailed him and pointed to the screen. "Can you tell us what that other ship is?"

The steward glanced and seemed to recognize it instantly. But he paused in replying. "That's the Mars liner," he said finally. "In just a few minutes the public address system will announce contact and change of ship."

"Change of ship?" Mel asked, puzzled. "I never heard anything about a change of ship."

"Oh, yes," the steward said. "This is only the shuttle that we're on now. We transfer to the liner for the remainder of the trip. I'm sure that was explained to you at the time you purchased your tickets." He hurried away.

Mel was quite sure no such thing had been explained to him when he purchased tickets. He turned back to the screen and watched the black ship growing swiftly larger now as it and the Martian Princess approached on contact courses.

The public address system came alive suddenly. "This is your Captain. All passengers will now prepare to leave the shuttle and board the Mars liner. Hand luggage should be made ready. All luggage stowed in the hold will be transferred without your attention. It has been a pleasure to have you aboard. Contact with the liner will be made in fifteen minutes."

From the buzz around him Mel knew that this was as much a surprise to everyone else as it was to him, but it was greeted with excitement and without question.

Even Alice was growing excited now and others crowded around them when it was discovered what they were viewing. "It looks *big*," said Alice in subdued voice. "Bigger than this ship by far."

Mel moved away and let the others have his place before the screen. His sense of uneasiness increased as he contemplated the approach of that huge black ship. And he was convinced its color *was* black, that it was not just the monotone of the view screen that made it so.

Why should there be such a transfer of passengers in mid-space? The Martian Princess was certainly adequate to make the journey to Mars. Actually they were more than a third of the way there, already. He wasn't sure why he felt so certain something was amiss. Surely there was no possibility that the great Connemorra Lines would plan any procedure to the detriment of the more than five thousand passengers aboard the ship. His uneasiness was pretty stupid, he thought.

But it wouldn't go away.

He returned to the crowd clustered at the viewing screen and took Alice by the arm to draw her away.

She looked quizzically at him. "This is the most exciting thing yet. I want to watch it."

"We haven't got much time," Mel said. "We've got a lot of things to get in our suitcases. Let's go down to our stateroom."

"Everyone else has to pack, too. There's no hurry."

"Fifteen minutes, the Captain said. We don't want to be the last ones."

Unwillingly, Alice followed. Their stateroom was a long way from the salon. The fifteen minutes were almost up by the time they reached it.

*   *   *   *   *

Mel closed the door to their room and put his hands on Alice's shoulders. He glanced about warily. "Alice—I don't want to go aboard that ship. There's something wrong about this whole thing. I don't know what it is, but we're not going aboard."

Alice stared at him. "Have you lost your mind? After all our hopes and all our planning you don't want to go on to Mars?"

Mel felt as if a wall had suddenly sprung up between them. He clutched Alice's shoulders desperately in his hands. "Alice—I don't think that ship out there is going to Mars. I know it sounds crazy, but please listen to me—we weren't told anything about the Martian Princess being merely a shuttle and that we'd transfer to another ship out here. No one was told. The Martian Princess is a space liner perfectly capable of going to Mars. There's no reason why such a huge ship should be used merely as a shuttle."

"That ship out there is bigger."

"Why? Do we need any more room to finish the journey?"

Alice shook herself out of his grasp. "I don't know the answers to those questions and I don't care to know them!" she said angrily.

"If you think I'm going to give up this vacation and turn right around here in space and go back home you're crazy. If you go back you'll go back alone!"

Alice whirled and ran to the door. Mel ran after her, but she was through the door and was melting into the moving throng by the time he reached the door. He took a step to follow, then halted. He couldn't drag her forcibly back into the stateroom. Maybe she'd return in a few minutes to pack her bags. He went back in the room and closed the door.

*   *   *   *   *

Even as he did so he knew that he was guessing wrong. Alice would be matching him in a game of nerves. She'd go on to the other ship, expecting him to pack the bags and follow. He sat down on the bed and put his head in his hands for a moment. A faint shudder passed through the ship and he heard the hollow ring of clashing metal. The unknown ship had made contact with the Martian Princess. Their airlocks were being mated now.

From the porthole he could see the incredible mass of the ship. He crossed the room and pressed the curtains aside. His impression had been right. The ship *was* black. Black, nameless, and blind. No insignia or portholes were visible anywhere on the hull within his range of vision.

He didn't know what he was going to do, but he knew above all else that he wasn't going to board that ship. He paced the floor telling himself it was a stupid, neurotic apprehension that filled his mind, that the great Connemorra Lines could not be involved in any nefarious acts involving five thousand people— or even one person. They couldn't afford such risk.

He couldn't shake it. He was certain that, no matter what the cost, he was not going to board that black ship.

He looked about the stateroom. He couldn't remain here. They'd certainly find him. He had to hide somewhere. He stood motionless, staring out the porthole. There was no place he could hide with assurance inside the ship.

But what about outside?

His thoughts crumpled in indecision as he thought of Alice. Yet whatever the black ship meant, he could help no one if he went aboard. He had to get back to Earth and try to find out what it was all about and alert the authorities. Only in that way could he hope to help Alice.

*   *   *   *   *

He opened the stateroom door cautiously and stepped out. The corridor was filled with hurrying passengers, carrying hand luggage, laughing with each other in excitement. He joined them, moving slowly, alert for crew members. There seemed to be none of the latter in the corridors.

Keeping close to the wall, he moved with the crowd until he reached the rounded niche that marked an escape chamber. As if pushed by the hurrying throng, he backed into it, the automatic doors opening and closing to receive him.

The chamber was one of scores stationed throughout the ship as required by law. The escape chambers contained space suits for personal exit from the ship in case of emergency. They were never expected to be used. In any emergency requiring abandonment of the vessel it would be as suicidal to go into space in a suit as to remain with the ship. But fusty lawmakers had decreed their necessity, and passengers received a perfunctory briefing in the use of the chambers and the suits—which they promptly forgot.

Mel wrestled now with what he remembered of the instructions. He inspected a suit hanging in its cabinet and then was relieved to find that the instructions were repeated on a panel of the cabinet. Slowly, he donned the suit, following the step by step instructions as he went. He began to sweat profusely from his exertions and from his fear of discovery.

He finally succeeded in getting the cumbersome gear adjusted and fastened without being detected. He did not know if the airlock of the chamber had some kind of alarm that would alert the crew when it was opened. That was a chance he had to take. He discovered that it was arranged so that it could be opened only by a key operated from within the suit. This was obviously to prevent anyone leaving the ship unprotected. Perhaps with this safeguard there was no alarm.

He twisted the lock and entered the chamber. He opened the outer door and faced the night of space.

*   *   *

He would not have believed that anything could be so utterly terrifying. His knees buckled momentarily and left him clinging to the side of the port. Sweat burst anew from every pore. Blindly, he pressed the jet control and forced himself into space.

He arced a short distance along the curve of the ship and then forced himself down into contact with the hull. He clung by foot and hand magnetic pads, sick with nausea and vertigo.

He had believed that by clinging to the outside of the hull he could escape detection and endure the flight back to Earth. In his sickness of body and mind the whole plan now looked like utter folly. He retched and closed his eyes and lay on the hull through the beginning of an eternity.

*   *   *   *   *

He had no concept of time. The chronometer in the suit was not working. But it seemed as if many hours had passed when he felt a faint shock pass through the hull beneath him. He felt a momentary elation. The ships had separated. The search for him—if any—had been abandoned.

Slowly he inched his way around the hull to get a glimpse of the black ship. It was still there, standing off a few hundred yards but not moving. Its presence dismayed him. There could be no reason now for the two ships to remain together. The Martian Princess should be turning around for the return to Earth.

Then out of the corner of his eye he saw it. A trace of movement. A gleam of light. Like a small moon it edged up the distant curvature of the hull. Then there were more—a nest of quivering satellites.

Without thought, Mel pressed the jet control and hurled himself into space.

The terror of his first plunge was multiplied by the presence of the searchers. Crewmen of the Martian Princess, he supposed. The absence of the space suit had probably been discovered.

In headlong flight, he became aware of eternity and darkness and loneliness. The sun was a hot, bright disc, but it illuminated nothing. All that his mind clung to for identification of itself and the universe around it was gone. He was like a primeval cell, floating without origin, without purpose, without destination.

Only a glimmer of memory pierced the thick terror with a shaft of rationality. Alice. He must survive for Alice's sake. He must find the way back to Alice—back to Earth.

He looked toward the Martian Princess and the searchers on the hull. He cried out in the soundless dark. The searchers had left the hull and were pursuing him through open space. Their speed far exceeded his. It was futile to run before them—and futile to leave the haven of the Martian Princess. His only chance of survival or success lay in getting to Earth aboard the ship. In a long curve he arced back toward the ship. Instantly, the searchers moved to close in the arc and meet him on a collision course.

He could see them now. They were not crewmen in spacesuits as he had supposed. Rather, the objects—two of them—looked like miniature spaceships. Beams of light bore through space ahead of them, and he suspected they carried other radiations also to detect by radar and infra red.

In the depths of his mind he knew they were not of the Martian Princess. Nor were there any crewmen within them. They were robot craft of some kind, and they had come from the great black ship.

He felt their searching beams upon him and waited for a deadly, blasting burst of heat or killing radiation. He was not prepared for what happened.

*   *   *   *   *

They closed swiftly, and the nearest robot came within a dozen feet, matching Mel's own velocity. Suddenly, from a small opening in the machine, a slender metal tentacle whipped out and wrapped about him like the coils of a snake. The second robot approached and added another binding. Mel's arms and legs were pinned. Frantically, he manipulated the jet control in the glove of the suit. This only caused the tentacles to cut deeply and painfully, and threatened to smash the shell of the suit. He cut the jets and admitted the failure of his frantic mission.

In short minutes they were near the ships again. Mel wondered what kind of reprimand the crewmen of the Martian Princess could give him, and what fantastic justification they might offer for their own actions.

But he wasn't being taken toward the Martian Princess. He twisted painfully in the grip of the robot tentacles and confirmed that he was being carried to the black stranger.

Soundlessly, a port slid open and the robots swept him through into the dark interior of the ship. He felt himself dropped on a hard metal floor. The tentacles unwound. Alone, he struggled to his feet and flashed a beam of light from the suit flashlight to the walls about him. Walls, floor and ceiling were an indistinguishable dark gray. He was the only object in the chamber.

While he strained his sight to establish features in the blank metallic surfaces a clipped, foreign voice spoke. "Remove your suit and walk toward the opening in the wall. Do not try to run or attack. You will not be harmed unless you attack."

There was no use refusing. He did as commanded. A bright doorway opened in the wall before him. He walked through.

It reminded him of a medical laboratory. Shelves and cabinets of hand instruments and electronic equipment were about. And in the room three men sat watching the doorway through which he entered. He gazed at the strangers as they at him.

They looked ordinary enough in their white surgeons' smocks. All seemed to be of middle age, with dark hair turning gray at the fringe. One was considerably more muscular than the other two. One leaned to overweight. The third was quite thin. Yet Mel felt himself bristling like a dog in the dark of the moon.

No matter how ordinary they looked, these three were not men of Earth. The certainty of this settled like a cold, dead weight in the pit of his stomach.

"You—" he stammered. There was nothing to say.

"Please recline on this couch," the nearest, the muscular one said. "We wish you no harm so do not be afraid. We wish only to determine if you have been harmed by your flight into space."

All three of them were tense and Mel was sure they were worried—by his escapade. Had he nearly let some unknown cat out of the bag?

"Please—," the muscular one said.

He had no alternative. He might struggle, and destroy a good deal of apparatus, but he could not hope to overwhelm them. He lay on the couch as directed. Almost instantly the overweight one was behind him, seizing his arm. He felt the sting of a needle. The thin one was at his feet, looking down at him soberly. "He will rest," the thin one said, "and then we shall know what needs to be done."

     *   *   *

The sleep had lasted for an eon, he thought. He had a sense of the passage of an enormous span of time when he at last awoke. His vision was fuzzy, but there was no mistaking the image before him.

Alice. His Alice—safe.

She was sitting on the edge of the bed, smiling down at him. He fought his way up to a half-sitting position. "Alice!" He wept.

Afterwards, he said, "Where are we? What happened? I remember so many crazy things—the vacation to Mars."

"Don't try to remember it all, darling," she said. "You were sick. Some kind of hysteria and amnesia hit you while we were there. We're home now. You'll soon be out of the hospital and everything will be all right."

"I spoiled it," he murmured. "I spoiled it all for you."

"No. I knew you were going to be all right. I even had a lot of fun all by myself. But we're going back. As soon as you are all well again we'll start saving up and go again."

He nodded drowsily. "Sure. We'll go to Mars again and have a real vacation."

Alice faded away. All of it faded away.

    *   *   *   *   *

As if from a far distance the walls of Dr. Martin's laboratory seemed to close about him and the lights slowly increased. Dr. Martin was seated beside him, his head shaking slowly. "I'm so terribly sorry, Mr. Hastings. I thought we were going to get the full and true event this time. But it often happens, as in your case, that fantasy lies upon fantasy, and it is necessary to dig through great layers of them before uncovering the truth. I think, however, that we shall not have to go much deeper to find the underlying truth for you."

Mel lay on the couch, continuing to stare at the ceiling. "Then there was no great, black ship out of space?"

"Of course not! That is one danger of these analyses, Mr. Hastings. You must not be deceived into believing that a newly discovered fantasy is the truth for which you were looking. You must come back and continue your search."

"Yes. Yes, of course." He got up slowly and was helped to the outer room by the Doctor and an attendant. The attendant gave him a glass of white, sweetish substance to drink.

"A booster-upper," laughed Dr. Martin. "It takes away the grogginess that sometimes attends such a deep sweep. We will look for you day after tomorrow."

Mel nodded and stepped out into the hall.

*   *   *

No great black ship.

No mysterious little robot ships with tentacles that whip out and capture a man.

No strange trio in surgeons' gowns.

And no Alice—

A sudden spear of thought pierced his mind. Maybe all that was illusion, too. Maybe he could go home right now and find her waiting for him. Maybe—

No. That was real enough. The accident. Dr. Winters. The scene in the icy room next to Surgery at the hospital. Dr. Martin didn't know about that. He would have called that a fantasy, too, if Mel had tried to tell him.

No. It was all real.

The unbelievable, alien organs of Alice.

The great, black ship.

The mindless robot searchers.

His nightmare had stemmed from all this that had happened out in space, which had somehow been wiped from his conscious memory. The nightmare had not existed in his boyhood, as he had thought. It was oriented in time now.

But what had happened to Alice? There was no clue in the memory unearthed by Dr. Martin. Was her condition merely the result of some freak heredity or gene mutation?

The surging turmoil in his mind was greater than before. There was only one way to quiet it—that was to carry out his original plan to go to Mars.

He'd go out there again. He'd find out if the black ship existed or not.

*   *   *   *   *

The girl in the ticket office was kind but firm. "Our records show that you were a vacationer to Mars very recently. The demand is so great and the ship capacity so small that we must limit vacation trips to no more than one in any ten-year period."

He turned away and went down the hall and out the doorway of the marble and brass Connemorra Lines Building.

He walked through town for six blocks and the thought of old Jake Norton came to his mind. Jake had been an old timer in the city room when Mel was a cub. Jake had retired just a few months ago and lived in a place in town with a lot of other old men. Mel hailed the nearest cab and drove to Jake's place.

"Mel, it's great to see you!" Jake said. "I didn't think any of the boys would remember an old man after he'd walked out for the last time."

"People remember real easy when they want favors."

"Sure," Jake said with a grin, "but there's not much of a favor I can do you any more, boy. Can't even loan you a ten until next payday."

"Jake, you can help me," said Mel. "You don't expect to ever take a trip to Mars, do you?"

"Mars! Are you crazy, Mel?"

"I went once. I've got to go again. It's about Alice. And they won't let me. I didn't know you could go only once in ten years."

Jake remembered. Alice had called him and all the other boys after they'd come back the other time. Mel had been sick, she said. He wouldn't remember the trip. They were asked not to say anything about it. Now Mel was remembering and wanted to go again. Jake didn't know what he should do.

"What can I do to help you?" he asked.

"I'll give you the money. Buy a ticket in your name. I'll go as Jake Norton. I think I can get away with it. I don't think they make any closer check than that."

"Sure—if it'll do you any good," Jake said hesitantly. He was remembering the anxiety in Alice's voice the day she called and begged him not to say anything that would remind Mel of Mars. No one ever had, as far as Jake knew.

He took the money and Mel waited at the old men's home. An hour later Jake called. "Eight months is the closest reservation I can get at normal rates, but I know of some scalpers who charge 50% more."

Mel groaned. "Buy it no matter what the cost! I've got to go at once!" He would be broke for the next ten years.

*　　*　　*　　*　　*

It was little different from the other time. There was the same holiday excitement in the crowd of vacationers and those who had come to see them off. It was the same ship, even.

All that was different was the absence of Alice.

He stayed in his stateroom and didn't watch the takeoff. He felt the faint rocking motion as the ship went down its long waterway. He felt the shift as the artificial gravity took over. He lay on the bed and closed his eyes as the Martian Princess sought the cold night of space.

For two days he remained in the room, emerging only for meals. The trip itself held no interest for him. He waited only for the announcement that the black ship had come.

But by the end of the second day it had not come. Mel spent a sleepless night staring out at the endless horizon of stars. Dr. Martin had been right, he thought. There was no black ship. He had merely substituted one illusion for another. Where was reality? Did it exist anywhere in all the world?

Yet, even if there were no black ship, his goal was still Mars.

The third day passed without the appearance of the black ship. But on the very evening of that day the speaker announced: "All passengers will prepare for transfer from the shuttle ship to the Mars liner. Bring hand luggage—"

Mel sat paralyzed while he listened to the announcement. So it was true! He felt the faint jar that rocked the Martian Princess as the two ships coupled. From his stateroom port Mel could see the stranger, black, ugly, and somehow deadly. He wished he could show Dr. Martin this "illusion"!

He packed swiftly and left the room. Mel joined the surprised and excited throng now, not hanging back, but eager to find out the secret of the great black ship.

The transition from one ship to the other was almost imperceptible. The structure of both corridors was the same, but Mel knew when the junction was crossed. He sensed the entry into a strange world that was far different from the common one he knew.

Far down the corridor the crowd was slowing, forming into lines before stewards who were checking tickets. The passengers were shunted into branching corridors leading to their own staterooms. So far everything was so utterly normal that Mel felt an overwhelming despondency. It was just as they had been told; they were transferring to the Mars liner from the shuttle.

The steward glanced at his ticket, held it for a moment of hesitation while he scanned Mel's face. "Mr. Norton—please come with me."

The steward moved away in a direction no other passengers were taking. Another steward moved up to his place. "That way," the second man said to Mel. "Follow the steward."

*　　*　　*　　*　　*

Mel's heart picked up its beat as he stepped out of the line and moved slowly down the corridor after the retreating steward. They walked a long way through branching silent corridors that showed no sign of life.

They stopped at last before a door that was like a score of others they had passed. There were no markings. The steward opened the door and stood aside. "In here please," he said. Mel entered and found himself alone. The steward remained outside.

The room was furnished as an office. It was carpeted and paneled luxuriously. A door leading from a room at his left opened and admitted a tall man with graying hair. The man seemed to carry an aura of power and strength as he moved. An aura that Mel Hastings recognized.

"James Connemorra!" Mel exclaimed.

The man bowed his head slightly in acknowledgement. "Yes, Mr. Hastings," he said.

Mel was dismayed. "How do you know who I am?" he said.

James Connemorra looked through the port beside Mel and at the stars beyond. "I have been looking for you long enough I ought to know who you are."

Something in the man's voice chilled Mel. "I have been easy enough to find. I'm only a news reporter. Why have you been looking for me?"

Connemorra sank into a deep chair on the opposite side of the room. "Can't you guess?" he said.

"It has something to do with what happened—before?" Mel asked. He backed warily against the opposite wall from Connemorra. "That time when I escaped from the Martian Princess rather than come aboard the black ship?"

Connemorra nodded. "Yes."

"I still don't understand. Why?"

"It's an old story." Connemorra shrugged faintly. "A man learns too much about things he should know nothing of."

"I have a right to know what happened to my wife. You know about her don't you?"

Connemorra nodded.

"What happened to her? Why was she different after her trip to Mars?"

James Connemorra was silent for so long that Mel thought he had not heard him. "Is everyone different when they get back?" Mel demanded. "Does something happen to everybody who takes the Mars trip, the same thing that happened to Alice?"

"You learned so much," said Connemorra, speaking as if to himself, "I had to hunt you down and bring you here."

"What do you mean by that? I came through my own efforts. Your office tried to stop me."

"Yet I knew who you were and that you were here. I must have had something to do with it, don't you think?"

"What?"

"I forced you to come by deception, so that no one knows you are here—except the old man whose name you used. Who will believe him that you came on the Martian Princess? Our records will show that a Jake Norton will be there on Earth. No one can ever prove that Mel Hastings ever came aboard."

*   *   *   *   *

Mel let his breath out slowly. His fear suddenly swallowed caution. He took a crouching step forward. Then he stopped, frozen. James Connemorra tilted the small pistol resting in his lap. Mel did not know how it came to be there. He had not seen it a moment ago.

"What are you going to do?" Mel demanded. "What are you going to do with all of us?"

"You know too much," said Connemorra, shrugging in mock helplessness. "What *can* I do with you?"

"Explain what I don't understand about the things you say I know."

"Explain to you?" The idea seemed to amuse Connemorra greatly, as if it had some utterly ridiculous aspect. "Yes, I might as well explain," he said. "I haven't had anyone interested enough to listen for a long time.

"Men have never been alone in space. We have been watched, inspected, and studied periodically since Neanderthal times by races in the galaxy who have preceded us in development by hundreds of thousands of years. These observers have been pleasantly excited by some of the things we have done, appalled by others.

"There is a galactic organization that has existed for at least a hundred thousand years. This organization exists for the purpose of mutual development of the worlds and races of the galaxy. It also exists to maintain peace, for there were ages before its organization when interstellar war took place, and more than one great world was wiped out in such senseless wars.

"When men of Earth were ready to step into space, the Galactic Council had to decide, as it had decided on so many other occasions, whether the new world was to be admitted as a member. The choice is not one which a new world is invited to make; the choice is made for it. A world which begins to send its ships through space becomes a member of the Council, or its ships cease to travel. The world itself may cease to exist."

"You mean this dictatorial Council determines whether a world is fit to survive and actually wipes out those it decides against?" gasped Mel in horror. "They set themselves up as judges in the Universe?"

"That's about the way they operate, to put it bluntly," said Connemorra. "You can call them a thousand unpleasant names, but you can't change the fact of their existence, nor the fact of their successful operation for a period as long as the age of the human race.

"They would never have made their existence known to us if we had not begun sending our ships into space. But once we did that we were entering territory staked out by races that were there when we crawled out of our caves. Who can say what their rights are?"

"But to pass judgment on entire worlds—"

"We have no choice but to accept that such judgment is passed."

"And their judgment of Earth—?"

"Was that Earth was not ready for Council membership. Earthmen are still making too many blunders to join creatures that could cross the galaxy at the speed of light when we were learning how to chip flint."

"But they didn't wipe us out!"

*   *   *   *   *

James Connemorra looked out at the stars. "I wonder," he said. "I wonder—"

"What do you mean?" Mel said in a tight voice.

"We have defects which are not quite like any they have encountered before. We have developed skills in the manufacture of artifacts, but we have no capacity for using them. For example, we have developed vast systems of communication, but these systems have not improved our communications they have actually blocked communication."

"That's crazy!" said Mel. "Do they suppose smoke signals are superior to the 3-d screens in our homes?"

"As a matter of fact, they do. And so do I. When a man must resort to smoke signals he is very certain that he has something to say before he goes to the trouble of putting the message in the air. But our fabulous screens prevent us from communicating with each other by throwing up a wall of pseudo-communication that we can't get through. We subject ourselves to a barrage of sound and light that has a communication content of almost zero.

"The same is true of our inventions in transportation. We have efficient means of travel to all parts of the world and now to the Universe itself. But we don't travel. We use our machines to block traveling."

"I can understand the first argument, but not this one!" said Mel.

"We move our bodies to new locations with our machines, but our minds remain at home. We take our rutted thoughts, our predispositions, our cultural concepts wherever we go. We do not touch, even with a fragment of our minds, that which our machines give us contact with. We do not travel. We move in space, but we do not travel.

"This is their accusation. And they're right. We are still doing what we have always done. We are using space flight for the boring, the trivial, the stupid; using genius for a toy, like a child banging an atomic watch on the floor. It happened with all our great discoveries and inventions: the gasoline engine, the telephone, the wireless. We've built civilizations of monumental stupidity on the wonders of nature. One race of the Galactics has a phrase they apply to people like us: 'If there is a God in Heaven He has wept for ten thousand years.'

*　*　*　*　*

"But all this is not the worst. A race that is merely stupid seldom gets out to space. But ours has something else they fear: destructiveness. They have plotted our history and extrapolated our future. If they let us come out, war and conflict will follow."

"They can't know that!"

"They say they can. We are in no position to argue."

"So they plan to destroy us—"

"No. They want to try an experiment that has been carried out just a few times previously. They are going to reduce us from what they term the critical mass which we have achieved."

"Critical mass? That's a nuclear term."

"Right. Meaning ready to blow up. That's where we are. Two not-so-minor nuclear wars in fifty years. They see us carrying our destructiveness into space, fighting each other there, infecting other races with our hostility. But if we are broken down into smaller groups, have the tools of war removed, and are forced to take another line of development—well, they have hopes of salvaging us."

"But they can't do a thing like that to us! What do they intend? Taking groups of Earthmen, deporting them to other worlds—breaking them apart from each other forever—?"

The coldness found its resting place in Mel's chest. He stared at James Connemorra. Then his eyes moved slowly over the walls of the room in the black ship and out to the stars. The black ship.

"This ship—! You transfer your passengers to this Galactic ship for deportation to other worlds! But they come back—"

"They are sent to colonies on other worlds where conditions are like those on Earth—with significant exceptions. The colonies are small, the largest are only a few thousand. The problems there are different than on Earth—and they are tough. The natural resources are not the same. The development of the resulting cultures will be vastly different from that of Earth. The Galactic Council is very interested in the outcome—which will not be known with certainty for a thousand years or so."

"But they come back," Mel repeated. "You bring them back!"

"For each Earthman who goes out, a replacement is sent back. The replacement is an android supplied by the Council."

"Android!" Mel felt his reason slipping. He knew he was shouting. "Then Alice—the Alice that died was an android, she was not my wife! My Alice is still alive! You can take me to her-"

Connemorra nodded. "Alice is still alive, and well. No harm has come to her."

"Take me to her!" Mel knew he was pleading, but in his anguish he had no pride.

Connemorra seemed to ignore his plea. "Earth's population is slowly being diluted by the removal of top people. The androids behave in every way like the individuals they replace, but they are preconditioned against the inherent destructiveness of Earthmen."

Blind anger seemed to rise within Mel. "You have no right to separate me from Alice. Take me to her!"

His rage ignited and he leaped forward.

The small gun in Connemorra's hand spurted twice. Mel felt a double impact in a moment of great wonder. It couldn't end like this, he thought. It couldn't end without his seeing Alice once more. Just once more—

*   *   *   *   *

He sank to the floor. The pain was not great, but he knew he was dying. He looked down at his hand that covered the great wound in his mid-section. There was something wrong.

He felt the stickiness, but the red blood was not welling out. Instead, a thick bubble of green ooze moved from the wound and spread over his clothes and his hand. An alien greenness that was like nothing human.

He had seen it once before.

Alice.

He stared up at Connemorra with wide, wondering eyes.

"Everything went wrong, my poor android," said Connemorra softly. "After your human was brought back to the ship we were forced to go through with the usual process of imprinting his mind content upon his android. But we had to wipe out all memory of the attempted escape from the Martian Princess. This was not successful. It still clung in the nightmares you experienced. And the psycho-recovery brought it all back.

"We tried to cover it with an amnesiac condition instead of the usual pre-printed memory of a Mars vacation. And all this might have worked if the Alice android had not been defective also. A normal android has protective mechanisms that make accidents and subsequent discovery impossible. But the Alice android failed, and you set out on a course to uncover us. I had to find a way to destroy you—murder.

"I'm truly sorry. I don't know how an android thinks or feels. Sometimes I'm afraid of all of you. You are like men, but I've seen the factories in which you are produced. There are many things I do not know. I know only that I had to obey the Galactic Council or Earth would have been destroyed long ago.

"And something else I know: Alice and Mel Hastings are content and happy. They are on a lovely world, very much like Central Valley."

He closed his eyes as he felt the life—or whatever it was— seeping out of him. It came out right, after all, he thought.

Like a wooden soldier with a painted smile, fallen from a shelf, he lay twisted upon the floor.

THE GREAT GRAY PLAGUE

ORIGINALLY PUBLISHED IN *ANALOG SCIENCE FACT AND SCIENCE FICTION*, FEBRUARY 1962

There is no enemy so hard to fight as a dull gray fog.
It's not solid enough to beat, too indefinite to kill,
and too omnipresent to escape.

THE GREAT GRAY PLAGUE

Dr. William Baker was fifty and didn't mind it a bit. Fifty was a tremendously satisfying age. With that exact number of years behind him a man had stature that could be had in no other way. Younger men, who achieve vast things at, say, thirty-five, are always spoken of with their age as a factor. And no matter what the intent of the connection, when a man's accomplishments are linked to the number of years since he was born there is always a sense of apologia about it.

But when a man is fifty his age is no longer mentioned. His name stands alone on whatever foundation his achievements have provided. He has stature without apology, if the years have been profitably spent.

William Baker considered his years had been very profitably spent. He had achieved the Ph. D. and the D. Sc. degrees in the widely separated fields of electronics and chemistry. He had been responsible for some of the most important radar developments of the World War II period. And now he held a post that was the crowning achievement of those years of study and effort.

On this day of his fiftieth birthday he walked briskly along the corridor of the Bureau building. He paused only when he came to the glass door which was lettered in gold: National Bureau of Scientific Development, Dr. William Baker, Director. He was unable to regard that door without a sense of pride. But he was convinced the pride was thoroughly justifiable.

He turned the knob and stepped into the office. Then his brisk stride came to a pause. He closed the door slowly and frowned. The room was empty. Neither his receptionist nor his secretary, who should have been visible in the adjoining room, were at their posts. Through the other open door, at his left, he could see that his administrative assistant, Dr. James Pehrson, was not at his desk.

He had always expected his staff to be punctual. In annoyance that took some of the glint off this day, he twisted the knob of his own office door and strode in.

He stopped just inside the room, and a warm wave of affection welled up within him. All nine members of his immediate staff were gathered around the table in the center of his office. On the table was a cake with pink frosting. A single golden candle burned brightly in the middle of the inscription: Happy Birthday, Chief.

The staff broke into a frighteningly off-key rendition of "Happy Birthday to You." William Baker smiled fondly, catching the eye of each of them as they badgered the song to its conclusion.

Afterward, he stood for a moment, aware of the moisture in his own eyes, then said quietly, "Thank you. Thank you very much, Family. This is most unexpected. None of you will ever know how much I appreciate your thoughtfulness."

"Don't go away," said Doris Quist, his blond and efficient secretary. "There's more. This is from all of us."

He opened the package she offered him. A genuine leather brief case. Of course, the Government didn't approve of gifts like this. If he observed the rules strictly, he ought to decline the gift, but he just couldn't do that. The faces of Doris and the others were glowing as he held up the magnificent brief case. This was the first time such a thing had occurred in his office, and a man hit fifty only once.

"Thanks so much for remembering," Baker said. "Things like this and people like you make it all worth while."

When they were all gone he sat down at his desk to take up the day's routine. He felt a little twinge of guilt at the great satisfaction that filled him. But he couldn't help it. A fine family, an excellent professional position—a position of prominence and authority in the field that interested him most—what more could a man want?

His meditation was interrupted by the buzzing of the interphone. Pehrson was on the other end. "Just reminding you, Chief," the assistant said. "Dr. Fenwick will be in at nine-thirty regarding the request for the Clearwater grant. Would you like to review the file before he arrives?"

"Yes, please," said Baker. "Bring everything in. There's been no change, no new information, I suppose?"

"I'm afraid not. The Index is hopelessly low. In view of that fact there can be no answer but a negative one. I'm sorry."

"It's all right. I can make Fenwick understand, I'm sure. It may take a little time, and he may erupt a bit, but it'll work out."

Baker cut off and waited while Pehrson came in silently and laid the file folders of the offending case on the desk. Pehrson was the epitome of owl-eyed efficiency, but now he showed sympathy behind his great horn-rimmed spectacles as he considered Baker's plight. "I wish we could find some way to make the Clearwater research grant," he said. "With just a couple of good Ph. D.'s who had published a few things, the Index would be high enough—"

"It doesn't matter. Fenwick is capable of handling his own troubles." Pehrson was a good man, but this kind of solicitousness Baker found annoying.

"I'll send him in as soon as he comes," Pehrson said as he closed the door behind him.

*　　*　　*　　*　　*

Baker sighed as he glanced at the folder labeled, Clearwater College. Jerkwater is what it should be, he thought. He almost wished he had let Pehrson handle Fenwick. But one couldn't neglect old friends, even though there was nothing that could be done for shortsighted ones.

Baker's memories shifted. He and Fenwick had gone to school together. Fenwick had always been one to get off into weird wide alleys, mostly dead ended. Now he was involved in what was probably the most dead ended of all. For the last three years he had been president of little Jerkwater—Clearwater College, and he seemed to have some hope that NBSD could help him out of the hole.

That was a mistake many people made. Baker sometimes felt that half his time was spent in explaining that NBSD was not in the business of helping people and institutions out of holes. It was in the business of buying for the United States Government the best scientific research available in the world.

Fenwick wanted help that would put Clearwater College on its feet through a research contract in solid state physics. Fenwick, thought Baker, was dreaming. But that was Fenwick.

The President of Clearwater College entered the outer office promptly at nine-thirty. Pehrson greeted him, and Doris showed him into Baker's office.

Dr. John Fenwick didn't look like a college president, and Baker, unknowingly, held this vaguely against him, too. He looked more like a prosperous small business man and gave the impression of having just finished a brisk workout on the handball court, and a cold shower. He was ruddy and robust and ill-equipped with academic dignity.

Baker pumped his hand as if genuinely glad to see him. "It's good to see you again, John. Come on over and sit down."

"I'll bet you hoped I'd break a leg on the way here," said Fenwick. He took a chair by the desk and glanced at the file folder, reading the title, Clearwater College. "And you've been hoping my application would get lost, and the whole thing would just disappear."

"Now, look, John—" Baker took his own seat behind the desk. Fenwick had always had a devilish knack for making him feel uncomfortable.

"It's all right," said Fenwick, waving away Baker's protests with a vigorous flap of his hand. "I know Clearwater isn't MIT or Cal Tech, but we've got a real hot physics department, and you're going to see some sparks flying out of there if you'll give us half a chance in the finance department. What's the good word, anyway? Do we get the research grant?"

Baker took a deep breath and settled his arms on the desk in front of him, leaning on them for support. He wished Fenwick wasn't so abrupt about things.

"John," Baker said slowly. "The head of your physics department doesn't even have a Ph. D. degree."

Fenwick brightened. "He's working on that, though! I told you that in answer to the question in the application. Bill, I wish you'd come down and see that boy. The things he can do with crystals would absolutely knock your hat off. He can stack them just like a kid stacking building blocks—crystals that nobody else has ever been able to manipulate so far. And the electrical characteristics of some of them—you wouldn't believe the transistors he's been able to build!"

"John," said Baker patiently. "The head of the physics department in any institution receiving a grant must have a Ph. D. degree. That is one absolutely minimum requirement."

"You mean we've got to wait until George finishes his work for his degree before we get the grant? That puts us in kind of a predicament because the work that we hoped to have George do under the grant would contribute towards his degree. Can't you put it through on the basis that he'll have his degree just as soon as the present series of experiments is completed?"

Baker wiped his forehead and looked down at his hands on the desk. "I said this is *one* minimum requirement. There are others, John."

"Oh, what else are we lacking?" Fenwick looked crestfallen for the first time.

"I may as well be blunt," said Baker. "There is no conceivable way in which Clearwater College can be issued a research grant for *anything*—and especially not for basic research in any field of physical science."

*   *   *   *   *

Fenwick just stared at him for a minute as if he couldn't believe what he had heard, although it was the thing he had expected to hear since the moment he sat down.

He seemed deflated when he finally spoke. "I don't think it was the intent of the Congressional Act that made these funds available," he said, "that only the big, plush outfits should get all the gravy. There are plenty of smaller schools just like Clearwater who have first rate talent in their science departments. It isn't fair to freeze us out completely—and I don't think it's completely legal, either."

"Clearwater is not being frozen out. Size has nothing to do with the question of whether an institution receives a grant from NBSD or not."

"When did you last give a grant to a college like Clearwater?"

"I am afraid we have never given a grant to a college—like Clearwater," said Baker carefully.

Fenwick's face began to grow more ruddy. "Then will you tell me just what is the matter with Clearwater, that we can't get any Government research contract when every other Tom, Dick, and Harry outfit in the country can?"

"I didn't state my case in exactly those terms, John, but I'll be glad to explain the basis on which we judge the qualifications of an institution to receive a grant from us."

Baker had never done this before for any unsuccessful applicant. In fact, it was the policy of the Bureau to keep the mysteries of the Index very carefully concealed from the public. But Baker wanted Fenwick to know what had hung him. It was the one more or less merciful thing he could do to show Fenwick what was wrong, and might be sufficient to shake him loose from his dismal association with Clearwater.

Baker opened the file folder and Fenwick saw now that it was considerably fuller than he had first supposed. Baker turned the pages, which were fastened to the cover by slide fasteners. Chart after chart, with jagged lines and multicolored areas, flipped by under Baker's fingers. Then Baker opened the accordian folds of a four-foot long chart and spread it on the desk top.

"This is the Index," he said, "a composite of all the individual charts which you saw ahead of it. This Index shows in graphical form the relationship between the basic requirements for obtaining a research grant and the actual qualifications of the applicant. This line marks the minimum requirement in each area."

Baker's finger pointed to a thin, black line that crossed the sheet. Fenwick observed that most of the colored areas and bars on the chart were well inside the area on Baker's side of the line. He guessed that the significance of the chart lay in this fact.

"I take it that Clearwater College is in pretty sad shape, chartwise," said Fenwick.

"Very," said Baker.

"Can you tell me how these charts are compiled?"

Baker turned back to the sheaf of individual charts. "Each item of data, which is considered significant in evaluating an applicant, is plotted individually against standards which have been derived from an examination of all possible sources of information."

"Such as?"

"For example, the student burden per faculty Ph. D. That is shown on this chart here."

"The what? Say that again," said Fenwick in bewilderment.

"The number of students enrolled, plotted against the number of doctorate degrees held by the faculty."

"Oh."

"As you see, Clearwater's index for this factor is dismally low."

"We're getting a new music director next month. She expects to get her doctorate next summer."

"I'm afraid that doesn't help us now. Besides, it would have to be in a field pertinent to your application to have much weight."

"George—"

"Doesn't help you at all for the present. You would require a minimum of two in the physics department alone. These two would have to be of absolutely top quality with a prolific publication record. That would bring this factor to a bare minimum."

"You take the number of Ph. D.'s and multiply them by the number of papers published and the years of experience and divide by the number of students enrolled. Is that the idea?"

"Roughly," said Baker. "We have certain constants which we also inject. In addition, we give weight to other factors such as patents applied for and granted. Periods of consultation by private industry, and so on. Each of these factors is plotted separately, then combined into the overall Index."

Baker turned the pages slowly, showing Fenwick a bleak record of black boundary lines cutting through nearly virginal territory on the charts. Clearwater's evaluation was reflected in a small spot of color near the bottom edge.

*   *   *   *   *

Fenwick stared at the record without expression for a long time. "What else do you chart?" he said finally.

"The next thing we evaluate is the performance of students graduated during the past twenty-five years."

"Clearwater is only ten years old," said Fenwick.

"True," said Baker, "and that is why, I believe, we have obtained such an anomalous showing in the chart of this factor."

Fenwick observed that the colored area had made a considerable invasion on his side of the boundary on this chart. "Why anomalous? It looks like we make a pretty good showing here."

"On the face of it, this is true," Baker admitted. "The ten-year record of the graduates of Clearwater is exceptional. But the past decade has been unusual in the scope of opportunities, you must admit."

"Your standard level must take this into account."

"It does. But somehow, I am sure there is a factor we haven't recognized here."

"There might be," said Fenwick. "There might be, at that."

"Another factor which contributes to the Index," said Baker, "is the cultural impact of the institution upon the community. We measure that in terms of the number and quality of cultural activities brought into the community by the university or college. We include concerts, lectures, terpsichorean activities, Broadway plays, and so on."

"Terpsichorean activities. I like that," said Fenwick.

"Primarily ballet," said Baker.

"Sure."

"Clearwater's record here is very low. It fact, there isn't any."

"This helps us get turned down for a research grant in physics?"

"It's a factor in the measurement of the overall status."

"Look," said Fenwick, "the citizens of Clearwater are so infernally busy with their own shindigs that they wouldn't know what to do if we brought a long-hair performance into town. If it isn't square-dancing in the Grange Hall, it's a pageant in the Masonic Temple. The married kids would probably like to see a Broadway play, all right, but they're so darned busy rehearsing their own in the basement of the Methodist Church that I doubt they could find time to come. Besides that, there's the community choir every Thursday, and the high school music department has a recital nearly every month. People would drop dead if they had any more to go to in Clearwater. I'd say our culture is doing pretty good."

"Folk activities are always admirable," said Baker, "but improvement of the cultural level in any community depends on the injection of outside influences, and this is one of the functions of the university. Clearwater College has not performed its obligation to the community in this respect."

Fenwick appeared to be growing increasingly ruddy. Baker thought he saw moisture appearing on Fenwick's forehead.

"I know this is difficult to face," said Baker sympathetically, "but I wanted you to understand, once and for all, just how Clearwater College appears to the completely objective eye."

Fenwick continued to stare at him without comment. Then he said flatly, "Let's see some more charts, Bill."

"Museum activities. This is an important function of a college level institution. Clearwater has no museum."

"We can't afford one, in the first place. In the second place, I think you've overlooked what we do have."

"There *is* a Clearwater museum?" Baker asked in surprise.

"Two or three hundred of them, I guess. Every kid in the county has his own collection of arrowheads, birds' eggs, rocks, and stuffed animals."

"I'm not joking, John," said Baker bleakly. "The museum aspect of the college is extremely important."

"What else?" said Fenwick.

"I won't go into everything we evaluate. But you should be aware of several other factors pertaining to the faculty, which are evaluated. We establish an index of heredity for each faculty member. This is primarily an index of ancestral achievement."

Fenwick's color deepened. Baker thought it seemed to verge on the purple. "Should I open the window for a moment?" Baker asked.

Fenwick shook his head, his throat working as if unable to speak. Then he finally managed to say, "Apart from the sheer idiocy of it, how did you obtain any information in this area?"

Baker ignored the comment, but answered the question. "You filled out forms. Each faculty member filled out forms."

"Yeah, that's right. I remember. Acres of forms. None of us minded if it was to help get the research grant. We supposed it was the usual Government razzmatazz to keep some GS-9 clerk busy."

"Our forms are hardly designed to keep people busy. They are designed to give us needed information about applicant institutions."

"And so you plot everybody's heredity."

"As well as possible. You understand, of course, that the data are necessarily limited."

"Sure. How do our grandpas stack up on the charts?"

"Not very well. Among Clearwater's total faculty of thirty-eight there were no national political figures through three generations back. There was one mayor, a couple of town councilmen, and a state senator or two. That is about all."

"Our people weren't very politically minded."

"This is a measure of social consciousness and contemporary evaluation."

Fenwick shrugged. "As I said, we aren't so good at politics."

"Achievements in welfare activities are similarly lacking. No notable intentions or discoveries, with the exception of one patent on a new kind of beehive, appear in the record."

"And this keeps us from getting a research grant in physics? What *did* our progenitors do, anyway? Get hung for being horse thieves?"

"No criminal activities were reported by your people, but there is a record of singular restlessness and dissatisfaction with established conditions."

*　　*　　*　　*　　*

"What did they do?"

"They were constantly on the move, for the most part. In the eighteenth and nineteenth centuries they were primarily pioneers, frontiersmen, settlers of new country. But when the country was established they usually packed up and went somewhere else. Rovers, trappers, unsettled people."

"This is not good?" Fenwick glanced at the chart that was open now. It was almost uncolored.

"I regret to say that such people are not classed as the stable element of communities," said Baker. "We cannot evaluate the index of hereditary accomplishment for the Clearwater faculty very high."

"It appears that our grandpas were among those generally given credit for getting things set up," said Fenwick.

"Such citizens are indeed necessary," said Baker. "But our index evaluates stability in community life and accomplishments with long-range effects in science and culture."

"We haven't got much of a chance then, grandpa being foot-loose as he was."

"Other factors could completely override this negative evaluation. You see, this is the beauty of the Index; it doesn't depend on any one factor or small group of factors. We evaluate the whole range of factors that have anything to do with the situation. Weaknesses in one spot may be counterbalanced by strength in others."

"It looks like Clearwater is staffed by a bunch of bums without any strong spots."

"I wouldn't say it in such terms, but the reason I am pointing these things out to you, John, is to try to persuade you to disassociate yourself from such a weak organization and go elsewhere. You have fine talents of your own, but you have always had a pattern of associating with groups like this one at Clearwater. Don't you see now that the only thing for you to do is go somewhere where there are people capable of doing things?"

"I *like* Clearwater. I like the people at the College. Where else are we in the bums category?"

Baker suddenly didn't want to go on. The whole thing had become distasteful to him. "There are a good many others. I don't think we need to go into them. There is the staff reading index, the social activity index, wardrobe evaluation, hobbies, children—actual and planned."

"I want to hear about them," said Fenwick. "That wardrobe evaluation—that sounds like a real fascinating study."

"Actually, it's comparatively minor," said Baker. "Our psychologists have worked out some extremely interesting correlations, however. Each item of a man's wardrobe is assigned a numerical rating. Tuxedo, one or more. Business suits, color and number. Hunting jackets. Slacks. Sport coats. Work shoes. Dress shoes. Very interesting what our people can do with, such information."

"Clearwater doesn't rate here?"

Baker indicated the chart. "I'm afraid not. Now, this staff reading index is somewhat similar. You recall the application forms asked for the number of pages of various types of material read during the past six months—scientific journals, newspapers, magazines, fiction."

"I suppose Clearwater is a pretty illiterate bunch," said Fenwick.

Baker pointed soundlessly to the graph.

"Hobbies and social activities are not bad," Baker said, after a time. "Almost up to within ten points of the standard. A few less bingo parties and Brownie meetings and that many more book reviews or serious soirees would balance the social activity chart. If the model railroad club were canceled and a biological activity group substituted, the hobby classification would look much better. Then, in the number of children, actual and planned, Clearwater is definitely out of line, too. You see, the standard takes the form of the well-known bell-shaped curve. Clearwater is way down on the high side."

"Too much biological activity already," Fenwick murmured.

Baker looked up. "What was that? I didn't hear what you said."

Fenwick leaned back and extended his arms on the desk. "I said your whole damned Index is nothing but a bunch of pseudo-intellectual garbage."

*   *   *   *   *

Baker felt the color rising in his face, but he forced himself to remain calm. After a moment of silence he said. "Your emotional feelings are understandable, but you must remember that the Index permits us to administer accurately the National Science Development Act. Without the scientific assurance of the Index there would be no way of determining where these precious funds could best be utilized."

"You'd be better off putting the money on the ponies," said Fenwick. "Sometimes they win. As it stands, you've set it up for a sure loss. You haven't got a chance in the world."

"You think Clearwater College could make better use of some of our funds than, say, MIT?"

"I wouldn't be surprised. Don't get me wrong. I'm not saying the boys at MIT or Cal Tech or a lot of other places couldn't come up with a real development in the way of a fermodacular filter for reducing internucleated cross currents. But the real breakthroughs—you've closed your doors and locked them out."

"Who have we locked out? We've screened and fine combed the resources of the entire country. We know exactly where the top research is being conducted in every laboratory in the nation."

Fenwick shook his head slowly and smiled. "You've forgotten the boys working in their basements and in their back yard garages. You've forgotten the guys that persuade the wife to put up with a busted-down automatic washer for another month so they can buy another hundred bucks worth of electronic parts. You've remembered the guys who have Ph. D.'s for writing 890-page dissertations on the Change of Color in the Nubian Daisy after Twilight, but you've forgotten guys like George Durrant, who can make the atoms of a crystal turn handsprings for him."

Baker leaned back in his chair and smiled. He almost wished he hadn't wasted the effort of trying to show Fenwick. But, then, he had tried. And he would always have regretted it if he hadn't.

"You're referring now to the crackpot fringe?" he said.

"I suppose so," said Fenwick. "I've heard it called that before."

"One of the things, above all else, which the Index was designed to accomplish," said Baker, "was the screening out of all elements that might be ever so remotely associated with the crackpot fringe. And believe me, you'll never know how strong it is in this country! Every two-bit tinkerer wants a handout to develop his world-shaking gadget that will suppress the fizz after the cap is removed from a pop bottle, or adapt any apartment-size bathtub for raising tropical fish."

"You ever heard of the flotation process?" said Fenwick abruptly.

Baker frowned at the sudden shift of thought. "Of course—"

"What would the world be like without the flotation process?"

"The metals industry would be vastly different, of course. Copper would be much scarcer and higher priced. Gold—"

"A ton of ore and maybe a pound of recovered metal, right?" said Fenwick. "Move a mountain of waste to get anything of value. Crush millions of tons of rock and float out the pinpoint particles of metal on bubbles of froth."

"That's a rough description of what happens."

"You've heard of high-grading."

"Of course. A somewhat colloquial term used in mining."

"The high-grader takes a pick and digs for anything big enough to see and pick up with his hands. He doesn't worry about the small stuff that takes sweat and machinery to recover."

"I suppose so. I fail to see the significance—"

"You're high-grading, Bill," said Fenwick. He leaned across the desk and spoke with bitter intensity. "You're high-grading and you should be using a flotation process."

Fenwick slowly drew back in his chair. Baker felt overwhelmed by the sudden intensity he had never before seen displayed in John Fenwick. Any reaction on his part seemed suddenly inadequate. "I fail to see any connection—," he said finally.

Fenwick looked at him steadily. "Human creativeness can be mined only by flotation methods. It's in low-grade ore. Process a million stupid notions and find a pin point of genius. Turn over enormous wastes of human thought and recover a golden principle. But turn your back on these mountains of low-grade material and you shut out the wealth of creative thought that is buried in them. More than that, by high-grading only where rich veins have appeared in the past, you're mining lodes that have played out."

"An ingenious analogy," said Baker, recovering with a smile now. "But it's hardly an accurate or applicable one. The human mind is not a piece of precious metal found in a mountain of ore. Rather, it's an intricate device capable of producing computations of unbelievable complexity. And we know how such devices that are superior in function are produced, and we know what their characteristics are. We also know that such a device does not 'play out'. If it is superior in function, it can remain so for a long time."

"High-grading," said Fenwick. "And the vein is played out. You'll never find the thing you're looking for until you develop means of processing low-grade material."

* * * * *

Baker watched Fenwick across the desk. He was weary of the whole thing. He certainly had no need to prove himself to this man. He had simply tried to do Fenwick a favor, and Fenwick had thrown it right back in his face. Yet there was a temptation to go on, to prove to Fenwick the difference between their two worlds. Fenwick belonged to a world compounded of inevitable failure. The temptation to show him, to try again to lift him out of it was born of a kind of pity for Fenwick.

Baker's own life had arrowed decisively, without waver, to a goal that was as correct as the tolerances of human error could make it. He often permitted himself the pride of considering his mind somewhat as a computer that had been programmed through a magnificent gene inheritance to drive irresistibly toward the precise goals he had reached. But Fenwick—Fenwick was still fumbling around in a morass of uncertainty. After years of erratic starts and stops he was now confusedly trying to make something out of that miserable little institution called Clearwater College.

It wasn't particularly friendship that urged Baker to show Fenwick. Their friendship was of a breed that Baker had never quite been able to define to his own satisfaction. It seemed to him there was a sort of deadly fascination in associating with a man who walked so blindly, who was so profoundly incapable of understanding his own blindness and peril.

"I'm going to show you," Baker said abruptly, "exactly what it would mean if we were to do as you suggest. I'll show you what it would be like to give attention to every halfwit and crackpot that comes begging for a handout." He switched the intercom and spoke into it. "Doris, please bring in the Ellerbee file. Yes—the crackpot section."

He switched off. "Doris has her own quaint but quite accurate way of cataloguing our various applications," he explained.

In a moment the secretary entered and placed the file on the desk. "There's a new letter in there," she said. "Dr. Pehrson initialed it. He said you didn't want to be bothered any more with this case."

"That's right."

Baker opened the file and shoved it toward Fenwick. "This boy has a gadget he wants us to look at. Doesn't really need any money, he says. That's the kind we really have to be on guard against. If we looked at his wonder gadget, we'd be pestered for a million-dollar handout for years to come."

"What's he got?" Fenwick asked.

"Some kind of communication device, he says. He claims it's nothing but a grown crystal which you hold in your hand and talk to anybody anywhere on Earth."

"Sounds like it wouldn't take much to find out whether he's got anything or not. Just let him put on a five-minute demonstration."

"But multiply that five minutes by a thousand, by ten thousand. And once you let them get their teeth into you, it doesn't stop with five minutes. It goes on into reams of letters and years of time. No, you have to stop this kind of thing before it ever starts. But take a look at some of this material in the file and you'll see what I mean."

Fenwick picked up the top letter as Baker pushed the file toward him. "He starts this one by saying, 'Dear Urban.' Is that what he calls you? What does he mean?"

"Who knows? He's a crackpot, I told you. Who cares what he means, anyway. We've got far more important things to worry about."

Fenwick scanned the letter a moment, then looked up, a faint smile on his face. "I know what he means. Urban—Pope Urban—was the one responsible for the persecutions of Galileo."

Baker shrugged embarrassedly. "I told you he was a crackpot. Delusions of grandeur and of persecution are typical."

"This boy may not be as crazy as he sounds. You're giving him a pretty good imitation of a Galileo treatment—won't even look at his device. He says here that 'Since you have previously refused to examine my device and have questioned my reliability as an observer, I have obtained the services of three unbiased witnesses, whose affidavits, signed and notarized, are attached. These men are the Fire Chief, the Chief of Police, and the Community Church Pastor of Redrock, all of whom testify that they did see my device in full operation this past week. I trust that this evidence will persuade you that an investigation should be made of my device. I fail to see how the bull-headedness and cocksureness of your office can withstand any more of the evidence I have to offer in support of my claims.'"

"A typical crackpot letter," said Baker. "He tries to be reasonable, but his colors are soon shown when he breaks down into vituperative language like a frustrated child."

Fenwick thumbed through the large pile of correspondence. "I'd say anybody would likely blow his stack a good deal harder than this if he'd been trying to get your attention this long. Why didn't he ever send you one of his gadgets in the mail?"

"Oh, he did," said Baker. "That was one of the first things he did."

"What did you do?"

"Sent it back. We always return these things by registered return mail."

"Without even trying it out?"

"Of course."

"Bill, that isn't even reasonable. These earlier letters of his describe the growing of these crystals. He tells exactly how he does it. He knows what he's talking about. I'd like to see him and see his crystal."

"That's what I was hoping you'd say! All we have to do is get Doris to give him a call and he'll be here first thing in the morning. You can be our official investigator. You can see what it's like dealing with a crackpot!"

*   *   *   *   *

James Ellerbee was a slim man, impetuous and energetic. Fenwick liked him on sight. He was not a technical man; he was a farmer. But he was an educated farmer. He had a degree from the State Agricultural College. He dabbled in amateur radio and electronics as a hobby.

"I'm certainly glad someone is finally willing to give me a break and take a look at my device," he said as he shook Fenwick's hand. "I've had nothing but a runaround from this office for the past eight months. Yet, according to all the publicity, this is where the nation's scientific progress is evaluated."

Fenwick felt like a hypocrite. "We get pretty overloaded," he said lamely.

They were in Baker's office. Baker watched smugly from behind his desk. Ellerbee said, "Well, we might as well get started. All you have to do, Mr. Fenwick, is hold one of these crystal cubes in your hand. I'll go in the other office and close the door. It may help at first if you close your eyes, but this is not really necessary."

"Wait," said Fenwick. Somehow he wanted to get away from Baker while this was going on. "I'd like to take it outside, somewhere in the open. Would that be all right?"

"Sure. Makes no difference where you try it," said Ellerbee. "One place is as good as another."

Baker waved a hand as they went out. "Good luck," he said. He smiled confidently at Fenwick.

As far as Fenwick could see, the crystal was not even potted or cased in any way. The raw crystal lay in his hand. The striations of the multitude of layers in which it was laid down were plainly visible.

Ellerbee dropped Fenwick off by the Jefferson memorial, then drove on about a mile. Still in sight, he stopped the car and got out. Fenwick saw him wave a hand. Nothing happened.

Fenwick glanced down at the crystal in his hand. About the size of a child's toy block. He could almost understand Baker's position. It *was* pretty silly to suppose this thing could have the powers Ellerbee said it had. No electric energy applied. It merely amplified the normal telepathic impulses existing in every human mind, Ellerbee said. Fenwick sighed. You just couldn't tell ahead of time that a thing wasn't going to pan out. He knew his philosophy was right. These had to be investigated—every lousy, crackpot one of them. You could never tell what you were missing out on unless you did check.

He squeezed harder on the crystal, as Ellerbee had told him to do.

It was just a little fuzzy at first, fading and coming back. Then it was there, shimmering a little, but steady. The image of Ellerbee standing in front of him, grinning.

Fenwick glanced down the road. Ellerbee was still there, a mile away. But he was also right there in front of him, about four feet away.

"It shakes you up a little bit at first," said Ellerbee. "But you get used to it after a while. Anyway, this is it. Are you convinced my device works?"

Fenwick shook his head to try to clear it rather than to give a negative answer. "I'm convinced *something* is working," he said. "I'm just not quite sure what it is."

"I'll drive across town," Ellerbee offered. "You can see that distance makes no difference at all. Later, I'll prove it works clear across the country if you want me to."

They arranged that proof of Ellerbee's presence on the other side of the city could be obtained by Fenwick's calling him at a drug store pay phone. Then they would communicate by means of the cubes.

It was no different than before.

The telephone call satisfied Fenwick that Ellerbee was at least ten miles away. Then, within a second, he also appeared to be standing directly in front of Fenwick.

"What do you want?" said Fenwick finally. "What do you want the Bureau to do about your device? How much money do you want for development?"

"Money? I don't need any money!" Ellerbee exploded. "All I want is for the Government to make some use of the thing. I've had a patent on it for six months. The Patent Office had sense enough to give me a patent, but nobody else would look at it. I just want somebody to make some use of it!"

"I'm sure a great many practical applications can be found," Fenwick said lamely. "We'll have to make a report, first, however. There will be a need for a great many more experiments—"

But most important of all, Baker would have to be shown. Baker would have to *know* from his own experience that this thing worked.

Fenwick suddenly wanted to get away from Ellerbee as much as he had from Baker a little earlier. There was just so much a man's aging synapses could stand, he told himself. He had to do a bit of thinking by himself. When Ellerbee drove up again, Fenwick told him what he wanted.

Ellerbee looked disappointed but resigned. "I hope this isn't another runaround, Mr. Fenwick. You'll pardon me for being blunt, but I've had some pretty raw treatment from your office since I started writing about my communicator."

"I promise you this isn't a runaround," said Fenwick, "but it's absolutely necessary to get Dr. Baker to view your demonstration. We will want to see your laboratories and your methods of production. I promise you it won't be more than two or three days, depending on Dr. Baker's busy schedule."

"O.K. I'll wait until the end of the week," said Ellerbee. "If I don't hear something by then, I'll go ahead with my plans to market the crystals as a novelty gadget."

"I'll be in touch with you. I promise," said Fenwick. He stood by the curb and watched Ellerbee drive away.

*   *   *   *   *

Fenwick moved slowly back to his own car and sat behind the wheel without starting the motor. It seemed a long time since nine-thirty yesterday morning, when he had come in to Baker's office to check on the grant he had known Baker wasn't going to give him. Now, merely by kicking Baker's refuse pile with his toe, so to speak, he had turned up a diamond that Baker was ready to discard.

Fenwick felt a sudden surge of revulsion. How was it possible for such a blind, ignorant fool as Baker to be placed in the position he was in? How could the administrative officers of the United States Government be responsible for such misjudgment? Such maladministration, if performed consciously, would be sheer treason. Yet, unconsciously and ignorantly, Baker's authority was perpetuated, giving him a stranglehold on the creative powers of the nation.

Fenwick tried to recall how he and Baker had become friends—so long ago, in their own college days. It wasn't that there was any closeness or common interest between them, yet they seemed to have drawn together as two opposites might. They were both science majors at the time, but their philosophies were so different that their studies were hardly a common ground.

Fenwick figuratively threw away the textbook the first time the professor's back was turned. Baker, Fenwick thought, never took his eyes from its pages. Fenwick distrusted everything that he could not prove himself. Baker believed nothing that was not solidly fixed in black and white and bound between sturdy cloth covers, and prefaced by the name of a man who boasted at least two graduate degrees.

Fenwick remembered even now his first reaction to Baker. He had never seen his kind before and could not believe that such existed. He supposed Baker felt similarly about him, and, out of the strange contradiction of their worlds, they formed a hesitant friendship. For himself, Fenwick supposed that it was based on a kind of fascination in associating with one who walked so blindly, who was so profoundly incapable of understanding his own blindness and peril.

But never before had he realized the absolute danger that rested in the hands of Baker. And there must be others like him in high Government scientific circles, Fenwick thought. He had learned long ago that Baker's kind was somewhere in the background in every laboratory and scientific office.

But few of them achieved the strangling power that Baker now possessed.

The Index! Fenwick thought of it and gagged. Wardrobe evaluation! Staff reading index! The reproductive ratio—social activity index—the index of hereditary accomplishment—multiply your ancestors by the number of technical papers your five-year old children have produced and divide by the number of book reviews you attend weekly—

Fenwick slumped in the seat. We hold these truths to be self-evident—that the ratio of sports coats to tuxedos in a faculty member's closet shall determine whether Clearwater gets to do research in solid state physics, whether George Durrant gives his genius to the nation or whether it gets buried in Dr. William Baker's refuse pile.

But not only George Durrant. Jim Ellerbee, too. And how many others?

Something had to be done.

Fenwick hadn't realized it before, but this was the thought that had been churning in his cortex for the last hour. Something had to be done about Bill Baker.

But, short of murder, what?

Getting rid of Baker physically was not the answer, of course. If he were gone, a hundred others like him would fight for his place.

Baker had to be shown. He had to be shown that high-grading was costing him the very thing he was trying to find. It must be proven to him that flotation methods work as well in mining human resources as in mining metal. That the extra trouble paid off.

This was known—a long time ago—Fenwick thought. Somewhere along the way things got changed. He glanced toward the Jefferson Memorial. Tom Jefferson knew how it should be, Tom Jefferson, statesman, farmer, writer, and amateur mechanic and inventor. It was not only every gentleman's privilege, it was also his duty to be a tinkerer and amateur scientist, no matter what else he might be.

Fenwick glanced in the distance toward the Lincoln Memorial. Abe had done his share of tinkering. His weird boot-strap system for hoisting river boats off shoals and bars hadn't amounted to much, but Abe knew the principle that every man has the right to be his own scientist.

And then there was Ben Franklin, the noblest amateur of them all! He had roamed these parts, too.

Somewhere it had been lost. The Bill Bakers would have laughed out of existence the great tinkerers like Franklin and Lincoln and Jefferson. And the Pasteurs and the Mendels—and the George Durrants and the Jim Ellerbees, too.

Fenwick started the car. Something had to be done about Bill Baker.

*　　*　　*　　*　　*

Baker leaned back in his chair and laughed heartily. "So it worked, did it? He showed you something that made you think he had a real working device."

"There was no 'think' about it," said Fenwick. "I saw it with my own eyes. That boy's got something terrific!"

Baker sobered and thumbed through the Ellerbee file again. "Any freshman math major could poke holes all through this mathematical explanation he offers. Right? Secondly, a device such as he claims to have produced violates all the basic laws of science. Why, it's even against the Second Law of Thermodynamics!"

"I don't care what it's against," said Fenwick. "It works. I want you to come with me to Ellerbee's and see for yourself. His device will revolutionize communications."

Baker shook his head sadly. "It's always tougher when they show you something that seems to work. Then you've got to waste a lot of time looking for the gimmick if you're going to follow it through. I just haven't got the time—"

"You've got to, Bill!"

"I'll tell you what I'll do. You go out there and look over his setup. If you can't find his gimmick in half a day, I'll come out and show it to you. But I warn you, some of these things are very tricky—like the old perpetual motion machines. You've got to have your wits about you. Is that fair enough?"

"Fair enough," Fenwick agreed.

Baker smiled broadly. "I'll do even more. If this Ellerbee device should prove to be on the level, I'll give you the research grant you want for Clearwater."

"I'm not so sure I want it on those terms," said Fenwick.

"Well, it's a purely academic matter. You won't have to worry about it. But, on the other hand, I'll expect you to agree that when Ellerbee is exposed you'll not persist in your request to this office."

"Well, now—"

"That's a fair offer. I'm giving you a chance to prove I'm wrong in setting up the Index to screen out people like Ellerbee—"

"—And institutions like Clearwater."

"And institutions like Clearwater," Baker agreed.

"All right," said Fenwick. "I'll gamble with you—for one more stake: If Ellerbee's device is on the level, you'll make a grant to Clearwater *and* other institutions of like qualifications, and you'll scrap that insane Index—"

Baker tapped the desk placatingly. "The grant to Clearwater, yes. As for the Index, if it should fail in its applicability to this clear-cut Ellerbee case I would be the first to want to know why. But I assure you there is no flaw in the Index. It has been tried too many thousands of times."

*   *   *   *   *

Ellerbee's place was in Virginia, in a dairying area in the hills. The last ten miles of the road were not the kind to attract visitors. The road was steep and narrow in places that turned sharply around the hillsides. No guardrails blocked the descent into the steep gullies. It was definitely a region for people who liked solitude. The farms that lay in the valleys of the hills were neat and well-cared for, however. The people Fenwick passed on the road didn't look like the recluse type.

Ellerbee's farm was one of the best looking in the vicinity. It had the look of being cared for by a man who could do everything. The huge barn and the corrals were as neat as a garden, and the large white frame farmhouse stood out like a monument against the green pasture.

A woman and two children were in the garden beside the house as Fenwick drove up. "May I help you? I'm Mrs. Ellerbee," the woman said.

Fenwick explained who he was and his purpose in coming. "Jim's been expecting you," the woman said. "His laboratory is the long white building back of the house. He's out there now."

Jim Ellerbee met him at the door. "You didn't bring Dr. Baker," he said almost accusingly.

"Later," said Fenwick. "I came, as I promised. Dr. Baker wants my report on your facilities and production methods. Then he will come up to make his own inspection."

There was doubt in Ellerbee's eyes, as if he was used to such stories. "Maybe it would be best if I marketed the crystals in any form I can," he said.

He led Fenwick through a number of rooms of expensive, precision electronic equipment. Then they passed through a set of double doors, which Fenwick observed acted as a thermal lock between the crystal growing room and the rest of the building. It reminded him of George Durrant's laboratory at Clearwater.

"This is where the crystals are grown," said Ellerbee. "I suppose you're familiar with such processes. Here we must use a very precisely controlled sequence of co-crystallization to get layers of desired thickness—"

Fenwick wasn't listening. He had suddenly observed the second man in the room, a rather small, swarthy man, who moved with quiet precision among a row of tanks on the far side of the room. There was a startling quality about the man that Fenwick was unable to define, a strangeness.

Ellerbee caught the direction of his glance. "Oh," he said. "You must meet my neighbor, Sam Atkins. Sam is in this as deep or even deeper than I am. I think perhaps he's more responsible for the communicator crystals."

The man turned as his name was mentioned, and came toward them. "You were the one who developed the crystals," he said in a soft, persuasive voice, to Jim Ellerbee.

"This is my setup," Ellerbee explained with a wave of his hand to indicate the laboratory surroundings. "But Sam has been working with me for about a year on this thing. When Sam moved in, we found we were both radio hams and electronic bugs. I'd been fooling around with crystal growing, trying to design some new type transistors. Then Sam suggested some experiments in co-crystallization—using different chemicals that will crystallize in successive layers in one crystal.

"We stumbled on one combination that made a terrific amplifier. Then we found it would actually radiate to a distant point all by itself. Finally, we discovered that its radiation was completely nonelectromagnetic. There is no way we have yet found of detecting the radiation from the crystal—except by means of another piece of the same crystal.

"I know it's against all the rules in the books. It just doesn't make sense. But there it is. It works."

Sam Atkins had turned away for a moment to attend to one of the tanks, but Fenwick found himself intensely aware of the man's presence. There was nothing he could put his finger on. He just knew, with such intense certainty, that Sam Atkins was *there*.

"What does Mr. Atkins do?" Fenwick asked. "Does he have a dairy farm, too?"

Ellerbee nodded. "His place is right next to mine. Since we started this project Sam has practically lived here, however. He's a bachelor, and so he takes most of his meals with us."

"Seems strange—" Fenwick mused, "two men like you, way out here in the country, doing work on a level with that of the best crystal labs in the country. I should think you'd both rather be in academic or industrial work."

Ellerbee smiled and looked up through the windows to the meadows beyond. "We're *free* out here," he said.

Fenwick thought of Baker. "You are that," he said.

"You said you wanted to investigate the whole production process. We'll start here, if you like, and I'll show you every step in our process. This tank contains an ordinary alum solution. We start building on a seed crystal of alum and continue until we reach a precise thickness. Here is a solution of chrome alum. You'll note the insulated tanks. Room temperature is maintained within half a degree. The solutions are held to within one-tenth of a degree. Crystal dimensions must be held to tolerances of little more than the thickness of a molecule—"

*   *   *   *   *

The gimmick to fool him and cheat him. Where was it? Fenwick asked himself. Baker was sure it was here. If so, where could it be? There was no trickery in the crystal laboratory— unless it was the trickery of precision refinement of methods. Only men of great mechanical skill could accomplish what Ellerbee and his friend were doing. Genius behind the milking machine! Fenwick could almost sympathize with Baker in his hiding behind the ridiculous Index. Without some such protection a man could encounter shocks.

The crackpot fringe.

Where else would credence have been given to the phenomenon of a crystal that seemed to radiate in a nonelectromagnetic way?

But, of course, it couldn't actually be doing that. All the books, all the authorities, and the known scientific principles said it couldn't happen. Therefore, it wouldn't have happened— outside the crackpot fringe.

If Ellerbee and Atkins weren't trying to foist a deliberate deception, where were they mistaken? It was possible for such men as these to make an honest mistake. That would more than likely turn out to be the case here. But how could there be a mistake in the production of a phenomenon such as Fenwick had witnessed? How could that be produced through some error when it couldn't even be done by known electronic methods—not just as Fenwick had seen it.

Throughout the morning Ellerbee led him down the rows of tanks, explaining at each step what was happening. Sometimes Sam Atkins offered a word of explanation also, but always he stayed in the background. The two farmers showed Fenwick how they measured crystal size down to the thickness of a molecule while the crystals were growing.

A sudden suspicion crossed Fenwick's mind. "If those dimensions are so critical, how did you determine them in the first place?"

"Initially, it was a lucky accident," said Sam Atkins.

"Very lucky," said Fenwick, "if you were able to accidentally obtain a crystal of fifteen layers or so and have each layer even approximately correct."

Sam smiled blandly. "Our first crystals were not so complex, you understand. Only three layers. We thought we were building transistors, then. Later, our mathematics showed us the advantage of additional layers and gave us the dimensions."

The mathematics that Baker said a kid could poke holes in. Fenwick didn't know. He hadn't checked the math.

Where was the gimmick?

In the afternoon they took him out for field tests again. A rise behind the barn was about a mile from a similar rise on Sam Atkins' place. They communicated across that distance in all the ways, including various kinds of codes, that Fenwick could think of to find some evidence of hoax. Afterwards, they returned to the laboratory and sawed in two the crystals they had just used. Then they showed him the tests they had devised to determine the nature of the radiation between the crystals.

He did not find the gimmick.

By the end of the day Ellerbee seemed beat, as if he'd been under a heavy strain all day long. And then Fenwick realized that was actually the case. Ellerbee wanted desperately to have someone believe in him, believe in his communication device. Not only had he used all the reasoning power at his command, he had been straining physically to induce Fenwick to believe.

Through it all, however, Sam Atkins seemed to remain bland and utterly at ease, as if it made absolutely no difference to him, whatever.

"I guess we've just about shot our wad," said Ellerbee. "That's about all we've got to show you. If we haven't convinced you by now that our communicator works, I don't know how we can accomplish it."

Had they convinced him? Fenwick asked himself. Did he believe what he had seen or didn't he? He had been smug in front of Baker after the first demonstration, but now he wondered how much he had been covered by the same brush that had tarred Baker.

It wasn't easy for him to admit the possibility of nonelectromagnetic radiation from these strange crystals, radiation which could carry sight and sound from one point to another without any transducers but the crystals themselves.

"You have to step out of the world you've grown accustomed to," said Sam Atkins very quietly. "This is what we have had to do. It's not hard now to comprehend that telepathic forces of the mind can be directed by this means. This is a new pattern.

Think of it as such. Don't try to cram it into the old pattern. Then it's easy."

A new pattern. That was the trouble, Fenwick thought. There couldn't really be any new patterns, could there? There was only one basic pattern, in which all the phenomena of the universe fit. He readily admitted that very little was known about that pattern, and many things believed true were false. But the Second Law of Thermodynamics. *That* had to be true—invariably true—didn't it?

If there was a hoax, Baker would have to find it.

"I'll be back with Dr. Baker in a couple of days," Fenwick said. "After that, the one final evidence we'll need will be to construct these crystals in our own laboratories, entirely on our own, based on your instructions."

Ellerbee nodded agreement. "That would suit us just fine."

* * * * *

"Hypnotism," said Baker. "It sounds like some form of hypnotism, and I don't like that kind of thing. It could merit criminal prosecution."

"There's no possible way I could have been hypnotized," said Fenwick.

"These crystals—obviously it has something to do with them. But I wonder what their game is, anyway? It's hard to see where they can think they're headed."

"I don't know," said Fenwick. "But you promised to show me the gimmick if I couldn't find it in half a day. I spent a whole day out there without finding anything."

Baker slapped the desk in exasperation. "You're not really going to make me go out there and look at this fool thing, are you? I know I made a crazy promise, but I was sure you could find where they were hoaxing you if you took one look at their setup. It's probably so obvious you just stumbled right over it without even seeing it was there."

"Possibly. But you're going to have to show me."

"John, look—"

"Or, I *might* be willing to take that Clearwater research grant without any more questions on either side."

Baker thought of the repercussions that would occur in his own office, let alone outside it, if he ever approved such a grant. "All right," he sighed. "You've got me over a barrel. I'll drive my car. I may have to stop at some offices on the other side of town."

"I might be going on, rather than coming back to town," said Fenwick. "I ought to have my car, too. Suppose I meet you out there?"

"Good enough. Say one o'clock. I'm sure that will give us more time than we need."

*   *   *   *   *

Baker was prompt. He arrived with an air of let's-get-this-over-as-quick-as-possible. He nodded perfunctorily as Ellerbee introduced his wife. He scarcely looked at Sam Atkins.

"I hope you've got your demonstration all set up," he said. He glanced at the darkening sky. "It looks like we might get some heavy rain this afternoon."

"We're all ready," said Ellerbee. "Sam will drive over to that little hill on his farm, and we'll go out behind the barn."

On the knoll, Baker accepted the crystal cube without looking at it. Clenching it in his fist, he put his hand in his pocket. Fenwick guessed he was trying to avoid any direct view and thus avoid the possibility of hypnotic effects. This seemed pretty farfetched to Fenwick.

Through field glasses Sam Atkins was seen to get out of his car and walk to the top of the knoll. He stood a moment, then waved to signal his readiness.

"Press the crystal in your hand," Ellerbee said to Baker. "Direct your attention toward Sam Atkins."

Each of them had a cube of the same crystal. It was like a party line. Fenwick pressed his only slightly. He had learned it didn't take much. He saw Baker hesitate, then purse his lips as if in utter disgust, and follow instructions.

In a moment the image of Sam Atkins appeared before them. Regardless of their position, the image gave the illusion of standing about four feet in front of them.

"Good afternoon, Dr. Baker," Sam Atkins said.

Fenwick thought Baker was going to collapse.

The director just stood for a moment, like a creature that had been pole-axed. Then his color began to deepen and he turned with robot stiffness. "Did you men hear anything? Fenwick ... did you hear ... did you see?"

"Sure," said Fenwick, grinning broadly. "Sam Atkins said good afternoon to you. It would be polite if you answered him back."

The image of Sam Atkins was still before them. He, too, was grinning broadly. The grins infuriated Baker.

"Mr. Atkins," said Baker.

"Yes, Dr. Baker," said Sam Atkins.

"If you hear me, wave your hands. I will observe you through the field glasses."

"The field glasses won't be necessary."

Both the image before them, and the distant figure on the knoll were seen to wave arms and gyrate simultaneously. For good measure, Sam Atkins turned a cartwheel.

Baker seemed to have partly recovered. "There seems to be a very remarkable effect present here," he said cautiously.

"Dr. Baker," Jim Ellerbee spoke earnestly, "I know you're skeptical. You don't think the crystals do what I say they do. Even though you see it with your own eyes you doubt that it is happening. I will do anything possible to test this device to your satisfaction. Name the test that will dispel your doubts and we will perform it!"

"It's not entirely a question of demonstration, Mr. Ellerbee," said Baker. "There are the theoretical considerations as well. The mathematics you have submitted in support of your claim are not, to put it mildly, sound."

"I know. Sam keeps telling me that. He says we need an entirely new math to handle it. Maybe we'll get around to that. But the important thing is that we've got a working device."

"Your mathematical basis *must* be sound!" Baker's fervor returned. Fenwick felt a sudden surge of pity for the director.

The demonstration was repeated a dozen times more. Fenwick went over on Sam Atkins' hill. He and Baker conversed privately.

"Do you see it yet?" Fenwick asked.

"No, I'm afraid I don't!" Baker was snappish. "This is one of the most devilish things I've ever come across!"

"You don't think it's working the way Jim and Sam say it is?"

"Of course not. The thing is utterly impossible! I am convinced a hypnotic condition is involved, but I must admit I don't see how."

"You may figure it out when you go through Ellerbee's lab."

*   *   *   *   *

Baker was obviously shaken. He spoke in subdued tones as Ellerbee started the tour of the crystal lab again. Baker's eyes took in everything. As the tour progressed he seemed to devour each new item with frenzied intensity. He inspected the crystals through a microscope. He checked the measurements of the thickness of the growing crystal layers.

The rain began while they were in the crystal lab. It beat furiously on the roof of the laboratory building, but Baker seemed scarcely aware that it was taking place. His eyes sought out every minute feature of the building. Fenwick was sure he was finding nothing to confirm his belief that the communicator crystals were a hoax.

Fenwick hadn't realized it before, but he recognized now that it would be a terrific blow to Baker if he couldn't prove the existence of a hoax.

Proof that the communicator crystals were all they were supposed to be would be a direct frontal attack on the sacred Index. It would blast a hole in Baker's conviction that nothing of value could come from the crackpot fringe. And, not least of all, it would require Baker to issue a research grant to Clearwater College.

What else it might do to Baker, Fenwick could only guess, but he felt certain Bill Baker would never be the same man again.

As it grew darker, Baker looked up from the microscope through which he had been peering. He glanced at the windows and the drenched countryside beyond. "It's been raining," he said.

Mary Ellerbee had already anticipated that the visitors would be staying the night. She had the spare room ready for Baker and Fenwick before dinner. While they ate in the big farmhouse kitchen, Ellerbee explained. "It would be crazy to try to get down to the highway tonight. The county's been promising us a new road for five years, but you see what we've got. Even the oldest citizen wouldn't tackle it in weather like this, unless it was an emergency. You put up for the night with us. You'll get home just as fast by leaving in the morning, after the storm clears. And it will be a lot more pleasant than spending the night stuck in the mud somewhere—or worse."

Baker seemed to accept the invitation as he ate without comment. To Fenwick he appeared stunned by the events of the day, by his inability to find a hoax in connection with the communicator crystals.

*　　*　　*　　*　　*

It was only when Baker and Fenwick were alone in the upstairs bedroom that Baker seemed to stir out of his state of shock.

"This is ridiculous, Fenwick!" he said. "I don't know what I'm doing here. I can't possibly stay in this place tonight. I've got people to see this evening, and appointments early in the morning."

"It's coming down like cats and dogs again," said Fenwick. "You saw the road coming in. It's a hog wallow by now. Your chance of getting through would be almost zero."

"It's a chance I have to take," Baker insisted. He started for the door. "*You* don't have to take it, of course."

"I'm not going to!" said Fenwick.

"But I must!"

Fenwick followed him downstairs, still trying to persuade him of the foolishness of driving back tonight. When Ellerbee heard of it he seemed appalled.

"It's impossible, Dr. Baker! I wouldn't have suggested your not returning if there were any chance of getting through. I assure you there isn't."

"Nevertheless I must try. Dr. Fenwick will remain, and I will come back tomorrow afternoon to complete our investigation. There are important things I must attend to before then, however."

Fenwick had the sudden feeling that Baker was in a flight of panic. His words had an aimless stream-of-consciousness quality that contrasted sharply with his usually precise speech. Fenwick was certain there was nothing sufficiently important that it demanded his attention on a night like this. He could have telephoned his family and had his wife cancel any appointments.

No, Fenwick thought, there was nothing Baker had to go *to*; rather, he was running *from*. He was running in panicky fear from his failure to pin down the hoax in the crystals. He was running, Fenwick thought, from the fear that there might be no hoax.

It seemed incredible that such an experience could trigger so strong a reaction. Yet Fenwick was aware that Baker's attitude toward Ellerbee and his device was not merely one aspect of Baker's character. His attitude in these things *was* his character.

Fenwick dared not challenge Baker with these thoughts. He knew it would be like probing Baker's flesh with a hot wire. There was nothing at all that he could do to stop Baker's flight.

Ellerbee insisted on loaning him a powerful flashlight and a hand lantern, which Baker ridiculed but accepted. It was only after Baker's tail-light had disappeared in the thick mist that Fenwick remembered he still had the crystal cube in his coat pocket.

"He's bound to get stuck and spend the night on the road," said Ellerbee. "He'll be so upset he'll never come back to finish his investigation."

Fenwick suspected this was true. Baker would seal off every association and reminder of the communicator crystals as if they were some infection that would not heal. "There's no use beating your brains out trying to get the NBSD to pay attention," Fenwick told Ellerbee. "You've got a patent. Figure out some gadgety use and start selling the things. You'll get all the attention you want."

"I wanted to do it in a dignified way," said Ellerbee regretfully.

You, too, Fenwick thought as he moved back up the stairs to the spare bedroom.

Fenwick undressed and got into bed. He tried to read a book he had borrowed from Ellerbee, but it held no interest for him. He kept thinking about Baker. What produced a man like Baker? What made him tick, anyway?

Fenwick had practically abandoned his earlier determination that something had to be done about Baker. There was really nothing that could be done about Baker, Bill Baker in particular—and the host of assorted Bakers scattered throughout the world in positions of power and importance, in general.

They stretched on and on, back through the pages of history and time. Jim Ellerbee understood the breed. He had quite rightly tagged Baker in addressing him as "Dear Urban." Pope Urban, who persecuted the great Galileo, had certainly been one of them.

It wasn't that Baker was ignorant or stupid. He was neither. Fenwick gave reluctant respect to his intelligence and his education. Baker was quick-witted. His head was stuffed full of accurate scientific information from diversified fields.

But he refused to be jarred loose from his fixed position that scientific breakthroughs could come from any source but the Established Authority. The possibility that the crackpot fringe could produce such a break-through panicked him. It *had* panicked him. He was fleeing dangerously now through the night, driven by a fear he did not know was in him.

Inflexibility. This seemed to be the characteristic that marked Baker and his kind. Defender of the Fixed Position might well have been his title. With all his might and power, Bill Baker defended the Fixed Position he had chosen, the Fixed Position behind the wall of Established Authority.

A blind spot, perhaps? But it seemed more than mere blindness that kept Baker so hotly defending his Fixed Position. It seemed as if, somehow, he was aware of its vulnerability and was determined to fight off any and all attacks, regardless of consequences.

Fenwick didn't know. He felt as if it was less than hopeless, however, to attempt to change Bill Baker. Any change would have to be brought about by Baker himself. And that, at the moment, seemed far less likely than the well-known snowball in Hades.

*   *   *   *   *

Fenwick knew he must have dozed off to sleep with the light still on in the room and Ellerbee's unread book opened over his chest. He did not know what time it was when he awoke. He was aware only of a suffocating sensation as if some ghostly aura were within the room, filling it, pressing down upon him. A wailing of agony and despair seemed to scratch at his senses although he was certain there was no audible sound. And a depression clutched at his soul as if death itself had suddenly walked unseen through the closed door.

Fenwick sat up, shivering in the sudden coolness of the room, but clammy with sweat over his whole body. He had never experienced such sensations before in his life. His stomach turned to a hard ball under the flow of panic that surged through all his nerves.

He forced himself to sit quietly for a moment, trying to release his fear-tightened muscles. He relaxed the panic in his stomach and looked slowly about the room. He could recall no stimulus in his sleep that had produced such a reaction. He hadn't even been dreaming, as far as he could tell. There was no recollection of any sound or movement within the house or outside.

He was calmer after a moment, but that sensation of death close at hand would not go away. He would have been unable to describe it if asked, but it was there. It filled the atmosphere of the room. It seemed to emanate from—

Fenwick turned his head about. It was almost as if there was some definite source from which the ghastly sensation was pouring over him. The walls—the air of the room—

His eyes caught the crystal on the table by the bed.

He could feel the force of death pouring from it.

His first impulse was to pick up the thing and hurl it as far as he could. Then in saner desperation he leaped from the bed and threw on his clothes. He grabbed the crystal in his hand and ran out through the door and down the stairs.

Jim Ellerbee was already there in the living room. He was seated by the old-fashioned library table, his hand outstretched upon it. In his hand lay the counterpart of the crystal Fenwick carried.

"Ellerbee!" Fenwick cried. "What's going on? What in Heaven's name is coming out of these things?"

"Baker," said Ellerbee. "He smashed up on the road somewhere. He's out there dying."

"Can you be sure? Then don't sit there, man! Let's get on our way!"

Ellerbee shook his head. "He'll be dead before we can get there."

"How do you know he cracked up, anyway? Can you read that out of the crystal?"

Ellerbee nodded. "He kept it in his pocket. It's close enough to him to transmit the frantic messages of his dying mind."

"Then we've got to go! No matter if we get there in time or not."

Ellerbee shook his head again. "Sam is on his way over here. He's in touch with Baker. He says he thinks he can talk Baker back."

"*Talk* him back? What do you mean by that?"

Ellerbee hesitated. "I'm not sure. In some ways Sam understands a lot more about these things than I do. He can do things with the crystals that I don't understand. If he says he can talk Dr. Baker back, I think maybe he can."

"But we can't depend on that!" Fenwick said frantically. "Can't we get on our way in the car and let Sam do what he thinks he can while we drive? Maybe he can get Baker to hold on until we get him to a doctor."

"You don't understand," said Ellerbee. "Dr. Baker has gone over the edge. He's *dying*. I know what it's like. I looked into a dying mind once before. There is nothing whatever that a doctor can do after an organism starts dying. It's a definite process. Once started, it's irreversible."

"Then what does Sam—?"

"Sam thinks he knows how to reverse it."

*   *   *   *   *

There wasn't much pain. Not as much as he would have supposed. He felt sure there was terrible damage inside. He could feel the warmth of blood welling up inside his throat. But the pain was not there. That was good.

In place of pain, there was a kind of infinite satisfaction and a growing peace. The ultimate magnitude of this peace, which he could sense, was so great that it loomed like some blinding glory.

This was death. The commitment and the decision had been made. But this was better than any alternative. He could not see how there could have been any question about it.

He was lying on his back in the wet clay of a bank below the road. It was raining, softly now, and he rather liked the gentle drop of it on his face. Somewhere below him the hulk of his wrecked car lay on its side. He could smell the unpleasant odor of gasoline. But all of this was less than nothing in importance to him now. Somewhere in the back of his mind was a remnant of memory of what he had been doing this day. He remembered the name of John Fenwick, and the memory brought a faint amusement to his bloody lips. There had been some differences between him and John Fenwick. Those differences were also less than nothing, now. All differences were wiped out. He gave himself up to the pleasure of being borne along on that great current that seemed to be carrying him swiftly to a quiet place.

After a time, he remembered two other names, also. James Ellerbee and Sam Atkins. He remembered a crystal, and it meant nothing. He remembered that it was in his pocket and that for some time he had felt a warmth from it, that was both pleasant and unpleasant. It was of no importance. He might have reached for it and thrown it farther from him, but his arm on that side was broken.

He was glad that there was nothing—nothing whatever—that had any magnitude of importance. Even his family—they were like fragments of a long-ago dream.

He lay waiting quietly and patiently for the swiftly approaching destination of ultimate peace. He did not know how long it would take, but he knew it could not be long, and even the journey was sweet.

It was while he waited, letting his mind drift, that he became aware of the intruder. In that moment, the pain boiled up in shrieking agony.

He had thought himself alone. He wanted above all else to be alone. But there was someone with him. He wasn't sure how he knew. He could simply *feel* the unwanted presence. He strained to see in the wet darkness. He listened for muted sounds. There was nothing. Only the presence.

"Go away!" he whispered hoarsely. "Go away, and leave me alone—whoever you are."

"No. Let me take you by the hand, William Baker. I have come to show you the way back. I have come to lead you back."

"Leave me alone! Whoever you are, leave me alone!" Baker was conscious of his own voice screaming in the black night. And it was not only terror of the unknown presence that made him scream, but the physical pain of crushed bones and torn flesh was sweeping like a torrent through him.

"Don't be afraid of me. You know me. You remember, we met this afternoon. Sam Atkins. You remember, Dr. Baker?"

"I remember." Baker's voice was a painful gasp. "I remember. Now go away and leave me alone. You can do nothing for me. I don't want you to do anything for me."

*   *   *   *   *

Sam Atkins. The crystal. Baker wished he could reach the cursed thing and hurl it away from him. That must be how Atkins was communicating with him. Yes, somehow it was possible. He had found no trick, no gimmick. Somehow, the miserable things worked.

But what did Sam Atkins want? He had broken in on a moment that was as private as a dream. There was nothing he could do. Baker was dying. He knew he was dying. There was no medicine that could heal the battering his body had taken. He had been slipping away into peace and release of pain. He had no desire to have it interrupted.

There was no more evidence of Sam Atkins' presence. It was there—and Baker wished furiously that Atkins would let his death be a private thing—but he was not interfering now.

There was the faint suggestion of other presences, too. Baker thought he could pick them out, Fenwick and Ellerbee. They were all gathered to watch him die through the crystals. It was unkind of them to so intrude—but it didn't really matter very much. He began drifting pleasantly again.

"William Baker." The soft voice of Sam Atkins shattered the peaceable realm once more. "We must do some healing before we start back, Dr. Baker. Give me your hand, and come with me, Dr. Baker, while we touch these tissues and heal their breaks. Stay close to me and the pain will not be more than you can endure."

The night remained dark and there was no sound, but Baker's body arched and twisted in panic as he fought against invisible hands that seemed to touch with fleeting, exploratory passes over him.

"I don't want to be healed," he whispered. "There is nothing that can be done. I'm dying. I want to die! Can't you understand that? I want to die! I don't want your help!"

He had said it. And the shock of it jolted even him in the depths of his half-conscious mind. Could a man really *want* to die?

Yes.

He had forgotten what terror he had left so far behind. He knew only that he wanted to move forever in the direction of the flowing peace.

Like probing fingers, Sam Atkins' mind continued to touch him. It scanned the broken organs of his body, and, in some kind of detached way, Baker felt that he was accompanying Atkins on that journey of exploration, even as Sam had asked.

They searched the skeleton and found the splintered bones. They examined the muscle structure and found the torn and shattered tissue. They searched the dark recesses of his vital organs and came to injury that Baker knew was hopeless.

"You built this once," Sam Atkins' voice whispered. "You can build it again. The materials are all here. The blood stream is still moving. The nerve tissue will carry your instructions. I'll supply the scaffolding—while you build—"

He remembered. Baker examined the long-untouched record of when he had done this before. He remembered the construction of cells, the building of organs, the interconnection of nerve tissue. He felt an infinite sadness at the present ruin. Yes—he could build again.

*   *   *   *   *

Sam Atkins' face was like that of a dead man. Across the table from him, Jim Ellerbee and John Fenwick watched silently. Faintly, between them was the crystal-projected image of Baker's body.

Fenwick felt the cold touch of some mysterious unknown prickle his scalp. Sam Atkins seemed remote and alien, like the practitioner of ancient and forbidden arts. Fenwick found the question tumbling over and over in his mind, who is this man? He felt as if the very life energy of Sam Atkins was somehow flowing out through the crystal, across space, to the distant broken body of Bill Baker and was supporting it while Baker's own feeble energy was consumed in the rebuilding of his shattered organs.

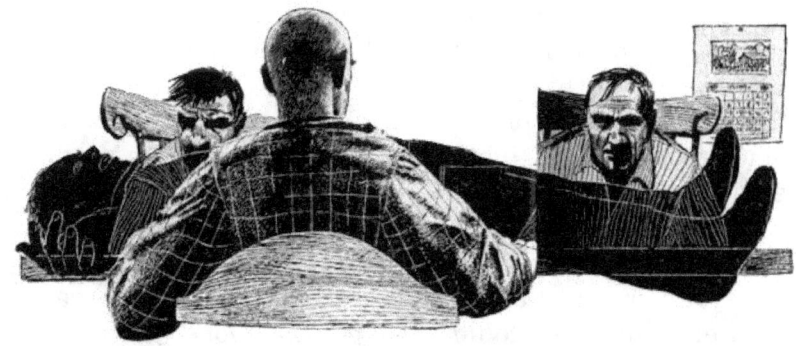

Though Fenwick and Ellerbee held their own crystals, Sam had somehow shut them out. They were in faint contact with

Baker, but they could not follow the fierce contact that Sam's mind held with him.

Ellerbee's face showed worry and a trace of panic. He hesitantly reached out to touch the immobile figure of Sam Atkins, who sat with closed eyes and imperceptible breath. Fenwick sensed disaster. He arrested the motion of Ellerbee's hand.

"I think you could kill them both," he whispered. The life force of one man, divided between two—it was not sufficient to cope with unexpected shocks to either, now.

Ellerbee desisted. "I've never seen anything like this before," he said. "I don't know what Sam's doing—I don't know how he's doing it—"

Fenwick looked sharply at Ellerbee. Ellerbee had discovered the crystals, so he and Sam said. Yet Sam was able to do things with them that Ellerbee could not conceive. Fenwick wondered just who was responsible for the crystals. And he resolved that some day, when and if Baker pulled out of this, he would learn something more about Sam Atkins.

Time moved beyond midnight and into the early morning hours of the day, but this meant nothing to William Baker. He was in the midst of eternity. Because the old pattern was there, and the ancient memories were clear, his reconstruction moved at a pace that was limited only by the materials available. When these grew scarce, Sam Atkins showed him how to break down and utilize other structures that could be rebuilt leisurely at a later time. There was remembered joy in the building and, once started, Baker gave only idle wonder to the question of whether this was more desirable than death. He did not know. This seemed the right thing to do.

In the presence of Sam Atkins everything he was doing seemed right, and a lifetime of doubts, and errors, and fears seemed distant and vague.

But Sam said suddenly, "It is almost finished. Just a little farther and you'll have to go the rest of the way alone."

Terror struck at Baker. He had reached a point where he was absolutely sure he could *not* go on alone without Sam's supporting presence. "You tricked me!" Baker cried. "You tricked me! You didn't tell me I would have to be reborn alone!"

"Doesn't every man?" said Sam. "Is there any way to be born, except alone?"

Slowly, the world closed in about Baker.

Light. Sounds.

Wet. Cold.

The impact of a million idiot minds. The coursing of cosmic-ray particles. The wrenching of Earth's magnetic and gravitational fields. Old and sluggish memories were renewed, memories meant to be buried for all of his life.

Baker felt as if he were suddenly running down a dark and immense corridor. Behind were all the terrors spawned since the beginning of time. Ahead were a thousand openings of light and safety. He raced for the nearest and brightest and most familiar.

"No," said Sam Atkins. "You cannot go that way again. It is the way you went before—and it led to this—to a search for death. For you, it will lead only to the same goal again."

"I can't go on!" Baker cried. The terrors seemed to be swiftly closing in.

"Take my hand a moment longer," said Sam. "Inspect these more distant paths. There are many of them that will be agreeable to you."

Baker felt calmer now in the renewed presence of Sam Atkins. He passed the branching pathway that Sam had forbidden, that had seemed so bright. He sensed now why Sam had cautioned him against it. Far down, in the depths of it, he glimpsed faintly a dark ugliness that he had not seen before. He shuddered.

Directly ahead there seemed to be the opening of a corridor of blazing brightness. Baker's calmness increased as he approached. "This one," he said.

He heard nothing, but he sensed Sam Atkins' smile, and nod of approval.

He remembered now for the first time why he had wanted to die. It was to avoid the very terrors by which he had been pursued through the dark corridor. All this had happened before, and he had gone down the pathway Sam had forbidden. Somehow, like a circle, it had come back to this very point, to this forgotten experience for which he had been willing to die rather than endure again.

It was very bewildering. He did not understand the meaning of it. But he knew he had corrected a former error. He was back in the world. He was alive again.

Sam Atkins looked up at his companions through eyes that seemed all but dead. "He's going to make it," he said. "We can get the car out and pick up Baker now."

*   *   *   *   *

They used Sam's panel truck, which had a four-wheel drive and mud tires. Nothing else could possibly get through. Fenwick left his own car at Ellerbee's.

It was still raining lightly as the truck sloshed and slewed through the muck that was hardly recognizable now as a road. For an hour Sam fought the wheel to hold the car approximately in the middle of the brownish ooze that led them through the night. The three men sat in the cab. Behind them, a litter and first-aid equipment had been rigged for Baker. Sam told them nothing would be needed except soap and water, but Fenwick and Ellerbee felt it impossible to go off without some other emergency equipment.

After an hour, Sam said, "He's close. Just around the next bend. That's where his car went off."

Baker loomed suddenly in the lights of the car. He was standing at the edge of the road. He waved an arm wearily.

Fenwick would not have recognized him. And for some seconds after the car had come to a halt, and Baker stood weaving uncertainly in the beam of the lights, Fenwick was not sure it was Baker at all.

He looked like something out of an old Frankenstein movie. His clothes were ripped almost completely away. Those remaining were stained with blood and red clay, and soaked with rain. Baker's face was laced with a network of scars as if he had been slashed with a shower of glass not too long ago and the wounds were freshly healed. Blood was caked and cracked on his face and was matted in his hair.

He smiled grotesquely as he staggered toward the car door. "About time you got here," he said. "A man could catch his death of cold standing out here in this weather."

*　　*　　*　　*　　*

Dr. William Baker was quite sure he had no need of hospitalization, but he let them settle him in a hospital bed anyway. He had some thinking to do, and he didn't know of a better place to get it done.

There was a good deal of medical speculation about the vast network of very fresh scars on his body, the bones which X rays showed to have been only very recently knit, and the violent internal injuries which gave some evidence of their recent healing. Baker allowed the speculation to go on without offering explanations. He let them tap and measure and apply electrical gadgets to their heart's content. It didn't bother the thinking he had to get done.

Fenwick and Ellerbee came back the next day to see him. The two approached the bed so warily that Baker burst out laughing. "Pull up chairs!" he exclaimed. "Just because you saw me looking a shade less than dead doesn't mean I'm a ghost now. Sit down. And where's Sam? Not that I don't appreciate seeing your ugly faces, but Sam and I have got some things to talk about."

Ellerbee and Fenwick looked at each other as if each expected the other to speak.

"Well, what's the matter?" demanded Baker. "Nothing's happened to Sam, I hope!"

Fenwick spoke finally. "We don't know where Sam is. We don't think we'll be seeing him again."

"Why not?" Baker demanded. But in the back of his mind was the growing suspicion that he knew.

"After your—accident," said Fenwick, "I went back to the farm with Ellerbee and Sam because I'd left my car there. I went back to bed to try to get some more shut-eye, but the storm had started up again and kept me awake. Just before dawn a terrific bolt of lightning seemed to strike Sam's silo. Later, Jim went out to check on his cows and help his man finish up the milking.

"By mid-morning we hadn't heard anything from Sam and decided to go over and talk to him about what we'd seen him do for you. I guess it was eleven by the time we got there."

Jim Ellerbee nodded agreement.

"When we got there," Fenwick went on, "we saw that the front door of the house was open as if the storm had blown it in. We called Sam, but he didn't answer, so we went on in. Things were a mess. We thought it was because of the storm, but then we saw that drawers and shelves seemed to have been opened hastily and cleaned out. Some things had been dropped on the floor, but most of the stuff was just gone.

"It was that way all through the house. Sam's bed hadn't been disturbed. He had either not slept in it, or had gone to the trouble of making it up even though he left the rest of the house in a mess."

"Sounds like the place might have been broken into," said Baker. "Didn't you notify the sheriff?"

"Not after we'd seen what was outside, in back."

"What was that?"

"We wanted to see the silo after the lightning had struck it. Jim said he'd always been curious about that silo. It was one of the best in the county, but Sam never used it. He used a pit.

"When we went out, all the cows were bellowing. They hadn't been milked. Sam did all his own work. Jim called his own man to come and take care of Sam's cows. Then we had a close look at the silo. It had split like a banana peel opening up. It hardly seemed as if a bolt of lightning could have caused it. We climbed over the broken pieces to look inside. It was still warm in there. At least six hours after lightning—or whatever had struck it, the concrete was still warm. The bottom and several feet of the sides of the silo were covered with a glassy glaze."

"No lightning bolt did that."

"We know that now," said Fenwick. "But I had seen the flash of it myself. Then I remembered that in my groggy condition that morning something had seemed wrong about that flash of lightning. Instead of a jagged tree of lightning that formed instantly, it had seemed like a thin thread of light striking *upward*. I thought I must be getting bleary-eyed and tried to forget it. In the silo, I remembered. I told Jim.

"We went back through the house once more. In Sam's bedroom, as if accidently dropped and kicked partway under the bed, I found this. Take a look!"

Fenwick held out a small book. It had covers and pages as did any ordinary book. But when Baker's fingers touched the book, something chilled his backbone.

The material had the feel and appearance of white leather— yet Baker had the insane impression that the cells of that leather still formed a living substance. He opened the pages. Their substance was as foreign as that of the cover. The message—printing, or whatever it might be called—consisted of patterned rows of dots, pin-head size, in color. It reminded him of computer tape cut to some character code. He had the impression that an eye might scan those pages and react as swiftly as a tape-fed computer.

Baker closed the book. "Nothing more?" he asked Fenwick.

"Nothing. We thought maybe you had found out something else when he worked to save your life."

*   *   *   *   *

Baker kept his eyes on the ceiling. "I found out a few things," he said. "I could scarcely believe they were true. I have to believe after hearing your story."

"What did you find?"

"Sam Atkins came from—somewhere else. He went back in the ship he had hidden in the silo."

"Where did he come from? What was he doing here?"

"I don't know the name of the world he was from or where it is located. Somewhere in this galaxy, is about all I can deduce from my impressions. He was here on a scientific mission, a sociological study. He was responsible for the crystals. I suppose you know that by now?" Baker glanced at Ellerbee.

Jim Ellerbee nodded. "I suspected for a long time that I was being led, but I couldn't understand it. I thought I was doing the research that produced the crystals, but Sam would drop a hint or a suggestion every once in a while, that would lead off on the right track and produce something fantastic. He knew where we were going, ahead of time. He led me to believe that we were exploring together. Do you know why he did this?"

"Yes," said Baker. "It was part of his project. The project consisted of a study of human reaction to scientific processes which our scientific culture considered impossible. He was interested in measuring our flexibility and reaction to such introductions."

Baker smiled grimly. "We sure gave him his money's worth, didn't we! We really reacted when he brought out his little cubes. I'd like to read the report he writes up!"

"Why did he leave so suddenly?" asked Fenwick. "Was he through?"

"No, that's the bad part of it. My reaction to the crystals was a shock that sent me into a suicidal action—"

Fenwick stared at him, shocked. "You didn't—"

"But I did," said Baker calmly. "All very subconsciously, of course, but I did try to commit suicide. The crystals triggered it. I'll explain how in a minute, but since Sam Atkins was an ethical being he felt the responsibility for what had happened to me. He had to reveal himself to the extent of saving my life—and helping me to change so that the suicidal drive would not appear again. He did this, but it revealed too much of himself and destroyed the chance of completing his program. When he gets back home, he's really going to catch hell for lousing up the works. It's too bad."

Jim Ellerbee let out a long breath. "Sam Atkins—somebody from another world—it doesn't seem possible. What things he could have taught us if he'd stayed!"

Fenwick wondered why it had to have been Baker to receive this knowledge. Baker, the High Priest of the Fixed Position, the ambassador of Established Authority. Why couldn't Sam Atkins—or whatever his real name might be—have whispered just a few words of light to a man willing to listen and profit? His bowels felt sick with the impact of opportunity forever lost.

*   *   *   *   *

"How did the crystals trigger a suicidal reaction?" asked Fenwick finally, as if to make conversation more than anything else.

Baker's face seemed to glow. "That's the really important thing I learned from Sam. I learned that about me—about all of us. It's hard to explain. I experienced it—but you can only hear about it."

"We're listening," said Fenwick dully.

"I saw a picture of a lathe in a magazine a few months ago," said Baker slowly. "You can buy one of these lathes for $174,000, if you want one. It's a pretty fancy job. The lathe remembers what it does once, and afterwards can do it again without any instructions.

"The lathe has a magnetic tape memory. The operator cuts the first piece on the lathe, and the tape records all the operations necessary for that production. After that, the operator needs only to insert the metal stock and press the start button.

"There could be a million memories in storage, and the lathe could draw on any one of them to repeat what it had done before at any time in its history."

"I don't see what this has got to do with Sam and you," said Fenwick.

Baker ignored him. "A long time ago a bit of life came into existence. It had no memory, because it was the first. But it faced the universe and made decisions. That's the difference between life and nonlife. Did you know that, Fenwick? The capacity to make decisions without pre-programming. The lathe is not alive because it must be pre-programmed by the operator. We used to say that reproduction was the criterion of life, but the lathe could be pre-programmed to build a duplicate of itself, complete with existing memories, if that were desired, but that would not make it a living thing.

"Spontaneous decision. A single cell can make a simple binary choice. Maybe nothing more complex than to be or not to be. The decision may be conditioned by lethal circumstances that permit only a 'not' decision. Nevertheless, a decision *is* made, and the cell shuts down its life processes in the very instant of death. They are not shut down for it.

"In the beginning, the first bit of life faced the world and made decisions, and memory came into being. The structures of giant protein molecules shifted slightly in those first cells and became a memory of decisions and encounters. The cells split and became new pairs carrying in each part giant patterned molecules of the same structure. These were memory tapes that grew and divided and spread among all life until they carried un-numbered billions of memories.

"Molecular tapes. Genes. The memory of life on earth, since the beginning. Each new piece of life that springs from parent life comes equipped with vast libraries of molecular tapes recording the experiences of life since the beginning.

"Life forms as complex as mammals could not exist without this tape library to draw upon. The bodily mechanisms could not function if they came into existence without the taped memories out of the ages, explaining why each organ was developed and how it should function. Sometimes, part of the tapes *are* missing, and the organism, if it endures, must live without instructions for some function. One human lifetime is too infinitesimally small to relearn procedures that have taken aeons to develop.

"Just as the lathe operator has a choice of tapes which will cause the lathe to function in different ways, so does new life have a choice. The accumulated instructions and wisdom of the whole race may be available, except for those tapes which have been lost or destroyed through the ages. New life has a choice from that vast library of tapes. In its inexperience, it relies on the parentage for the selection of many proven combinations, and so we conclude certain characteristics are 'dominant' or 'inherited,' but we haven't been able to discover the slightest reason why this is so.

"A selection of things other than color of eyes, the height of growth to be attained, the shape of the body must also be made. A choice of modes of facing the exterior world, a choice of stratagems to be used in attaining survival and security in that world, must be made.

"And there is one other important factor: Mammalian life is created in a universe where only life exists. The mammal in the womb does not know of the existence of the external universe. Somewhere, sometime, the first awareness of this external universe arises. In the womb. Outside the womb. Early in fetal life, or late. When and where this awareness comes is an individual matter. But when it comes, it arrives with lethal impact.

"Awareness brings a million sensory invasions—chemical, physical, extrasensory—none of them understood, all of them terrifying.

"This terrible fear that arises in this moment of awareness and non-understanding is almost sufficient to cause a choice of death rather than life at this point. Only because of the developed toughness, acquired through the aeons, does the majority of mammalian life choose to continue.

"In this moment, choices must be made as to how to cope with the external world, how to understand it so as to diminish the fear it inspires. The library of genetic tapes is full of possible solutions. Parental experience is examined, too, and the very sensory impacts that are the source of the terror are inspected to a greater or lesser extent to see how they align with taped information.

"A very basic choice is then made. It may not be a single decision, but, rather, a system of decisions all based on some fundamental underlying principle. And the choice may not be made in an instant. How long a time it may occupy I do not know.

"When the decision has been made, reaction between the individual and the external universe begins and understanding begins to flow into the data storage banks. As data are stored, and successful solutions found in the encounter with the world, fear diminishes. Some kind of equilibrium is eventually reached, in which the organism decides how much fear it is willing to tolerate to venture farther into areas of the unknown, and how much it is willing to limit its experience because of this fear.

"When the decision has been made, and the point of equilibrium chosen, a personality exists. The individual has shaped himself to face the world.

"And nothing short of a Heavenly miracle will ever change that shape!"

"You have said nothing about how the crystal caused you to attempt suicide," said Fenwick.

"The crystal invalidated the molecular tape I had chosen to provide my foundation program for living. The tape was completely shattered, brought to an end. There was nothing left for me to go on."

*　　*　　*　　*　　*

"Wait a minute!" said Fenwick. "Even supposing this could happen as you describe it, other programs could be selected out of the great number you have described."

"Quite true. But do you know what happens to an adult human being when the program on which his entire life is patterned is destroyed?"

Fenwick shook his head. "What is it like?"

"It's like it was in the beginning, in that moment of first awareness of the external universe. He is aware of the universe, but has no understanding of it. Previous understanding—or what he thought was understanding—has been invalidated, destroyed. The drive to keep living, that was present in that first moment of awareness, has weakened. The strongest impulse is to escape the terror that follows awareness without understanding. Death is the quickest escape.

"This is why men are inflexible. This is why the Urbans cannot endure the Galileos. This is why the Bill Bakers cannot face the Jim Ellerbees. That was what Sam Atkins wanted to find out.

"If a man should decide his basic program is invalid and decide to choose another, he would have to face again the terror of awareness of a world in which understanding does not exist. He would have to return to that moment of first awareness and select a new program in that moment of overwhelming fear. Men are not willing to do this. They prefer a program—a personality—that is defective, that functions with only a fraction of the efficiency it might have. They prefer this to a basic change of programs. Only when a program is rendered absolutely invalid—as mine was by the crystal communicator—is the program abandoned. When that happens, the average man drives his car into a telephone pole or a bridge abutment, or he steps in front of a truck at a street intersection. I drove into a gully in a storm."

"All this would imply that the tape library is loaded with genetic programs that contain basic defects!" said Fenwick.

Baker hesitated. "That's not quite true," he said finally. "The library of molecular tapes does contain a great many false solutions. But they are false not so much because they are defective as because they are obsolete. All of them worked at one time, under some set of circumstances, however briefly. Those times and circumstances may have vanished long since."

"Then why are they chosen? Why aren't they simply passed over?"

"Because the individual organism lacks adequate data for evaluating the available programs. In addition, information may be presented to him which says these obsolete programs are just the ones to use."

Fenwick leaned against the bed and shook his head. "How could a crazy thing like that come about?"

"Cultures become diseased," said Baker. "Sparta was such a one in ancient times. A more psychotic culture has scarcely existed anywhere, yet Sparta prevailed for generations. Ancient

Rome is another example. The Age of Chivalry. Each of these cultures was afflicted with a different disease.

"These diseases are epidemic. Individuals are infected before they emerge from the womb. In the Age of Chivalry this cultural disease held out the data that the best life program was based on the concept of Honor. Honor that could be challenged by a mistaken glance, an accidental touch in a crowd. Honor that had to be defended at the expense of life itself.

"Pure insanity. Yet how long did it persist?"

"And our culture?" said Fenwick. "There is such a sickness in our times?"

*   *   *   *   *

Baker nodded. "There's a disease in our times. A cultural disease you might call the Great Gray Plague. It is a disease which premises that safety, security, and effectiveness in dealing with the world may be obtained by agreement with the highest existing Authority.

"This premise was valid in the days when disobedience to the Head Man meant getting lost in a bog or eaten by a saber-toothed tiger. Today it is more than obsolete. It is among the most vicious sicknesses that have ever infected any culture."

"And you were sick with it."

"I was sick with it. You remember I said a molecular program is chosen partly on the basis of data presented by parental sources and the spears of invasion from the external world. This data that came to me from both sources said that I could deal with the world by yielding to Authority, by surrounding myself with it as with a shell. It would protect me. I would have stature. My world-problems would be solved if I chose this pattern.

"I chose it well. In our culture there are two areas of Authority, one in government, one in science. I covered myself both ways. I became a Government Science Administrator. You just don't get any more authoritative than that in our day and time!"

"But not everyone employs this as a basic premise!" exclaimed Fenwick.

"No—not everyone, fortunately. In that, may be our salvation. In all times there have been a few infected individuals—Pope Urban, for example. But in his time the culture was throwing off such ills and was surging forward under the impetus of men like Galileo.

"In our own time we are on the other end of the stick. We are just beginning to sink into this plague; it has existed in epidemic form only a few short decades. But look how it has spread! Our civil institutions, always weak to such infection, have almost completely succumbed. Our educational centers are equally sick. Approach them with a new idea and no Ph. D. and see what happens. Remember the Greek elevator engineer who did that a few years ago? He battered his way in by sheer force. It was the only way. He became a nuclear scientist. But for every one of his kind a thousand others are defeated by the Plague."

Fenwick was grinning broadly. He suddenly laughed aloud. "You must be crazy in the head, Bill. You sound just like me!"

Baker smiled faintly. "You are one of the lucky ones. You and Jim. It hasn't hit you. And there are plenty of others like you. But they are defeated by the powerful ones in authority, who have been infected.

"It's less than fifty years since it hit us. It may have five hundred years to run. I think we'll be wiped out by it before then. There must be something that can be done, some way to stamp it out."

"Well," said Fenwick. "You could give Clearwater enough to get us on our feet and running. That would be a start in the right direction."

"An excellent start," said Baker. "The only trouble is you asked for less than half of what you need. As soon as I get back to the office a grant for what you need will be on its way."

*   *   *   *   *

William Baker stayed in the hospital two more days. Apart from his family, he asked that no visitors be admitted. He felt as if he were a new-born infant, facing the world with the knowledge of a man—but innocent of experience.

He remembered the days before the accident. He remembered how he dealt with the world in those days. But the methods used then were as impossible to him now as if he were paralyzed. The new methods, found in that bright portal to which Sam Atkins had helped guide him, were untried. He knew they were right. But he had never used them.

He found it difficult to define the postulates he had chosen. The more he struggled to identify them, the more elusive they seemed to become. When he gave up the struggle he found the answer. He had chosen a program that held no fixed postulates. It was based on a decision to face the world as it came.

He was not entirely sure what this meant. The age-old genetic wisdom was still available to guide him. But he was committed to no set path. Fresh decisions would be required at every turn.

A single shot of vaccine could not stem an epidemic. His immunity to the sickness of his culture could not immunize the entire populace. Yet, he felt there was something he could do. He was just not sure what it was.

What could a single man do? In other times, a lone man had been enough to overturn an age. But William Baker did not feel such heroic confidence in his own capacity.

He was not alone, however. There were the John Fenwicks and the Jim Ellerbees who were immune to the great Plague. It was just that William Baker was probably the only man in the world who had ever been infected so completely and then rendered immune. That gave him a look at both sides of the fence, which was an advantage no one else shared.

There was something that stuck in his mind, something that Sam Atkins had said that night when Baker had been reborn. He couldn't understand it. Sam Atkins had said of the molecular program tape that had been broken: When you cease to be fearful of Authority, you become Authority.

The last thing in the whole world William Baker wanted now was to be Authority. But the thought would not leave his mind. Sam Atkins did not say things that had no meaning.

*   *   *   *   *

Baker's return to the office of NBSD was an occasion for outpouring of the professional affection which his staff had always tendered him. He knew that there had been a time when this had given him a great deal of satisfaction. He remembered that fiftieth birthday party.

Looking back, it seemed as if all that must have happened to some other man. He felt like a double of himself, taking over positions and prerogatives in which he was a complete impostor.

This was going to be harder than he had anticipated, he thought.

Pehrson especially, it appeared, was going to be difficult. The administrative assistant came into the office almost as soon as Baker was seated at his desk. "It's very good to have you back," said Pehrson. "I think we've managed to keep things running while you've been gone, however. We have rejected approximately one hundred applications during the past week."

Baker grunted. "And how many have you approved?"

"Approval would have had to await your signature, of course."

"O.K., how many are awaiting my signature?"

"It has been impossible to find a single one which had a high enough Index to warrant your consideration."

"I see," said Baker. "So you've taken care of the usual routine without any help from me?"

"Yes," said Pehrson.

"There's one grant left over from before I was absent. We must get that out of the way as quickly as possible."

"I don't recall any that were pending—" said Pehrson in apology.

"Clearwater College. Get me the file, will you?"

Pehrson didn't know for sure whether the chief was joking or not. He looked completely serious. Pehrson felt sick at the sudden thought that the accident may have so injured the chief's mind that he was actually serious.

He sparred. "The Clearwater College file?"

"That's what I said. Bring a set of approval forms, too."

Pehrson managed to get out with a placid mask on his face, but it broke as soon as he reached the safety of his own office. It wasn't possible that Baker was serious! The check that went out that afternoon convinced him it was so.

When Pehrson left the office, Baker got up and sauntered to the window, looking out over the smoke-gray buildings of Washington. The Index, he smiled, remembering it. Five years he and Pehrson had worked on that. It had seemed like quite a monumental achievement when they considered it finished. It had never been really finished, of course. Continuous additions and modifications were being made. But they had been very proud of it.

Baker wondered now, however, if they had not been very shortsighted in their application of the Index. He sensed, stirring in the back of his mind, not fully defined, possibilities that had never appeared to him before.

His speculations were interrupted by Doris. She spoke on the interphone, still in the sweetly sympathetic tone she had adopted for her greetings that morning. Baker suspected this would last at least a full week.

*   *   *   *   *

"Dr. Wily is on the phone. He would like to know if you'd mind his coming in this afternoon. Shall I make an appointment or would you rather postpone these interviews for a few days? Dr. Wily would understand, of course."

"Tell him to come on up whenever he's ready," said Baker. "I'm not doing much today."

President George H. Wily, Ph. D., D.Sc., of Great Eastern University. Wily was one of his best customers.

Baker guessed that he had given Wily somewhere around twelve or thirteen million dollars over the past decade. He didn't know exactly what Wily had done with all of it, but one didn't question Great Eastern's use of its funds. Certainly only the most benevolent use would be made of the money.

Baker reflected on his associations with Wily. His satisfaction had been unmeasurable in those exquisite moments when he had had the pleasure of handing Wily a check for two or three million dollars at a time. In turn, Wily had invited him to the great, commemorative banquets of Great Eastern. He had presented Baker to the Alumni and extolled the magnificent work Baker was doing in the advancement of the cause of Science. It had been a very pleasant association for both of them.

The door opened and Doris ushered Wily into the room. He came forward with outstretched hands. "My dear Baker! Your secretary said you had no objection to my coming up immediately, so I took advantage of it. I didn't hear about your terrible accident until yesterday. It's so good to know that you were not more seriously hurt."

"Thanks," said Baker. "It wasn't very bad. Come and sit down."

Wily was a rather large, beetle-shaped man. He affected a small, graying beard that sometimes had tobacco ashes in it.

"Terrible loss to the cause of Science if your accident had been more serious," Wily was saying. "I don't know of anyone who occupies a more critical position in our nation's scientific advance than you do."

This was what had made him feel safe, secure, able to cope with the problems of the world, Baker reflected. Wily represented Authority, the highest possible Authority in the existing scientific culture.

But it had worked both ways, too. Baker had supplied a similar counterpart for Wily. His degrees matched Wily's own. He represented both Science and Government. The gift of a million dollars expressed confidence on the part of the Government that Wily was on the right track, that his activity was approved.

A sort of mutual admiration society, Baker thought.

"I suppose you are interested in the progress on your application for renewal of Great Eastern's grants," said Baker.

Wily waved the subject away with an emphatic gesture. "Not business today! I simply dropped in for a friendly chat after learning of your accident. Of course, if there is something to report, I wouldn't mind hearing it. I presume, however, the processing is following the usual routine."

"Not quite," said Baker slowly. "An increasing flood of applications is coming in, and I'm finding it necessary to adopt new processing methods to cope with the problem."

"I can understand that," said Wily. "And one of the things I have always admired most about your office is your ability to prevent wastage of funds by nonqualified people. Qualifications in the scientific world are becoming tighter every day. You have no idea how difficult it is to get people with adequate backgrounds today. Men of stature and authority seem to be getting rarer all the time. At any rate, I'm sure we are agreed that only the intellectual elite must be given access to these funds of your Bureau, which are limited at best."

Baker continued to regard Wily across the desk for a long moment. Wily was one of them, he thought. One of the most heavily infected of all. Surround yourself with Authority. Fold it about you like a shell. Never step beyond the boundaries set by Authority. This was George H. Wily, President of Great Eastern University. This was a man stricken by the Great Gray Plague.

"I need a report," said Baker. "For our new program of screening I need a report of past performance under our grants. The last two years would be sufficient, I think, from Great Eastern."

Wily was disturbed. He frowned and hesitated. "I'm sure we could supply such a report," he said finally. "There's never been any question—"

"No question at all," said Baker. "I just need to tally up the achievements made under recent grants. I shall also require some new information for the Index. I'll send forms as soon as they're ready."

"We'll be more than glad to co-operate," said Wily. "It's just that concrete achievement in a research program is sometimes hard to pin point, you know. So many intangibles."

"I know," said Baker.

When Wily was gone, Baker continued sitting at his desk for a long time. He wished fervently that he could talk with Sam Atkins for just five minutes now. And he hoped Sam hadn't gotten too blistered by his mentors when he returned home after fluffing the inquiry he was sent out on.

There was no chance, of course, that Baker would ever be able to talk with Sam again. That one fortuitous encounter would have to do for a lifetime. But Sam's great cryptic statement was slowly beginning to make sense: When you cease to be fearful of Authority, you become Authority.

Neither Baker or Wily, or any of the members of Wily's lock-step staff were Authority. Rather, they all gave obeisance to the intangible Authority of Science, and stood together as self-appointed vicars of that Authority, demanding penance for the slightest blasphemy against it. And each one stood in living terror of such censure.

The same ghost haunted the halls of Government. The smallest civil servant, in his meanest incivility, could invoke the same reverence for that unseen mantle of Authority that rested, however falsely, on his thin shoulders.

The ghost existed in but one place, the minds of the victims of the Plague. William Baker had ceased to recognize or give obeisance to it. He was beginning to understand the meaning of Sam Atkins' words.

He was quite sure the grants to Great Eastern were going to diminish severely.

* * * * *

Within six months, the output from Clearwater College was phenomenal. The only string that Baker had attached to his grants was the provision that the National Bureau of Scientific Development be granted the privilege of announcing all new inventions, discoveries, and significant reports. This worked to the advantage of both parties. It gave the college the prestige of association in the press with the powerful Government agency, and it gave Baker the association with a prominent scientific discovery.

During the first month of operation under the grant, Fenwick appointed a half dozen "uneducated" professors to his physical science staff. These were located with Baker's help because they had previously applied to NBSD for assistance.

The announcement of the developments of the projects of these men was a kind of unearned windfall for both Baker and Fenwick because most of the work had already been done in garages and basements. But no one objected that it gave both Clearwater and NBSD a substantial boost in the public consciousness.

During this period, Baker found three other small colleges of almost equal caliber with Clearwater. He made substantial grants to all of them and watched their staffs grow in number and quality of background that would have shocked George Wily into apoplexy. Baker's announcements of substantial scientific gains became the subject of weekly press conferences.

And also, during this time, he lowered the ax on Great Eastern and two other giants whose applications were pending. He cut them to twenty per cent of what they were asking. A dozen of the largest industrial firms were accorded similar treatment.

Through all this, Pehrson moved like a man in a nightmare. His first impulse had been to resign. His second was to report the gross mismanagement of NBSD to some appropriate congressman. Before he did either of these things the reports began to come in from Clearwater and other obscure points.

Pehrson was a man in whom allegiance was easily swayed. His loyalty was only for the top man of any hierarchy, and he suddenly began to regard Baker with an amazed incredulity. It seemed akin to witchcraft to be able to pull out works of near genius from the dross material Baker had been supporting with his grants. Pehrson wasn't quite sure how it had been done although he had been present throughout the whole process. He only knew that Baker had developed a kind of prescience that was nothing short of miraculous, and from now on he was strictly a Baker man.

Baker was happy with this outcome. The problem of Pehrson had been a bothersome one. Civil Service regulations forbade his displacement. Baker had been undecided how to deal with him. With Pehrson's acceptance of the new methods, the entire staff swung behind Baker, and the previous grumblings and complaints finally ceased. He stood on top in his own office, at least, Baker reflected.

George H. Wily was not happy, however. He waited two full days after receiving the announcement of NBSD's grant for the coming year. He consulted with his Board of Regents and then took a night plane down to Washington to see Baker.

He was coldly formal as he entered Baker's office. Baker shook his hand warmly and invited him to sit down.

"I was hoping you'd drop in again when you came to town," said Baker. "I was sorry we had to ask you for so much new information, but I appreciate your prompt response."

Wily's eyes were frosty. "Is that why you gave us only two hundred thousand?" he asked.

Baker spread his hands. "I explained when you were here last that we were getting a flood of applications. We have been forced to distribute the money much more broadly than in other years. There is only so much to go around, you know."

"There is just as much as you've ever had," snapped Wily. "I've checked on your overall appropriation. And there is no increase in qualified applicants. There is a decrease, if anything.

"I've done a little checking on the grants you've made, Baker. I'd like to see you defend your appropriation for that miserable little school called Clearwater College. I made a detailed study of their staff. They haven't a single qualified man. Not one with a background any better than that of your elevator operator!"

Baker looked up at the ceiling. "I remember an elevator man who became quite a first rate scientist."

Wily glared, waiting for explanation, then snorted. "Oh, *him*—"

"Yes, *him*," said Baker.

"That doesn't explain your wasting of Government funds on such an institution as Clearwater. It doesn't explain your grants to—"

"Let me show you what does explain my grants," said Baker. "I have what I call the Index—with a capital I, you know—"

"I don't care anything about your explanations or your Index!" Wily exclaimed. "I'm here to serve notice that I represent the nation's interest as well as that of Great Eastern. And I am not going to stand by silently while you mismanage these sacred funds the way you have chosen to do in recent months. I don't know what's happened to you, Baker. You were never guilty of such mistakes before. But unless you can assure me that the full normal grant can be restored to Great Eastern, I'm going to see that your office is turned inside out by the Senate Committee on Scientific Development, and that you, personally, are thrown out."

Wily glared and breathed heavily after his speech. He sat waiting for Baker's answer.

Baker gave it when Wily had stopped panting and turned to drumming his fingers on the desk. "Unless your record of achievement is better this year than it has been in recent years, Great Eastern may not get any allotment at all next year," he said quietly.

Wily shaded toward deep red, verging on purple, as he rose. "You'll regret this, Baker! This office belongs to American Science. I refuse to see it desecrated by your gross mismanagement! Good day!"

Baker smiled grimly as Wily stormed out. Then he picked up the phone and asked Doris to get Fenwick at Clearwater. When Fenwick finally came on, Baker said, "Wily was just here. I expected he would be the one. This is going to be it. Send me everything you've got for release. We're going to find out how right Sam Atkins was!"

He called the other maverick schools he'd given grants, and the penny ante commercial organizations he'd set on their feet. He gave them the same message.

It wasn't going to be easy or pleasant, he reflected. The biggest guns of Scientific Authority would be trained on him before this was over.

*   *   *   *   *

Drew Pearson had the word even before it reached Baker. Baker read it at breakfast a week after Wily's visit. The columnist said, "The next big spending agency to come under the fire of Congressional Investigation is none other than the high-echelon National Bureau of Scientific Development. Dr. William Baker, head of the Agency, has been accused of indiscriminate spending policies wholly unrelated to the national interest. The accusers are a group of elite universities and top manufacturing organizations that have benefited greatly from Baker's handouts in years past. This year, Baker is accused of giving upwards of five million dollars to crackpot groups and individuals who have no standing in the scientific community whatever.

"If these charges are true, it is difficult to see what Dr. Baker is up to. For many years he has had an enviable record as a tight-fisted, hard-headed administrator of these important funds. Congress intends to find out what's going on. The watchdog committee of Senator Landrus is expected to call an investigation early next week."

Baker was notified that same afternoon.

*　　*　　*　　*　　*

Senator Landrus was a big, florid man, who moved about a committee hearing chamber with the ponderous smoothness of a luxury liner. He was never visited by a single doubt about the rightness of his chosen course—no matter how erratic it might appear to an onlooker. His faith in his established legislative procedures and in the established tenets of Science was complete. Since he wore the shield of both camps, his confidence in the path of Senator Robert Landrus was also unmarred by questions.

Baker had faced him many times, but always as an ally. Now, recognizing him as the enemy, Baker felt some small qualms, not because he feared Landrus, but because so much was at stake in this hearing. So much depended on his ability to guide the whims and uncertainties of this mammoth vessel of Authority.

There was an unusual amount of press interest in what might have seemed a routine and unspectacular hearing. No one could recall a previous occasion when the recipients had challenged a Government handout agency regarding the size of the handouts. While Landrus made his opening statement several of the reporters fiddled with the idea of a headline that said something about biting the hand that feeds. It wouldn't quite come off.

Wily was invited to make his statement next, which he did with icy reserve, never once looking in Baker's direction. He was followed by two other university presidents and a string of laboratory directors. The essence of their remarks was that Russia was going to beat the pants off American researchers, and it was all Baker's fault.

This recital took up all of the morning and half the afternoon of the first day. A dozen or so corporation executives were next on the docket with complaints that their vast facilities were being hamstrung by Baker's sudden switch of R & D funds to less qualified agents. Baker observed that the ones complaining were some of those who had never spent a nickel on genuine research until the Government began buying it. He knew that Landrus had not observed this fact. It would have to be called to the senator's attention.

By the end of the day, Landrus looked grave. It was obvious that he could see nothing but villainy in Baker's recent performance. It had been explained to him in careful detail by some of the most powerful men in the nation. Baker was certainly guilty of criminal negligence, if not more, in derailing these funds which Congress had intended should go to the support of the nation's scientific leaders. Landrus felt a weary depression. He hadn't really believed it would turn out this bad for Baker, for whom he had had a considerable regard in times past.

"You have heard the testimony of these witnesses," Landrus said to Baker. "Do you wish to reply or make a statement of your own, Dr. Baker?"

"I most certainly do!" said Baker.

Landrus didn't see what was left for Baker to say. "Testimony will resume tomorrow at nine a.m.," he said. "Dr. Baker will present his statement at that time."

*   *   *   *   *

The press thought it looked bad for Baker, too. Some papers accused him openly of attempting to sabotage the nation's research program. Wily and his fellows, and Landrus, were commended for catching this defection before it progressed any further.

Baker was well aware he was in a tight spot, and one which he had deliberately created. But as far as he could see, it was the only chance of utilizing the gift that Sam Atkins had left him. He felt confident he had a fighting chance.

His battery of supporters had not even been noticed in the glare of Wily's brilliant assembly, but Fenwick was there, and

Ellerbee. Fenwick's fair-haired boy, George, and a half dozen of his new recruits were there. Also present were the heads of the other maverick schools like Clearwater, and the presidents—some of whom doubled as janitors—of the minor corporations Baker had sponsored.

Baker took the stand the following morning, armed with his charts and displays. He looked completely confident as he addressed Landrus and the assembly.

"Gentlemen—and ladies—" he said. "The corner grocery store was one of America's most familiar and best loved institutions a generation or two ago. In spite of this, it went out of business because we refused to support it. May I ask why we refused to continue to support the corner grocery?

"The answer is obvious. We began to find better bargains elsewhere, in the supermarket. As much as we regret the passing of the oldtime grocer I'm sure that none of us would seriously suggest we bring him back.

"For the same reason I suggest that the time may have come to reconsider the bargains we have been getting in scientific developments and inventions. Americans have always taken pride in driving a good, hard, fair bargain. I see no reason why we should not do the same when we go into the open market to buy ideas.

"Some months ago I began giving fresh consideration to the product we were buying with the millions of dollars in grants made by NBSD. It was obvious that we were buying an impressive collection of shiny, glass and metal laboratories. We were buying giant pieces of laboratory equipment and monstrous machines of other kinds. We were getting endless quantities of fat reports—they fill thousands of miles of microfilm.

"Then I discovered an old picture of what I am sure all unbiased scientists will recognize as the world's greatest laboratory—greatest in terms of measurable output. I brought this picture with me."

Baker unrolled the first of his exhibits, a large photographic blowup. The single, whitehaired figure seated at a desk was instantly recognized. Wily and his group glanced at the picture and glared at Baker.

"You recognize Dr. Einstein, of course," said Baker. "This is a photograph of him at work in his laboratory at the Institute for Advanced Study at Princeton."

"We are all familiar with the appearance of the great Dr. Einstein," said Landrus. "But you are not showing us anything of his laboratory, as you claimed."

"Ah, but I am!" said Baker. "This is all the laboratory Dr. Einstein ever had. A desk, a chair, some writing paper. You will note that even the bookshelves behind him are bare except for a can of tobacco. The greatest laboratory in the world, a place for a man's mind to work in peace. Nuclear science began here."

Wily jumped to his feet. "This is absurd! No one denies the greatness of Dr. Einstein's work, but where would he have been without billions of dollars spent at Oak Ridge, Hanford, Los Alamos, and other great laboratories. To say that Dr. Einstein did not use laboratory facilities does not imply that vast expenditures for laboratories are not necessary!"

"I should like to reverse your question, Dr. Wily, and then let it rest," said Baker. "What would Oak Ridge, Hanford, and Los Alamos have done without Dr. Einstein?"

*   *   *   *   *

Senator Landrus floated up from his chair and raised his hands. "Let us be orderly, gentlemen. Dr. Baker has the floor. I should not like to have him interrupted again, please."

Baker nodded his thanks to the senator. "It has been charged," Baker continued, "that the methods of NBSD in granting funds for research have changed in recent times. This is entirely correct, and I should first like to show the results of this change."

He unrolled a chart and pinned it to the board behind him. "This chart shows what we have been paying and what we have been getting. The black line on the upper half of the chart shows the number of millions of dollars spent during the past five years. Our budget has had a moderately steady rise. The green line shows the value of laboratories constructed and equipment purchased. The red line shows the measure of new concepts developed by the scientists in these laboratories, the improvement on old concepts, and the invention of devices that are fundamentally new in purpose or function."

The gallery leaned forward to stare at the chart. From press row came the popping of flash cameras. Then a surge of spontaneous comment rolled through the chamber as the audience observed the sharp rise of the red line during the last six months, and the dropping of the green line.

Wily was on his feet again. "An imbecile should be able to see that the trend of the red line is the direct result of the previous satisfactory expenditures for facilities. One follows the other!"

Landrus banged for order.

"That's a very interesting point," said Baker. "I have another chart here"—he unrolled and pinned it—"that shows the output in terms of concepts and inventions, plotted against the size of the grants given to the institution."

The curve went almost straight downhill.

Wily was screaming. "Such data are absolutely meaningless! Who can say what constitutes a new idea, a new invention? The months of groundwork—"

"It will be necessary to remove any further demonstrators from the hearing room," said Landrus. "This will be an orderly hearing if I have to evict everyone but Dr. Baker and myself. Please continue, doctor."

"I am quite willing for my figures and premises to be examined in all detail," said Baker. "I will be glad to supply the necessary information to anyone who desires it at the close of this session. In the meantime, I should like to present a picture of the means which we have devised to determine whether a grant should be made to any given applicant.

"I am sure you will agree, Senator Landrus and Committee members, that it would be criminal to make such choices on any but the most scientific basis. For this reason, we have chosen to eliminate all elements of bias, chance, or outright error. We have developed a highly advanced scientific tool which we know simply as The Index."

*   *   *   *   *

Baker posted another long chart on the wall, speaking as he went. "This chart represents the index of an institution which shall remain anonymous as Sample A. However, I would direct Dr. Wily's close attention to this exhibit. The black median line indicates the boundary of characteristics which have been determined as acceptable or nonacceptable for grants. The colored areas on either side of the median line show strength of the various factors represented in any one institution. The Index is very simple. All that is required is that fifty per cent of the area above the line be colored in order to be eligible for a grant. You will note that in the case of Sample A the requirement is not met."

Fenwick couldn't believe his eyes. The chart was almost like the first one he had ever seen, the one prepared for Clearwater College months ago. He hadn't even known that Baker was still using the idiotic Index. Something was wrong, he told himself— all wrong.

"The Index is a composite," Baker was saying; "the final resultant of many individual charts, and it is the individual charts that will show you the factors which are measured. These factors are determined by an analysis of information supplied directly by the institution.

"The first of these factors is admissions. For a college, it is admission as a student. For a corporation, it is admission as an employee. In each case we present the qualifications of the following at college age: Thomas Edison, Michael Faraday, Nicholai Tesla, James Watt, Heinrich Hertz, Kepler, Copernicus, Galileo, and Henry Ford. The admissibility of this group of the world's scientific and the inventive leaders is shown here." Baker pointed to a minute dab of red on the chart.

"Gentlemen of the Committee," he said, "would you advise me to support with a million-dollar grant an institution that would close its doors to minds like those of Edison and Faraday?"

The roar of surf seemed to fill the committee room as Landrus banged in vain on the table. Photographers' flashes lit the scene with spurts of lightning. Wily was on his feet screaming, and Baker thought he heard the word, "Fraud!" repeated numerous times. Landrus was finally heard, "The room will be cleared at the next outburst!"

Baker wondered if he ever did carry out such a threat.

But Wily prevailed. "No such question was ever asked," he cried. "My organization was never asked the ridiculous question of whether or not it would admit these men. Of course we would admit them if they were known to us!"

"I should like to answer the gentleman's objection," Baker said to Landrus.

The senator nodded reluctantly.

"We did not, of course, present these men by name. That would have been too obvious. We presented them in terms of their qualifications at the age of college entrance. You see how many would have been turned down. How many, therefore, who are the intellectual equals of these men are also being turned down? Dr. Wily says they would be admitted if they were known. But of course they could not be known at the start of their careers!"

*   *   *   *   *

Baker turned the chart and quickly substituted another. "The second standard is that of creativeness. We simply asked the applicants to describe ten or more new ideas of speculations entertained by each member of the staff during the past year. When we received this information, we did not even read the descriptions; we merely plotted the degree of response. As you see, the institution represented by Sample A does not consider itself long on speculative ideas."

A titter rippled through the audience. Baker saw Wily poised, beet-red, to spring up once more; then apparently he thought better of it and slumped in his seat.

"Is this a fair test?" Baker asked rhetorically. "I submit that it is. An institution that is in the business of fostering creativeness ought to be guilty of a few new ideas once in a while!"

He changed charts once more and faced the listeners. "We have more than twenty such factors that go into the composition of the Index. I will not weary you with a recital of all of them, but I will present just one more. We call this the area of communication, and it is plotted here for Sample institution A."

Again, a dismal red smudge showed up at the bottom of the sheet. Fenwick could hardly keep from chuckling aloud as he recalled the first time he had seen such a chart. He hoped Baker was putting it over. If the reaction of the gallery were any indication, he was doing so.

"A major activity of scientists in all ages has been writing reports of their activities. If a man creates something new and talks only to himself about it, the value of the man and his discovery to the world is a big round zero. If a man creates something new and tells the whole world about it, the value is at a maximum. Somewhere in between these extremes lies the communicative activity of the modern scientist.

"There was a time when the scientist was the most literate of men, and the writing of a scientific report was a work of literary art. The lectures of Michael Faraday, Darwin's account of his great research—these are literate reading still.

"There are few such men among us today. The modern scientists seldom speak to you and me, but only to each other. To the extent their circle of communication is limited, so is their value. Shall we support the man who speaks to the world, or the man who speaks only in order to hear his own echo?"

He had them now, Fenwick was convinced. He could quit any time and be ahead. The gallery was smiling approval. The press was nodding and whispering to each other. The senators wouldn't be human if they weren't moved.

Baker swept aside all these charts now and placed another series before the audience. "This is the Index on an institution to whom we have given a sizable grant," he said. "Is there anyone here who would question our decision?

"This institution would have accepted every one of the list of scientists I gave you a moment ago. They would have had their chance here. This institution has men in whom new ideas pop up like cherry blossoms in the spring. I don't know how many of them are good ideas. No one can tell at this stage, but, at least, these men are *thinking*—which is a basic requirement for producing scientific discovery.

"Finally, this institution is staffed by men who can't be shut up. They don't communicate merely with each other. They talk about their ideas to anyone who comes along. They write articles for little publications and for big ones. They are in the home mechanics' journals and on publishers' book lists.

"Most important of all, these are some of the men responsible for the red line on the first curve I showed you. These are the men who have produced the most new developments and inventions with the least amount of money.

"I leave it to you, gentlemen. Has the National Bureau of Scientific Development chosen correctly, or should we return to our former course?"

There were cheers and applause as Baker sat down. Landrus closed the hearing with the announcement that the evidence would be examined at length and a report issued. Wily hurried forward to buttonhole him as the crowd filed out.

*   *   *   *   *

"It was a good show," Fenwick said, "but I'm still puzzled by what you've done. This new Index is really just about as phony as your old one."

They were seated in Baker's office once more. Baker smiled and glanced through the window beyond Fenwick. "I suppose so," Baker admitted finally, "but do you think Wily will be able to convince Landrus and his committee of that no matter how big a dinner he buys him tonight?"

"No—I don't think he will."

"Then we've accomplished our purpose. Besides, there's a good deal of truth buried in the Index. It's no lie that we can give them scientific research at a cheaper price than ever before."

"But what was the purpose you were trying to accomplish?"

Baker hesitated. "To establish myself as an Authority," he said, finally. "After today, I will be the recognized Authority on how to manage the nation's greatest research and development program."

Fenwick stared, then gasped. "Authority—you? This is the thing you were trying to fight. This is the great Plague Sam Atkins taught you—"

Baker was shaking his head and laughing. "No. Sam Atkins didn't tell me that one man could become immune and fight the Plague head on all by himself. He taught me something else that I didn't understand for a long time. He told me that he who ceases to fear Authority becomes Authority.

"To become Authority was the last thing in the world I wanted. But finally I recognized what Sam meant; it was the only way I could ever accomplish anything in the face of this Plague. You can't tell men of this culture that it is wrong to put themselves in total agreement with Authority. If that's the program on which they've chosen to function, the destruction of the program would destroy them, just as it did me. There had to be another way.

"If men are afraid of lions, you don't teach them it's wrong for men to be afraid of beasts; you teach them how to trap lions.

"If men are afraid of new knowledge-experiences, you don't teach them that new knowledge is not to be feared. There was a time when men got burned at the stake for such efforts. The response today is not entirely different. No—when men are afraid of knowledge you teach them to trap knowledge, just as you might teach them to trap lions.

"I can do this now because I have shown them that I am an Authority. I can lead them and it will not fracture their basic program tapes, which instruct them to be in accord with Authority. I can stop their battle against those who are not possessed of the Plague. It may even be that I can change the course of the Plague. Who knows?"

Fenwick was silent for a long time. Then he spoke again. "I read somewhere about a caterpillar that's called the Processionary Caterpillar. Several of them hook up, nose to fanny, and travel through a forest wherever the whims of the front caterpillar take them.

"A naturalist once took a train of Processionary Caterpillars and placed them on the rim of a flower pot in a continuous chain. They marched for days around the flower pot, each one supposing the caterpillar in front of him knew where he was going. Each was the Authority to the one behind. Food and water were placed nearby, but the caterpillars continued marching until they dropped off from exhaustion."

Baker frowned. "And what's that got to do with—?"

"You," said Fenwick. "You just led the way down off the flower pot. You just got promoted to head caterpillar."

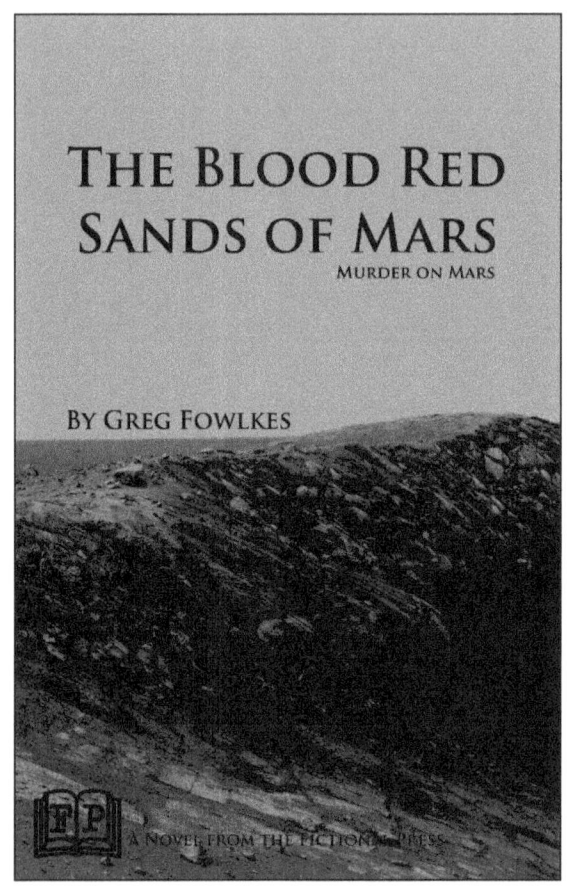

THE BLOOD RED SANDS OF MARS
MURDER ON MARS

A NOVEL BY GREG FOWLKES

THE BLOOD RED SANDS OF MARS

The wind was blowing again against the west wall of the hut. He could hear the grains of sand abrading the thin aluminum skin that protected him from the outside. Through the window, half frosted from the continuous onslaught of sand and dust, he could see clouds of dust obscuring the sky. The sky was a pastel pink, a color no sky had any right to be. The wind, despite its 120 kph. velocity, made only a thin howl as it blew over the half buried cylinder of the hut.

McKernan lay on his cot trying not to admit that he was awake. It was a losing battle. After a few minutes he surrendered and glanced over at the clock sitting on the crate next to his bed. The dim red digits of the LED display read 7:58. It was too early to get up, too late to go back to sleep. He rolled over, shivering at the cold. The temperature couldn't have been more than ten degrees Celsius inside the hut. For the twentieth time he thought to himself that he would have to fix the heater before winter—if he could get the parts. Either that, or put in more insulation—if he could find that. The cold finally forced the decision to get up.

Standing, he felt the cold plastic floor beneath his bare feet. With his foot he fished the worn and patched pants from beneath the cot and pulled them on. He dug underneath his pillow and came up with a switchblade knife that he stuck in his pocket before drawing on the turtleneck sweater that had lain next to his pants. The cold feel of the cloth did nothing to dispel the cold from his body. From the crate he picked up a shoulder holster with a small automatic pistol and put it on. McKernan drew the weapon, worked the slide once, and after examining it perfunctorily, placed it back in the holster. Satisfied, he pulled on a worn pair of leather boots and placed another knife in a sheathe between his skin and the boot top.

Dressed, he went over to the shelf that served as counter and table. He put a pan of beans onto the heating unit and got a soysteak from the small refrigerator that held up one end of the shelf. The steak went into the frying pan on the other heating element. An egg would have been nice, but at the current price of three dollars apiece it was an extravagance that he would have to put off for a while.

As the food cooked he drew a liter of water from the spigot in the corner of the hut and watered the plants in the garden under the window. The carrots and tomatoes were doing nicely. He smiled briefly because it would be good to have fresh vegetables for a change. The big, leafy oxygen plants were doing well, too. He would be able to cut down on his oxygen ration this month and save some money.

He took the beans off the heating element and replaced them with the coffee pot. The beans were still half cold, but he wasn't in the mood to hassle with them. He only had the two heating elements, and he didn't want to have to wait for his coffee. He forced down the beans and then wolfed down the steak. It almost tasted like real beef, but then maybe his memories were fading. As usual, the coffee tasted terrible and tepid, too. The air pressure in the hut was too low for water to boil properly.

He finished his meal and scraped the remnants of food into the pressure vessel that served as a compost heap. The gauge on its neighbor showed that he had almost half a tank of methane. He'd be able to sell that soon and use the money for something useful, like a still. Completing his rounds, the gauges on the life support systems showed that everything was still working at keeping him alive. He went back to the pots and scrubbed them clean with sand. That, at least, was plentiful and cheap.

He checked his watch against the clock. It was time to get going. Pulling on his jacket he went to the airlock at the corridor end of the hut. After checking the gauge to make sure that there was pressure on the other side, he undogged the latches and stepped through. Closing the door behind him, he repeated the process with the outer hatch, latching both doors behind him. The outer door he locked with a heavy padlock.

He had entered a low tubular corridor made of the same aluminum foil and plastic foam construction as the hut. The walls, however, were even thinner, and no pretense was made of heating it. He could see his breath condensing in front of him as he began to walk down its length. It was a hell of a way to live, he reflected, not for the first time. But then, it had been hell living in L.A. where he'd been born, with brown air, rats, a chronic shortage of water, and overcrowded tenements. He had made his choice, but sometimes it seemed as though life was a continual shiver.

The corridor was pierced at regular intervals by hatches identical to his own. The huts behind the hatches were identical, too, except for the modifications the owners had made to make them more livable. This part of the city was old, dating back a couple of decades to the first days of the settlement when it had been part of a scientific base. The scientists had departed, at least from that corridor, and been replaced by those who had the money to buy or rent the huts from the Trust Authority. Maintenance was pretty much left up to the residents.

Along the sides and overhead ran the pipes and conduits that pumped in the gases, liquids, and power necessary for sustaining life. The whole system looked as jury rigged and fragile as it actually was, though surprisingly few people died whenever the system failed. Martians were a cautious lot. One didn't talk much about injuries. Accidents on Mars didn't leave many.

A hundred meters down the tube he came to an airlock. Going through the same ritual that he had used on his front door, he went through to another length of corridor indistinguishable from the one he had just left. Continuing on, he passed through two more airlocks until he entered a corridor that sloped downward. The hatches were farther apart, and larger. Signs overhead indicated the businesses or functions that were carried out behind them. The air was warmer because the corridor was buried beneath the sand which provided insulation. At the end of the tunnel was a larger airlock set into a wall of fused silica bricks, the first substantial piece of construction he had met that morning.

Passing through the portal was like entering another world, which in a way he had. This was the public Mars, the planet seen by the corporation men and the officials of the Trust Authority. It was also the planet seen by tourists, the brave new colony, man's first outpost on another planet. The tourists didn't really care to see the hut town. They were part of the same world as the corporation men and the government types. It still took a great deal of money or power to reach Mars.

The difference was more than one of degree. For one thing, the temperature was a comfortable twenty. For another, the walls were flat and met the floors and ceilings at right angles, unlike the inflated skins of the huts and corridors. With a little imagination it could almost be an enclosed shopping mall on earth, though the presence of fused silica blocks was more prevalent than any architect would allow.

The most important difference, however, was the sight of people scurrying along. He hadn't met anyone in the outer corridors. People rarely lingered there because of the cold. Now, McKernan could see at least twenty people and it was still fairly early. No airlocks interrupted this corridor. Extending for two hundred meters in either direction, it was twenty meters wide and ten high, the largest enclosed volume on the planet. Arrayed along its length were the offices and store fronts of the corporations that owned Mars, as well as the more prosperous saloons and bordellos.

One day the Trust Authority promised that the whole city would be like that, with apartments and condominiums for the ordinary workers, but neither the Authority or the corporations had yet come up with the money. For the moment all that existed was the one street of a few blocks.

McKernan headed towards the Authority's offices which dominated one end of the mall, but turned aside at the last moment when he noticed that a small, dark doorway was open. He knew that he should resist the temptation, but he was not in a very disciplined mood. He went through the doorway into the darkness beyond.

Finnegan's was the only real, honest bar on Mars. There were any number of saloons and even a cocktail lounge in the Mars Sheraton, but only one quiet, dark place where a man could drink in peace. McKernan felt the need for some of that peace at the moment.

He sat down on one of the stools before the only mahogany bar on Mars. Finnegan, himself, was behind the bar, though in fact he almost always was, no matter what the hour. The bartender looked up and greeted the newcomer, "Good morning, constable. Beer or whiskey?"

"It's too early for beer. It's too early for whiskey, but give me a shot, anyway."

Finnegan poured out a shot glass of amber liquid and placed it before McKernan and then stood back polishing a glass while he studied the man opposite him.

McKernan knocked back half the glass before he spoke. When he did, there was a bitter edge to his voice. "Sometimes I wonder if it's worth it, Finnegan. I could be back on a planet fit for human life."

"Could you, now, constable?" Finnegan said, putting down the glass and picking up another in equally gleaming condition. "If mother earth was such a bed of roses, why are you here?"

He breathed on the glass and examined it against the light for a moment, then looked at McKernan with the same intentness. "You're here because you're not the sort to live off the dole or to spend your life with another man being your boss. Instead you'll spend your life trying to make this planet a fit place to live and retire in twenty years with a nice pension. Now drink up and get to work, laddy."

"Yeah, sure. Sorry to burden you with my problems. Early morning depression, I guess. See you." He finished off the shot and left five dollars in Authority script on the bar.

The bite of the whiskey so early in the morning didn't really help his disposition, but it did give him enough courage to make it to the office. The morning ritual at Finnegan's was becoming too much of a habit. His three years on Mars were beginning to show.

The jail wasn't in the brick part of the Authority building, but in the complex of pneumatic architecture that sprawled behind it. The huts were old—older than his own—but dated back to the days when governments had not begrudged a few billions for exploration, back before space had to show a profit. For that reason, they were sound and well insulated, though a bit tacky looking.

The jail consisted of two huts joined together, one for offices, the other for the two makeshift cells and storage. Ferris was the only one there when he walked in, a young kid, younger than he had been himself when he had come to Mars. He was still impressed enough with his responsibilities and had not yet been worn down by the grim realities to take his job in any way but seriously.

Ferris greeted him with a solemn, "Good morning, sir," with a stress on the sir. As a three year veteran of Mars, Ferris looked on his boss with more than a touch of awe.

"Anything exciting happen overnight?" McKernan didn't really expect much. A few fights in the saloon district, a knifing maybe if things got out of hand. Petty thievery, or perhaps not so petty. He looked at Ferris and saw a flash of excitement in his eyes that the younger man was trying hard to suppress in order to match the hard bitten image he had of his superior.

"Yes, sir. We've got a murder on our hands."

"Another knifing down at Thelma's?" he asked, naming an infamous saloon and bordello that figured in a quarter of all the police reports.

"No. A prospector was found out on his claim yesterday, over on the far side of Olympus Mons. He was shot, Inspector."

That was bad, McKernan thought. People on Mars weren't supposed to have guns. With the thin skins of most buildings and a hostile atmosphere outside that would support life exactly as long as you could hold your breath, they were dangerous, and not just to the targets. The Authority had made them illegal and the corporations had been more than willing to agree. They weren't easy to get—not something that could be picked up casually or made, like a knife. Even without the details it sounded like the work of a real criminal and not just a squabble over a claim or a woman.

"Okay. Let me have the report. I'll take a look at it."

He took the folder from Ferris who looked a bit crestfallen. He probably expects me to go rush off to the outside and track down the murderer like an Indian scout, McKernan thought. He'd learn in time. Mars was a big planet and a dangerous one, but because of its nature there were also very few places that a man could run to and none where he could hide indefinitely.

He was leafing through the report when he came to his door. For the thousandth time he read, "Inspector Erik McKernan, Chief Constable." Mother would have been proud, he thought sardonically. She had hated the L.A. cops like all the other residents of the barrio. He went through the door into the little cubicle that was his real home. There, sitting at his desk, he began to read the report, sketchy though it was, to look for some explanations.

Available now! Visit www.TheFictionalPress.com for more information, or buy it in both print and electronic format at your favorite online bookstore!

Other Science Fiction Novels by Greg Fowlkes

The Fictional Detective

The Blood Red Sands of Mars: Murder on Mars

The Laws of Magic: A Wizard at Law Novel.

The Ghost in the Machine: A wizard at Law novella

Ice Vikings

Cargo from Paradise

Tequila Visions

Also From Resurrected Press
SCIENCE FICTION AUTHORS RESURRECTED

FYFE RESURRECTED - THE STORIES OF H. B. FYFE
Stories from the Golden Age of Science Fiction by the author of D-99. dealing with the interaction of humans and aliens on far off worlds in ways that were as creative as they were imaginative.

SCHMITZ RESURRECTED - SELECTED STORIES OF JAMES H. SCHMITZ
Includes "An Incident on Route 12", "Watch the Sky", "The Other Likeness", "The Star Hyacinths", "Oneness", "The Winds of Time", "Ham Sandwich" and "Gone Fishing".

SHECKLY RESURRECTED - THE EARLY STORIES OF ROBERT SHECKLEY
Resurrected Press has collected some of the best of these from the 50's including "Warrior Race", "The Leech", "Watchbird", "Warm", "Diplomatic Immunity", "The Hour of Battle", "Besides Still Waters", "Keep Your Shape", "One Man's Poison", 'Ask a Foolish Question", "Cost of Living", "Death Wish Forever".

DICK RESURRECTED - THE EARLY STORIES OF PHILIP K. DICK
Early stories from the author of the novels that inspired "Blade Runner," "Total Recall," and "A Scanner Darkly".

HAMILTON RESURRECTED - CLASSIC STORIES OF EDMOND HAMILTON
Edmond Hamilton was one of the most popular writers during the 30's and 40's, the period that saw the first flowering of modern science fiction.

SMITH RESURRECTED - SELECTED STORIES OF EVELYN E. SMITH TON
During an era when women rarely appeared in science fiction magazines, Evelyn E. Smith appeared regularly in the pages of Galaxy and Fantastic Universe. Resurrected Press is proud to return these stories to print.

The Fictional Detective
by Greg Fowlkes

Who killed Ezekial O. Handler?

A beautiful dame, a hard-boiled private eye — and a dead body.

It started like any other case. When a famous writer dies in a mysterious car crash, private detective Frank Slade is called in to find answers, but all he finds is more questions. Who killed Ezekial Handler? Who is Janet Nielsen and why is she so interested in finding out? Who is leaving the neatly typed clues? And as Slade tries to find answers to these questions he starts to wonder if the ultimate answer will threaten his very existence.

Read about it in
The Fictional Detective

Visit www.thefictionaldetective.com

About Resurrected Press

This classic book was handcrafted by Resurrected Press. Resurrected Press is dedicated to bringing high quality classic books back to the readers who enjoy them. These are not scanned versions of the originals, but, rather, quality checked and edited books meant to be enjoyed!

Introducing The Fictional Press

The Fictional Press is a small, independent press specializing in the publication of fictional works by emerging authors. If you are interested in bringing your fictional works to life in print as well as electronically, contact us! We can help!

www.ingramcontent.com/pod-product-compliance
Lightning Source LLC
Chambersburg PA
CBHW070356260626
47161CB00001B/163